"Now," Agrona said. "We can finally proceed. If it pleases you, my lord?"

She and Vivian both turned and looked over their shoulders. I'd been so focused on the two of them that I hadn't realized a third figure was sitting on the steps in the exact center of the amphitheater.

Instead of a robe, shadows wrapped around his body, curling, writhing, and wisping around him like smoke hovering over a fire. Slowly, the darkness began to spread out from him, unrolling like a carpet over the steps, smothering the soft, rainbow flashes of color in the stone, and staining everything a horrible, unending black. All I could see of his features were his eyes—one a vivid blue, the other that burning Reaper red that I hated more than anything else—but I shivered with fear all the same.

Because somehow, someway, Loki, the evil Norse god of chaos, was here at Mythos Academy.

"My lord?" Agrona asked again.

"Proceed," Loki answered, his voice booming through the auditorium, louder than any clap of thunder. "Kill the Frost girl—now."

MIDNIGHT FROST

JENNIFER ESTEP

KENSINGTON PUBLISHING CORP.
www.kensingtonbooks.com

KTEEN BOOKS are published by

Kensington Publishing Corp.
119 West 40th Street
New York, NY 10018

All Kensington titles, imprints, and distributed lines are available at special quantity discounts for bulk purchases for sales promotions, premiums, fund-raising, educational, or institutional use.

Special book excerpts or customized printings can also be created to fit specific needs. For details, write or phone the office of the Kensington special sales manager: Kensington Publishing Corp., 119 West 40th Street, New York, NY 10018, attn: Special Sales Department; phone 1-800-221-2647.

KENSINGTON and the KTeen logo are Reg. U.S. Pat. & TM Off.

ISBN-13: 978-0-7582-8149-4
ISBN-10: 0-7582-8149-8

First KTeen Trade Paperback Printing: August 2013

10 9 8 7 6 5 4 3 2 1

Printed in the United States of America

First Electronic Edition: August 2013

ISBN-13: 978-0-7582-8151-7
ISBN-10: 0-7582-8151-X

As always, to my mom, my grandma, and Andre,
for all their love, help, support, and patience
with my books
and everything else in life

ACKNOWLEDGMENTS

Any author will tell you that her book would not be possible without the hard work of many, many people. I want to thank some of the folks who helped bring Gwen Frost and the world of Mythos Academy to life:

Thanks to my agent, Annelise Robey, for all her helpful advice.

Thanks to my editor, Alicia Condon, for her sharp editorial eye and thoughtful suggestions. They always make the book so much better.

Thanks to everyone at Kensington who worked on the project, and thanks to Alexandra Nicolajsen and Vida Engstrand for all their promotional efforts.

And, finally, thanks to all the readers out there. Entertaining you is why I write books, and it's always an honor and a privilege. I hope you have as much fun reading about Gwen's adventures as I do writing them.

Happy reading!

Library of Antiquities

1 Balcony of Statues
2 Check Out Counter
3 Artifact Case
4 Raven's Coffee Cart
5 Entrance
6 Book Stacks
7 Study Area
8 Offices
9 Staircase

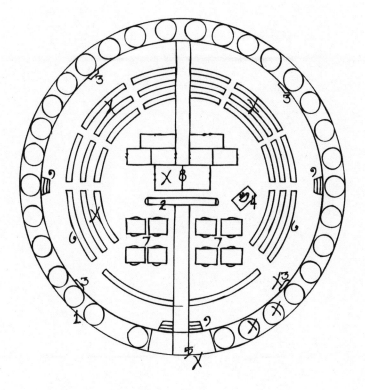

Chapter 1

I was trapped.

I paced from one side of the room to the other, pivoted on my sneaker heel, and hurried back the other way. A few steps later, I reached the opposite wall, so I turned and repeated the process. Back and forth, and back and forth, I stalked, my mind drifting from one thing to the next.

My friends at Mythos Academy. My search for artifacts. What Agrona, Vivian, and the rest of the Reapers of Chaos were plotting next. Where Logan was.

My heart twinged at the thought of Logan, and my foot caught in the bottom part of a net that was draped over the back of my desk chair. I stumbled forward, barely managing to catch myself before I slammed face-first onto my bed.

I staggered back up onto my feet and glared at the net. Oh sure, it looked all innocent hanging there, like a patch of light gray seaweed had sprouted out of the back of my chair. Supposedly, it had belonged to Ran, the Norse goddess of storms. Truth be told, it wasn't all that impressive, as far as artifacts went. The seaweed was gnarled, knotted, and seemed so thin, threadbare, and brittle that it would probably crumble to dust if you so much as breathed on it. But I'd learned the hard way that looks were often deceiving, especially in the mythological world. Still, I supposed I should be grateful I hadn't crushed the net by tromping all over it.

I'd had the net for a couple of days now, ever since I'd found it at the Crius Coliseum, and I still didn't know what was so special about it. I hadn't even gotten any big vibes off the net with my psychometry magic, which let me know, see, and feel an object's history.

But finding powerful mythological artifacts and keeping them safe from Reapers was the latest mission that Nike, the Greek goddess of victory, had given to me. Most folks knew me as Gwen Frost, that weird Gypsy girl who touched stuff and saw things, but I was also Nike's Champion, the girl picked by the goddess to help carry out her wishes here in the mortal realm.

Me, a Champion. I still couldn't believe it sometimes. But Nike was very, very real, just like the rest of the mythological world, with all its gods, goddesses, magic, creatures, artifacts, and warrior whiz kids.

More and more thoughts crowded into my mind, but I pushed them aside. Instead, I slid the chair even closer to the desk so I wouldn't trip over the net again and resumed my pacing. Back and forth, and back and forth, from one side of my prison to the other . . .

"Will you stop all that bloody stomping around?" a voice with a cool English accent growled a few minutes later. "You are making it *impossible* for me to get in my mid-afternoon, pre-killing-Reaper nap."

I looked at the wall, where a sword in a black leather scabbard was hanging next to my posters of Wonder Woman, Karma Girl, and The Killers. A purplish eye on the hilt was open wide and glaring at me, while the rest of the sword's features—a nose, an ear, and a mouth— were turned down into a petulant pout.

"Really, Gwen," Vic, my talking sword, chastised me again. "Some of us are trying to sleep. Isn't that right, fuzzball?"

An agreeing bark sounded from a basket in the corner. Nyx, the Fenrir wolf pup I was taking care of, was as cute as she could be with her dark gray fur and purplish eyes, but she had an annoying habit of going along with just about whatever Vic said.

"Fine," I grumbled and plopped down on my bed. "I'll stop pacing."

Okay, okay, so I wasn't *really* trapped. But my dorm room sure felt like a prison these days, especially since there was almost always a Protectorate guard stationed outside. I pushed aside a curtain and stared out one of the picture windows. Aiko, a thin, petite, twentysomething Ninja, was leaning against a tree on the lawn below, just like she had been ever since I'd come back to my room an hour ago. Aiko shifted on her feet, causing the folds of her gray robe to billow out around her slender figure and giving me a brief glimpse of the short sword and silver throwing stars hooked to her belt.

I sighed and let the curtain fall back into place. Aiko was outside to protect me from any Reapers who might try to kill me, something that had happened more than once within the walled confines of Mythos Academy.

Still, I didn't like being watched all the time, even if it was for my own good. It made me feel weak and helpless and just . . . trapped.

Suddenly, the room felt unbearably hot and stuffy, and I couldn't draw enough air down into my lungs. Even though my room was on the large side compared to some of the others at the academy, the ceiling seemed to swoop down and the walls seemed to creep closer the longer I stared at them, like they were all slowly sliding toward me, getting ready to surge forward and crush me in their cold, indifferent embrace.

I shivered and dropped my gaze to the floor, but even it seemed to ripple, as though it was trying to rise up to meet the ceiling. I sighed. My Gypsy gift was acting up and making me see things that weren't really there. I stared at the floor, determined to control my psychometry, but once again, the boards rose and fell like the ocean waves I'd seen when I'd touched Ran's net.

I bolted off my bed. "I need some air," I said. "I'll be back soon."

Vic and Nyx didn't say anything as I stalked over to the door, opened it, and peered out into the hallway. I expected to see a guy with hazel eyes, dark brown hair, and tan skin leaning against the wall, but Alexei Sokolov, my friend and the Russian Bogatyr warrior who served as my guard, wasn't waiting to walk me across campus. That was a little strange, since Alexei took his assignment super seriously, but I wasn't about to overlook my good luck.

I stepped outside, shut the door behind me, and hurried away from my room as fast as I could.

*   *   *

Despite the fact that Aiko was outside my dorm, it was easy enough for me to go to the common kitchen that all the girls in Styx Hall shared, open one of the windows, and crawl outside. I slid from one tree to the next until I was out of sight of Aiko and the dorm before I stepped onto one of the ash-gray cobblestone paths that wound across campus.

It was late January, and the air was bitterly cold. The blustery gusts of wind kicked up the hard bits of snow that littered the ground, while the thick gray clouds cast the landscape in shifting shadows, even though it was only late afternoon. I stuffed my hands into my jacket pockets and tucked my chin down into the dark gray, snowflake-patterned scarf wrapped around my neck, trying to stay warm.

Since it was so cold, I was the only one walking across campus. I thought about heading up the hill to the main quad and going over to the Library of Antiquities, but it was sure to be full of kids studying. I didn't feel like being gawked at, so I veered onto a path to my left. I wound up in the amphitheater.

The amphitheater was really two pieces put together—a stage at the bottom and then a series of long, flat shallow steps that climbed up the hill above it. The steps, which also served as seats, arced out and up into an enormous semicircle, until it almost seemed like each row was a pair of arms reaching around to hug the stage close.

The shadows seemed even deeper here, but the theater's bone-white stone glimmered like a ghost in the wintry darkness. Sparks of soft lilac, silvery gray, and forest green were embedded in the stone, giving it a pale, opalescent sheen and making it seem as if a hundred thousand fireflies were slowly winking on and off. It was a beautiful sight, and some of the tension and worry drained out of my body. Plus, the amphitheater was empty, just like I'd hoped it would be. I wasn't in the mood for any sort of company.

I walked over to the stage, which was surrounded by four columns, one at each corner. Stone chimeras crouched on round globes on the very tops of the columns, their heads turned to stare out at the steps, almost as if they were waiting for a crowd to gather for some show. I hesitated, a bit of unease bubbling up in my stomach, but when the chimeras didn't turn and glare at me, I climbed up the steps, walked to the middle of the stage, and sat down on the edge. I let out a deep sigh.

Alone—I was finally alone.

I closed my eyes and breathed—in and out, in and out—just enjoying this moment of peace, quiet, and solitude—

Something skittered off to my left.

My eyes snapped open, and my hand dropped to my side, but I only came up with empty air. I'd left Vic in my room, so the sword wasn't strapped to my waist as usual. I frowned. Why had I left him behind? That wasn't like me. I usually took Vic everywhere I went, especially now, with the Reapers on the verge of declaring another Chaos War against the Pantheon.

The noise sounded again, like boots scuffling over stone. I turned my head to the left and realized there was someone else on stage with me—a boy about my own age with ink-black hair and a lean, muscled body.

Logan freaking Quinn.

The guy I loved.

The one who'd stabbed me in the chest—and left me behind.

He wore boots, jeans, and a black leather jacket over a light blue sweater that brought out the intense color of his icy eyes. He looked the same as I remembered, the same as I'd imagined him a hundred times since he'd left Mythos, since he'd left me.

Logan?" I asked, my voice a hoarse, hopeful whisper. "Logan!"

I scrambled to my feet. I opened my arms and started to run toward him when I realized that Logan was holding a sword—and that his eyes were now glowing that eerie Reaper red.

I stopped short. The last time Logan's eyes had been that horrible color had been a few weeks ago during a Reaper ambush at the Aoide Auditorium. He'd attacked and almost killed me before I used my psychometry to undo the murderous magic the Reapers had done.

I thought I'd saved Logan from the Reapers, from Loki, but now, it looked like he was here to finish the job.

"Oh, go on, Gwen," a mocking, sneering voice called out. "Go say hello to your boyfriend. He's oh so glad to see you."

I whirled around. A girl now sat in the middle of one of the auditorium steps. A black Reaper robe hid her clothes from sight, but she wasn't wearing a mask so I could see her face. Frizzy auburn hair, amazing golden eyes, pretty features. Vivian Holler, Loki's Champion, the Reaper girl who'd murdered my mom.

"What are you doing here?" I hissed.

Vivian grinned at me. "Nothing much. Just watching Logan finally follow through with what he started. Isn't that right, Logan?"

I looked at the Spartan. He didn't say anything, although his fingers slowly tightened around the hilt of the sword. After a moment, he started twirling the weapon in his hand, getting a feel for the sword, just like he'd done at the auditorium before he'd attacked me.

"No," I whispered. "No, no, no."

"Oh yes, yes, yes, Gypsy," another voice purred.

I looked back at the steps. A woman with golden hair and bright green eyes was now sitting beside Vivian, wearing the same sort of black robe that she did. Agrona Quinn, Logan's traitorous stepmom and the head of the Reapers.

I frowned. How had Agrona and Vivian gotten here? And how had they managed to work their foul magic on Logan again? He was supposed to be with his dad, Linus, recovering from all of the terrible things that had happened at the auditorium. He was supposed to be *safe*.

"What's going on?" I asked.

I backed away from Logan and eased toward the far side of the stage, hoping I could run down the steps before he caught me. Logan would cut me to ribbons with his sword, especially since I didn't have Vic to defend myself with. But more than that, I didn't want to fight Logan—not again.

"Ah, ah, ah," Vivian called out. "Stay right where you are, Gwen."

A soft *click* sounded. My head snapped back to the

Reaper girl, who now had a crossbow trained on me. I froze. Where had she gotten that from?

"Excellent," Agrona purred again.

She waved her left hand, causing a large, heart-shaped ruby to sparkle in a ring on her finger. Did Agrona still have some of the Apate jewels left? Was that how she was controlling Logan again? I thought that I'd smashed all of the jewels she was wearing at the auditorium, but she must have gotten her hands on some more of them.

"Now," Agrona said. "We can finally proceed. If it pleases you, my lord?"

She and Vivian both turned and looked over their shoulders. I'd been so focused on the two of them that I hadn't realized a third figure was sitting on the steps in the exact center of the amphitheater.

Instead of a robe, shadows wrapped around his body, curling, writhing, and wisping around him like smoke hovering over a fire. Slowly, the darkness began to spread out from him, unrolling like a carpet over the steps, smothering the soft, rainbow flashes of color in the stone and staining everything a horrible, unending black. All I could see of his features were his eyes—one a vivid blue, the other that burning Reaper red I hated more than anything else—but I shivered with fear all the same.

Because somehow, someway, Loki, the evil Norse god of chaos, was here at Mythos Academy.

"My lord?" Agrona asked again.

"Proceed," Loki answered, his voice booming through the auditorium, louder than any clap of thunder. "Kill the Frost girl—now."

"With pleasure." This time, it was Logan who spoke. Only it wasn't his voice—it was Loki's.

I looked at him in horror, but Logan was already running toward me.

"No, Logan," I said, holding my hands up and backing away from him. "Don't. Please don't. Not again—"

Logan surged forward and ran his sword through my chest.

Agonizing pain exploded like a bomb in my heart, and I screamed and screamed from the sharp, brutal force of it. Logan smiled, yanked his sword out of my chest, and stabbed me with it again.

And again, and again, and again . . .

I woke up screaming.

One second, I was on the amphitheater stage with Logan killing me, and Vivian, Agrona, and Loki all happily watching. The next, I was lying in bed in my dorm room, wrestling with the pillow I'd buried my face in.

I slapped the pillow off the bed, sat up, and gulped down breath after breath. My eyes darted around my room, but everything was the same. Bed, desk, bookcases, fridge, TV. Vic hanging on the wall, Nyx curled up in her basket in the corner, Ran's seaweed net draped over the back of my chair.

Real—this was *real*. Everything else had been a dream. Just a dream.

Vic's eye snapped open, and he regarded me with a sympathetic expression. "Another nightmare?"

I slid to the floor and leaned back against the side of the bed. Nyx hopped out of her basket and raced over to me. I scooped up the pup and cradled her in my arms.

Nyx licked my cheek, and I felt her warm concern wash over me.

"Gwen?" Vic asked again. "Another nightmare?"

"Something like that."

"Did he stab you again this time?"

"Oh yeah."

My chest ached, as though Logan really had hurt me again, and I buried my face in Nyx's fur until the sensation faded away, and I was reasonably sure I wasn't going to cry.

"How did it start?" Vic asked. "The nightmare?"

Calmer now, I rewound the images in my mind. Thanks to my psychometry, I never forgot anything I heard, saw, or felt, not even my dreams. Sometimes it was a blessing, being able to recall a cherished memory, but with the nightmares I'd been having lately, it seemed more like a curse.

"I was in here, pacing back and forth, and I felt like I needed to escape . . ."

I told Vic the rest of it. When I finished, the sword frowned in thought, while Nyx licked my fingers, trying to let me know she was here for me too.

The weird thing was that I really had gone to the Crius Coliseum a few days earlier, and I really did have Ran's net draped over my desk chair. In fact, I'd talked about the net and how useless it seemed with Alexei and Daphne Cruz, my best friend, when we'd had dinner in the dining hall earlier. We'd come back to my dorm room to hang out for a while, and after they'd left, I'd decided to lie down on my bed to rest for a few minutes before taking a shower and getting ready for bed. Instead, I'd fallen asleep, and the image of the net had somehow led to my recurring nightmare of Logan stabbing me in the chest.

Just like he'd done for real a few weeks ago.

"Well, obviously, you still have some issues with the Spartan and what he did to you," Vic finally said. "And who wouldn't? Do you want to talk about it?"

He'd been asking me that ever since I'd had the first nightmare a couple of weeks ago, but once again, I shook my head. I didn't want to talk about it. I didn't even want to *think* about it, even though my refusal to deal was probably causing some of my nightmares. After a moment, I sighed, suddenly tired—of Reapers, of fighting, and most especially of all the horrible memories that I could never, ever forget, not even when I went to sleep.

"Gwen?" Vic asked again.

"I'm fine now," I said. "It was just a dream. It wasn't real."

This time.

Vic gave me a sympathetic look, which I ignored. The sword had been extra nice to me ever since Logan left. All of my friends had, which only reminded me all the more that he was gone.

Still, despite my words, the nightmare had shaken me, and once again, I felt that desperate need to escape, to go someplace where no one was watching me, to go someplace where no one would think to look for me or try to hurt me. I glanced at the clock on my nightstand. Just after eight. I still had some time before the dorms locked down for the night at ten.

I gave Nyx one more hug, carried her back over to her basket, and helped her settle down inside it. Then, I shrugged into my jacket and grabbed my gloves and scarf. I also plucked Vic off the wall and belted the sword and his scabbard around my waist. Unlike in my dream, I wasn't going to be so stupid as to not take a weapon with me, even if my destination wasn't that far away and campus was supposedly safer these days.

"Where are we going?" Vic asked.

"You'll see."

I opened the door and left my dorm room.

For real, this time.

Chapter 2

I'd told Alexei I was staying put in my room for the rest of the night, so he'd gone back to his own dorm instead of standing guard outside my door. Good. I didn't want him to know where I was going. I didn't want anyone to know. Seriously, it was that sad and pathetic.

I didn't bother crawling out a window like I had in my dream. Instead, I walked down the steps and right out the front door of Styx Hall.

One thing that was the same in real life as in my nightmare was the weather. Because of the cold, snow, and blustering winds, campus was as deserted as I'd imagined it had been—except for the members of the Protectorate.

Men and women of all shapes, sizes, and ethnicities could be seen patrolling the academy grounds, standing guard under trees and peering into the shadows that had spread out over the landscape. After the Reaper attack at the band concert, security on campus had been seriously beefed up, and members of the Protectorate could be seen here twenty-four-seven now. I doubted it would help, though. Try as they might, the Protectorate couldn't be everywhere at once. Sooner or later, the Reapers would strike here again, and all I could do was to wait for it to happen—and try to survive.

Another thing that was the same was Aiko, who was standing below my windows, just as she had in my dream. I waved at the Ninja, and she lifted her hand and waved back. I liked Aiko. She read comic books and graphic novels, just like I did.

I stepped onto the path outside my dorm and hurried across campus. Aiko watched me go but didn't follow, since her orders were to keep an eye on my dorm—not necessarily on me. That was Alexei's job. I felt bad about not keeping my promise to him to stay inside, but I couldn't sit in my room for the rest of the night. Not after the nightmare. So I headed toward Hephaestus Hall, one of the boys' dorms.

All of the Mythos dorms required a student ID card in order to get inside, and your card only let you in to the dorm where you lived. But if you leaned on the front bell long enough, someone would eventually get fed up enough to buzz you inside without checking to make sure you really belonged there. We kids were totally lazy that way. I only had to hold down the bell for thirty seconds before the door clicked open.

"Enough already!" a male voice rumbled from deeper inside the dorm. "We're trying to watch the game!"

I grinned, opened the door, and stepped through before the guy came to investigate. Judging from the alternating cheers and groans I heard coming from the common room, everyone in the dorm was watching the game, which made it easy for me to climb the steps to the fifth floor. I paused at the top of the stairs, wondering if someone might actually be in his room, studying, but everything was still and quiet. Since the coast was clear, I crept down the hallway until I reached the last door.

I stopped and cocked my head to the side, listening, but no sounds came from the other side. Then again, I hadn't expected them to—I knew exactly how empty this particular room was. I reached into my messenger bag and drew out my wallet. It only took me a minute to slide my driver's license in between the lock and the frame and pop open the door. I slid through to the other side and shut the door behind me.

The room was dark, so I hit the switch on the wall. Lights blazed on, revealing the same furniture that all of the kids had. A bed, a desk, some bookcases, a flat-screen TV mounted on one of the walls. The only thing that was different about the room was all the trophies he'd won. Dozens of little gold men holding swords, spears, and other weapons peeped out at me from the desk, the bookcases, and a shelf above the bed. There was even a life-sized trophy stuffed in the corner, a staff clutched in his hands like the man was about to step forward and bash me over the head with it. I shivered and looked away. Somehow, the fact that none of the trophies actually had distinct faces made them even creepier.

A loud sigh sounded, and I realized that Vic was awake. The sword had gone to sleep, as was his habit when he was in his scabbard. I pulled the sword free of the leather and held him up so that we were face-to-face. The sword glanced around the room.

Vic sighed again. "Really? You're going to come in here and mope again?"

"I'm not moping," I said in a defensive voice.

"Really?" Vic asked again, his voice made even more sarcastic by his biting English accent. "Because I think that sitting on the Spartan's bed and staring at his things definitely qualifies as moping. *Brooding*, even. Especially when you've done it a dozen times since he left."

I looked out over Logan's room. Maybe Vic was right. Maybe I was moping over the Spartan and the fact that he'd left Mythos—that he'd left *me*.

I'd first come in here two weeks ago hoping to find some clue as to where Logan had gone. He had asked me not to look for him, and I'd wanted to respect his wishes. Really, I had. I wasn't planning to track him down and beg him to come back or anything crazy like that. But I figured that maybe my heart wouldn't hurt quite as much if I at least knew where he was—and that he was okay. So I'd snuck into his room, determined to use my magic to flash on his things until I figured out where he'd gone with his dad, Linus. The first thing I had found had been a note propped up on his desk:

Seriously, Gypsy girl.
Stop looking for me.
Love,
Logan

I didn't know whether to smile or grumble that he knew me so well.

After I found the note, I abandoned my plan to find out where Logan was. But I couldn't keep myself from sneaking into his room, especially after the nightmares started. If I closed my eyes and touched his myth-history book or one of the trophies he'd won, I could feel, see,

and hear the *real* Logan and not the Reaper-crazed mur-
derer he'd turned into in my nightmares—the one who
seemed to take such evil delight in stabbing me to death
over and over again. By using my psychometry on one
of his leather jackets or the swords he had lined up in
the back of his closet, I could almost pretend he was still
here with me, getting ready to meet me at the dining hall
for lunch or come to the gym for early morning weapons
training. It almost made me feel better about things.

Almost.

"Well, if you're determined to spend the rest of the
night in here brooding, then I'm going back to sleep,"
Vic said. "Wake me when there's something to kill."

The sword snapped his eye shut. I sighed and slid him
back into his scabbard. At least he wasn't going to
mouth off to me anymore. Or worse, stare at me with
such pity in his eye.

I walked over and sat down on the bed, right next to
a photo. I picked up the glossy paper, which showed me
sitting on the steps outside the Library of Antiquities,
my arms around Logan. He had the same black hair and
blue eyes as in my dream, but the teasing, mischievous
grin that stretched across his face was something that
never appeared in my nightmares. It was a welcome
sight, one I never got tired of, especially given the hor-
rific images my brain kept conjuring up of him.

He smiled up at me, and I ran my fingers over his
face.

"Oh Spartan," I whispered. "I wish you really were
sitting on the library steps right now. I wish I was there
with you too."

Logan kept grinning at me. Of course, he never an-

swered when I talked to him like this, and he hadn't re-
sponded to any of my voice mails or texts either. Sometimes he seemed like a wonderful dream I'd had—one
that was gone forever. Maybe that's why the nightmares
were so terrible, because he wasn't here to show me that
he wasn't that monster, even though I knew the goodness in his heart. Maybe that's the reason I snuck into
his room so often. So I could remind myself just how
real Logan was—and hope that he'd come to his senses
and come back to the academy soon.

That he'd come back to me soon.

I snorted. Yeah, Vic was right. Nightmares or not, I
was being totally, utterly pathetic.

A pretty silver frame embossed with flowers and vines
also lay on the bed. Logan had been going to frame the
photo of us and give it to me for Valentine's Day. I'd
used my psychometry to flash on the picture and the
frame. He'd been smiling as he'd picked out the frame
in one of the Cypress Mountain shops and thinking
about how nice the photo of us would look on my desk
next to the ones I had of my mom and Professor Metis.

I sighed, and my hand crept up to the necklace
around my throat. Six silver strands wrapped around
my neck, the diamond-tipped points joining together to
form a snowflake in the middle of the delicate, beautiful
design. A Christmas gift from Logan. One that I almost
always wore, despite the bad memories associated with
it—the ones of him attacking me.

For a moment, my chest ached, and I let go of the
necklace and massaged a spot right over my heart. Two
scars slashed across my skin there. One was from
Logan's attack, while the other had been made by Pre-

ston Ashton, a Reaper boy who'd stabbed me. Daphne and Professor Metis had both used their healing magic to try to get rid of my scars, but it hadn't worked. Metis said that sometimes powerful artifacts left behind marks that would never, ever fade—just like my memories of the battles would never, ever disappear.

I also had two marks on my hands—one from the fight with Logan, while the other was where Vivian had cut me with the Helheim Dagger when she'd used the artifact and my blood to free Loki. The strange thing was that the marks on my hand exactly matched the ones over my heart—right down to their size, shape, and the odd, off-center X they made as they slashed over each other. I wondered how many more scars I would get before Loki was dead—or I was.

Thinking about Vivian, Preston, and the other Reapers made anger bubble up in my chest, burning away my melancholy. But the truth was that I wasn't just angry at the Reapers—I was pissed at Logan too.

I knew that he had felt he had to leave Mythos, that he thought he couldn't trust himself not to hurt me again, that he needed some time to sort out everything that had happened. In my head, I *knew* that. But in my heart, it felt like he'd abandoned me—like he'd left me to fight the Reapers and face the nightmares alone.

I let out a bitter laugh. Maybe I wasn't angry so much as I was jealous. Because if I never saw another Reaper again, it would be too soon. But there was nothing I could about that—or anything else.

Nothing at all.

So I slid the photo of me and Logan into the frame, then hugged the silver to my chest, as though it would ease my anger, as though it would soothe the hollow ache inside me, as though it were a shield that would protect me, as though the small bit of metal would keep my heart from breaking any more than it already had.

It didn't, of course, but at least I felt that I could breathe again and that the walls weren't closing in on me. So I sat there on Logan's bed, holding the photo of us, for a while longer.

Chapter 3

I made it back to my dorm right before the ten o'clock curfew, but I didn't sleep much that night. Every time I started to drift off, I would jerk awake, worried that I'd have another nightmare about Logan and the Reapers. Finally, I gave up trying to sleep, wrapped myself in my comforter, curled up in the padded window seat, and stared out into the dark of the night. That way if Vivian and the rest of the Reapers attacked, at least I'd see them coming.

But no Reapers appeared, the sun came up, the way it always did, and I had to face another day.

Weapons training with my friends Oliver and Kenzie in the gym. Morning classes. Lunch with Oliver and Alexei. Afternoon classes. A quick visit off-campus to see my Grandma Frost. Same-old, same-old, right up until it was time for me to go work my shift at the Library of Antiquities.

Normally, I would have been sprawled across my bed, reading through my latest stash of comic books and eating some sinfully sweet treat that Grandma Frost had baked for me. But right now, I was in another dorm room, one where the walls, the ceiling, and the curtains were all pink. I shifted on the bed, wrinkling the comforter, which was also, you guessed it, pink. Sunlight streaming in through the lace curtains slanted across the bookcase in the corner, highlighting the volumes there. Even her myth-history books had pink covers on them. How had she managed that?

I didn't consider myself a tomboy, but I certainly was no girly-girl, and being around so much pink made me a little queasy. If I didn't have nightmares already, I certainly would now. No doubt the next time I dreamed about Logan killing me, he'd be wearing a pink leather jacket. I snorted at the thought.

A pair of fingers snapped in front of my face, followed by a shower of princess pink sparks. I jerked away from the explosion of magic and looked up to find Daphne Cruz standing in front of me, her hands on her hips and her foot tapping out a quick rhythm on the pink rug on the floor.

"Gwen? Are you even paying attention to me?"

"Sure," I said in a bright voice. "I was just waiting for you to try on the next dress."

Daphne's black eyes narrowed, and more sparks shot out of her fingertips. Like all Valkyries, Daphne always gave off more magic whenever she was angry, upset—or aggravated, in this case, by me and my complete lack of fashion sense.

She'd asked me over here to help her pick out something to wear for a big date that she had planned for next weekend with her boyfriend, band geek Carson Callahan. I'd been sitting on Daphne's bed for the last hour, watching her try on dresses, sweaters, and the occasional pair of pink designer jeans, all with matching purses, jewelry, and other accessories.

"Well?" she demanded. "What do you think of this one?"

She twirled around, causing her blond hair to dance around her shoulders and the short skirt on her pink dress to swirl out around her legs. The rich color of the fabric made me long for some of Grandma Frost's homemade strawberry ice cream.

"Um . . . it's very . . . pink?"

Daphne rolled her eyes. "Of *course*, it's pink. Is there any other color? But do you like this pink dress better than the raspberry one I tried on a minute ago? Or what about the cotton candy skirt I showed you before that? I think I have a bubblegum sweater in my closet somewhere too . . ."

Daphne stalked over to her closet and started grabbing even more clothes out of the depths, tossing them aside until she found the ones she wanted. With her great Valkyrie strength, the garments flew all over the room, landing on the bookcase, the TV, and even on the computer monitors, servers, and hard drives on her desk that she loved to tinker with in her spare time.

I ducked down just in time to avoid getting hit in the face by a baby pink turtleneck. Desperate, I glanced at Vic for help, since I'd propped him up on the bed when I'd first come into the room. But the sword's mouth was open, and he was snoring softly. Vic wasn't into fashion any more than I was. I'd brought Nyx along too, and the wolf pup was crouched down on the floor on the far side of the room, getting ready to pounce on a stuffed Hello Kitty that was propped up against the bottom of one of the bookcases. Even the plush toy had on a pink dress.

"There it is!" Daphne said, stepping away from the closet, a pale cashmere sweater in her hands. "What do you think about this?"

She held the sweater up over the dress she was wearing, and the color made her amber skin seem even lovelier than usual.

"I like it," I said. "It's very . . . pink."

I winced again, but Daphne beamed at me.

"It *is* one of my favorite sweaters," she said, holding it up to her chest again and admiring her reflection in the mirror over her vanity table. "I don't know why I didn't think of it before. Thanks, Gwen."

"Sure. No problem."

"And I'm sure it will be just perfect for the restaurant where Carson is taking me."

"Yeah. Perfect."

Daphne must have picked up on my less-than-enthusiastic voice because she abruptly spun back around to face me. "I'm sorry. I shouldn't be talking about Carson and some stupid date that he's taking me on. Not with Logan . . ."

Her voice trailed off, and this time, she winced.

"Not with Logan gone," I finished.

"I'm sorry, Gwen. This was a dumb idea, wasn't it? I just wanted to cheer you up—"

I held up my hand, cutting her off. "No, it's fine. Just because Logan isn't here doesn't mean that life doesn't go on. That *we* don't go on. I'm glad that you and Carson are so happy together. And coming here today helped take my mind off . . . other things."

Namely, my nightmares, although I didn't tell her that. I hadn't told Grandma Frost or Professor Metis about them either. Vic and Nyx were the only ones who knew that I dreamed about Logan stabbing me over and over again, if only because they were with me in my room every night and had to listen to my screams.

Daphne chewed her lower lip in doubt, and more sparks of magic flickered in the air around her. I made myself smile at her, hoping to convince her that I was having a great time. Yeah, maybe it hadn't been the easiest thing in the world, hearing her chatter on about her date with Carson, especially since my one and only date with Logan had ended with me getting arrested by the Protectorate a few weeks ago. But she was just trying to be a good friend, and I wasn't going to ruin her fun because I was tired, cranky, and worried about problems I couldn't fix.

"Are you sure?" Daphne asked, tossing her sweater aside and plopping down on the bed beside me. "Because we can totally do something else."

"I'm sure," I replied in a firm voice. "Besides, we've only been through half your closet. We can't stop now."

Daphne arched an eyebrow. "Your sarcasm is noted."

She reached down, grabbed a pillow off the bed, and threw it at me, but I laughed and easily ducked down out of the way.

An alarm on my cell phone beeped, reminding me that I had fifteen minutes to get my butt in gear and get over to the library.

"And fun time is officially over," I said, making a face and getting up off the bed. "Gotta go slave away in the library. You know Nickamedes will be on my case if I'm so much as one minute late."

On the floor, Nyx let out a fierce growl and finally pounced on the stuffed toy, tearing into it with her baby teeth. Vic's eye snapped open at the sound of the fabric ripping, and he stared at the wolf pup.

"Way to go, fuzzball," Vic said. "You're getting much better at pouncing on things. I approve. Soon, you'll be ready to take on some Reapers."

Nyx puffed up with pride and spent the next two minutes racing from one side of the room to the other, the Hello Kitty plushie hanging out of her mouth as she showed off her prize to me, Vic, and Daphne.

"You know that was my favorite toy, right?" Daphne groused.

"Well, just think," I chirped. "Now you can buy a new one . . . that's wearing even *more* pink."

Daphne gave me a shove, careful not to hurt me with her Valkyrie strength. I laughed and tossed a pillow back at her.

Nyx plopped down on her butt, tilted her head back, and let out a triumphant, if slightly squeaky, howl. She'd totally killed Hello Kitty, and she knew it. And even Daphne had to smile at that.

Daphne offered to walk with me over to the library, but I told her to stay put and finish going through her closet. She reluctantly agreed.

Usually, Alexei would have been waiting outside Daphne's dorm, Valhalla Hall, to walk with me wherever I was going, but he'd texted me to say he was busy with something and he'd meet me at the library. So I looped my gray messenger bag over my chest, clipped a purple leash to the collar Nyx was wearing, per Linus Quinn and the Protectorate's rules, and headed out.

It was even colder today than it had been yesterday, and the whistling winter wind cut through my thick layers of clothes like they weren't even there. But campus was much livelier this afternoon, as kids went to their after-school clubs, sports, and activities, headed over to the dining hall to get some supper, or trudged toward the library to finally get started on that essay that was due, like, first thing in the morning.

I walked along the cobblestone path winding up the hill and stepped onto the main quad, which featured the five buildings where students spent most of their time— English-history, math-science, the gym, the dining hall, and the Library of Antiquities.

I tucked my chin down into my scarf and hurried over to the library. Despite the cold, I stopped a moment at the bottom of the main steps, where two gryphon statues sat.

Eagle heads, wings, lions' bodies, long tails, curved beaks, sharp talons. The gryphons seemed like they were about a breath away from breaking free of their stone shells and attacking anyone who so much as glanced at them funny. But it wasn't just how fierce they looked that made them seem special to me. There was some sort of presence, some spark of life, deep inside the stone. I'd felt it before when I'd touched the statues, and I could sense it now. But instead of filling me with dread like it used to, the fact that the gryphons were watching over me gave me a sense of comfort and peace. As if maybe they really would spring to life and help if something terrible happened here.

Another cold blast of wind swept across the quad, making me shiver, so I gave the gryphons a small salute, then left the statues behind, hurried up the steps, and headed into the library.

It might be cold, dark, and gloomy outside, but the high dome that arced over the main space gave the inside of the library a bright, airy feel. Stacks of books ringed the bottom floor, while a wide aisle cut through the middle of them and led to a series of glassed-in offices in the center of the enormous room. Acres of marble made up the floor and the walls, but my gaze drifted up to the second floor and the statues there—the ones of all the gods and goddesses of all the cultures of the world.

The statues circled the entire balcony, each facing out toward the center of the library, as if they were watching over the students studying below. Slender columns separated the statues from each other, although it sometimes seemed to me as if the gods and goddesses were leaning around the columns and whispering to each other about all the happenings below. Then again, that might have just been my psychometry playing tricks on me, like it so often did, especially where statues were concerned.

I walked down the main aisle, but instead of going behind the checkout counter, logging on to the computer system, and getting to work, I veered off to my right, where a freestanding coffee cart was shoved in between some study tables and the stacks behind them. I got in line and breathed in, enjoying the rich, dark aroma of the hot espresso mixed with the softer scents of chocolate, vanilla, and cinnamon that flavored the air.

Maybe it was the cold outside, but I wasn't the only one who wanted a drink or a snack, and several kids were ahead of me in line. As I stood there, I was aware of eyes on me. Except this time, it wasn't the statues who were watching me—it was my fellow students.

I knew what they saw when they looked at me—a girl with violet-colored eyes and frizzy, wavy brown hair who was wearing not-so-designer jeans, sneakers, and a gray T-shirt and sweater under her purple plaid jacket. Nothing really out of the ordinary or impressive, but the students started talking all the same.

"Look. There's Gwen Frost."

"Is that a real Fenrir wolf she has with her? It's so cute!"

"I wonder what she's up to now?"

"The Gypsy girl? Probably trying to figure out how to stop the Reapers. They say she's Nike's Champion . . ."

Those whispers and more swirled around me like the bits of snow had outside. I grimaced, but there was nothing I could do but pretend I didn't hear everyone talking about me or the chimes on their phones as they texted their friends about the latest Gwen Frost sighting. Daphne had told me that someone had even come up with an app so everyone could track me around campus with their phones. As if I didn't have enough problems already without everyone knowing exactly where I was all the freaking time.

Oh yeah, everyone seemed to be watching every move I made, and it had only gotten worse since the Reaper attack at the winter band concert. Now, all the kids at

Mythos knew that I was Nike's Champion—and that I was supposed to save us all.

They didn't know the details, though. That all I had to do was find some mysterious magical artifact that would supposedly let me kill Loki, who was pretty much all-powerful and evil incarnate.

No pressure or anything.

Nyx cocked her head to the side, staring up at the other kids. She gave a tentative little growl, hoping that someone would drop to their knees and pet her, but the low sound only made the other students shy away from her. I couldn't blame them for that, though. Most kids at the academy weren't used to mythological creatures like Fenrir wolves, Nemean prowlers, and Black rocs trying to do anything but kill them.

I was the last one in line, and, finally, it was my turn to order. I scanned the menu tacked up beside the cash register.

"Give me a bottled water, a jumbo pretzel with nacho cheese sauce, and a dark chocolate brownie," I said.

Silence.

I peered around a display of blueberry muffins. A woman sat on a stool behind the cash register, reading through a celebrity gossip magazine as if it was the most interesting thing ever. The woman was old—even older than Grandma Frost—with a shock of long, white hair that seemed to flow into the long, white gown she wore. Her eyes were as black, bright, and shiny as a bird's, while dark wrinkles streaked across her face, almost like the thin grooves were filled with shadows instead of just sagging skin. She licked her thumb and turned another page in her magazine, completely ignoring me, even though I'd stepped up to the counter as soon as the Viking in front of me had left.

I sighed. Raven was here today. I should have known.

Raven ran the coffee cart, one of the many odd jobs she had at the academy, along with being on the security council, overseeing members of the Protectorate when they cleaned up crime scenes, and watching over any Reapers being kept in the prison in the math-science building. I didn't know exactly *why* Raven had all of these jobs, since she didn't seem particularly qualified for any of them and was always scanning through some magazine or another, but everything important always seemed to get done, and I guess that's all the Powers That Were really cared about.

I cleared my throat, and Raven finally put down her magazine. I repeated my order, and she moved from one side of the cart to the other, heating up my pretzel and cheese sauce in the small microwave and handing them to me, along with my bottled water and brownie. I reached into my jeans pocket, drew out a ten-dollar bill, and handed it across the counter to her, careful not to let my fingers brush hers. Not only could I flash on objects, but my psychometry also kicked in whenever I touched another person. Right now, I had no desire to see how bored Raven was sitting at the coffee cart making hot peppermint chocolate for folks.

Still, as I looked at her, it seemed like her face flickered for a moment, as though there was something underneath her features the same way there was something lurking beneath all the statues on campus.

"One day I'm going to figure out what you're hiding with all of those wrinkles," I said.

Raven raised her bushy eyebrows at me, but she didn't say anything. She'd never said anything to me, so I had no idea what her voice sounded like, whether it would be light and lilting or the cackle and crackle of an old crone.

She handed me my change, sat down on her stool, and stuck her nose back in her magazine. I rolled my eyes, grabbed my food, and hurried down the main aisle to the checkout counter. Nyx trotted along beside me, her toenails *click-click-clicking* against the floor.

I stepped behind the counter, laid my food down on it, and put my messenger bag on the floor next to a large gray wicker basket. Grandma Frost had given me the basket so Nyx would have a comfy place to hang out while I was working. I crouched down and unclipped the leash from around the wolf's neck, although I left the collar on her.

"I have to go to work now, so stay in your basket, okay?" I murmured, rubbing her tiny ears between my fingers.

Nyx leaned into my hand and let out a contented sigh. Then, she plopped down on her cute, pudgy, baby belly, tucked her tail over her nose, and closed her violet-colored eyes. She'd been coming to the library with me for several days now, so she knew the drill.

"The fuzzball has the right idea," Vic said, his half of a mouth stretching into a wide, loud yawn. "Wake me when there are Reapers to kill."

"I wouldn't *dream* of doing anything else."

Vic glared at me, picking up on the sarcasm in my voice. "Hmph!" he huffed, then snapped his eye shut.

I left Vic in his scabbard and propped the sword up

next to Nyx. Despite his snit, I knew that Vic would give a shout and let me know if he or Nyx needed anything, and that Nyx would come running to get me if something happened to Vic. I liked that the two of them could watch each other's backs, especially these days, when we all knew that Reapers could attack anywhere, anytime—even in the Library of Antiquities.

I plopped down on a stool and logged in to the computer system. Then, I opened my bag of food and arranged it on the counter. I dunked my pretzel into the warm, nacho cheese sauce and was about to take a big bite when a door opened in the glass office complex behind me, and the sharp *tap-tap-tap* of wing tips on marble sounded. A moment later, a shadow fell over me, and someone cleared his throat.

"Yes, Nickamedes?"

"You are late, Gwendolyn," he said. "At this point, do I even have to say *again*? Perhaps it would be more appropriate to say *as usual*, or *as always*, or even *for the umpteenth time*."

"I'm not late," I protested, waving my pretzel in his direction. "I've been in the library for ten minutes already. I was at the coffee cart. See?"

Nickamedes sniffed. "Standing in line is not the same thing as actually being behind the counter working."

I rolled my eyes. Sometimes, I thought the two of us were just destined to disagree.

"And will you please look at me when I am speaking to you?"

I pressed my lips together, raised my head, and looked up at him. The head librarian was handsome, for a guy in his forties, with ink-black hair and blue eyes. You could tell how lean and muscled his body was, despite the dark blue sweater vest, shirt, tie, and black corduroy pants he wore. I wasn't trying to be rude by ignoring him and concentrating on my food. Really, I wasn't. But Nickamedes looked so much like his nephew that it made my heart clench. Because the librarian was yet another reminder that Logan was gone.

"Thank you," Nickamedes said, crossing his arms over his chest. "Now, as I was saying, you are late *again*, and I think that..."

I immediately dropped my gaze back down to my food. Okay, okay, so I was totally tuning out his lecture, but only because it was the same one he'd given me a dozen times before. Besides, I was hungry. I started to lean forward to take a bite of my pretzel, when the librarian snatched it out of my hand.

"Hey!" I said. "I was eating that!"

"Correction, you *were* going to eat that," Nickamedes said. "Right now, you are going to shelve books."

He put my pretzel down on top of its bag on the counter, grabbed a stack of books off a metal cart, and dumped them in my arms.

"But—"

"No buts," Nickamedes said. "Books now, food later."

The librarian crossed his arms over his chest and gave me a pointed stare. He was standing between me and my food, so there was no way I could grab my pretzel, shove it into my mouth, and take it into the stacks with me. Even if I did, Nickamedes would complain about how I was getting crumbs all over his precious books. There was just no winning with him.

"Now, if you please, Gwendolyn."

"Yes, master," I sniped.

Nickamedes's eyes narrowed at my snide tone, but I didn't care. I gave my food one more longing look before I tightened my grip on the books and trudged back into the stacks.

Chapter 4

I spent the next half hour shelving books. By the time I got back to my food, the warm, soft pretzel and ooey, gooey cheese sauce were a hard, cold, congealed mess. So I dumped them in the trash and made do with my brownie and bottled water.

I'd just finished licking the last of the dark chocolate crumbs off my fingers when Nickamedes stepped behind the counter. He'd been over to Raven's coffee cart too, judging from the blueberry muffin and water bottle he was holding. A professor came over and asked him a question. Nickamedes took a swig of his water, then put his bottle on the counter right next to mine. I edged my bottle away from his and turned mine so that the label faced out toward the rest of the library so I would know which one was which. I had no desire to accidentally ingest his germs. I might catch something awful, like, you know, *punctuality*. I also noticed that the librarian didn't wait to eat *his* muffin as he looked up something in the computer system for the professor.

I was still shooting Nickamedes angry, jealous glances when Oliver Hector stepped up to the checkout counter.

Sandy blond hair, green eyes, great smile, muscular body. The Spartan was cute, but, more important, he was my friend. Oliver watched me watching the librarian.

"You know, if I were Nickamedes, I'd be glad that you just had touch magic, instead of the ability to shoot fire out your eyeballs," Oliver drawled. "Because Nickamedes would be totally toasted right now."

I rolled my eyes, but I had to laugh. "Yeah, well, if I had that power, I'd save it to use on Reapers. I wouldn't mind melting off Vivian's face. Or Agrona's."

"I don't think any of us would mind that," Oliver said.

I thought about my recurring nightmare. Maybe next time instead of letting Logan attack me, I could try to throw myself off the amphitheater stage and fight Vivian and Agrona instead. No doubt they would still kill me in my dream, but that wouldn't be as bad as Logan murdering me again—and having to stare into his Reaper red eyes while he did it.

Oliver walked around the counter, slung his bag down next to mine, and hopped up on a stool that was sitting against the glass wall behind me.

I frowned. "What are you doing?"

He shrugged. "Alexei had some meeting with the other Protectorate guards that's running long, so he asked me to keep an eye on you until he gets here."

I sighed. "I am perfectly capable of taking care of myself, you know. I think I've proven that enough already."

"I know," Oliver replied. "But I also know that all of the Reapers are gunning for you, Gwen. So just relax and let us watch your back, okay?"

I sighed again. He was right, but sometimes it made me feel so helpless, so *useless*, always being watched over by somebody, whether it was Alexei, Oliver, Daphne, or one of my other friends. I was a target for the Reapers, and now they were too, just because they were my friends. I didn't know what I would do if something happened to one of them because of me—because they'd taken an arrow or a dagger meant for me. But no matter what I said or did, my friends insisted on sticking by me, telling me we were all in this together. It made me want to scream at their stubbornness—and cry because of their loyalty.

"All right, all right," I groused. "You can stay. But only because you're so cute, and I need some eye candy to look at."

His grin widened. "Oh Gypsy. You say the sweetest things."

I rolled my eyes again. Oliver laughed.

The next two hours dragged by. I did all my usual chores. Shelved books. Helped kids locate reference material for their homework assignments. Even dusted a few of the artifact cases in the stacks.

Cleaning off the cases made me think about Ran's net, which I'd shoved into the bottom of my messenger bag for safekeeping. Of course, I'd shown the net to Professor Metis when Alexei, Daphne, and I had brought it back from the Crius Coliseum a few days ago, but Metis didn't know what was so special about it any more than I did. So she'd told me to hang on to it for now. I didn't know what good the net would do, stuffed in among my comic books and the tin I had that was shaped like a giant chocolate chip cookie, but like Metis had said, at least we'd know where it was.

Since I didn't have anything else to do, I decided to take another look at the net. I reached into my bag, drew out a small white card that had been in the artifact case with the net, and scanned through the words on the front, even though I'd read them a dozen times already.

This net is thought to have belonged to Ran, the Norse goddess of storms, and was rumored to be among her favorite fishing gear. Despite its fragile appearance, the net is quite strong and can hold much more than it should be able to, given its relatively small size. The braided seaweed itself is thought to have the unusual property of making whatever is inside it seem much lighter than its actual weight . . .

The card went on to talk about some of the creatures Ran had supposedly caught and tamed with the net, but I skimmed over the rest of the words.

Instead, I reached back into my bag and grabbed the thin, threadbare net itself. To my surprise, it had folded up quite easily, and I'd looped it over and over again, until the whole thing was no bigger and not much thicker than a belt. I threaded my fingers through some of the loops and reached for my magic.

But the only thing I saw was the endless rise and fall of the blue-gray ocean, and the only thing I felt was a smooth, constant motion, as if I was bobbing up and down like a fishing lure riding the tops of the waves. The sharp tang of the sea filled my nose, while the sounds of the swells slapping against each other echoed in my ears. I licked my lips and tasted salt. Even more of it seemed to be crusted in my hair, and I could almost feel gritty bits of sand sticking to my skin, as though I'd spent the day at the beach.

It wasn't unpleasant, though. In fact, the sensations were some of the nicest I'd experienced with my magic in a long time. So nice, so calm, so soothing, that I could have let the waves carry me away—and all my fears, worries, and heartache along with them.

But I had a job to do, so instead I concentrated, focusing on the net and all of the images, memories, and emotions attached to it, but the scene and the feelings didn't change. After a few more seconds, I opened my eyes, unwound my fingers from the gray seaweed, and stuffed the net and the card back into my bag.

"Anything new?" Oliver asked, watching me.

I shook my head. "Nothing I haven't seen before."

"But Nike showed it to you, so it has to be important, right?"

"I guess. Although I have no idea what I'm supposed to do with a mythological fishing net when we're hundreds of miles away from the ocean."

My eyes drifted upward, searching for inspiration— or some sort of clue. For months, I'd only been able to see darkness whenever I'd gazed up at the ceiling inside the Library of Antiquities. But a few weeks ago, Nike had shown me the amazing fresco hidden beneath the shadows—one of me and my friends fighting the Reapers in some great battle. Each of us had been holding a weapon or some other object, and those were the artifacts that Nike had asked me to find and keep out of the

Reapers' hands. So far, though, Ran's net had been the only thing I'd been able to identify and track down.

But once again, shadows obscured the fresco. No help there. At least not tonight.

"But it looks like the net in my drawing, right?" Oliver asked.

I couldn't draw to save my life, but Oliver had some mad art mojo so he'd happily sketched the fresco for me, based on my own crude drawings and descriptions. His detailed sketch was also nestled inside my messenger bag for safekeeping.

"Your drawing is perfect, and this is definitely the right net," I said. "It's not your fault I'm too dumb to understand what the big deal is about it."

"Don't worry, Gwen. You'll figure it out. You always do. I have faith in you."

"Well, it's a good thing one of us does," I grumbled.

Oliver grinned at my sarcasm.

Since I'd struck out with the net, I shelved a few more books and dusted a couple more artifact cases, but my mind wasn't on the tasks, and I was only going through the motions, just like I had ever since Logan had left. More than once, I found myself staring off into space, wondering where he was and what he was doing. If he was okay. If he was cold or hungry or scared or tired.

If he was thinking about me.

After about two minutes of that, I'd shake off my sorrow and get angry at for myself for obsessing about him. Vic was right. I really needed to quit brooding and get on with killing Reapers. Or at the very least, finish my homework for tomorrow.

Easier said than done. Because five minutes later, instead of reading through my myth-history book like I should have been, I found myself thinking about Logan again.

Finally, I couldn't stand it any longer, so I turned around on my stool and faced Oliver, who was messing with his phone.

"So..." I said in a light voice, trying not to let on how important this was to me. "Have you heard anything from Logan?"

Oliver froze. He looked at me, then glanced down at the screen. Guilt flickered in his green eyes.

"You're texting with him right now, aren't you?"

Oliver winced. He typed something else on his phone, then slid the device into his pants pocket. He didn't answer my question.

"How is he? Where is he? Is he okay? Is he ever coming back to the academy?"

They were the same questions I'd asked everyone a hundred times already. The same ones I thought about late at night in my room, especially after I'd had one of my nightmares.

Oliver sighed. "Logan needs some time, Gwen. He needs some space, from the academy and everything that happened. But yes, to answer your question, he's fine. At least, that's what he says when he texts me." He hesitated. "If it helps at all, he asks about you all the time."

"And what do you tell him?" I asked in a soft voice.

He hesitated again. "That you miss him. That we all miss him. That we need him, and that he should get his ass back here as soon as he can."

"And what does he say to that?"

Oliver shrugged. "Nothing. Just...nothing. I don't

know when he's coming back. I don't know if he's *ever* coming back. Not after what the Reapers did to him. And especially not after what he did to you."

I let out a breath. The thought that Logan might never return was one I hadn't let myself dwell on too much, but now, it was all I could think about, like a cold fist wrapped around my heart and slowly crushing it, crushing me, from the inside out. Suddenly, it was too small behind the checkout counter. Too cramped, too cluttered, and much too crowded for me to catch my breath.

Oliver noticed my stricken expression. "I didn't mean that, Gwen. It's not your fault Logan's gone."

But it was, and we both knew it. I shook my head, grabbed some books, and disappeared into the stacks before Oliver could see how much I was hurting.

Thankfully, Oliver decided not to follow me. I went back to a remote part of the stacks, the spot where Vic's case had once been. I stood there, eyes closed, books clutched to my chest, trying to breathe. In and out, in and out, in and out, like my mom had taught me to do whenever I was worried, nervous, scared, or upset.

Worried? Check. Upset? Definitely. And once again, I felt that spurt of anger at Logan for not being here, for leaving me behind to deal with everything.

It took a few minutes, but my heart stopped aching, and the pressure in my lungs slowly eased. I still felt cold inside, though—cold, dull, and empty. My anger was gone, or at least iced over for the moment, and I couldn't even cry. My tears seemed to be as frozen as the rest of me felt deep down inside.

Once again, I went through the motions, shelving the books I'd grabbed. When that was done, I wandered up the stairs to the second floor. It was quieter here, and the only sound was the faint scuffle of my sneakers on the marble. Oliver would probably get worried and come looking for me at some point, but for now, I enjoyed the silence—and the solitude.

Eventually, I wound up in a familiar spot in the circular pantheon—in front of Nike's statue.

The Greek goddess of victory looked the same in her marble form as when she appeared to me in real life. Her hair twisted into ringlets and falling down past her slim shoulders. A white, toga-like gown wrapped around her slender, muscled body. Wings arching up over her back. A crown of laurels resting on top of her head. Features that were somehow strong, cold, terrible, and beautiful all at the same time.

Normally, I said a few words to the goddess whenever I came up here to her statue, but I didn't feel like it tonight. Instead, I curled up into a ball at the base of the statue and leaned my head back against the cool, smooth marble.

After a while, I felt calmer, like I had the strength to go downstairs and face the rest of the night, but I stayed where I was. Since I was on the second floor, I had a bird's-eye view of all the students studying below—including the guy standing by the checkout counter.

I wasn't sure what drew my attention to him. Maybe it was the way he just stood there, as though he were waiting for someone to come and help him. Maybe it was the furtive looks he kept giving Oliver, who was still sitting behind the counter and texting on his phone again, oblivious to everything else. Or maybe it was the fact that he didn't have anything in his hands. No text-books, no notepads, no pens, not even a tablet that he was using to idly surf the web instead of doing his homework like he should have been. But something about the guy just seemed . . . wrong.

I scooted over to the edge of the balcony so I could get a better look at him. Jeans, green sweater, brown boots, brown leather jacket. He had on the same clothes as everyone else, right down to the designer logos that covered the expensive fabrics. So I studied his face. Brown hair, dark eyes, tan skin.

Wait a second. I knew him. Jason Anderson. A Viking and a second-year student like me. He sat two desks over from me in English-lit. I'd never paid much atten-tion to Jason before, except to say hello or ask him to pass me a book or a copy of the latest pop quiz we were taking. But something about him made me keep watch-ing him now.

Jason tentatively put one hand on the counter, then another one—and then he reached out and grabbed my water bottle.

I frowned. What was he doing messing with my drink? As I watched, Jason slid a small white pouch out of his jeans pocket. He glanced around to make sure no one was watching him, then dropped the bottle down by his side and held the pouch up over it. Some sort of white powder dropped into the water. Jason quickly swirled around the liquid inside so the powder dissolved in it.

I sucked in a breath. Was he—could he be—was he *poisoning* my water?

Jason put the bottle back on the counter where it had

been. He started to turn around, but then he spotted the second bottle—the one that belonged to Nickamedes. Jason must not have been sure which water was mine because he glanced around again, then did the same thing to that bottle. White powder, shake the water around until the poison dissolved, then set it down like he'd never even picked it up to start with.

"Reaper," I muttered.

Jason glanced around a final time, making sure no one had seen what he'd done. Then, he turned, went over to the study table where he'd been sitting, and gathered up his things. Now that his mission was complete, he was leaving the library, leaving the scene of the crime.

My eyes narrowed. Not if I could help it.

I scrambled to my feet and started to run.

Chapter 5

I ran into the stairwell and raced down the steps as fast as I could. I was in such a rush that I jumped down the last five steps, almost falling on my face before I managed to right myself at the last second. I drew in a breath and hurried along the back wall of the library. More than a few couples stood in the shadowy stacks, eagerly macking on each other, but I didn't have time to be disgusted by the PDAs. My focus was on stopping the Reaper boy—nothing else mattered right now.

I broke free of the stacks and skidded to a halt in the middle of the main aisle. Jason had been walking toward the open double doors that led out of the library. He'd been texting on his phone, and his head snapped up at the *squeak-squeak-squeak* of my sneakers on the floor.

"You!" I screamed, pointing my finger at him. "Jason Anderson! Stop right there!"

The Reaper froze. He was in the middle of the study tables, and all the kids stared at him, then me, wondering what was going on.

I slowly walked toward him, not sure what other

tricks he might be plotting. Jason blinked and stuffed his phone into his jacket pocket. His hand also dropped down, and he fumbled with a zipper on his backpack. I picked up my pace and charged at him, not wanting to give him the chance to draw a weapon on me, especially since Vic was still in his spot behind the checkout counter.

I put my shoulder down and barreled into the Reaper, laying him out like a linebacker would a quarterback, and we both went down in a heap, slip-slip-sliding across the slick floor. All sorts of things slid out of his open backpack—books, pens, his laptop, a sword encased in a red leather scabbard.

"Gwen!" Oliver's voice rang out above the confused shouts of the other kids.

"Reaper!" I yelled back, surging to my feet. "He's a Reaper!"

Jason reached out, snatched up his sword, pulled the weapon free of the scabbard, and got back on his feet.

"Die, Gypsy!" Jason hissed at me.

He raised his sword high, and I ducked to one side. The blade sliced by my shoulder and sank into the top of one of the study tables, right in front of where Helena Paxton, a mean-girl Amazon, had been sitting. Helena shrieked, pushed her chair back, and stumbled away.

Jason cursed and struggled to pull his weapon free of the wood. I snatched up one of Helena's books off the table, darted forward, and slammed it into the side of his head. He cursed again and lashed out at me with his fist. I turned, so that the blow only dug into my shoulder, but I still yelped as pain exploded in the joint and shot down into my arm, making me lose my grip on the book, which clattered to the floor. He definitely packed a punch with his great Viking strength. I started to throw myself forward again, but Jason managed to pull his weapon free. I stopped short. He grinned, realizing that I didn't have a sword, and he crept even closer to me.

"Now what you are going to do, Gypsy?" he taunted.

Jason raised his blade for another strike, and I lurched to the side—

A pencil zipped through the air and embedded itself in Jason's shoulder, causing him to arch back and scream with pain. It was quickly followed by two more pencils, a roll of tape, and a metal stapler that beaned him in the side of the head with a loud, satisfying *thwack*.

I looked past the Reaper. Oliver stood behind the checkout counter, his green eyes narrowed, already reaching for one of the computer keyboards. Spartans had the freaky ability to pick up any weapon—or any object—and automatically know how to kill someone with it. In Oliver's hands, that keyboard could be as deadly as a battle-ax.

But the Spartan wasn't the only one on my side now.

My fight with Jason had stunned the other students, but their surprise had quickly worn off. Chairs scraped back, shouts rose up, and the other kids started digging into their bags, drawing out the swords, staffs, and spears that were their weapons of choice. Oliver yanked the keyboard off the counter and headed toward the Reaper. Jason's eyes flicked from one kid to another, and he realized he was going to be seriously outnumbered in another minute.

"This isn't over, Gypsy!" Jason hissed again.

Then, he turned and ran toward the back of the library.

For a second, I froze, surprised that he wasn't going to stand and fight, but then I bolted into action, running after him. Jason had headed toward the right side of the library, away from Oliver, who was rushing toward him from the left, the keyboard still clutched in his hand.

"I've got him!" I yelled. "You circle around! We have to cut him off before he reaches one of the side doors and gets outside!"

Oliver nodded, turned, and raced in that direction.

Out of the corner of my eye, I noticed Nickamedes standing behind the checkout counter holding his bottle of water—the water that had been poisoned along with mine. I immediately veered in that direction.

"Stop!" I yelled. "Don't drink that!"

"Gwendolyn?" Nickamedes said, his brow furrowing as he stared at the chaos in and around the study tables. "What's going on? What are you doing? Why are all the students drawing their weapons instead of studying?"

I slapped the water bottle out of the librarian's hand. "Don't drink that!"

Nickamedes looked at me like I'd lost my mind, but I was already moving past him, reaching down, grabbing Vic, and pulling the weapon free from his scabbard. The sword's eye snapped open, and he fixed his purplish gaze on me.

"Reaper?" he asked in a hopeful voice.

"Uh-huh."

I felt the sword's mouth curve into a smile against the palm of my hand.

"Fuzzball!" Vic barked. "Time to fight!"

Nyx scrambled up out of her basket and let out a fierce growl, like a soldier obeying her general's orders.

"Gwendolyn?" Nickamedes asked again, his blue eyes going back and forth between the three of us.

"Reaper! Poison! Chase!" That was all I managed to get out before I rounded the counter, headed toward the back of the library, and started to run again.

Those moments at the checkout counter had cost me, and I didn't see Oliver or Jason as I darted into the back half of the building. The lights were turned down low on this side of the library, making the shadows seem that much darker and even more sinister than usual. But instead of charging blindly down the aisles, I slowed, eased up beside a bookcase, and peered around it.

Nothing—I saw and heard nothing.

Rows of books stretched out as far as I could see before the shadows swallowed them up at the far end of the aisle. A few glass artifact cases squatted here and there in front of the shelves, the metal and jewels inside gleaming like dull stars. I drew in several long, slow breaths, trying to calm my racing heart, and straining to hear any footsteps, any rustles of clothing, or any other whispers of movement that would tell me where Jason was.

Nothing—once again, I saw and heard nothing.

Well, if Jason wasn't going to come to me, I'd have to find him instead. So I tightened my grip on Vic and eased down the aisle, looking in front of and behind me, and peering left and right through the rows of books on either side. Nyx trotted along behind me like a pup-sized sentry. The Fenrir wolf was quiet, although her toenails softly scraped against the floor. I thought about calling out to Oliver, but I didn't want to give away my position to Jason—

I started to move over to the study tables on this side of the library when Nyx let out a fierce growl and a sword zoomed out of the darkness. I jumped to my left, and the blade bounced off the side of one of the book-cases, throwing red sparks everywhere.

I whirled around. Jason was behind me. Jeans, sweater, nice features. He looked the same as before with one no-table difference—his eyes were glowing red. A bright, fiery, intense red that told me exactly how much he hated me—and just how much he wanted to kill me.

He let out a wild battle cry and raised his weapon for another strike.

Clash-clash-clang!

Back and forth, we fought through the study tables. Nyx danced all around us, trying to get into the battle, but Jason and I were moving too fast for that. He cursed every time I blocked one of his attacks, but I didn't bother responding to him.

All I wanted to do right now was kill him.

"Gwen!" Oliver's voice drifted out of the stacks to me.

"Over here!" I yelled back.

Jason lashed out with his sword, causing me to jump back. He glanced over his shoulder and saw the same thing I did—Oliver running out of the stacks, still clutching that keyboard.

Jason lunged forward. The attack caught me by surprise, and I stumbled back a few more steps. My hip hit the side of one of the study tables, and I growled with pain. I raised Vic, expecting Jason to try to end me while my defenses were down, but, instead, he turned and ran again. I started after him, but my legs got tangled up in a chair, and it took me a few precious seconds to free myself, even though I knew any delay on my part would let him escape.

But I'd forgotten I wasn't the only one fighting the Reaper—Nyx was too.

I don't know how she did it, since she was actually behind me, but the Fenrir wolf pup sank down on her haunches and sprang through the air, leaping farther than I'd ever seen her go before—and landing on the back of one of Jason's legs.

Nyx let out another growl and sank her needle-sharp baby teeth into his calf. Jason yelped in pain and staggered forward, his leg almost buckling beneath him. Nyx drew back and bit him again. Jason managed to shake her off, sending the wolf pup sliding across the floor, but he was limping as he headed toward one of the side doors, shoved it open, and staggered out.

Oliver finally reached me. "Gwen! Are you okay!"

"I'm fine. We have to get him!"

He nodded, and we pushed through the door after our enemy. Nyx scrambled to her feet and chased after us, as well.

The wolf pup must have done more damage to Jason than I'd realized, because he hadn't made it very far, having only hobbled down a set of steps and then a few feet out onto the quad, leaving a trail of blood drops behind him. Oliver threw away his keyboard, leaped onto the balcony wall, then launched himself through the air and onto Jason's back. The two guys hit the snowy ground with an audible *thud.*

Jason tried to attack Oliver, but the Spartan slapped his sword away. The Reaper managed to throw Oliver off of him, and both guys sprang back up onto their feet.

I raced down the steps, Vic still clutched in my hands, and Oliver and I both slowly advanced on Jason. Nyx was there too, her violet eyes fixed on him, teeth bared, and growls rumbling out of her tiny throat like a car engine steadily churning. Jason turned to run, but once again, his leg almost went out from under him. He yelped with pain and pulled up short.

"It's over," I said. "You're hurt, and we're not. Give it up."

He turned to face us. His eyes, which were still that horrible Reaper red, zoomed from me to Oliver and back again. Instead of answering me, Jason reached into his jeans pocket. I tensed, expecting him to come up with a dagger or maybe a throwing star, but all he pulled out was a red paper pouch. He wasted no time in ripping it open with his teeth.

Oliver started forward, but I held up my hand, stopping him. That pouch probably had the same kind of white powder in it that I'd seen Jason dump into the water bottles. Maybe you had to eat the poison for it to work, or maybe it just had to touch your skin or get in your nose or eyes. Either way, he could easily douse us with it, and I didn't want to take that risk.

Jason realized we weren't going to be dumb enough to charge him, and his mouth twisted down into an angry, sullen pout. Behind us, more lights turned on inside the library, and more shouts and yells cut through the night air.

"It's over," I repeated. "The Protectorate guards will be here any second. You're done. Give it up."

Jason stared at me, considering my words. He looked at Oliver again, then his red gaze dropped to the pouch in his hand. He hesitated a second longer, then raised it up, and I realized what he was going to do—poison himself, sacrifice himself, to the evil god.

"Don't do it," I warned. "Loki isn't worth it. Trust me. You've already ruined your life by serving him. Don't let him take away what's left of it too."

"As if I could go back to the other Reapers after failing my mission. And of course Loki is worth it," Jason sneered. His voice, which I remembered being so soft and kind, was now harsh with hate. "You'll realize that soon enough—when you and all of your stupid friends are cowering at his feet. That day is coming, Gypsy—sooner than you think."

Even as I started forward to try to stop him, I knew it was already too late. Jason drew in a breath, tipped the contents of the pouch into his mouth, and swallowed them. He grimaced, as though the powder left a bad taste behind. After a moment, his eyes bulged, and he reached up and started clawing at his throat.

"Burns . . ." he rasped. "It . . . burns . . ."

His legs went out from under him, and he collapsed on the cold, snow-dusted grass. I went over to him, but it was no use. Jason started convulsing, and a strange smell filled the air—almost like the sharp tang of a pine tree. As quickly as he started convulsing, the Reaper stopped. His head lolled to the side, and a bit of white foam trickled out the side of his mouth.

I watched as the fierce red light burning in Jason's eyes dimmed, dulled, and finally died—and so did he.

Chapter 6

I don't know how long I stood over Jason's body, staring into his sightless eyes as if they would tell me something important.

As if they would actually let me understand why someone would willingly choose to serve a god who wanted to hurt, kill, and enslave other people. As if looking into his eyes would tell me why he'd sacrificed himself for such a horrible creature as Loki. Was it the power the evil god promised his followers? A desire to be as cruel as Loki himself was? Or something else entirely? I didn't know, and I didn't understand. I didn't know if I would *ever* understand—or maybe I just didn't want to.

"Gwen?" Oliver said, putting a hand on my shoulder. "Are you okay?"

I let out a breath. "Yeah. We're alive, and he's not. I guess that's all that matters, right?"

"Of course that's all that matters," Vic said. "Don't you think so, fuzzball?"

Nyx let out a yippy growl, agreeing with him.

Oliver slung his arm around my shoulders, and I

moved closer to him, glad he was here with me. After a moment, I stepped away from him and stared down at Jason's body again.

"Do you think—do you think I should touch him?" I asked. "Before his memories completely fade away?"

Oliver shook his head and pointed at the red paper pouch in Jason's hand. "No. We don't know how that poison works or what other kind he might have on him. It could be on his skin, on his clothes. It's not worth the risk. The Protectorate guards will look through his back-pack and check out his phone and laptop. Hopefully, that will tell them exactly what he was up to and who he was working with. Maybe it will even give the Protectorate some leads on where Vivian and Agrona might be."

"And what if that's not enough?"

Oliver shrugged. "It'll have to be—"

A phone started ringing. Oliver and I looked at each other, then at the dead boy. It was his phone. I hesitated, then dropped to my knees beside him.

"Gwen? What are you doing?" Oliver asked.

"Don't worry. I'll be careful."

I pulled down the edge of my hoodie sleeve and used it to fish Jason's phone out of his jacket pocket, careful not to touch the phone with my bare fingers, before get-ting back up onto my feet. Still using my sleeve, I tapped the screen to accept the call and held the phone up close to my ear.

"Finally!" Vivian Holler's voice filled my ear. "I was starting to think you were never going to pick up. Is it done yet?"

I didn't know who I'd expected to be on the other end of the line, but hearing the Reaper girl's voice startled me so much that I almost lost my grip on the phone. For one crazy moment, I wondered if this was some twisted new version of my nightmare. But it couldn't be that— otherwise Logan would have been here, stabbing me to death again.

"Jason?" Vivian asked again. "Are you there? Did Gwen drink the poison?"

I finally found my voice. "So sorry to disappoint, Viv. But I'm not dead yet."

Oliver's eyebrows shot up in his face at the realization of who I was talking to.

But Vivian must have been just as surprised to hear my voice as I'd been to hear hers because she didn't say anything. Instead, I heard a faint *rasp-rasp-rasping* sound. I frowned. It almost sounded like she was jogging across a lawn or something.

"Well, that's too bad," Vivian finally sniped. "Do me a favor, though. Put Jason on the phone. I want to tell him exactly what I plan to do to him for his failure to poison you."

I stared down at his body. "That's going to be a bit difficult, since he's already dead."

"Good," she snarled. "You've saved me the trouble of killing him."

I didn't respond.

"Oh, come on, now, Gwen," Vivian said. "Why are you looking so glum? You've managed to make it through another day. Even if Oliver is the one standing next to you, instead of your precious Logan."

I whirled around, my gaze zooming from one side of the quad to the other. The streetlights along the cobblestone paths cast out golden glows, but shadows cloaked the rest of the area. Still, I knew Vivian was here some-where—watching me. That was the only way she could have known Oliver was outside with me.

Oliver tapped me on the shoulder. *What's wrong?* he mouthed. I shook my head. I didn't want him darting off and trying to find Vivian. It would be all too easy for her to ambush him—and me too.

"Logan's fine," I said, trying to make my voice strong and confident. "He's waiting inside the library for me right now."

"Liar," Vivian countered. "I know he's not at Mythos anymore. In fact, I know *exactly* where he is—with Agrona and the rest of the Reapers. She captured him yesterday morning."

Logan captured by the Reapers? It was my nightmare come true all over again. Still, I tried not to let her hear my panic.

"You're lying."

Vivian laughed. "Sure, go ahead and believe that. Whatever helps you sleep at night, Gwen. Anyway, I gotta go. Catch you later. Or maybe I should just say *kill you later.*"

She laughed again and hung up on me.

Once again, I searched the quad, looking for any movement in the shadows, but I still couldn't spot her.

"Gwen?" Oliver asked. "Are you okay?"

I whirled around to face him. "Where's Logan? Where is he *right now*?"

Oliver shrugged. "He's with his dad. That's all I really know. Why?"

I told him everything Vivian had said. Oliver listened, then shook his head.

"Relax, Gwen. Of course, she was lying. She was just trying to rattle you. I was texting with Logan earlier. There's no way the Reapers have him."

"But how can you be sure it's really him?" I persisted.

"Because I can tell by his tone and the things we're talking about. Stuff only Logan would know. So relax, okay? Vivian is just messing with your head. Logan is safe. Trust me."

Oliver put his hands on my shoulders. Sincerity and surety blazed in his green eyes. After a moment, I forced myself to nod. He was right. Vivian was jerking my chain—nothing else.

Oliver bent down, picked up Nyx, and cradled her in the crook of his arm. She let out a happy yip and licked him on the cheek. He rubbed her head a moment before looking at me again.

"Now, come on," he said. "There's nothing else we can do here. We both know Vivian is long gone. So let's go back inside, find Nickamedes, and tell him what happened."

Oliver was right, but that didn't keep me from searching the quad a final time for the Reaper girl before sighing and following him up the steps and back inside.

Oliver and I made it back to the main part of the library. Coach Ajax, Aiko, and a few other Protectorate guards had converged in the center of the room and were examining the part of the aisle where I'd fought the Reaper. Nickamedes stood behind the counter, talking on his phone. Ajax nodded his head at me and Oliver. We waved back at the big, burly coach.

Most of the students had cleared out, and the few who remained were gathering up their things. Helena Paxton shot me a pointed, nasty look as she picked up her book—the one I'd hit the Reaper with—from where I'd dropped it on the floor. I ignored her. I had other things to worry about right now—like why Jason had tried to poison me.

Okay, okay, so I knew *why*. Well, sort of. The Reapers wanted me dead because they had this strange idea that I was going to kill Loki—something that Nike believed, as well. If I was dead, then obviously I wouldn't even get the chance to try to kill Loki—as if I even knew how I was supposed to do that in the first place.

No, what I really wondered was *why now*? Why here, tonight, in the library? Why had it suddenly become so important to murder me? But in the end, I supposed it didn't really matter. Jason wasn't the first Reaper who'd tried to kill me, and he wouldn't be the last.

Still, I eyed my poisoned water bottle. It was sitting on the counter where Jason had left it. If I hadn't been upset, if I hadn't gone up to the second-floor balcony, if I hadn't seen what he was doing, I might have picked up the bottle and chugged down the rest of the water before my psychometry kicked in. Then, I would have been as dead as Jason was. This wasn't the first time I'd escaped death, but the knowledge that it could have just as easily been me lying outside on the quad made me shiver all the same.

Vic's eye snapped open at the shuddering motion that swept through my body. I was still clutching the sword, and he looked at me, then at the water bottle.

"You fought well tonight, Gwen," he said, picking up on my dark thoughts. "You did what you had to in order to survive—that's all. And there was nothing you could have done to change that boy's mind."

"Vic's right," Oliver chimed in. "The Reaper made his choice—not you."

Nyx let out a low, serious yip, agreeing with them. The wolf pup was still secure in the Spartan's arms.

I shrugged. Maybe that was true, but it didn't feel that way. Yes, I'd wanted to kill Jason, but now that he was gone, I just felt hollow and empty inside. A boy was dead because of me—but not in the way I'd expected.

Oh, I'd killed Reapers before in battle, and I'd even used my psychometry to pull all of the magic, all of the life, out of Preston Ashton so I could heal the mortal wound he'd given me. I'd done those things in the heat of the moment, because it had been them or me, and I'd just wanted to survive, like Vic had said. But this—this was different. Jason had free will, the same free will we all had, the same free will that Nike and Metis were always going on and on and *on* about. But I'd forced him to make a choice between surrendering or death—and he'd chosen death. I didn't know if that made things better or worse, but right now, it felt like worse.

"Gwendolyn," Nickamedes said, waving his hand at me. "Come here, please."

I sighed and looked at Vic, then Oliver, then Nyx. "Great. Not only is that boy dead, but now I'm probably going to get another lecture from Nickamedes about ruining the peace and quiet of his precious library."

Oliver grinned at me. "That does sort of seem to be your thing, Gypsy."

I punched him in the shoulder as I passed. "Shut up, Spartan."

I walked over to Nickamedes. He murmured something into his phone, then snapped it shut and put it down on the counter. He reached up and wiped a bit of sweat off his forehead, as though he were hot.

"I just got off the phone with Aurora," he said, referring to Professor Metis. His voice took on a harsh, raspy note. "She's on her way over here. What happened? What tipped you off that boy was a Reaper? And did you really have to chase him through the middle of the library?"

I sighed. There it was. The beginning of the lecture I knew was coming. There was nothing to do now but listen to him, so I went around the counter, slid Vic back into his scabbard, and propped the sword up next to Nyx's basket.

Nickamedes drew in a breath. "Because I have to say that not only did you upset your fellow students, but you also . . ."

And it went on from there. How I'd disturbed the peaceful, studious atmosphere of the library. How I'd frightened the other students. How I'd put my classmates in jeopardy by chasing after the Reaper instead of quietly alerting someone that I suspected there was a bad guy in the library.

"And most important, you didn't wait for me," Nickamedes said. "I would have come and helped you if only you'd waited—"

The librarian stopped in mid-sentence. I kept staring down at the checkout counter, rubbing my thumb over a rough spot in the wood. I'd learned it was better to keep my mouth shut until Nickamedes got done lecturing me. To let him get it all out of his system at once. Like Daphne, his bark was almost always worse than his bite.

But instead of picking up his train of thought and telling me how reckless I'd been once again, Nickamedes stood there, still and silent. I tapped my finger on the counter, wanting him to get on with things. Because in addition to his lecture, I'd probably have to listen to several more, including one from Alexei. The Bogatyr would be upset that he hadn't been around to protect me from Jason and his poisonous plot—

Nickamedes sucked in another breath. I thought he was finally going to start up his rant again, but once more, he didn't say anything.

"Gwendolyn..." he finally said, his voice even harsher and raspier than before. "You'll have to excuse me. I don't feel...very well..."

My gaze flicked up to his face. I noticed more beads of sweat on his forehead, the ruddy flush in his cheeks, and the faint, upset gurgle of his stomach. His blue eyes seemed dull and unfocused, and he was swaying from side to side, as though he was having a hard time keeping his balance.

"Nickamedes?" I asked.

The librarian collapsed without another word.

"Nickamedes? Nickamedes!"

I rushed forward, and dropped to my knees beside the sick librarian.

"Nickamedes? What's wrong? Are you okay—"

My gaze caught on a piece of plastic that had rolled underneath the counter—the bottle of water I'd slapped out of the librarian's hand when I'd been chasing after Jason. The bottle was empty now, the water having pooled underneath the counter. A sick feeling filled my stomach, and I turned back to Nickamedes.

"The water," I asked, leaning forward and shaking his shoulders to try to get him to talk to me. "Did you drink any of your water in the last few minutes?"

"I just . . . had a sip . . ." he mumbled, his head lolling to one side.

Poisoned—Nickamedes had been poisoned.

He must have taken a drink from his own spiked water bottle while I was running down to the first floor and through the stacks. I'd been so focused on trying to stop Jason that I'd never considered someone else— Nickamedes—might drink the poisoned water meant for me.

For a moment, my mind went completely, utterly, horribly blank. There was nothing but shock—and growing fear. Then, the moment passed, the gears in my mind started grinding together again, and all I could think about was the terrible thing that had happened— because of me.

"Metis!" I screamed. "Somebody get Metis!"

"Gwen?" Oliver asked, peering over the counter, still holding Nyx. "What's wrong?"

"Nickamedes drank the poisoned water. Go get Metis! Right now!"

Oliver's eyes widened, and he hurried away. All I could do was lean over Nickamedes again.

The librarian looked at me. "Not . . . your fault . . ." he rasped.

I shook my head. "Don't try to talk. Save your strength. Metis will be here any second, and she'll fix you."

Nickamedes gave me a weak smile. "Not much . . . she can do . . . against poison . . ."

I bit my lip to keep from screaming. Instead, I made myself crouch there and talk to Nickamedes, telling him how happy he should be that I'd just chased the Reaper through the library this time, instead of knocking over some of the stacks like I'd done in the past. The librarian stared at me, but his eyes seemed to get brighter and glassier with every passing second. I didn't know if he was hearing me or not, but I kept up my constant stream of chatter.

Fabric whispered, and I looked up from Nickamedes's face long enough to see Coach Ajax ordering Aiko and the other Protectorate guards to form a semicircle around the counter, face outward, and draw their weapons as if more Reapers might storm into the library. But they wouldn't—the Reapers had already done all the damage they needed to tonight. Bitter laughter bubbled up in my throat like acid, but I managed to swallow it.

I don't know how long I huddled there, babbling nonsense to Nickamedes, but finally—*finally*—I heard footsteps hurrying across the floor. A second later, Metis was there, along with Daphne, Carson, and Alexei. Metis dropped to her knees on the other side of Nickamedes and took her hand in his. A second later, a golden glow enveloped them both as Metis channeled her healing power into the sick librarian.

Daphne put her hands on my shoulders and pulled me up and out of the way.

"C'mon, Gwen," she said. "Let Metis do her thing."

Daphne kept her arm around my shoulders, and we watched Metis work on Nickamedes. The librarian didn't have any visible injuries so I couldn't actually see his wounds knit together and disappear like I did when Metis used her magic to heal cuts and scrapes. The only thing visible was the golden glow that flowed from Metis into Nickamedes and back again.

Minutes ticked by. Nobody moved. Nobody spoke. Finally, Metis dropped her hand, and the golden, healing glow of her magic disappeared. I looked at Nickamedes. He wasn't sweating anymore, and his eyes were closed, as though he were sleeping peacefully. I let out a quiet sigh of relief. So did Daphne and the rest of my friends. Nickamedes would be okay now—

Metis slumped against one of the metal book carts, her shoulders sagging and exhaustion grooving deep lines around her mouth. Her black hair drooped out of its usual bun, her bronze skin seemed unnaturally pale, and she looked almost as sick as Nickamedes had when he'd first collapsed. I frowned. I'd never seen Metis look so worn out from healing someone. Oliver must have put Nyx down sometime while Metis had been working on the librarian, because the pup tiptoed forward and gave the professor's hand a tentative lick. Metis smiled and scratched Nyx's head, but if anything, she looked even more weary than before.

"Professor?" I asked.

Metis stared down at Nickamedes, a troubled look on her face. "He's stable—for now."

That sick feeling ballooned up in my stomach again, choking the hope I'd felt a moment ago. "For now? What does that mean?"

She looked up at me, pain, weariness, and sorrow glinting in her green eyes. "It means that if we can't figure out what kind of poison the Reapers used, then Nickamedes will die."

Chapter 7

Nickamedes? Die?

It didn't seem possible. It didn't seem *real*. He couldn't die. Not like this. Not when the Reaper had been trying to kill *me*.

For a moment, I swayed from side to side, just like the librarian had done. Then, all of my seesawing emotions, all of the pain and fear and worry I'd felt these past few weeks, disappeared into the burning ball of anger that roared to life in my chest. The Reapers had already taken my mom away from me. Nyx's mom, Nott. Logan. They weren't getting anyone else—not if I could help it.

I shrugged off Daphne's arm, got down on my hands and knees, and peered under the counter.

"Gwen?" Daphne asked. "What are you doing?"

I didn't answer her. There was only one thing I was focused on right now—Nickamedes's water bottle.

I used the edge of my hoodie sleeve to fish the bottle out of the shadows, careful not to touch any of the water that had leaked out of it. The plastic rolled to a stop right beside the stool I always sat on whenever I was working in the library. Before anyone could ask me what I was doing, I grabbed the water bottle, closed my eyes, and reached for my magic.

I was dimly aware of someone, maybe Carson, gasping in surprise, but I ignored my friends' shock and focused on the bottle. But I only saw the same things I had from the balcony—Jason Anderson dropping the poison into the water. I concentrated, and, a moment later, Nickamedes's face filled my mind, along with the memory of him reaching for the bottle and taking a swig. He'd just started to put the bottle to his lips a second time when something caught his attention—me screaming at the Reaper. After that, all I felt was his surprise and confusion at why I was fighting a boy in the middle of the library. The final image was of me smacking the bottle out of his hand, not realizing it was already too late . . .

That was all there was. Just a chain of events. Nothing useful, like why Jason had tried to kill me or what poison he'd used.

I opened my eyes and got to my feet, the empty bottle clutched in my hand. I looked at it a moment, then turned and threw it against the glass wall as hard as I could. But, of course, the plastic only bounced off and clattered across the floor, adding to my anger and frustration.

I stood there, fuming for a moment, before I snapped around, marched past the counter, and headed toward the back of the library.

"Gwen? Gwen!" Daphne shouted. "Where are you going?"

"You'll see."

I drew in a breath and started to run. I knew what I had to do now, and I didn't want my friends trying to stop me. I raced through the stacks, rammed my shoulder into one of the side doors to open it, and hurried outside. Then, I pounded down the nearest set of steps and ran across the quad.

The dead Reaper boy lay in the same position as before, although now two Protectorate guards wearing gray robes were standing over him. The guards both stopped talking at the sight of me sprinting toward them. I ignored them and fell to my knees beside Jason, the dusty snow melting into my jeans.

"Gwen!" Oliver shouted behind me. "No! It's too dangerous! Don't do it!"

But he was too late, and I didn't care how dangerous it was. I reached for Jason's hand and let the memories come.

Jason Anderson had been dead for the better part of twenty minutes, and much of the warmth had already fled from his body, along with his memories. But I gripped his hand that much tighter and let myself fall into the few images that remained.

Most of the flickers and flashes were of him fighting and running through the library, trying to get away from me and Oliver. I concentrated on the images, but all that filled Jason's mind was a mix of anger that he hadn't been able to poison me and his growing fear that he wouldn't be able to escape and that there was only one option left to him—taking the last pouch of poison. He knew it would be kinder than what Vivian, Agrona, and the other Reapers would do to him if he reported his failure.

My stomach roiled at his grim determination to do whatever was necessary to avoid capture, but I forced myself to clutch his hand in mine and go that much deeper into what was left of his memories. It was almost like watching a movie in reverse. Jason dying, being chased through the library, poisoning the water bottles, and sidling up to the checkout counter in the first place. Once again, I didn't see or feel anything I didn't already know, and the memories were getting fainter and fuzzier with every passing second.

I was just about to admit defeat and let go of his hand when a final memory popped into my head—one of him sitting at a study table looking through a reference book. I almost let the ordinary image slide by and disappear into the growing darkness of his mind when a wave of emotion hit me—heart-quickening excitement.

I frowned. Why would Jason be so thrilled to look through some boring old reference book? I loved books, but even I didn't get excited about something like that. So I zoomed in on the memory, pulling up every single detail I could.

Jason didn't actually read the book so much as he kept shooting little glances all around him, holding his breath and hoping no one would notice the book or what he was up to. Every time he did look at the book, he would skim a few paragraphs, then nod his head, as if he'd already memorized the information and was reviewing it one more time for some important test—killing me. It almost seemed as if he were making himself look at the book and then deliberately glance away over and over again, although I couldn't imagine why. So I forced myself to focus that much harder, trying to see each small detail and learn as much as I could from the open pages in front of him.

It was a thick book, old, dusty, and worn. Probably some obscure reference volume that got pulled off the shelf once a year when some kid needed a source for a term paper. Not exactly helpful, since there were hundreds of thousands of those in the library. I could search for a year and not come across the book.

The next time he glanced at the book, I noticed that the corner of the top right page had been turned back and that a few sentences on that page had been highlighted with a red marker. My eyes narrowed. Nickamedes would *so* not like that. I'd heard him give more than one student an ear-blistering lecture about dog-earing pages and marking passages.

My heart squeezed at the thought of Nickamedes, but I kept concentrating. Jason turned back to the book again, and I spotted some sort of plant on the left page, although I had no idea what kind of flower, herb, or weed it might be.

Jason's heart quickened that much more, and he snapped the book shut, wincing at the loud *crack* it made. His hand was splayed across the cover, hiding the title, although I managed to pick out two words printed in dull gold foil on the worn brown leather—*Plants* and *Poison*.

No big shock there. What was a surprise was the next image that popped into my mind—one of my own face.

The sight startled me so much that I almost lost the rest of the memory, but I managed to hold on to it. I was pushing one of the squeaky metal carts down the main aisle, heading into the stacks so I could shelve some more books. Jason got to his feet, walked over, and held the book out to me.

"Would you mind putting this away?" he asked.

"Sure," I heard myself say. "Just add it to the pile."

More anger exploded in me. It was bad enough that Jason had tried to poison me and had succeeded in sickening Nickamedes instead. But to actually ask me to shelve the book that he'd used to plot my murder? That was cold, even for the Reapers.

In the memory, Jason smiled at me. I pushed the cart past him, but he kept watching me. After a moment, he went back to his chair, happy at the thought that I'd be hurting before the night was through . . .

The memory flickered and faded away. I kept reaching out with my psychometry, trying to go even further back into Jason's thoughts, but there was nothing left but darkness. So I went forward, sorting through all of the images and feelings again, but there was nothing new. Just the same memories I'd seen before of me and Oliver chasing him; his last, awful act of poisoning himself; and the blaze of hot, pulsing, agonizing pain that had followed. After a few more seconds, even those thoughts and feelings faded, and I knew I wouldn't learn anything else from the dead boy.

I opened my eyes, dropped Jason's cold hand, got to my feet, and stalked back toward the steps. By this point, Daphne, Carson, and Alexei had joined Oliver, and the four of them followed me as I hurried up the steps, toward the side door, and back into the library.

"Gwen?" Daphne asked. "Slow down and talk to us. You're acting like a crazy person."

I let out a hard, brittle laugh. "Crazy? You haven't even seen my *crazy* yet. And neither have the Reapers."

Pink sparks of magic exploded out of the Valkyrie's fingertips like fireworks, letting me know how worried she was about me. She bit her lip and fell in step beside me.

"You took a big risk touching the Reaper like that," Oliver said, his voice cold, clipped, and angry. "I told you before that we didn't know what other kind of poison he might have on him. But you went ahead and did it anyway, Gwen, just like you always do. And for what?"

I stopped and whirled around so that I was face-to-face with him. "For *Nickamedes*. That's who I did it for. Just like I would do the same thing if it had been any one of you lying poisoned on the floor instead of him."

Oliver winced, but he wasn't done arguing with me. "Your killing yourself by being reckless isn't going to help Nickamedes."

"I'm not killing myself," I snapped. "I am trying to figure out what sort of poison the Reaper used. And if I have to be reckless to do it, well, so be it. All that matters to me right now is saving Nickamedes. So you can either help me, or you can stay the hell out of my way. Which is it going to be, Spartan?"

Oliver took in my tight, balled fists, my stiff shoulders, my narrowed eyes, my flushed face. After a moment, his gaze softened with understanding.

"All right," he said, holding his hands out to his sides

in a placating gesture. "All right. You win. You just—you worry me, Gwen. You worry us all."

I looked at my friends. Daphne and her crackling shower of pink sparks. Alexei and his stoic, impassive features. Carson and the concern that blackened his dark eyes. Oliver and the tension that tightened his face.

I drew in a deep breath to calm my anger and slowly let it out. "You're right. It was reckless. I'm sorry I scared you, but it was the only way I could think of to figure out what kind of poison the Reaper used."

"And did you figure it out?" Carson asked, peering through the snowflakes that had stuck to the lenses of his black glasses.

"Not yet," I said. "But I'm going to. Now, come on. We've got work to do."

Chapter 8

My friends and I went back to the main part of the library. By this point, the Protectorate guards had moved Nickamedes out from behind the counter and laid him down on top of one of the study tables. The librarian's eyes were still closed, and his face was peaceful, like he was taking a nap—but I knew better. Metis was standing by his side, holding his hand in hers. Once again, the golden glow of her healing magic enveloped them both. I watched them for a second longer, then moved past them.

I went back around the checkout counter, plopped onto my stool, and logged on to the library's computer system. Vic was still propped up next to Nyx's basket. The sword's purplish eye snapped open, and he regard me with a serious expression, but he didn't say anything. Nyx had curled up in her basket once again, and she raised her head and let out a worried growl, picking up on the tension in the air.

"Gwen?" Alexei asked, his Russian accent a bit more pronounced than usual. His hazel eyes fixed on my face. "You want to tell us what you're doing now?"

"What Nickamedes taught me to do," I murmured, turning away from him to stare at the computer screen.

"And what would that be exactly?"

"The Reaper had a book in the library earlier tonight," I said. "Before he poisoned the water bottles. I'm going to find that book and see what he was looking at."

"How can we help?" Carson asked.

The band geek's soft voice penetrated some of my anger, fear, and concern. I looked up and realized that all of my friends were standing in a row in front of the counter. Daphne. Carson. Oliver. Alexei. All of them ready and willing to do whatever I asked of them. And I realized that they were as worried about Nickamedes as I was—and that I didn't have to do this alone.

I grabbed a pen and a piece of paper, scribbled down my login and password, and handed it to Daphne. "Here. Start searching through the catalog of the library's books. Look for anything with the words *Plants* and *Poison* in the title. That's what the Reaper was looking at, and I'm willing to bet that's where he got the idea for whatever poison he used."

She took the slip of paper from me. "Got it. It shouldn't be too hard for me to figure out a search program to make things go a little quicker."

"You are our resident computer genius," Carson said.

Daphne grinned. "Don't you know it, babe."

She leaned over and planted a loud, smacking kiss on his cheek, then came around the counter, dragged a stool over to the nearest computer, and hopped up onto it. A moment later, she started typing, a furious shower of pink sparks exploding out of her fingertips with every key she hit.

"And us?" Carson asked. "What do you want the three of us to do?"

"Once Daphne's compiled the list, we can all spread out and start grabbing the books off the shelves," I said. "We'll bring the books back here to the center of the library, look at them, and see if any of them match the book I saw the Reaper staring at. Hopefully, once we find the book, we'll find the poison he used too—and the antidote."

The library was quiet as we worked. Coach Ajax and the Protectorate guards were still clustered around Metis and Nickamedes, so nobody paid us any attention. They probably thought we were wasting our time. Maybe we were, but it was the only thing I could think of to do to help the librarian. I'd worked in the Library of Antiquities for months now. Surely, all those long hours of finding reference materials, shelving books, and dusting artifact cases had to amount to *something*—and I was hoping that something would be enough to save Nickamedes.

It only took Daphne about ten minutes to compile a list of all of the books with the words *Plants* and *Poison* in the title. Unfortunately, there were dozens of them, spread out all over the first floor. I tore Daphne's list into five sections and handed everyone a piece. We each grabbed a metal cart and headed into the stacks.

I raced from one aisle to the next, grabbing all of the books on my list and dumping them onto my cart. When my cart was full, I pushed it back to the center of the library. Carson and Oliver were already there, standing next to a study table covered with books. The guys were flipping through the books one by one and then tossing them aside when it became clear they weren't what we were looking for. Nickamedes would have pitched a fit if he saw the way the guys were casually throwing the books onto the next closest study table—and the fact that more than a few were missing the mark and falling to the floor. But the books would recover from being tossed around a little—the librarian might not if we didn't figure out which poison the Reaper had used.

"Remember," I said. "Look for any red highlights and dog-eared pages. That's what I saw in Jason's book."

Carson and Oliver nodded and went back to flipping through the books and tossing them aside. I added my books to the pile they'd made and pushed the empty cart back into the stacks.

Up and down, and back and forth, I raced through the library as fast as I could. Every once in a while, I caught sight of Daphne doing the same thing, her long, blond ponytail swishing from side to side, or Alexei smoothly moving from one aisle to the next, his dark brown hair glinting under the library lights. My friends waved at me, but none of us stopped working—not even for a second.

There was no time for that—not when Nickamedes's life depended on us finding an answer.

I don't know how long I moved through the stacks, grabbing book after book after book. I focused on each of them a moment, but they were only reference materials. Nobody had any real emotional attachment to them, which meant that I didn't get any big flashes off them with my psychometry. All I saw were the hundreds of kids who had touched the volumes over the years, and all I experienced was their supreme boredom, weariness, and frustration from using the books to finish their homework.

Of course, all of those flickers of weariness and frustration didn't make me feel any better, and my movements became more hurried, awkward, and frantic as my fear and worry for Nickamedes grew. But there was nothing I could do but keep moving, keep grabbing books, and keep flashing on them.

Finally, I got down to the last book on my part of the list. I found it easily enough and grabbed it off the shelf—

An image of the Reaper boy popped into my mind.

I was so surprised that I almost dropped the book, but I managed to cradle it to my chest. I closed my eyes and concentrated, and I saw the same thing that I had before—Jason leaning over the book at one of the study tables. This was it. This was the book he'd been looking at.

I opened my eyes and stared down at the title on the brown cover: *Healing, Medicinal, and Poisonous Properties of Mythological Plants.*

My fingers trembling, I opened the book and flipped through the pages until I came to the passage that Jason had highlighted in red:

> *Serket sap is an evergreen plant that is known*
> *in the mythological world for its intense*
> *poisonous properties. It is named after the*

Egyptian goddess who is associated with poisons. Serket sap can be administered in a variety of ways, including boiling it to create a dark green liquid, but the most popular method involves drying the plant's leaves and roots, then grinding them up into a fine white powder in order to more easily use it . . .

I stared at the left page and the picture of the small green plant, which resembled a miniature pine tree with both leaves and needles sprouting from its thin brown trunk. It looked harmless, but according to this description, it was anything but. I snapped the book shut, left the cart where it was, and ran back to the study tables.

By this point, even more of the Protectorate guards had gathered in the library, but I pushed past them to where Metis was still standing beside Nickamedes.

"Here," I said, thrusting the book into her hands. "This is what they used to poison Nickamedes—Serket sap."

Metis looked at me, her green eyes sharp. "Are you sure?"

I nodded. "This is the book I saw the Reaper boy looking at. This is the poison he used. It has to be. Look at this page in the middle."

Metis opened the book to the appropriate page, and I pointed to the drawing and highlighted passage. My fingers brushed hers, and my psychometry kicked in, letting me feel Metis's worry for Nickamedes—and something else I never would have guessed.

I froze, wondering if I was imagining things, but the emotions washed over me again, even stronger than before. Metis's cold, agonizing dread that she wouldn't be able to save Nickamedes mixed with a warm, soft, fizzy feeling that could only mean one thing—love.

Metis? In love with Nickamedes? When had that happened? And how?

I was so shocked that I pulled my hand away from hers. The professor nodded and closed the book. She didn't seem to realize that I'd flashed on her—and what I'd felt.

"All right. Thank you, Gwen. We'll take it from here." Metis turned to Ajax. "Let's go. We need to get Nickamedes over to the infirmary and get started on an antidote."

Ajax nodded, and several of the Protectorate guards stepped forward. They helped Ajax transfer Nickamedes to a flat, plastic board, the sort that paramedics use, strapped him down to it, and hefted the board onto their shoulders, as if he were some ancient king they were transporting. A moment later, the guards left the library, carrying Nickamedes along with them.

And all I could do was just stand there, watch them go, and hope he would be okay.

Chapter 9

"What is taking so long?" I growled. "It's been *hours* now."

"Actually, it's only been about ninety minutes," Carson pointed out.

I glared at him, and he winced and slouched down a little more in his chair.

Daphne rolled her eyes. "Ignore her, Carson. She's just a little crazy right now. Well, crazier than usual. It's going to take as long as it takes, Gwen. You're just wearing yourself out pacing back and forth like that."

"I am not pacing," I muttered.

"Yes, you are," Oliver said. "You have been ever since we came in here."

Here was the waiting room of the school's infirmary, which was located in a square, three-story building not too far from my dorm. I'd expected the infirmary to be in the bottom of the math-science building, right next to the morgue and the prison, but my friends had led me over here instead.

I'd never paid too much attention to this building before, since it was made out of the same dark gray stone as most everything else at Mythos. But it was a calm, soothing space, at least on the inside. The white marble floor had a hint of blue in it, like veins running near the surface of someone's skin. Or maybe the sheen of color was simply the stone reflecting back the pale blue paint that covered the walls. Each wall featured several windows, while a series of round skylights had been set into the ceiling, although all I could see through the glass right now was darkness.

A long reception desk squatted near the back of a room, with a set of double doors behind it that led to the patient rooms. Apparently, manning the infirmary was another one of Raven's odd jobs. She'd been sitting behind the desk when we'd arrived, her black boots propped up on top of the smooth wood. She'd glanced up at me and my friends, then gone back to her magazine. Every once in a while, she turned a page, but other than that, she was silent as usual.

White wicker chairs with thick cushions clustered together in the middle of the room, along with a couple of blue plaid couches. Daphne and Carson were huddled together on one of the couches, while Oliver and Alexei were sitting side by side in the chairs. I'd taken Vic and Nyx back to my dorm room before hurrying over here with the others. My friends alternated between talking to each other and texting on their phones, but I kept pacing.

Still, with every lap I made around the waiting room, my gaze was inevitably drawn to the small marble statues that could be found everywhere, from the wall recesses to the end tables cluttered with magazines to the far side of the reception desk, right next to Raven's elbow. The infirmary was like the dining hall in that all the statues had a similar theme. But instead of harvest and food gods who watched over the students as they ate, here in the infirmary, all of the statues were of figures associated with healing. Like Apollo and Asklepios, two Greek gods. As always, the statues seemed to be watching me, but their expressions were all closed-off and neutral, and I couldn't tell what, if anything, might be happening to Nickamedes.

I started to take another turn around the room when a faint *jingle-jingle-jingle* caught my attention. A moment later, an older woman with iron-gray hair and warm, kind violet eyes stepped through the open doorway.

"Grandma!" I threw myself into her arms.

Grandma Frost was wearing a white sweater with black pants and shoes with toes that slightly curled up. Layers of green, purple, and gray scarves peeked out of the various folds of her coat. Each one of the scarves was fringed with silver coins that made a merry sound as I hugged her tight.

She pulled back and cradled my face in her hands, and I felt a wave of love flow from her and wash over into me. Suddenly, everything seemed a little brighter and more hopeful, and I felt much calmer. Like everything would be okay now that she was here, even though I knew that wasn't really the case.

"It's okay, pumpkin," Grandma murmured, smoothing down my frizzy hair. "Everything's going to be all right. You'll see."

Her arms tightened around me, and I felt a force stir in the air around her—this old, knowing, watchful force that seemed to hug me right along with Grandma Frost. Like me, Grandma was a Gypsy, which meant that she'd been gifted with magic by Nike, just like I had. In her case, that power was the ability to see the future. I wondered if she'd just gotten a glimpse of Nickamedes's future, but by the time I pulled back to ask her, the force had vanished, and her eyes were as clear as mine, instead of being distant like they got when she was looking at something only she could see.

"I'm glad you're here," I whispered.

Grandma patted my hand. "I'm glad to be here. Now, tell me everything. Ajax filled me in on some of it when he called, but I want to hear it from you, pumpkin."

I led her over to one of the waiting room couches. She sat down and took my hand again, and I told her everything—including how the Reaper had really been trying to poison me instead of Nickamedes. My voice cracked a little on that last part, but Grandma tightened her grip on my cold fingers, and another wave of love and understanding surged through me.

"It's not your fault, pumpkin," she said. "Not that boy doing what he did, and not Nickamedes being hurt either."

I bit my lip and looked away from her, not wanting her to see the guilt in my eyes—especially when it came to Nickamedes. The librarian used to be in love with my mom, Grace, and when I'd first come to Mythos, he'd asked Metis to assign me to work with him in the library so he could look out for me in his own way. I couldn't help thinking he shouldn't have done that. He would have been so much better off if I hadn't been there tonight, if I'd never even set foot in the library to start with—

One of the double doors that led back into the infirmary opened, and Metis stepped into the waiting room. We all surged to our feet and hurried forward, clustering around her.

"What happened?"

"Did you get the poison out of his system?"

"Is Nickamedes going to be okay?"

One after another, the questions tumbled out of our lips. Metis held up her hands, and we slowly quieted down.

"Finding out which poison the Reaper used was an enormous aid," she said. "It's helped me figure out the best course of treatment for Nickamedes, including a way to slow the progression of the poison."

"Slow, but not stop?" Daphne asked, picking up on what she hadn't said.

Metis sighed. "Yes, slow, not stop. Poison is a tricky thing, especially a magic-based poison like this one. Basically, poisons like these eat up all of the magic you use to try to get rid of them. All my healing magic is doing right now is keeping the Serket sap from causing any more damage to Nickamedes. But eventually, the poison will build up a resistance to my magic and start to overcome it. When that happens, the poison will once again follow its normal progression and will start doing further damage to him—until he finally dies from it."

I closed my eyes. I wasn't touching any of my friends, but I could feel the agonizing grief rolling off them—it mirrored my own emotions perfectly. After a moment, I forced myself to open my eyes and look at Metis again.

"So there's no . . . cure?" I barely got the words out through the hard lump in my throat. "No way to save him?"

Metis sighed, a little deeper and sadder than before. "There is an antidote."

"So what's the problem? Go mix it up or get it or whatever and give it to him."

She shook her head. "It's not that easy. The only known antidote to Serket sap is Chloris ambrosia, named after the Greek goddess of flowers."

Chloris ambrosia? I'd never heard of it, and neither had anyone else, judging from the blank looks on my friends' faces.

"Oh sure," Carson piped up. "It's sort of like the honeysuckle that grows around here."

We all looked at Carson, who blushed.

"My dad owns wineries in California," he said. "He's always talking about grapes and plants and things like that."

Metis nodded. "That's right. Chloris ambrosia is a flowering vine that is similar to honeysuckle. The only problem is that it's very rare. In fact, there's only one place in the United States where it's supposed to grow—in the Rocky Mountains."

"So what's the problem?" I repeated. "We go there, pick this flower, and bring it back so you can cure Nickamedes with it. No sweat."

Metis stared at me. "The problem is that the only place the flower is known to grow is in some ruins on the top of a mountain above the Denver branch of Mythos Academy."

Alexei narrowed his hazel eyes. "You mean the Eir Ruins?"

Metis nodded again, her mouth flattening out into a grim line. Oliver crossed his arms over his chest. Daphne started muttering, while Grandma Frost sighed, as if she'd known that was what the professor would say all along. Maybe she had, with her ability to see the future.

"Okay, so what's the deal with the ruins?" I asked. "And why do you all look like it would be the worst idea ever to go there?"

Carson peered at me through his glasses. "The Eir Ruins are supposed to be a place of great power, of great magic."

"So?"

"So . . . tons of people have gone up to the ruins, but some of the folks have come back . . . different," he said.

Daphne snorted. "You mean, most of them were so scared that all they did was babble on about ghosts and spirits and how they barely survived."

"The ruins have a reputation," Oliver added. "You don't go up there unless you absolutely have to."

"Okay, so basically the ruins are some Mythos version of a haunted house," I said. "So what? We've been through worse."

"It's not the ruins I'm concerned about," Metis said. "It's the Reapers' trap."

We all froze for a moment.

Finally, Alexei spoke. "What do you mean? How could it be a trap?"

The professor took off her silver glasses and pinched the bridge of her nose. "Because the poison is working too slowly on Nickamedes. Serket sap is usually fatal within a few minutes, but it was longer than that before Nickamedes even showed any symptoms. And now, my magic is keeping the poison at bay, even though that's not usually possible. I think . . . I think the Reaper gave Nickamedes a small, diluted dose of the poison—on purpose."

"But why would the Reapers do that?" Oliver asked. "It doesn't make sense."

I thought back to when I'd seen the Reaper poison the water bottles, and I remembered something I hadn't thought too much about before. Jason had used white pouches on the bottles, but outside on the quad, he'd had a red paper pouch. And after he'd swallowed the poison inside, he'd been dead in a few minutes, just like Metis had said. Even when Vivian had called, she'd asked him if it was done, if I'd been poisoned—not if I was actually *dead* yet.

I looked at the professor, and I started to pick up on her train of thought. "Jason wanted to poison me, but he didn't want to kill me, did he? Not right away. Instead, he wanted to give you guys enough time to figure out what kind of poison he'd used. Maybe that's even why he kept looking at the book so much in the library—so I could flash on it and see him reading it when you guys finally found it back in the stacks. Once you did, he knew that you'd go rushing out to the ruins to find the antidote, and when you got there, the Reapers would be waiting."

Metis nodded. "That's what I think. That the Reapers want to lure us out to the ruins so they can attack us."

I frowned. "But why? Why go to all that trouble

when they could attack us here? They've done it before."

When they could just kill me, and be done with it. That was the other dark thought that filled my mind, but I didn't share it with the others.

"That, I don't have an answer to." Metis sighed again. "But even if it's not a trap, you can't just go find the flower. Chloris ambrosia has powerful healing properties, but there's a catch—it has to be picked under a midnight moon. That's the only time the flowers on the vine bloom, and the flowers are what I need to make the antidote."

"So let me get this straight," I said. "Not only do we have to get to the ruins, figure out how to survive whatever creepy magic mumbo jumbo may or may not be there, and thwart a likely Reaper attack, but we also have to pick this mythological flower at precisely the right moment or Nickamedes will die anyway. Does that about sum it up?"

Metis nodded. "Unfortunately."

We all fell silent once more, and the only sounds were the crinkle of Raven's magazine as she turned another page and the faint *beep-beep-beep* of a heart monitor somewhere deeper in the infirmary. I wondered if that was Nickamedes's heart beating—and how long it would be until that sound stopped altogether.

Not for the first time tonight, I wished that Logan was here. He wouldn't have been able to do anything—not any more than Metis was already doing for Nickamedes—but his being here would have comforted me, would have made me feel like the odds weren't stacked quite so high against us and that we had a chance to save Nickamedes after all.

Logan wasn't here—but I was. And I knew what I had to do—as Nike's Champion, and more important, as Nickamedes's friend.

"How long?" I asked. "How long does he have?"

"I won't know until we run some more tests to see exactly how much of the poison he ingested and how strong it is," Metis said. "But I would say a week. Maybe less."

Silence. Complete, utter, absolute, frightening silence descended over the waiting room once more.

I looked at Metis. The professor was putting on a brave face, but anguish tightened her features. How could I not have realized how much she cared about him before? Once again, I wondered how long she'd been in love with the librarian—and why she didn't tell him how she felt. They'd make a terrific couple. But the love Metis had for Nickamedes made me even more determined to save him—for her.

"Well," I finally said. "If it's a fight the Reapers want, then that's what we're going to give them."

"Gwen?" Metis asked.

I straightened up. "How soon can we get to Denver?"

Chapter 10

The answer to my question was several hours.

To my surprise, Carson had made all the arrangements. Apparently, his dad did a lot of business with wineries in North Carolina and the surrounding states, and Mr. Callahan was always traveling back and forth from one side of the country to the other. Lucky for us, Carson's dad had flown in a few days before and was currently over in Ashland, visiting some winery there. He'd told Carson to take the jet to wherever he needed.

After a mad dash back to our dorm rooms to pack, we'd gone over to the small airport in Cypress Mountain and had flown out in the wee hours of the morning. Daphne, Carson, Oliver, and Alexei had all pulled out pillows and blankets from the overhead bins, curled up in their seats, and gone to sleep, but I'd stayed awake. Partly because I'd never flown before and was a little freaked out by the whole experience, but mostly because I didn't want to have another nightmare and wake everyone else up with my screaming.

But the exhaustion finally caught up with me. One moment, I was staring out the window, worrying about

Nickamedes and wondering whether the Reapers had really captured Logan or not. The next, I woke up with Daphne standing over me, poking her finger into my shoulder.

"Wakey, wakey," she said. "We're here."

I sat up. I'd been using my coat as a blanket, and it slipped off my chest and landed on the floor. "We're in Denver already?"

"Not Denver, a suburb," Daphne said. "Ajax had us land here because he thought it would be a less obvious place for us to start from than the Denver airport. He's trying to throw the Reapers off our trail for as long as possible."

Coach Ajax was the only adult who'd come with us. Metis had to stay at the academy so she could keep using her magic on Nickamedes to fight off the poison until we returned with the antidote. Grandma Frost also remained behind to help Metis and keep an eye on Nyx. It wasn't out of the realm of possibility that the Reapers might attack again while we were away, and I was glad Grandma was going to watch Metis's back. Still, I missed her already. It was a dangerous mission I was on, but I wasn't a little girl anymore, and I couldn't go crying to my grandma every time something terrible happened. I was a Champion now—Nike's Champion— and it was up to me to stop Bad, Bad Things from happening—even if I wasn't sure I was the right person for the job.

But I had to try, for Nickamedes—especially when he was suffering because of me.

Ajax, Oliver, Alexei, and Carson were already grabbing their things, so I got up and did the same. At least,

I tried to. I had to wait for Daphne to clear all five of her suitcases out of the way first.

Somehow, she had managed to pack a month's worth of clothes in the time we'd had to go back to our rooms and grab our gear before leaving the academy. All of her luggage was pink, of course. It matched the long, heavy coat, gloves, earmuffs, and boots she was wearing, not to mention the oversized patent leather purse hanging off her arm.

"I know I forgot *something*," Daphne muttered, opening and closing another one of her bags.

"The only things in your closet that you didn't pack were the hangers that everything was on," I sniped. "We're not going to be gone that long, you know."

"And I know that you should always pack for every possible situation," Daphne sniffed.

I rolled my eyes.

Finally, Daphne hoisted her bags out of the way with one hand, and I managed to grab my stuff, which had been buried under hers. I pulled Vic out of my messenger bag. The sword gave a loud, jaw-cracking yawn and opened his eye. Then, he started blinking rapidly and moving his mouth up and down and wiggling his jaw from side to side.

"What are you doing?" I asked.

"What do you think I'm doing? I'm trying to pop my bloody ear," Vic said. "The change in altitude is killing me, I tell you. Killing me!"

I wanted to point out that the sword was the one who killed things, not the other way around, but I kept quiet. Finally, a minute later, something *squeaked* deep inside the metal, and Vic's face relaxed.

"There," he said. "All better. Now, time to take care of the jet lag. Wake me when there are Reapers to kill."

His purplish eye snapped shut. I thought about shaking him awake, so he'd be as cranky and sleep-deprived as I was, but I decided against it. I didn't want to listen to him complain all the way to . . . wherever it was we were going next.

I slid Vic back into my messenger bag, looped it across my chest, grabbed my duffel bag full of clothes, and plodded down the plane's stairs with the others.

The sun was just creeping up over the tops of the mountains, banishing the gray and lavender twilight that streaked across the sky. A bluish haze colored the Rockies themselves, softening the sharp edges of the tall, rugged peaks, before giving way to the snow that crowned the very tops of the mountains. My breath frosted in the air like a cloud of diamonds, and I suddenly realized how frigid it was, but the landscape was so beautiful that I didn't mind the cold.

"Come on," Daphne said. "Quit gawking. We need to get moving."

I shouldered my bags and followed the others across the tarmac. We stepped into a hangar, and heat blasted over my face, chasing away the chill. We all trailed after Coach Ajax, who was leading the way. Right before we got to the door that would let us enter the rest of the airport, Ajax turned and held his hands out wide.

"We all know the Reapers are probably already tracking us," Ajax rumbled in his deep voice. "What we don't know is how many spies the Reapers have, who they might be, or when they might decide to attack. So watch each other's backs—now more than ever. I want at least two of you together at all times with your weapons handy. Don't let yourselves get separated from each other."

"Why do they think we're here?" I asked. "And who is they and where exactly is here?"

"We're going to the Denver branch of Mythos Academy," Ajax said. "It's located higher up in the Rockies, in a suburb called Snowline Ridge. We should arrive as classes are starting. We'll take the day to prepare, then set out for the Eir Ruins tomorrow."

"And what are you telling the people at the academy about why we've suddenly shown up?" Alexei asked.

Ajax shrugged. "That this is a special field trip for students who are interested in transferring to the Denver branch. We do these on occasion."

"In the middle of the winter semester?" Oliver asked. "Don't you think that's a little weak as far as excuses go?"

The coach shrugged again. "It was the best excuse Metis and I could come up with on such short notice. Besides, the Reapers know why we're here. There's nothing we can do about that."

He was right. The Reapers had wanted us to come here, and now, all that was left to do was to see how things played out—and try to survive whatever trap the Reapers had in mind.

We walked through the airport and stepped outside to a car rental station. Ajax must have called ahead, because a black Cadillac Escalade was waiting by the curb. Ajax signed some paperwork, took the keys from one of the workers, and got behind the wheel. Alexei slipped into the front passenger seat. Oliver and I sat in the middle row, with Daphne and Carson in the back.

Nobody spoke as Ajax drove away from the airport—we were all too busy staring out the windows, already looking for the Reapers we knew were coming. But all we saw were modest homes and quiet streets.

We'd been driving for about ten minutes when Oliver's phone beeped, and he pulled it out of his pants pocket and stared at the screen.

"Who's that?" I asked.

He typed out a quick message. "Just Kenzie, wondering if we'd landed yet."

Kenzie Tanaka was another one of our Spartan friends at Mythos. He'd stayed behind to help Metis with Nickamedes, so it made sense that he'd texted Oliver, wanting an update.

"How's Nickamedes?"

Oliver hit some more buttons on his phone, sending my question. It beeped again a minute later. "No change, according to Kenzie. Everything's quiet there, so far."

I let out a breath. Well, at least he hadn't gotten any worse. If everything went according to Ajax's plan, we'd hike up to the ruins tomorrow. Then, the day after that, we'd head back to Mythos, hopefully with the ambrosia flowers.

Oliver texted something to Kenzie. He started to put the phone away, but it beeped again.

"Who is it now?"

Oliver frowned, as if he didn't like what the screen said this time. "Just Kenzie again. He forgot to tell me something."

I wanted to ask if he'd heard from Logan, but I kept my mouth shut. Before we'd left the infirmary, Metis had said that she had already called Linus Quinn and told him what had happened to Nickamedes. Ajax and the other Protectorate guards had swept the academy grounds, but there had been no sign of Vivian or any other Reapers. Still, I couldn't help worrying that Vivian and Agrona really did have Logan, despite all my friends' assurances that he was safe with his dad.

Oliver typed in another message and put away his phone. Silence descended over the car once again, so I stared out the window. I didn't know where we were in relation to Denver, but mountains ringed the horizon as far as I could see, although gray clouds had begun to gather around some of the higher peaks, as though a snowstorm was blowing in from the west. I didn't see the future like Grandma Frost did, but I couldn't help wondering if it was a sign all the same—that Reapers weren't the only things we had to worry about.

We'd been riding for about thirty minutes, when Ajax steered the car off the main road and onto a smaller highway. Ten minutes after that, we pulled into a parking lot that fronted a train station. A sign read *Snowline Ridge Runner—Tourist trains departing daily*. The image of a red train climbing up a green mountain had been carved into the wood, complete with white puffs of smoke coming out of the engine.

"What are we doing here?" I asked.

"The roads up to the academy are narrow, winding, and littered with switchbacks," Ajax said. "There are dozens of spots along the way that would be the perfect place for an ambush, and we'd be sitting ducks in any kind of vehicle. Metis and I agreed it would be safer if we took the train. Lots of Mythos folks use it to get down to Denver and then back up the mountain to the academy again. We have a better chance of blending in with the crowd this way, especially since some of the students were in the city yesterday attending a weapons tournament and are returning to the academy this morning."

"That sounds like you and your buses, Gwen," Carson said in a cheery voice.

"Yay for public transportation," I said.

We got out of the car, grabbed our bags, and headed into the train station. The inside was nicer than I expected, with lots of gleaming wooden benches and old-fashioned brass rails running alongside them, dividing the seats into various sections. The walls were made out of the same light, varnished wood as the benches, while the floor was an off-white marble with flecks of gold shimmering in it. A series of ticket counters took up the back wall, but a wide strip of white marble ran above the windows—one that featured dozens of carvings.

Many of the figures were the same creatures I walked by on a daily basis at the academy—dragons, basilisks, gargoyles, chimeras, even a Minotaur. But there were other figures depicted too—bears, wolves, buffalo, coyotes, rabbits, porcupines. All ten feet tall and frighteningly lifelike, as though they were about to bust out of their stone shells and leap down into the middle of the floor.

Once I spotted the carvings, I noticed all of the other things I'd missed before. Two suits of armor, both clutching giant battle-axes, stood on either side of the water fountains, while a series of paintings of some bloody mythological battle hung on the wall beside the doors that led out to the tracks. Small wooden carvings of mythological creatures perched in glassed-in recesses in the walls, all staring out at the passengers who milled through the waiting area.

The carvings, the statues, the paintings, the suits of armor. In a way, it was eerily familiar—and strangely comforting. When I'd first gone to Mythos, I hadn't thought I belonged at the academy, but now I couldn't imagine not being part of the mythological world. The carvings and statues told me I was in my element—so to speak.

We had thirty minutes to wait until the train arrived. The others pulled out their cell phones and started checking their messages, but I wandered over and plucked a brochure out of a rack next to one of the ticket counters. I got a vague flash of other people flipping through the pages, but that was all. The sort of small vibe I would expect, since dozens of folks had grabbed the same slip of paper before putting it back into its slot on the rack.

I scanned through the photos and realized that Snowline Ridge seemed very similar to Cypress Mountain. Both suburbs housed a variety of expensive designer shops, coffeehouses, and bookstores. The only difference was that Snowline Ridge also featured a high-end ski resort that catered to tourists. There was no mention of the academy in the brochure.

I was almost finished reading the information when I got the sense that someone was watching me. It felt as if I could see someone hovering at the edge of my vision, staring right at me. But when I snapped my head in that direction, all I saw was the usual ebb and flow of folks moving through the station. No one seemed to be paying any attention to me at all.

I sighed and slid the brochure back into the rack. I started to head over to my friends when I noticed a girl leaning against the wall a few feet away. She was about my age, seventeen or maybe even a year younger, and her glossy black hair was pulled back into a sleek, short ponytail. She wore black boots and designer jeans topped by a white turtleneck sweater and a forest-green leather jacket that made her look both tough and pretty at the same time. A dark green messenger bag lay on the floor at her feet.

She wasn't the only kid in the station. In fact, I spotted several folks who had to be Mythos students, judging from their pricey clothes and expensive jewelry. Not to mention the colorful sparks of magic that the Valkyries were giving off. But the regular passengers didn't notice the cracks and hisses around them, despite the fact that one Valkyrie was practically dripping blue sparks all over the newspaper the older guy sitting next to her was reading. Daphne had told me once that unless you were a warrior, you just couldn't see the sparks. Apparently, something in our ancient warrior DNA let us spot the colorful flashes that regular mortals couldn't. So that was why Daphne and the other Valkyries didn't worry about giving off magic in public.

It seemed like all of the other kids were gossiping with each other, and more than a few eyed my friends, wondering who they were and why they were taking the train. Everyone seemed to be friendly enough with each other—except when it came to the girl I'd noticed earlier.

The other kids looked at the girl, but nobody approached her and nobody said anything to her. Nobody gave her so much as a cheerful wave or even a polite nod. The girl pretended that she couldn't see the other kids deliberately avoiding her, but her jaw was clenched, and her whole body was tense with anger—and pain.

She reminded me of, well, *me.* Back when I'd first come to Mythos, I'd been that exact same girl—the one standing all alone, watching the other kids around me, hoping that someone would at least notice me.

She spotted me watching her and turned her head in my direction. Her eyes were a bright, vivid green. The girl scowled at me, crossed her arms over her chest, and looked away.

She had to be one of the Mythos students going up to Snowline Ridge—I just wondered if she was also a Reaper. That might explain why she seemed to be here by herself. Maybe she'd been the only Reaper sent to the station and was busy watching me and my friends instead of hanging out with her own.

Or maybe I was just being paranoid.

So she was standing by herself. That didn't mean she was a Reaper. Still, my gaze kept going back to the girl, who kept right on scowling at me.

"What are you looking at?" she finally growled.

I shrugged. "Nothing. Just killing time."

"Well, go kill it somewhere else. Or I'll make you wish you had."

I raised an eyebrow at her. "Really?"

"Yeah. Really."

A flash of purple caught my eye, and I looked down. Vic was sticking out of the top of my messenger bag. The sword had woken up from his latest nap, but instead of yawning like usual, he was glaring at the girl.

"Put me up against her throat, and I'll make her take back her snotty words real quick," Vic muttered.

The girl's scowl deepened. "What did you say?"

"Nothing. Nothing at all."

"Nothing!" Vic huffed in an indignant voice. "I'll show her nothing—"

I reached down and clamped my hand over the sword's mouth to muffle the sound of his voice. Vic would totally make me pay for this later, but right now, I needed him to be quiet. It was one thing for the Reapers to know we were coming. It was another for the sword to start shouting threats and telling everyone exactly where we were.

The girl's eyes narrowed, and she looked past me. A second later, Daphne stepped up beside me. The Valkyrie crossed her arms over her chest and gave the other girl a cool once-over.

"Problem, Gwen?"

"No problem," I said.

"Good," Daphne replied. "The train's almost here. Ajax wants us to head on outside."

"Right behind you."

Daphne stared at the girl a moment longer before striding back over to Carson and the others. I followed her.

Still, I couldn't help glancing over my shoulder. The

girl was still scowling at me. But for a moment, I almost thought I saw a flicker of sadness in her eyes, and her mouth seemed to turn down that much more. For some reason, the expression made me want to go back over to her and find out what she was so upset about.

"Come on, Gwen!" Daphne called out.

But my friends were waiting, so I put the girl out of my mind and followed them onto the platform.

Chapter 11

Fifteen minutes later, the train pulled out of the station. The engine's whistle pierced the early morning air, sounding as high and sharp as a Black roc's screech. Or maybe it only seemed that way because I knew the Reapers would probably be waiting for us up at the academy and then at the Eir Ruins—if we even made it that far.

Like the station, the train itself featured long, padded wooden benches with brass rails running alongside them. There were even a few tables bolted to the floor here and there throughout the car, so folks could face each other. I was sitting by myself. Oliver and Alexei were on the bench across from me, with Daphne and Carson sitting in front of me. Coach Ajax was in front of Oliver and Alexei, leaning his elbows on one of the tables, dwarfing the wood with his large frame and muscled body. The sunlight streaming in through the windows made his skin gleam like polished onyx.

I had my messenger bag next to me on the bench, with Vic propped up so that he could look out the large picture windows. The sword eyed the passing scenery,

when he wasn't busy shooting me dirty looks for clamp-
ing my hand over his mouth earlier.

The car we were in wasn't all that crowded. A few
other kids were sprawled over the benches in the front,
while two adults—a man and a woman—were at a table
behind them. Everyone was engrossed in their phones or
the laptops they'd opened up the second the train had
left the station. I eyed the other passengers, but no one
seemed to be paying me or my friends any attention. In
fact, none of the other folks in the car even glanced in
our direction. Normally, I would have thought that was
a good thing, but something about the complete lack of
attention struck me as being strange. Or perhaps that
was just my paranoia showing through again.

To my surprise, the girl I'd seen inside the station was
also in our car, although she made sure to sit in the
back, five rows away from anyone else. She had her
back to the window, and her legs stretched out on the
bench in front of her. She noticed me looking at her
again, scowled, and pointedly turned her head and
stared out the window.

"Who's that?" Oliver asked, leaning across the aisle
so he could talk to me. "She doesn't seem like she's a
member of the Gwen Frost fan club."

I shrugged. "Don't know. Don't care."

Alexei touched his arm, and Oliver leaned back to see
what he wanted.

We rode in silence for about thirty minutes. The trip
was pleasant enough. The train rocked from side to side
in a soothing way, although every once in a while, the
gears would grind together, making the car shudder and
the windows rattle as the engine struggled up the moun-

tain. According to Ajax, it was a ninety-minute ride up to Snowline Ridge, and the others soon took off their jackets, wadded them up to use as pillows, got comfortable, and drifted off to sleep.

The day had barely started, and I was already tired, but try as I might, I couldn't go to sleep, not without worrying that I might have another nightmare. So I stared out at the passing scenery instead.

In some ways, the Rockies were a lot like the Appalachian Mountains back home. Lots of trees, lots of stone outcroppings, lots of rocky ridges. But everything here seemed bigger, more jagged and rugged, the mountain peaks so tall and sharp that they resembled needles you might prick your finger on if only you could reach out and touch the tops of them. There was more snow here too, a couple of inches on the ground, and fresh flakes swirled all around and through the dense, towering pines like bits of hard, white confetti. But it wasn't just the snow and scenery that were different. I felt . . . a wildness in the landscape that I didn't back at the North Carolina academy. Or perhaps it was because Mythos was home and this wasn't—

A hand touched my shoulder.

My head snapped to the side, even as my fingers fumbled across the seat, straining to reach Vic's hilt—but it was only Coach Ajax looming over me. I let out a breath.

"I'm going to the snack car to get some coffee," Ajax said. "Want anything?"

I shook my head. "Thanks, but I'm good."

"Well, I'm starving," Daphne piped up.

"Me too," Carson said.

The two of them got up and followed Ajax. The coach walked to the front of the car, swaying from side to side with the motion of the train. He reached the door and hit the button so he could step forward into the next car; then he, Daphne, and Carson disappeared from sight. Oliver and Alexei slept on, their heads close together as they leaned on each other. The two guys made a cute couple. They'd met over winter break and had been totally into each other, although they hadn't officially started dating until a few weeks ago.

The minutes ticked by, and I started to wonder what was taking Ajax, Daphne, and Carson so long. I leaned over into the aisle. Through the glass in the doors at the front, I could see folks standing in the middle of the aisle in the next car up. That must be the line for the snack car. Looked like my friends weren't the only ones who'd wanted some breakfast. I sighed, leaned back, and stared out the windows again.

Another five minutes passed. Then, one of the girls in the front of the car got up and headed toward the back. At first, I wondered why, until I remembered that was where the bathrooms were. Still, I tensed up as the other girl approached me. Something about her seemed a little . . . off.

She glanced down and realized I was staring at her. The girl hesitated, then gave me a small smile. I nodded at her. But instead of nodding back, her eyes slid past me and fixed on Vic. For a moment, something sparked in her gaze. I couldn't tell exactly what it was, but it almost seemed like . . . satisfaction.

Her smile widened, and she stared at Vic a second longer before she noticed I was watching her watch my sword. Her features twisted into a grimace, and her gaze snapped straight ahead, as though I'd caught her doing something she shouldn't. Yeah, it was weird that she'd noticed Vic. Then again, it was weird for me to have a sword on a train, even this train that catered to Mythos students. And I still couldn't put my finger on what was bugging me about her so much, other than her curious interest in Vic.

It was only when she took a step past me that I realized she had one of her hands down by her side, instead of putting both of them on top of the brass rails for balance as she made her way to the back. I frowned, wondering why she would walk like that when the train was shuddering so much right now. The car rocked again, and the girl lurched to her right—letting me see the glint of silver underneath her long, black coat.

The girl froze for a moment, realizing that I'd noticed something. Then, she gave a small shrug, as though it were no big deal. She took another step forward, then another. I turned my head, following her movements.

She'd almost gone all the way past me when she abruptly whirled back in my direction. The girl whipped out a sword from underneath her coat, raised it high, and brought it down—aiming for my head.

Instinct took over, and I immediately ducked down and to my right.

Clang!

The girl's sword hit the top of the brass rail in front of me instead of driving deep into my skull. I scrambled to my feet, bumping my knees against the back of the bench in front of me.

But the girl was quick—Amazon quick. She stepped back, twirled the sword around in her hands, and raised it again for another strike. Since there was no way I could reach out, grab Vic, and use him to block her blow, I put my hands on the brass railing behind me, hefted myself up off the ground, and kicked out with my feet, catching her in the stomach.

The Reaper girl let out a loud *oof!* as the air hissed out of her lungs, but she didn't go down. I braced myself on the seats, pushed up, and kicked her again. This time, she staggered to the side—and landed right on top of Oliver and Alexei.

"Hey!" Oliver snapped. "I'm sleeping here!"

"What the—" Alexei muttered.

I didn't bother yelling about how I was getting attacked by yet another Reaper. The guys would figure that out soon enough. Looked like Ajax's plan to travel on the down low hadn't worked quite as well as he and Metis had thought it would.

While the girl scrambled up off Oliver's lap, I reached over and grabbed Vic.

"Look," I said, slipping out from behind the bench so that I was standing in the middle of the aisle. "A Reaper. Do you forgive me now?"

The sword eyed the girl, who was once again raising her sword and charging at me. "I'll let you know after we kill her."

I didn't have time to respond before the Reaper was on me.

Clash-clash-clang!

Up and down the aisle we fought, each one of us trying to drive her sword into the other. I ducked under the Reaper girl's swing and shoved past her, putting myself between her and my friends. I glanced over my shoulder. Behind me, I could see Oliver trying to crawl over the benches in order to get behind the Reaper girl, while Alexei was struggling to pull his two swords out of his black backpack. I knew my friends wanted to help me, but there wasn't time. Besides, I wanted to fight the Reaper, wanted to take my pain, anger, worry, and fear out on her. So I stepped up and focused on my enemy.

The girl was unbelievably quick, like all Amazons are, but the constant lurching of the train was messing with her balance more than it was mine. It made all of her attacks miss the mark by just that much. Through the windows, I could see a large curve coming up ahead, and I knew the train would lurch to the left. So I parried the girl's blows and waited for the right moment.

A minute later, the train screeched around the curve just as the girl raised her sword over her head. Her vicious strike, along with the train's rocking, put her even that much more off balance, and she almost fell onto one of the benches before she managed to right herself.

I leaned into the curve and let the train's momentum carry me forward into the girl—and help me bury Vic's sharp point in her stomach.

She sucked in a breath that was equal parts pain and surprise. The train swayed the other way, and I pulled the blade free.

The girl's sword fell to the floor, and she pressed her hands to her stomach, her breath coming in short, painful gasps. She looked down in disbelief at all the blood gushing out of her wound, then back up at me.

For a moment, a spark of Reaper red fire shimmered in her eyes. Then, it was abruptly snuffed out, like a light that had been turned off. The girl pitched forward onto one of the tables, her head cracking against the window, even as her legs went out from under her. She didn't move after that.

Breathing hard, I stared down at the dead Reaper. I didn't know her, had never seen her before, but the thing that struck me the most was that she appeared to be about the same age as Jason Anderson. Just a kid. Just like me. And now she was dead like he was—all because of me.

"Gwen?" Oliver slid free of the bench he'd been trying to crawl over, stepped forward, and put a hand on my shoulder.

"I'm okay," I said. "She didn't hurt me."

Not on the outside anyway, even though killing her had caused another little painful crack to zigzag across my heart. I wondered how many more cracks it could take before it crumbled completely.

Naturally, the fight had attracted the attention of the other passengers, and they scrambled to their feet and turned around to see what had caused all the commotion.

I let out a breath and raised Vic. "So do you forgive me now?"

"I might," the sword said. "If you live through the rest of the fight."

I frowned. "Rest of the fight? What are you talking about?"

Vic rolled his eye forward.

I looked in that direction and got my answer a second later. Because the folks in the front of the car weren't getting up because they were concerned about the battle. Oh no. They were getting to their feet because they were all wearing long, black coats, just like the Reaper girl.

And because they all held sharp, curved swords, just like hers—and because every single person's eyes were glowing that bright, eerie Reaper red.

Chapter 12

Oliver and Alexei realized what was happening the same time I did. Oliver cursed, while Alexei finally pulled his twin swords out of his backpack. Oliver grabbed my shoulder and shoved me behind him, so that I was standing in between him and Alexei.

"We need to get out of here," Alexei said.

The Bogatyr turned toward the back of the car. He hadn't taken two steps in that direction before the door hissed open, and more people entered from that side, also wearing long, black coats and carrying swords. The fiery red glow from the Reapers' eyes seemed to darken the inside of the train, despite the sunlight streaming in through the windows.

Alexei stopped short, and I almost rammed into him from behind.

"Trapped," he said in a voice loud enough for Oliver to hear. "Exit's blocked."

"Same on my side," Oliver said, reaching down and grabbing a magazine from the slot on the back of one of the benches.

"Well, then," Alexei said, twirling his swords. "Let's clear a path."

"My pleasure," Oliver replied, rolling the magazine into a long, thin, tight tube.

The two guys rushed forward to meet our enemies.

Clash-clash-clang!

Alexei's twin swords smashed against the blade of the Reaper in front of him. Even though he could only maneuver from one side of the aisle to the other, Alexei never stopped moving, never stopped fighting, never stopped attacking. Bogatyrs had incredible endurance that way.

On his side of the car, Oliver ducked under a Reaper's wide swing. The Spartan might not have had a traditional weapon, but he didn't need one. He whipped the rolled-up magazine this way and that, slamming it into his opponent's chest, throat, and face.

Thwack-thwack-thwack.

The Reaper choked and sputtered, trying to suck air back down into his lungs. While he was distracted, Oliver plucked the Reaper's sword out of the other guy's hand, flipped it around, and then stabbed the Reaper in the chest with his own weapon. I couldn't see Oliver's face, but he was probably grinning.

Logan would have been.

But as soon as that Reaper toppled to the floor, another stepped up to take his place—and all I could do was stand in the middle and watch my friends fight another battle for me.

I turned first one way, then the other, but the aisle wasn't quite wide enough for me to get to the Reapers from where I was standing. At least, not without me pushing past Oliver or Alexei, and I couldn't risk doing that for fear of spoiling their concentration. But I was determined to help my friends, so I hopped up onto the bench on my left and started crawling over it toward the back of the car, where the majority of the Reapers seemed to be coming from.

"Gwen!" Alexei said, spotting me out of the corner of his eye and realizing what I was up to. "Stay put! Stay behind me!"

I didn't bother answering him. I couldn't stay put, and I couldn't just stand there and do nothing. Not while he and Oliver were fighting so many Reapers. I might not be the best or most skilled warrior, but I was no coward, especially when it came to helping my friends.

As I heaved myself across the benches, I noticed the girl who'd been sitting in the back of the train. She was standing up on her bench just like I was. The girl kept looking back and forth between the Reapers and Alexei, as though she was watching an intense sporting match. She didn't move to attack my friend, but she didn't try to help him either. Since the girl seemed to be staying where she was and out of the fight, I put her out of my mind and kept climbing over the benches as fast as I could.

A Reaper girl who looked about my age moved to attack me, but I swung Vic and sliced the sword across her chest. Blood spurted out of her wound and spattered onto my hand, sliding across my skin like warm drops of rain. I gritted my teeth and ignored the awful sensation.

"Get her, Gwen!" Vic crowed, not having any problems with the blood that covered his blade. "Get her!"

I lashed out with the sword again, this time stabbing the blade deep into her stomach. The Reaper girl screamed and lurched back into the boy behind her, but he put his arms on her shoulders and shoved her forward. I put one hand down on a brass rail, bracing myself, and kicked her in the chest, sending her flying right back into the boy. They both fell to the floor. I could hear the boy yelling as he tried to shove the dead girl off him, but since he wasn't an immediate threat, I continued climbing over the benches.

Behind me, I could hear Oliver and Alexei shouting to each other as they counted off the Reapers they killed.

"One down!" Alexei said.

"Two down!" Oliver chimed in.

"Three!"

"Four!"

I finally managed to crawl to the back of the car and an open space that was reserved for storing luggage. I'd just put my feet down on the floor when the Reaper boy finally managed to push the dead girl off him. He scrambled to his feet and charged at me.

I didn't have time to raise my sword, so I stepped forward and punched him in the face. The blow didn't have much of an effect on the Reaper, but it made him hesitate long enough for me to shove Vic into his stomach. The boy screamed and fell to the floor.

Out of the corner of my eye, I saw one of the Reapers who'd been attacking Alexei turn in my direction, reach underneath his coat, and pull out a small crossbow. He leveled the weapon at my head.

Thwang!

Even as I started to move, I knew I couldn't duck out of the way in time to keep the arrow from hitting me—

Something moved off to my right, a shadow flitted in front of my eyes, and I heard the distinct sound of wood hitting flesh. I blinked.

Smack!

The arrow had stopped a foot from my face.

Eyes wide, my head snapped to the side, and I realized that the angry girl from the train station was there—and that she was holding the arrow in her hand like it was a football she'd just plucked out of midair.

"You're welcome," she said in a snide voice.

Then, she tossed the arrow up in the air, grabbed it by the end, and threw it at the Reaper with the crossbow. The arrow sank into his throat. The man clawed at the projectile, trying to rip it free, even as his legs went out from under him, and he dropped to the floor.

"A Spartan," I whispered. "You're a Spartan."

"Yeah, and you and your friends seem to be in a lot of trouble," the girl sniped.

She stepped in front of me and picked up the dead Reaper's crossbow. A second later, she slammed the heavy wood into the side of another Reaper's face. I shook my head, stepped up, and got back into the fight.

Together, the girl and I advanced on the Reapers who were clustered in front of Alexei and climbing up onto the benches so they could swarm around and attack him all at once. She'd step up and hit one with the crossbow, then slide to the side, leaving me enough room to move forward and kill the Reaper with Vic. When the crossbow finally splintered, then shattered, she used one of the broken pieces as a dagger, stabbing it into everyone she could reach.

Logan would have *definitely* approved.

Seeing that we had a handle on the Reapers on this side of the car, Alexei whirled around to help Oliver deal with the ones who were attacking him. Working together, the four of us cut through the rest of them. Three minutes later, it was over, and all the Reapers were dead.

We stood there, weapons clutched tight in our hands, blood everywhere, bodies stacked up two and three deep at our feet, with even more Reapers sprawled over the benches and tables. For a moment, the only sounds were our harsh, raspy breaths and the grind of the gears as the train kept chugging up the mountain.

"Well," Vic said in a cheery voice. "That's the way to start the day off right. Blood before breakfast. Always a treat, if you ask me."

The Spartan girl gave me a strange look, like she thought I was the one who was talking. Please. As if I would ever say such gruesome things—or could manage an English accent right now.

"Shut up, Vic," I muttered.

I looked at Oliver and Alexei. "You guys all right?"

They both nodded, and we all stared at the Spartan girl.

"I'm fine," she sniped again. "Thanks for asking."

Alexei stepped forward, probably to start searching the bodies, when the door at the front of the car hissed open. We all tensed and whirled around toward the opening.

Daphne stepped inside, with Carson and Coach Ajax right behind her.

"I can't believe they were out of blueberry bagels already—"

Her voice cut off, and she stopped in the middle of the aisle. Carson ran into her back and bounced off. Daphne's black eyes fixed on the dead Reapers, then her gaze flicked to Alexei, Oliver, and finally me.

"So," I asked. "How was breakfast?"

Daphne arched an eyebrow. "Obviously not as exciting as yours."

I grimaced at her words.

Chapter 13

Ajax shouldered past Carson and Daphne. The coach went from one Reaper to another, looking at them all in turn. Finally, he shook his head.

"I thought they'd at least wait until we got to the ruins before they attacked," he rumbled. "I'll have to call ahead and report this. Everybody stays in here where I can see you until we get to Snowline Ridge. Understand?"

We all nodded.

Ajax pulled out his cell phone and moved to the front of the car. He punched in some numbers and started talking in a low voice, probably alerting the members of the Protectorate about the battle—and the fact that they needed to come and deal with the blood and bodies.

We took turns using the bathrooms, cleaning the Reapers' blood off our hands, clothes, and weapons as best we could. Once that was done, Alexei and Oliver moved from body to body, pulling out the Reapers' wallets and looking at their driver's licenses, credit cards, and more. But they were just names that went with dead faces. None of the information told us anything important about the Reapers, like why they'd decided to attack us now—or what they might have planned next. I even leaned down and touched a few of the dead Reapers' hands, but the only flashes I got off them were of the battle—nothing useful. Ajax also went through the other cars on the train, in case Vivian or Agrona might be on board, hiding in the midst of the other passengers, but they were nowhere to be found.

"What do you think they wanted?" Carson asked, leaning down to peer at a guy who wore the same sort of black glasses he did.

"Other than killing us?" Daphne said. "I think that's enough for them. Don't you?"

Carson's words made me think back to the way the first Reaper girl's eyes had fixed on Vic. Sure, maybe she hadn't expected me to have the sword propped up in the seat beside me, but it seemed like there had been something more to her sharp gaze than just curiosity. I couldn't imagine what it could be, though, or what her interest in Vic could have to do with the attack.

Daphne turned to the mystery girl, who was leaning against the back wall of the car, her arms crossed over her chest once again. "And then there's you. Gwen says you're a Spartan. Female Spartans are rare. I've never met one before."

The girl shrugged. "Not so rare to me, since my mom and dad were both Spartans. Lucky for you, you get to meet me first, Valkyrie."

Pink sparks of magic crackled around Daphne's fingers, and she narrowed her eyes at the other girl. I stepped in between them, trying to diffuse the situation before things got any crazier.

"Well, thank you," I said. "For saving me. For fighting with us against the Reapers. You didn't have to do that."

The girl laughed, although it was a harsh, bitter sound. "Oh, you know us Spartans. We can't resist a good fight."

"What's your name?"

The girl glared at me, as though I'd asked her to reveal her deepest, darkest secret. Finally, when she realized that I was serious and expected her to, you know, actually *answer* me, she let out a long, deep sigh, as if giving me the information was some sort of cruel torture I'd devised specifically for her.

"Rory Forseti."

My mouth dropped open in surprise. I didn't know what name I'd expected her to give, but it hadn't been that one—because Forseti had been my dad, Tyr's, last name. Tyr Forseti. My parents had been married, but I had my mom's last name of Frost since that was the tradition for the women in our family.

It took me a moment to close my gaping jaw and gather my thoughts. "Forseti?" I asked, wondering if I'd heard her right. "F-o-r-s-e-t-i?"

The girl's eyes narrowed, and her hands balled into fists like she was thinking about stepping forward and attacking me the same way she had the Reapers. "Well, give you a gold star, for being able to spell. You got a problem with that name?"

Alexei stepped forward, shielding me from her. "You're the one who's going to have a problem if you take another step toward Gwen."

She let out another angry, bitter laugh. "In case you

didn't notice, dude, I'm the one who saved your precious little princess from getting an arrow through her skull."

"Princess?" I asked.

Rory gave a loud, derisive snort. "Yeah. You. Princess. You and your little entourage. I saw them hovering around you at the station. You'd think that you were some sort of princess or something the way they were hanging all over you."

My eyes widened, my lips twitched, and my shoulders started to shake. I tried to contain it—really, I did—but I couldn't help it. I started laughing. And once I started, I couldn't stop. I knew it was crazy, that my laughter was crazy, that I should try to bottle it up the way I had all of my other emotions lately, but I just couldn't do it.

My friends looked at me, then each other. Daphne shrugged. She didn't know why I was laughing, and neither did any of the guys.

"What's so funny?" Rory muttered.

"Princess!" I managed to get out the word between fits of laughter. "You think I'm a bloody princess!"

The laughter kept coming and coming until tears streamed out of the corners of my eyes, and my stomach ached from the force of it.

Rory glared at me again. "If I'd known you were crazy, I would have let the Reapers put you out of your misery—and mine too."

I wiped the tears away and finally managed to get my giggles under control. "You don't understand. If there's one thing I'm not, it's definitely a princess. That's more Daphne's thing than mine."

"Hey!" Daphne snapped.

I looked at her. "C'mon. You know it's true. How many bags did you bring for this trip?"

She sniffed. "Just because you want to spend the rest of your life wearing hoodies, sneakers, and ratty T-shirts doesn't mean the rest of us should suffer."

I rolled my eyes. "Oh no."

Rory looked at the Valkyrie. "Your name's Daphne?"

She straightened up. "Daphne Cruz. From the North Carolina academy."

One by one, Daphne introduced everyone, including Coach Ajax, who'd finished his phone call.

Rory glanced at my friends before her green eyes fixed on me once more. "And what's the princess's name?"

"Gwen," I said. "Gwen Frost."

Rory froze, just as I had a moment ago. A shadow passed over her pretty face, and for a moment, her whole body tensed up, like she was debating whether or not to throw herself forward and attack me. Something that looked a lot like hate blazed in her eyes, and I felt a wave of anger surge off her, as hot as a furnace blasting heat in my face.

"Maybe you've heard of her," Carson said in a helpful voice.

"Yeah," Rory muttered. "I've heard of her all right."

And from the sound of her voice, it hadn't been anything good. It was bad enough that all the kids back home watched my every move now, but I'd never considered that word of who I was would make its way through the rest of the mythological world. I should have known it would, though. Sometimes, I thought Mythos kids gossiped even better than they wielded weapons. I wondered what this meant for our welcome at the academy. Ajax had wanted to pass our group off as some kids taking a field trip, but that wasn't going to happen now—if it had ever even been possible to start with.

Rory gave me another dark look, then plopped down on her bench, crossed her arms over her chest, and turned her head toward the windows, pointedly ignoring me and my friends. The others and I sat down, as well, making sure we were as far away from the blood and Reapers' bodies as we could get. I tried to catch Rory's gaze, but she stared out the windows with the same sort of intense, single-minded determination she'd shown during the fight. She might have saved my life, but it was obvious she wasn't happy about it. I wondered why. I'd never seen or met her before today, so I had no idea why she'd have such an obvious grudge against me. Usually, I had to be around people for at least a few minutes before I pissed them off.

Maybe it was her dislike of me or maybe it was the fact that the train was now filled with dead Reapers, but I couldn't help feeling there was a giant ax swinging back and forth over my head. All that was left to do now was to see when it would finally fall.

About fifteen minutes later, the train pulled into the station at Snowline Ridge. My friends and I grabbed our things and stepped off the car. Waiting on the platform was a group of men and women, all wearing black coveralls with the hand-and-scales symbol of the Protectorate stitched into the collars in white thread. The Protectorate members waited for us to get clear of the train before they boarded, pushing metal carts into the car where the Reapers' bodies were.

The other folks on the train had finally realized something had happened, and more than a few kids held their phones out and up, taking photos of me and my friends before they started texting furiously. Someone must have known someone who knew something about me, because within two minutes, everyone's phones started chirping, and the whispers drifted over to me.

"Her name is Gwen Frost . . ."

"She's supposed to be a Champion . . ."

"Apparently, she's always in some sort of trouble with the Reapers . . ."

Well, there went Ajax's hopes of our staying incognito for as long as possible. I grimaced. Maybe things weren't going to be all that different here at the Colorado academy after all. Reapers trying to kill me? Check. Everyone staring at me? Check. Kids whispering about me behind my back? Double-check. So far, it was like I hadn't even left home.

The only person who seemed as miserable as I did was Rory. The Spartan girl stood off to one side of the platform by herself. Once again, I noticed how the other kids took pains to avoid her—when they weren't openly sneering and snickering at her.

"Of course *she* was on the train with the Reapers . . ."

"Keeping it in the family, I suppose . . ."

"I don't know why they even let her come to school with us . . ."

From the sound of things, the other kids thought Rory had something to do with the Reapers. But why would they think that? She'd helped us fight them. If she'd really been one of them, she would have joined in the attack—and let that arrow punch right through my skull. I frowned and looked at Rory, but once again, she wouldn't meet my gaze.

"Come on," Ajax said, interrupting my thoughts. "It's just a short walk to the academy from here. We need to get there, get settled in, and start making plans for tomorrow."

We shouldered our bags and followed the stream of students through the station and out into town. Ajax walked in front, with Carson and Daphne behind him, then me, then Oliver and Alexei bringing up the rear.

In many ways, Snowline Ridge was pretty much a carbon copy of Cypress Mountain. Designer shops, coffee-houses, and expensive cafés lined the wide streets, each storefront window showcasing luxury clothes, jewelry, electronics, and more. I even spotted a couple of parking lots full of Aston Martins and BMWs, along with sturdy SUVs and expensive pickup trucks with four-wheel drives to help navigate the icy roads in these parts. I guess the students here couldn't have cars on campus either.

But there were plenty of differences that let me know this wasn't home. For one thing, walking down the streets was like stepping back in time to the Old West. Many of the old-fashioned, wooden storefronts looked like they'd come straight out of some cowboy movie, right down to life-sized carvings of grizzly bears that stood guard on either side of the swinging saloon doors you pushed through to get inside. Then, there were the items the shops sold—custom-made cowboy boots, turquoise lariat ties, ten-gallon hats, diamond-crusted belt buckles the size of dinner plates. Everything had a

Western feel to it, and I half-expected some tumble-weeds to come rolling down the street, despite the snow underfoot.

Finally, we left the shops behind and reached the edge of the academy grounds. Just like at home, a stone wall ringed the entire academy, although the main iron gate stood open to let the returning students back onto campus. My friends stepped through the gate without even glancing around, but I stopped and peered up.

Sure enough, two statues perched on top of the stone wall on either side of the gate. But they weren't the sphinxes I expected—these statues were gryphons.

Eagle heads, lion bodies, wings, curved beaks, sharp talons. These statues looked as fierce, majestic, and life-like as the ones back home.

It was almost as if the statues could hear my thoughts, because as I watched them, they began to move. Their wings twitched, the feathers ruffled back and forth in the cold winter wind, their talons dug a little more into the stone at their feet, and their eyes narrowed as they glared down at me—

"C'mon on, Gwen!" Daphne said. "It's freezing out here!"

I blinked, and the gryphons were simply stone once more. Well, the figures might be different, but it seemed as though these statues would be watching me as closely as the ones back home did. In a strange way, that comforted me.

"Gwen!" Daphne yelled again.

I gave the gryphons a little salute with my hand, then hoisted my bags higher onto my shoulder and followed my friends onto the grounds.

Chapter 14

The more we walked, the more I got an extreme sense of déjà vu.

Just like back home, a series of ash-gray cobblestone paths wound every which way across the grounds. I imagined that all of the lawns would be as smooth, green, and manicured as they were at Mythos, except for the fact that they were buried under a couple of inches of snow right now. We also passed several dorms that could have been carbon copies of the ones in North Carolina. So far, the only big difference I could see between the two academies were the dense pine trees that dotted the grounds like rows of soldiers, instead of the sprawling maples and oaks I was used to. Well, that and the fact that the hills were a lot steeper here. We'd barely been walking for five minutes, and I could already feel the burn in my legs.

"What's wrong?" Alexei asked, noticing me glancing around.

"I think it's weird how much this academy looks like our academy," I said. "If it weren't for all the snow, I'd think I was back home."

He shrugged. "They all pretty much look like this. Dorms, stone paths, a main quad with several buildings."

"Really? Every single one of them?"

Alexei shrugged again. "All the ones I've been to. St. Petersburg, London, New York, North Carolina, and now here. But there are always some differences. You'll see."

We walked on. We finally crested the hill we'd been climbing, and I blinked in surprise.

Because before me lay the main quad of Mythos Academy—sort of.

Like Alexei had said, it looked a lot like our quad. Five main buildings arranged in a starlike pattern, a series of paths winding in between the structures. Math-science, English-history, a dining hall, a gym, a library. They were even arranged in the same spots as they were back home, and the outsides looked remarkably similar. Same dark gray stone, same gloomy outlines, same statues covering them all.

But the more I looked, the more I noticed the differences Alexei had mentioned. Instead of being smooth and unbroken, the stone of the buildings looked like boulders that had been piled on top of each other. The rocks were more black than gray and interspersed with dark logs that were thicker around than I was tall. Wide windows were set into all of the structures, I supposed to take advantage of the sweeping views of the pine trees that ran up to and seemed to merge into the mountain above. Everything seemed rough and raw, as if the buildings themselves were hollow rocks and tree trunks that had broken off the jagged mountain peak above and had finally tumbled to a stop here.

A series of bells rang out, the high, clear sounds

booming like claps of thunder throughout the quad and bouncing from one structure to the next. A minute later, the doors of the dining hall opened, and students started pouring out.

"Breakfast just ended, and everyone's heading to their morning classes," I murmured.

"That's right," Ajax said. "Come on. There's someone I need to speak to about making the arrangements for our trip tomorrow."

The coach set off across the quad, and we all fell in line behind him. I wasn't all that surprised when Ajax headed for the Library of Antiquities. A silver plaque on the front told me what the building was, but I would have known anyway. Oh, the shape was a bit different, since this library had three large wings joined together by a large, square tower in the middle, but it was still the largest and most impressive structure on the quad.

The others trooped up the steps, but once again, I lingered behind. A pair of gryphons perched on boulders on either side of these steps, and they looked just as fierce as the ones I'd come to think of as my protectors back home. It took me a moment to realize they were actually a bit smaller, although their features were that much sharper, as if whoever had carved the statues hadn't finished sanding down the stone and smoothing out the anger in the gryphons' expression. But it wasn't just their appearance that was different. It was the feeling that radiated off them—the same sort of intense wildness I'd felt ever since we'd stepped off the plane.

Oh, I imagined that if I touched these gryphons, they would break free of their stone shells just like I always thought the ones back home would. But instead of attacking, I got the sense that these creatures would immediately spread their wings, take to the sky, and revel in the freedom of the open horizon. I don't know why I thought that, but once the idea was in my mind, I couldn't get rid of it, and it almost seemed as if I could feel the wind tearing through my hair—

A hand clamped down on my arm, and a shower of pink sparks exploded, making me twitch my nose to hold back a sneeze.

"Oh, come on, Gwen," Daphne said. "Stop staring at everything. You're acting like you've never been to a different academy before."

I tried to pull my arm out of her firm grip, but it was no use. Not with her Valkyrie strength. "You're forgetting that you're right—I never have been to a different academy before."

She glanced around. "Well, I don't see what's so fascinating about it. Now, come on. Everyone else is inside already."

Daphne strong-armed me up the steps, inside the building, down a hallway, and into the main space of the Library of Antiquities.

Once again, I was struck by a serious sense of déjà vu—because this library looked eerily similar to the one I'd been in last night. A second-floor balcony ringed with statues of gods and goddesses. A main aisle that led to the checkout counter in the middle of the library. Study tables on either side, with shadow-filled stacks sitting all around them. There was even a coffee cart parked off to one side, although no students were gathered around it since it was still so early.

But there were differences here too. The inside of the

library was square and only five stories tall, making it seem short and squat in comparison to the one back home. The tower that I'd noticed outside took up the center of the library, with the three wings sticking out from it, like spokes on a wheel. More thick logs of lumber were stacked on top of each other, forming the walls and the supports for the floors above. Colorful rugs with a variety of Native American symbols stitched on them covered the floor, seeming like carvings that had been burned into the stone. I looked down and realized I was standing on the chin of Coyote. I murmured my apologies and stepped off the rug.

But perhaps the most impressive feature was an enormous stone fireplace to the right of the checkout counter. It was made out of the same dark boulders as everything else and was easily thirty feet wide and flanked by cushioned chairs and couches. I could picture students gathered there, studying in front of the crackling flames. All put together, the library reminded me of some rustic hunting lodge. It wasn't home, but I liked the look and feel of it all the same.

Daphne let go of my arm and headed over to where Carson was standing with the others. I slowly turned around, looking from one side to the other.

Finally, I peered up. Instead of being a dome, the ceiling here was divided into three sections, one for each wing, and they all rose up and flowed into the square ceiling that made up the tower in the middle. I tipped my head back even more, wondering if there was a fresco on the ceiling here too and if perhaps I could see it, since it was so much lower. There was a painting, and shadows cloaked much of it just like they did back home, but to my surprise, parts of the ceiling were crystal-clear—and the images revealed were all artifacts.

Sigyn's bow. The Horn of Roland. The Swords of Ruslan. The artifacts that Daphne, Carson, and Alexei carried were as clear as day to me, along with Vic, who was in my hand. I even saw something that looked like Ran's fishing net, which I still had stuffed in my messenger bag. It looked like the same fresco as in the library back home, although this time, all I could make out were the artifacts—and not my friends carrying them.

My gaze dropped to the second-floor balcony. It took me a moment to find Nike's statue in the square pantheon, even though it was in more or less the same place here as it was back home. I stared at the goddess, and it seemed that her statue shimmered, as though it was some sort of heat mirage. I blinked, and I noticed that Nike's head was tilted back, her gaze locked on the artifacts that I could still see on the ceiling. I blinked again, and the goddess's eyes were fixed on me once more. I frowned. It almost seemed as if she was trying to warn me about something—

"Beautiful, isn't it?" a low voice murmured.

I whirled around to find a man standing a few feet behind me. "Excuse me?"

He jerked his head upward. "The fresco on the ceiling. It's beautiful, isn't it? The landscape of the mountains and the academy nestled in the middle of them."

Was that what he saw? Because that definitely wasn't what I had gotten a glimpse of. Not here and not at home either. But if there was one thing I'd learned during these last few months, it was to keep my mouth shut with strangers—no matter how nice and harmless they might seem.

"Sure," I said. "I've never seen anything like it."

"Me either," the man said, smiling at me.

He was on the short side, several inches shy of six feet tall, and whip-thin. His hair and eyes were a light hazel, but his skin was much darker, a rich, reddish brown, as though he'd spent a lot of time outdoors over the years and had a ruddy tan that would never, ever fade. A small brown goatee clung to his chin, softening the sharp point of his face. He wore a dark blue, three-piece suit that reminded me of something Nickamedes would wear, although he had on a pair of sturdy brown hiking boots instead of the glossy wing tips the librarian almost always favored.

The man's smile widened as he kept looking at me. "Are you new here? I don't think I've ever seen you before. Can I help you find something in the library?"

I opened my mouth to answer him when someone interrupted me.

"Covington! There you are!" Ajax's voice rumbled through the library, and the coach walked down the aisle in our direction.

To my surprise, Ajax clapped the other man on his shoulder, almost sending Covington barreling into one of the bookcases before he managed to recover his balance.

"Ajax! What a surprise. It's good to see you," Covington said, returning Ajax's clap with a much weaker one of his own. "How are things in North Carolina? When I got your message that you were flying out here on the spur of the moment, I was worried something was wrong."

Ajax grimaced. "Unfortunately, something is wrong. Is there someplace private where we can talk?"

Covington nodded. "Of course. Just let me finish helping this young lady, and I'll be right with you."

"Actually, I'm with him." I pointed my finger at Ajax. "And so are my friends."

The others realized that Ajax and I were talking to someone, and they headed in our direction. Covington's gaze took us all in. He kept the smile fixed on his face, but I could tell he was wondering who we were and why we were there. I was wondering the same thing about him. Sure, he seemed nice enough, but I'd learned the hard way that was what Reapers did—they pretended to be your friend right before they stabbed you in the back. Vivian had done it to me, and Agrona had done the same thing to Logan by marrying and pretending to love his dad.

"Covington is a friend," Ajax said, noticing my questioning glance. "We need him to prepare for the next part of our journey."

"Journey?" Covington asked. "What journey?"

Ajax sighed. "Not here. Let's go somewhere more private."

"Certainly. I know just the place."

Covington gave us all one more curious look before he gestured for us to follow him.

Covington led us deeper into the library. Instead of heading for the checkout counter like I thought he might, the librarian skirted around that area and veered left into one of the wings. Eventually, he reached a door set into one of the walls, unlocked and opened it, and ushered us all inside. We stepped into a conference room. A long table, chairs clustered all around it, a pitcher of water and glasses perched on a silver tray on a small counter. Nothing all that interesting—except for the gryphon carving.

It took up almost the entire back wall. A gryphon with its wings spread wide, its head thrown back, and its beak wide open as if it was about to let out a screech, swoop down from the sky, and attack. And it wasn't the only gryphon in here. More images of the creature could be seen on the other walls, although those carvings were much smaller, but no less fierce-looking.

As soon as I stepped into the room, it seemed as if all of the gryphons' eyes swiveled around to me. I shivered and took a seat at the end of the table, as far away from the carvings as I could get.

"So," Covington asked when we were all finally settled, "you want to tell me what you're doing here? With five students in tow? I heard a rumor about some students being the target of a Reaper attack on the train this morning. I'm guessing that was you and your kids?"

Ajax nodded. "We're here on behalf of a friend. Nickamedes."

Covington nodded back. "I know him. He's my counterpart in the Library of Antiquities at the North Carolina academy. We exchange e-mails, books, and even artifacts from time to time."

"He's been poisoned, and we're here searching for a cure."

Ajax drew in a breath and explained everything to his friend. The Reaper boy poisoning Nickamedes, our hurried journey here, the attack on the train. To my surprise, the coach didn't say much about me or my friends. He introduced us, but he only gave Covington our first names. It made me wonder if Ajax didn't entirely trust his friend—and if so, why not. Then again, we'd all been fooled by the Reapers. Maybe the coach was just being extra cautious, even though I thought it was far too late for that.

When Ajax finished, Covington let out a low whistle. "Chloris ambrosia flowers aren't easy to come by."

"I know," the coach replied. "That's why we need to go up to the Eir Ruins—tomorrow."

Covington frowned. "You want to go the ruins? With your . . . students?"

Ajax nodded. "I know what you're thinking, and believe me, I know how dangerous the ruins are supposed to be. But it's the only place where the ambrosia flowers grow, and Nickamedes will die without them. So can you help us? Please?"

Covington studied his friend. "And if I don't?"

Ajax gave him a level stare. "Then, we'll go on our own."

Covington kept staring at Ajax, then his hazel eyes roamed over the rest of us. We all looked back, showing him the same determination to go to the ruins with or without his help. When he realized we were serious, he nodded.

"Okay, okay, I'll help. Don't worry about that." He hesitated. "It won't be easy, though. I know someone who can guide you to the ruins, and I'll be happy to accompany you myself, but I don't know of any other professors or staff members who would be willing to go. Especially not tomorrow."

"What's wrong with tomorrow?" Ajax asked.

"A storm is blowing in," Covington said. "We're supposed to get a foot of snow sometime in the next twenty-four to forty-eight hours. Maybe more."

Of course it was supposed to snow. As if this wouldn't be hard and dangerous enough already. I wondered if the Reapers had looked at the weather forecast and had factored in the brewing snowstorm when they'd decided to try to poison me. Probably. I wouldn't put it past them. That would be just the twisted sort of thing that Vivian and Agrona would think of—to make us all suffer as much as possible while we tried to get the antidote for Nickamedes.

"Well, we'll just have to risk the storm. And the fewer people who know where we're going, the better," Ajax said. "The Reapers already know we're here and that we have to go to the ruins to get the ambrosia flowers. But just because we're walking into a trap doesn't mean we can't be careful."

Covington nodded. "Understood. I'll start making the arrangements immediately. We'll leave tomorrow."

He stood up, and so did Ajax. The two men shook hands. Covington gave us all a polite nod, then left the conference room.

"So not only do we have to hike up to some creepy ruins, but now, it's going to snow buckets on us too? Terrific," Daphne said.

"Afraid you'll get your pink snowsuit all messed up?" Oliver teased.

She glared at him. "The only thing that's going to get messed up is your face, Spartan. The second I shove my fist through it."

Oliver raised an eyebrow. "Bring it on, Valkyrie."

"Enough," I said. "That's enough. It's bad enough we know the Reapers are lurking around waiting to attack us again. Can we please not snipe at each other too?"

Daphne turned her glare to me, but I glared right back at her. After a moment, she sighed.

"All right," she said. "All right. I'm just a little stressed."

"We all are," Carson said in a soft voice. "But we'll be okay, as long as we stick together."

I flashed him a grateful smile. We were all silent for a moment before Ajax spoke.

"Well," he said. "I have to help Covington with the arrangements. You guys can hang out in the library while we work."

I nodded. Hopefully, we would have a quiet day here, and I could gather my thoughts and prepare for what was to come tomorrow—another trap set by the Reapers, most likely.

Chapter 15

We trooped back out into the main part of the library. Covington waved at Ajax, and the two men disappeared into the glass office complex behind the checkout counter. My friends and I settled ourselves in the cushioned chairs in front of the fireplace. Even though no logs were burning, everyone else seemed perfectly happy to lean back in the chairs, close their eyes, and doze, but I couldn't sit still. Too much on my mind, too many things to worry about, and too many unanswered questions.

So I took off my coat, pulled Vic out of my messenger bag, and belted the sword around my waist, just in case there were any more Reaper attacks today. I also spent a few minutes fiddling with my bag and making sure that Ran's net was still safely tucked away inside, even though I doubted I'd have need of it anytime soon. After that, there wasn't anything left for me to do but start pacing back and forth through the chairs and study tables.

"Relax, Gwen," Oliver finally said, cracking one eye open at me. "Try to get a little rest. We'll have a tough enough day tomorrow."

"I know, I know," I grumbled. "But I hate that we have to sit here all day. I'm going to call my grandma and see how Nickamedes is doing."

Oliver nodded and went back to his dozing. I pulled my cell phone out of my jeans pocket and headed for the edge of the stacks. I stopped there, making sure to keep the others in sight, then hit the number that would speed-dial Grandma Frost. She answered on the second ring.

"Hello, pumpkin." Her warm, familiar voice flooded the line. "I thought it was about time for you to call."

"Hi, Grandma. How are you? How are Metis and Nickamedes?"

"We're all okay," she said. "I'm in the infirmary, sitting with Nickamedes and reading a book. He's asleep right now."

"How is he?"

"The same," she said. "No better, no worse."

"And Metis?"

"She's in the next room, sleeping. She's wearing herself out, coming in here and healing him every few hours, but so far, she's keeping the poison at bay."

I let out a breath. Well, that was something, I supposed.

"How are you, pumpkin?" Grandma Frost asked. "Where are you now?"

I filled her in on everything that had happened since we'd left the academy, including the Reaper attack on the train.

"There was something else," I said, finishing up my story. "I met someone today. A girl. Her name is Rory Forseti."

Grandma didn't say anything. For a moment, the only sound was the faint buzz of static over the line.

"Grandma? Did you hear me?"

After a moment, she sighed. "I heard you, pumpkin. I thought you might run into Rory out there."

My hand tightened around the phone. "Her last name is Forseti—just like my dad's was. Am I—are we—related?"

For a moment, I thought that Grandma wasn't going to answer me, but she finally let out another soft sigh.

"Yes," she said. "She's your cousin. Her father and your father were brothers."

My dad, Tyr, had died when I was two. My mom and grandma had always claimed that he'd passed away from cancer, but ever since I'd learned about the mythological world, I'd had a sneaking suspicion that he'd been killed, probably by Reapers, just like my mom had been murdered by Vivian. But so much had been going on that I hadn't thought to ask my grandma about him.

I didn't have any real memories of my dad, and my mom had only had a few photos of him that she'd shared with me. From the pictures I'd seen, Tyr Forseti had been a tall man with sandy hair, blue eyes, and a face that always seemed to have a hint of sadness in it, even when he had his arms wrapped around my mom and was smiling for the camera.

"Are there any others?" I asked. "Any other Forsetis?"

"No, as far as I know, Rory is the last Forseti. Her parents are both dead, and she lives with her mother's sister, her aunt," Grandma said.

"Why didn't you tell me about her?"

"Tyr . . . your father . . . didn't get along with the rest of his family," she answered. "Let the girl explain it all. It's more her story to tell than mine anyway, especially since she has to live with the consequences of it every day."

I frowned. "Consequences of what—"

Something rustled off to my left. I hadn't been paying attention to where I was walking, and I'd drifted back into the stacks while I'd been talking to Grandma Frost. Now, I was about halfway down one of the aisles, with books all around me.

Out of the corner of my eye, I could see someone watching me from the next shelf over.

I couldn't tell much about the figure. The stacks were actually shelves that had been carved out of the lumber logs, and the thickness of the wood cast deep shadows. The figure seemed to be tall, so I assumed it was a guy. He appeared to be wearing dark clothes, judging from the glimpses of his jeans and long coat that I got through the rows of books that separated us, but he was standing too far back in the shadows for me to get a good look at his face.

I was going to change that, though. No doubt he was some spy sent here to follow me and my friends since the Reapers had failed to kill us on the train. Maybe if I could sneak up on him, I could question him and get some answers as to what the Reapers were up to and why—and where Vivian and Agrona were hiding. Logan might not be here, but I wasn't going to let that stop me from tracking them down—and making Vivian and Agrona pay for what they'd done to him.

"Pumpkin?"

"I have to go, Grandma," I said. "I'll call you again later tonight, okay?"

"Just be careful. I love you, pumpkin."

"I love you too."

I hung up the phone. But instead of putting it away, I kept fiddling with it. I started pacing up and down the aisle, as though I were totally distracted and checking my text messages, even though I didn't have any. With every pass I made, I crept a little closer to the end of the aisle—and so did the guy on the other side.

He was keeping pace with me, and I was going to make him pay for it. When I was in range, I planned to grab Vic, charge around the end of the bookshelf, and put the sword up against the Reaper's throat. Okay, okay, so it wasn't much of a plan, but it was better than letting some Reaper creep spy on me and report back to Vivian and Agrona.

I finally got close enough to the end of the aisle to put my plan into action. I hit a few more buttons on my phone, scrolling through screen after screen, before sliding it back into my jeans pocket. I took a step forward, like I was going back to the center of the library, but at the last second, I pivoted, grabbed Vic from his scabbard around my waist, raised the sword high, and darted around the end of the bookcase and over into the next aisle, ready to attack whomever was watching me . . .

Empty—the aisle was completely, utterly empty.

I looked right and left and in front and behind me, but no one was there. I even peered through the rows of books, looking into the stacks on either side, but those aisles were as empty as this one was.

"Gwen?" Vic asked. He'd woken up when I'd

abruptly yanked him out of his scabbard. "What are you doing? Are there Reapers to fight?"

I let out the breath I'd been holding. The Reaper must have realized that I was onto him and had slipped away into the stacks. He could be anywhere by now—if he'd really even been there to start with.

I thought I'd seen someone watching me, but now, I didn't know. Because it had been a long day already, and I was still jumpy and on edge from the Reaper attack this morning. Maybe someone had been watching me—or maybe I was imagining things the way I so often did. Either way, there was nothing for me to do but go back to my friends.

"Gwen?" Vic asked again. "Is something wrong?"

"Nothing," I told the sword. "It's nothing. Just a false alarm. Go back to sleep."

Vic yawned again, and his eye snapped shut once more.

I sighed. I didn't know what was worse—the Reapers or my paranoia. With Vic still in my hand, I turned to head back to my friends—and slammed into someone creeping up behind me.

Chapter 16

Still thinking about the mystery figure, I immediately went into attack mode and raised Vic high. The only problem was that hitting the figure had thrown me off balance, and I staggered back. My shoulder slammed into one of the bookcases, making me wince with pain—and drop Vic.

The sword skittered across the floor. I threw myself down and forward, reaching, reaching, reaching for Vic—

A black boot came down on top of the sword, stopping it from skidding any farther along the floor. My head snapped up, and I realized it wasn't a Reaper looming over me—it was Rory Forseti.

"Geez, Princess. Kind of hard to fight when you're on your knees on the floor, isn't it?" Rory sniped.

I let out a breath and scrambled to my feet. "You scared me."

Rory's eyes dropped to Vic. "Apparently so."

She leaned down and grabbed the sword. Instead of handing Vic back to me, she held up the weapon, studying the hilt. I tensed, wondering if maybe she really was a Reaper after all—and if she was about to use my own weapon against me.

Vic's eye snapped open, and he regarded Rory with a cold, suspicious glare. "What you looking at, chickie?" he asked.

Rory jumped and almost dropped the sword. Her eyes bulged, and all of the color drained from her face. Vic had just given her a good scare. I snickered.

That snapped Rory out of her fright. She glared at me. Still, it took her a moment to work up the courage to raise Vic once more and peer even closer at the weapon.

"There's—there's some guy's face in the hilt of your sword," she said, an awed note in her voice.

Vic rolled his eye. "Well, aren't you the observant one?"

I held out my hand. "His name is Vic, he talks, and he belongs to me."

"Yes, if you don't mind, chickie, hand me back to the Gypsy," he said. "I want to get the rest of my nap in, just in case we run across any more Reapers today."

Eyes wide, Rory stared at Vic a moment longer before carefully passing him over to me. I took the weapon from her and slid the sword back into the scabbard strapped to my waist.

We stood there, staring at each other, and I studied her again. Black hair, green eyes, round face, pretty features. I wondered if she looked like her mom or her dad—my uncle.

"What are you doing here?" I asked.

She shrugged. "I snuck out of weapons training in the gym. I was bored."

Of course she was bored. Rory was like Logan, Oliver, Kenzie, Nickamedes, and Coach Ajax; she didn't need a weapon to fight—or kill. She'd already proven that on the train when she'd whaled on all of those Reapers with just a crossbow and then the broken bits of it.

Rory kept looking at me, her eyes scanning my features just like I'd done to her. I leaned against the shelf closest to me and stared right back at her. There were so many things I wanted to ask her—about her parents, about my dad, about why all the other kids had looked right through her as if she didn't even exist. But I decided to play it cool, so I kept my mouth shut, even though I wanted to know all of her secrets—all of our family's secrets—just the way I always did.

"So you're the famous Gwen Frost," she finally said.

"And you're a Forseti."

Her mouth tightened. "You got something against the Forsetis?"

"That depends. You got something against me?"

Her scowl deepened. "Why would you say that?"

"Because it seems like you think you know everything there is to know about me, and I don't know anything about you." I drew in a breath. "Except for the fact that we're cousins."

Rory didn't bat an eye at the news. "Yeah. So your dad and my dad were brothers. So what? It's not like that makes us family. Not really."

"But don't you want to know about me?" I asked. "About my dad? About the rest of my family?"

She let out a bitter laugh. "Not if they're anything like my parents. And besides, I know all about you already.

Everybody's been talking about you for weeks now. Ever since we heard about that Reaper attack at the coliseum near the North Carolina academy. Supposedly, you're some kind of great warrior, Nike's Champion, and all that." She sniffed. "I haven't been impressed so far."

My eyes narrowed. "Is that why you saved my life on the train? Because you weren't impressed? Because you didn't think I could defend myself?"

Her eyes glittered with a cold, hard light. "I saved your life because the Reapers wanted you dead. Anything they want, I want the opposite."

"Really?" I asked. "Then why did the other kids talk about you like you were working with the Reapers when we got off the train? Why would they think that when you had just helped me and my friends defeat a bunch of them?"

She tilted her head to the side and looked at me. "You really don't know, do you? About the Forsetis?"

"My dad died when I was two. I don't even remember him, and my mom didn't talk about him a lot."

Rory let out another bitter laugh. "Of course she didn't. Be glad about that. She did you a favor."

Every word this girl said only made me angrier. "Look. All I want is some information about my dad. And you too, if you want to share. My mom was murdered by Reapers last year, so it's just been me and my grandma ever since. But now I come here, and I find out that I have a cousin—one who seems to know a lot more about my dad than I do. Can you blame me for being curious?"

After a moment, she gave me a grudging nod. "No, I suppose not."

"So why don't you lose the attitude and tell me what you know?"

She studied me for several moments, staring into my face as if she could judge whether or not I was telling the truth just by looking at me, and I started to wonder what other magic she might have besides her Spartan fighting skills. Maybe she was even a Gypsy like me, gifted with magic by one of the gods.

"You want to know about the Forsetis?" Rory snapped. "Get your friends, Princess, and I'll show you exactly what the family name means around here."

Rory and I walked out of the stacks. My friends were still sitting in front of the fireplace, trying to nap, but they all sat up at the sound of our footsteps on the floor. They looked at Rory, then me.

"Well, well, well," Oliver said. "Looks like Gwen's made a new friend."

"Shut it, Spartan," Rory snapped. "Or I'll make you eat your own fist."

Oliver straightened up in his chair. "I'd like to see you try."

I rolled my eyes at them. "Again, with the sniping. Can we please cut it out?"

Oliver and Rory ignored me and kept right on glaring at each other. Rory opened her mouth, probably to challenge Oliver to a fight, but a door in the glass office complex squeaked open, cutting her off. Ajax and Covington stepped outside and walked over to the fireplace.

"Is something wrong?" the librarian asked, looking from me to Rory and back again.

"Oh, everything's just fine and dandy," I said. "In

fact, Rory just offered to show me and my friends around campus while you and Ajax work."

Covington frowned. "She did?"

Rory started to open her mouth again, but I clapped her on the back, almost sending her tumbling into Alexei's lap.

"You bet she did," I said.

Rory scowled at my lie, but she didn't contradict me. "Yeah. That's me. Campus tour guide."

Covington frowned, as if he was searching for a reason not to believe her. Rory glared at him, her fists clenched as though she'd like nothing more than to step forward and punch him. I wondered at her hostile reaction to him. What did she have against the librarian?

But in the end, Covington's face smoothed out. "Well, why don't you show Gwen and the others around and then go over to the dining hall and get some lunch? Ajax and I should be finished by the time you're done."

Rory rolled her eyes, but she didn't say anything else. Instead, she deliberately turned away from Covington, like he hadn't even spoken to her.

I looked at Ajax, who nodded. While my friends and I gathered up our things, Ajax gestured for me to come over to him.

"Be careful," he said. "You don't know this girl. We might be on campus now, but that doesn't mean we're safe."

"Don't worry," I said. "I'll be careful. We'll all stay together. We'll walk around campus awhile, then go get some lunch, like Covington suggested. Everything will be fine."

"Okay," the coach rumbled. "Just stick together and keep your weapons with you at all times. If you need anything—anything at all—Covington and I will be here in the library."

"Got it."

Ajax told us to leave our luggage in one of the librarians' offices, although we all kept our weapons like he'd said. I also slung my messenger bag over my shoulder to take with me since Ran's net was in the bottom of it, along with Oliver's drawing of the artifacts.

"Come on," Rory muttered when we'd finished putting everything away. "Let's get this over with."

She walked out of the library, and we all fell in step behind her.

Chapter 17

We'd barely made it outside and down the library steps before Daphne scooted up beside me.

"Are you sure this is a good idea, Gwen?" she asked. "We don't know anything about this girl. She could be a Reaper, just like Vivian was."

"I don't think she's a Reaper," I said in a low voice.

"Why not?"

I told her what Grandma Frost and Rory had both said to me. Daphne was quiet for a moment, thinking. Sparks of magic dripped from her fingertips, and the winter wind swirled them through the air like shimmering pink snowflakes.

"Just because she's related to you doesn't mean you guys are automatically going to be besties," Daphne pointed out.

"I know. But she knows something about my dad—something important. Grandma Frost said as much, and I want to know what it is. Besides, it beats sitting in the library all day, doesn't it?"

Daphne shrugged. She couldn't argue with that.

We followed Rory around the quad. She made a long,

slow circuit, taking us past all of the buildings. Through the windows, I could see other students sitting in their classes, their heads bent over their books, or their eyes fixed on the professors lecturing in front of them. They were doing the same things the kids at the North Carolina academy would be doing—the same things *we* should have been doing right now. I was surprised at how homesick the sights made me.

I started to ask Rory if we were going to walk around in circles all day, when a series of bells chimed. A few moments later, students started streaming out of the buildings. A few kids headed down the hill toward their dorms, but the majority made a beeline for the dining hall.

"Come on," Rory said. "Time for lunch. Oh, joy."

She led us over to the dining hall. My friends looked at me, but I shrugged. I didn't know what Rory was up to, but we could at least get something to eat.

We entered the dining hall, but I didn't get the same sense of déjà vu that I had from the rest of the buildings. I'd expected the area to be filled with round tables covered with white linens, fine china, and gleaming silverware like at home. But instead, the tables were long rectangles made out of the same large logs I'd noticed inside the library. More of the lumber made up the walls, interspersed with those familiar, blackish boulders. Only a few paintings decorated the walls, most of them mountainous landscapes, once again giving everything a rustic Western vibe.

The only thing that was sort of similar to home was the open-air garden in the middle of the enormous room. But instead of grapevines, the garden here featured a variety of evergreen trees that somehow grew in the middle of dense boulder formations. A narrow creek ribboned through the garden, tumbling down a tower of rocks before forming a small pool at the bottom. A variety of stone statues hovered around the edge of the water. Animals, mostly, bears, rabbits, and ducks, although I also spotted an image of Coyote in the mix. A pair of gryphons perched on either side of the top of the waterfall, looking down at the many figures below as though they were protecting the other creatures from harm.

Rory led us over to the far right side of the room, where the lunch line was. We'd come in behind all of the other kids, so we were at the very back. My friends and I grabbed some glass trays and fell in line. We went down the line, and the others filled up their trays with one dish after another, but mine remained empty.

Liver, veal, escargot, some sort of seafood salad with steamed clams. All of it artfully arranged in small white china bowls and garnished with carrots cut into the shapes of sunflowers, green peppers that had been curlicued like ivy vines, and pepper flakes that looked like bits of red snow resting on top of the mounds of steaming food.

I sighed. I'd hoped that the food here would be a little more, well, *normal*, but it was the same fancy stuff they served at home. For some reason, the Mythos kids loved to eat caviar and other froufrou food like that. Finally, I spotted some cheeseburgers, although technically, the sign said they were bison burgers. I didn't really want to eat bison, but since it was the closest thing to recognizable food on the menu, I grabbed a burger, along with some cheese fries, a buttermilk ranch dipping sauce, a bottle of cranberry juice, and a big piece of dark chocolate fudge for dessert.

Finally, we made it to the end of the line. All of my other friends had already paid and were waiting for Rory and me to do the same. The Spartan girl was in front of me, and she slowed her steps, as though she didn't actually want to pay for her food, but she eventually made it over to the cash register.

The woman sitting behind the register perked up at the sight of Rory. She wasn't that much older than us—probably in her mid-twenties—but she was exceptionally pretty, with long, glossy black hair, green eyes, and porcelain skin. She wore a white chef's uniform, and I wondered if she'd helped cook the food.

"Hi, Rory," the woman said. "How's school going today?"

"Hey, Aunt Rachel," Rory muttered. "Everything's fine."

Aunt Rachel? This must be the aunt whom Grandma Frost had told me about—the one Rory lived with. Her mother's sister. The only family she had left. Well, besides me.

Rachel's eyes flicked to me, and she noticed how close I was standing to her niece. Her face brightened a little more. "Who's your new friend?"

"Hi there," I said in a cheery voice, just to needle Rory. "I'm Gwen."

Rory shot me another dirty look, but Rachel didn't notice it. Instead, she reached over and took my hand in hers.

Her feelings and emotions hit me a moment later.

Normally, I was careful about touching people, since

my psychometry kicked in the second my hand brushed across someone else's, but Rachel caught me off guard with her impromptu, enthusiastic handshake. I thought about pulling back but decided not to. I had a lot of questions and not a lot of time to get answers to them since we'd be leaving in the morning to trek to the ruins. I wanted to know more about Rory, and flashing on Rachel was one way to find out. Besides, worst-case scenario, it would tell me whether or not they were Reapers and how much I could trust them.

Rachel's feelings blazed into my mind. For a moment, I was overwhelmed by images of her. Laughing, talking, smiling, growing up over the years, even learning how to fight as a Spartan. But the deeper I sank into her memories, the more I noticed another person in them—an older girl who resembled her. That must be her sister—Rory's mom. All three of them looked just alike. I could also feel all of Rachel's love for her older sister—and how much she looked up to her.

But there was a darkness in the other girl—a darkness that Rachel worried about more and more as the years passed. A darkness that only intensified when she met a boy her own age, and the two of them had Rory. At first, Rachel thought that Rory would be enough to pull her sister out of the darkness—but she wasn't. The images grew more and more disjointed after that, turning into a wall of solid red in Rachel's mind—a wall of blood.

Her sister's blood.

In front of me, I was dimly aware of Rachel looking at Rory. Suddenly, the memories and feelings changed, and I saw Rory growing up over the years—and all the love that Rachel had for her niece.

But the main thing I felt was how tired Rachel was—and how very sad. She was trying to do the best she could with Rory, but she was constantly worrying that she wasn't doing a good enough job, that her love wasn't enough for Rory, that it wasn't enough to help ease the pain of losing her parents.

Rory's parents were dead? When? How?

Before I could look for the answer, Rachel pulled her hand away from mine, and the memories and feelings vanished. I blinked, trying to get my bearings and sort through all of the images and emotions I'd seen and felt at the same time.

I must have had a strange look on my face, because Rachel's eyes narrowed with suspicion. But I gave her a bright smile, paid for my food, and walked over to the table where my friends were sitting. Footsteps smacked on the floor, and Rory hurried up beside me.

"What was that about?" she hissed. "What did you do to my aunt?"

"Nothing," I said. "She didn't feel a thing."

I didn't add that I'd felt everything Rachel was experiencing at the moment, especially her last, strongest emotion—her surprise and happiness that Rory seemed to have a new friend. I wondered what she would think when she realized who I was—and that Rory and I weren't exactly friends.

Rory gave me another suspicious look, but she sat down at the table with us. Nobody said anything, and we all dug into our food.

The bison cheeseburger was surprisingly good. Really, I couldn't even tell it wasn't regular old beef. The meat had a bit of a spicy red pepper seasoning, and the heat pleasantly warmed my mouth. The lettuce and other vegetables had a nice, fresh crunch to them, while the thick layer of mayonnaise on the grilled bun provided a bit of a cool contrast. The fries were hot and crispy, with just the right amount of bacon and melted cheese on them, and the ranch dipping sauce was the perfect blend of creamy tartness. The only thing that was disappointing was the fudge, which was satisfying, but not nearly as rich and sinfully decadent as what Grandma Frost made.

I was so busy stuffing my face that I didn't notice the dirty looks coming our way—at least not immediately.

I was finishing the last bite of my fudge when a surge of emotion washed over me—anger. Hot, burning, sizzling anger. At first, I thought it was directed at me, that there was some Reaper in here, so I turned around in my seat, trying to see who was glaring at me and why. I spotted a group of guys staring at our table. It took me another minute to realize they were actually glaring at Rory—and they weren't the only ones.

We were sitting at a table at the back of the dining hall, but everyone who walked by shot Rory a dirty look. I heard the mutters too.

"Reaper girl . . ."

"Can't believe she came back for another semester . . ."

"Why doesn't she just drop out . . ."

Rory also heard the angry whispers. Her shoulders tensed up, her knuckles went white around her fork, and her gaze flicked back and forth, as though she expected one of the other kids to attack her at any time.

Once again, I had a strange, sick sense of déjà vu. The whole thing reminded me of how the kids at Mythos had treated me a few weeks ago, when I'd been falsely accused of being a Reaper, when Vivian had blamed me for all the evil things she'd done—including killing some of our classmates.

Finally, the stares and mutters weren't enough, and a couple of guys approached our table.

"Well, well, well, look who's actually eating in the dining hall for a change," one of the guys sneered.

"Well, well, well," Rory sniped back. "Look who's still failing English lit—and every other class. That would be you, Duke."

Duke's face turned a mottled red with anger. He was a tall guy with a thick, beefy build, the sort who would have played linebacker at my old public high school. He wasn't carrying a weapon, but I got the vibe that he was a Viking from the way he kept cracking his knuckles, as though he was looking forward to driving them through Rory's face. Vikings were strong and had a rep for using their fists to solve problems instead of weapons.

"Yeah, well," he snarled. "I might not be as smart as you, but at least my parents aren't Reapers. At least they didn't go on a killing spree in the library. You can't say the same about yours, though, can you?"

I froze. So did all of my friends. We glanced at each other, then at Rory. Her parents had been Reapers? They'd killed people? On campus?

Well, that would explain why the other students treated Rory like she was no better than the dirt under their boots.

Rory's face was completely blank and closed off as she pushed her chair back and faced Duke. "I've told you before not to talk about my parents."

Duke's hands curled into fists. "I'll talk about them however I want to. And you too, you Reaper bitch."

Reaper bitch.

Those were the same words that had been spray-painted on my dorm room door and walls more than once. They made me see red now, just like they had then. Because I'd learned something when I'd touched Rachel—that she and Rory weren't Reapers any more than I was.

"Hey," I said, pushing my chair back and getting to my feet, as well. "Leave her alone. She wasn't doing anything to you."

Duke looked at me, and he sneered again. "Who's your friend, Rory? I haven't seen her or any of these other losers around before."

"This is Gwen," Rory said in a loud voice, making sure all the kids at the nearby tables heard her. "My cousin. Her dad was a Forseti. My dad's brother, as a matter of fact."

Hatred flashed in Duke's dark eyes. "Oh," he sneered. "Another Forseti. So your dad was a Reaper too, huh?"

Chapter 18

For a moment, the air left my lungs, my vision went dark, and white spots swam before my eyes. The world seemed to grind to a screeching halt before abruptly sputtering back into gear.

My dad had been—he'd been—my dad had been a *Reaper*?

It wasn't possible. It couldn't be. It just—it just could not *be*.

Rory looked at me, a mixture of anger and pity in her eyes, and I knew it was true. Every awful word that Duke had said was true. Her parents had been Reapers—and so had my dad.

How long had he been a Reaper? Had he killed people? Had my mom known? Had Grandma Frost known? All of these questions slammed into my mind one after another, the force of them making me wobble on my feet.

"What's the matter?" Duke taunted. "Don't like hearing the truth about your horrible family?"

He stepped toward me, but Rory moved in front of me, blocking him. She lifted her chin and glared at him.

Duke sneered at her, and his hand curled into a fist again, as though he was thinking about hitting her.

Another chair scraped back from the table, and Alexei moved in front of both of us.

"That's enough," he said in a chillingly quiet voice. "Walk away."

"Yeah, dude," Oliver said, moving to stand beside Alexei. "Get lost. Now."

Daphne and Carson got to their feet, as well, and Duke realized he was outnumbered. Still, he glared at Rory like he'd love nothing more than to wade through my friends to get to her—and me too.

"Whatever," he finally muttered. "She's not worth it anyway. None of the Forsetis are."

He stalked over to his friends, and they all sat down at their table and put their heads together. From the laughter, curses, and jeers, I knew they were talking about us—about my *dad*.

Suddenly, the dining hall seemed hot, small, and stuffy. I couldn't breathe, and what air I did manage to draw in came right back out in a series of choked gasps. I reached down, fumbled for my messenger bag, and straightened up.

"Gwen?" Daphne asked, her black eyes full of concern.

I shook my head. "I just—I need to be alone for a few minutes. Okay?"

Alexei started to come with me, whether I wanted him to or not, but Oliver put a hand on his arm.

"It's okay," Oliver said. "Let her go."

I hurried out of the dining hall without another word.

* * *

I wound up in the Library of Antiquities, just like I usually did back home whenever something was on my mind. Some new torture the Reapers had put me through, some horrible new secret I'd learned, some new way my heart had been broken once more.

I wasn't really paying attention to where I was going, so I was halfway down the main aisle before I spotted Ajax and Covington standing behind the checkout counter, talking. I didn't want them to see me and wave me over, so I slipped into the stacks and headed up to the second level to Nike's statue. I threw my messenger bag down and curled up in a ball on the floor at her feet.

Vic was sticking out of the top of the bag, and he opened his purplish eye and regarded me with a serious, pitying expression.

"I take it you heard all that in the dining hall?" I asked.

"I did. I'm sorry, Gwen."

"Did you know? About my dad?"

Vic winced, telling me what I already suspected. He'd known this whole time that my dad had been a Reaper, and he'd never said a word to me—not one *word*. I wondered what else he knew that I didn't, how many other secrets he'd been keeping to himself.

He opened his mouth. "But it's not as bad as you think—"

"Shut up, Vic," I muttered. "I don't want to hear it right now."

Vic stared at me a moment longer, then slowly closed his eye.

I didn't bother raising my head and speaking to Nike. She wouldn't answer me. Not now, not here. Besides, I didn't want to talk about things. Not yet. Just when I thought I knew all there was to know about my family, something else like this popped up. I wondered how many more secrets I could take before I started screaming and never stopped—

A shoe scuffed on the floor behind me.

My head snapped around, and I stretched my hand out toward Vic, ready to draw the sword and defend myself against the Reaper that was no doubt sneaking up on me.

Even as I reached for the sword, I cursed myself. *Stupid, stupid, stupid, Gwen!* Ajax had told us to stick together, but I'd rushed off in a snit like a complete idiot, just like I always did, and some Reaper had seen this as an opportunity to try to kill me, probably the mysterious figure I'd noticed in the stacks earlier . . .

I blinked and stopped my hasty scramble, my arm stretched out in midair—because the balcony was empty. My gaze zoomed left and right, and up and down, but the scene didn't change, and no Reapers erupted out of the shadows. I slowly lowered my hand. I kept looking around, peering at all of the logs, rocks, and statues, but no one was there. Still, I felt someone was watching me—a real, live someone and not just all the statues that had their heads turned in my direction.

I scooted around so that my back was pressed up against Nike's feet and made sure Vic was within easy reach, just in case any Reapers appeared. Then, I went back to my brooding.

I hadn't been sitting by the statue long, maybe five minutes, when boots scuffed on the floor again. I tensed, but this person wasn't trying to hide her approach. She rounded the corner and stepped into view. She hesitated a moment before squaring her shoulders, walking over, and plopping down beside me.

"I thought I might find you here," Rory said.

"Yay for you, Nancy Drew," I muttered.

"Your goddess, huh?" she said, twisting her neck so she could look up at the statue.

"Yeah."

We didn't speak for a few moments. Right now, I *never* wanted to speak to her again. But once more, the questions bubbled up in my mind, and I couldn't keep myself from wanting to know the answers, from wanting to know every last part and ugly truth of this deep, dark, dirty family secret that had been shoved out into the light for everyone to see—including me.

"You could have just told me," I finally said, my voice cracking a little on the words.

She grimaced. "I know. I'm sorry about that. It's just . . . it hurts, you know? It hurts so *much*."

I did know, but it still took me a moment to gather the courage to ask my questions. "What happened?"

She shrugged. "I don't know. Not really. One day, I'm just a girl, going through my first semester at Mythos Academy, dealing with classes and professors and stuff. The next day, my parents are dead. Then, it comes out that my parents were Reapers, had always been Reapers, and that they were trying to steal a bunch of artifacts from the library when Covington caught them. But instead of surrendering, they tried to fight their way free and killed some kids before Covington managed to take them out."

So that was why she didn't like the librarian—he'd

killed her parents. Yeah, they'd been Reapers, but he was still responsible for their deaths.

Rory sucked in a breath and finished her story. "And if all that's not bad enough, I also find out that my parents had been secret Reaper assassins for years. The rest... well, you saw the rest in the dining hall."

"I'm sorry," I said. "That's awful."

She shrugged again, trying to pretend she didn't care, trying to pretend it didn't matter, trying to pretend it didn't hurt. "The funny thing is that my parents were always talking about how important it was for me to learn how to fight. To be a good Spartan so I could protect other people from Reapers. And then, they turn out to be Reapers themselves. And not just any Reapers—but some of the worst of the worst."

"I'm sorry," I repeated. I didn't know what else to say. No words would make it better. Not for her—and not for me either.

Rory let out a bitter laugh. "And you know what the really twisted thing is? I still love them. They were my parents, and they were Reapers, but I still love them anyway. I still wish they were here with me instead of being dead. What kind of person does that make *me*?"

"Just a girl," I said. "Just a girl."

Rory picked at a loose thread on her jeans. She wouldn't meet my gaze. If I hadn't thought she would run away, I would have put my hand on hers and used my psychometry to show her that she wasn't the only one who'd been betrayed, fooled, and hurt by the Reapers.

"And my dad?" I finally asked. "What do you know about him?"

She hesitated. "Not much. Just what my dad, Tyson,

told me about him. Apparently, they had some kind of big fight when they were younger, and your dad took off. My dad never heard from him again, but he always seemed sad that he had lost his brother."

I was guessing there was a lot more to the story than what she knew. I'd have to ask Grandma Frost.

"My dad ... a Reaper." The words tasted cold and bitter in my mouth. "It doesn't seem possible. It doesn't seem *real*."

Rory laughed again, but it wasn't a happy sound. "Tell me about it."

"But your aunt seems nice. She's not a Reaper. And neither are you."

Rory kept tugging at that loose thread on her jeans. "Yeah, Rachel's great. She didn't know about them being Reapers either, so she was just as clueless as I was. But word got out about them trying to steal the artifacts and killing those other students."

"And now all the other kids take it out on you—they hate you for it."

She shrugged. "I can handle it. I'm a Spartan."

Her words made me smile. "I know a Spartan guy who would say the exact same thing if he were here. His name is Logan."

Rory eyed me. "And why isn't he here? Why isn't he part of your adoring entourage?"

"It's complicated."

She snorted. "Isn't it always?"

"You have no idea."

We didn't speak for a few moments. Finally, Rory turned to me again.

"So what's your story? The real story? Because I gotta say, I've heard some strange stuff about you."

I let out the same sort of harsh laugh that she had earlier. "Strange doesn't even begin to cover it. One day, I'm just a girl going to public school who has no idea the mythological world even exists. Then, I have a freak-out with my magic, my mom gets murdered, and I get shipped off to Mythos Academy. I find out that I'm descended from a long line of Nike's Champions and that I'm pretty much supposed to save the world from Loki. Only, I end up freeing Loki instead against my will, and now, I've got to figure out some way to stop him. Oh yeah, and the Reapers tried to put Loki's soul into my boyfriend's body, which made my boyfriend go all crazy, stab me in the chest, and almost kill me. Now, my boyfriend's gone, but I still have nightmares about him trying to murder me."

Rory let out a low whistle. "And I thought my life sucked."

"Sucks isn't a strong enough word," I said. "Not by a long shot."

Chapter 19

Rory and I didn't talk after that, but we didn't get up and go our separate ways either. Instead, we sat there by Nike, both of us thinking about all of our problems. But it wasn't an awkward silence. In fact, it felt kind of... nice to be with someone who was going through some of the same things I was.

Yeah, I had my friends, and I knew I could talk to them—or Grandma Frost or Metis—about anything, but they'd all grown up in the mythological world. None of my friends had ever had their whole lives turned upside down by family secrets—not like Rory and I had. Well, none of them except for Logan, but he wasn't here right now. Once again, I worried if the Reapers might have captured him, but I made myself push the thought aside. Oliver had assured me over and over again that Logan was okay, and there was nothing I could do but believe him.

Finally, Rory spoke again. "So why are you and your friends really here?" she asked. "I know you didn't come for some transfer visit like that coach of yours is claiming. And you wouldn't believe some of the rumors that have been going around campus about you guys."

I looked at the Spartan girl, wondering if I could really trust her. But then, I thought of everything I'd seen when I'd flashed on Rachel. Rory was more like me than she realized.

"We're going up to the Eir Ruins tomorrow," I said. "One of our friends has been poisoned. We have to find some ambrosia flowers to make an antidote for him, and the ruins are the only place where they grow. But of course, the Reapers know we're coming. We think they poisoned our friend to lure us out here and that they'll be waiting to ambush us up at the ruins, especially since they didn't kill us on the train."

Rory snorted. "That sounds like Reapers, all right. Always up to something. But the ruins are actually cool."

"You've been up to the ruins? Aren't they supposed to be haunted or something?"

She shrugged. "It's just a pile of rocks and lots of flowers, trees, and herbs everywhere. I don't see what's so creepy about them. Aunt Rachel and I go to the ruins all the time to pick fresh herbs for the dining hall kitchen. I like it because it's quiet up there, you know? Someplace you can sit and think and be by yourself."

I knew exactly what she meant. That was the reason I wound up in the Library of Antiquities so often. The stacks were a great place to lose yourself and get away from everything—at least for a little while.

But now it was time for me to go back to my friends. No doubt they were worried since I'd rushed out of the dining hall, especially since Ajax had told us to stick together. Plus, we needed to start preparing for the trip to the ruins tomorrow. And every second I sat here feeling sorry for myself was another one in which Nickamedes got a little worse as the poison slowly took its toll on him.

"Come on," I said, getting to my feet and heading for the stairs. "Time to go back to the real world."

Rory grinned, stood up, and followed me.

We went downstairs to the first floor. My friends were sitting in the comfy chairs around the fireplace once more. Carson, Alexei, Daphne. They all relaxed when they realized I was okay. Oliver was busy texting on his phone again, and he gave me a distracted wave.

Daphne got to her feet and came over to me. "Are you all right?" she whispered.

"I'm fine," I said, making myself smile at her even though I didn't really feel like it. "I'll deal with it later. Right now, we need to focus on our trip to the ruins, finding the ambrosia flowers, and getting them back to Nickamedes in time."

Daphne nodded, but she still reached out and hugged me. My back cracked, and I winced at the crushing pressure of her grip, but I returned her hug. She was just trying to comfort me. She was a good friend that way.

I sat down on a couch next to Oliver, who was still messing with his phone. Rory hovered outside the ring of chairs, clearly wanting to join us but not sure if she'd be welcome. I gestured at the empty chair a few feet away from me. Rory hesitated a moment longer before stepping forward and plopping down in it.

She'd barely settled herself before footsteps sounded, and Rachel stepped into view. She'd been heading for the checkout counter, but she caught sight of Rory and veered in our direction. Her eyes roamed over our group before they stopped on her niece.

"Rory?" she asked. "What are you doing here?"

"I could ask you the same thing," Rory said. "Shouldn't you be in the dining hall helping the other chefs clean up after lunch?"

"I got a call to come over here instead," Rachel said. "Covington wants to talk to me about guiding some folks up to the Eir Ruins tomorrow."

Rory's face darkened at the mention of the librarian.

"Rachel!" Covington's voice drifted out of the glass office complex. "There you are."

The librarian stepped around the checkout counter, with Ajax behind him. The coach gestured for us to follow him, and we all walked back to the conference room we'd been in earlier. When we were all inside, including Rachel and Rory, Covington shut the door.

The librarian's gaze went from me to Rory to Rachel and back again. "Well, it looks like some of you have met. But for the rest of you, this is Rachel Maddox. She works in the dining hall."

"She's a *chef*," Rory interrupted him. "The best chef at this miserable school. Not some random lunch lady."

Covington paused. Rachel winced and gave him an apologetic look. Everyone had heard the anger in Rory's voice.

"Er, yes," he finally continued. "Rachel is a chef. She's also familiar with the Eir Ruins, and she's agreed to serve as our guide tomorrow."

"How do you know so much about the ruins?" Ajax asked.

"My parents had a summer cabin close to the ruins," Rachel answered. "My sister and I used to go exploring there when we were kids. Rory and I still go up there quite a bit."

Rachel smiled at her niece, but then her eyes cut to me, and the softness in her face vanished. She'd probably seen the kids in the dining hall confronting me and Rory. That meant Rachel knew exactly who I was—another Forseti.

"Anyway, I thought I would show you some images of the ruins so you can prepare yourselves for what we might find there," Covington said.

The librarian powered up a laptop in the corner, pulled a white film screen down over one of the walls, and dimmed the lights. He hit a button on his computer, and a series of images appeared on the screen.

The Eir Ruins were perched on top of a beautiful, snow-covered mountain. They were larger than I'd thought they'd be, seeming to stretch from one side of the mountain to the other, although it was probably just the photos that made them seem so vast. The ruins were actually a series of buildings clustered together around a courtyard full of flowers. A small stream flowed through the middle of the courtyard, feeding into a broken fountain, before trickling out the far side, although the water seemed still and frozen in the photos. Perhaps they'd been taken in the winter, although I couldn't imagine how that many flowers could survive in such a cold climate.

"Legend has it that the ruins were once the winter home of Eir, the Norse goddess of healing," Covington said, clicking through some more photos. "Of course, what we are interested in is the main courtyard. Well, it's more like a garden, really. All sorts of plants and flowers bloom there all year long. There's also a stream that winds through the area."

The next photo showed a stone statue of a goddess, which I assumed was Eir. Short hair, sharp nose, curvy body. She wasn't nearly as beautiful as Nike, but there was ... a kindness in her face, one I could sense even through the photo.

"After Rachel guides us to the ruins, we'll make camp and search for the ambrosia flowers," Covington said. "Rachel believes they should be located somewhere in this area in the main courtyard."

The librarian hit a button on his computer, and another image appeared, this time a close-up shot of several colorful wildflowers that had grown up through some small cracks in the stone courtyard.

"After we locate the ambrosia flowers, we will wait until midnight to pick them, as per Professor Metis's instructions," Covington said. "Then, we will rest until dawn and hike back down the mountain. Rachel, do you want to say a few words about what everyone can expect on the trip?"

She nodded, got up from her chair, and stepped to the front of the room.

"The journey itself isn't all that dangerous," Rachel said. "It's about a two-hour hike from Snowline Ridge up to the top of the mountain where the ruins are located. Now, I'm sure you've all heard the stories. Locals claim the ruins are filled with all sorts of strange magic and curious creatures. I've never seen anything like that, but we still need to be careful. The winter weather has eroded many spots along the trail, so twisted ankles and broken legs are always a concern. We've been lucky in that it hasn't snowed much in the last few weeks, so hiking shouldn't be too difficult, but there is a storm front blowing in. We need to be off the mountain before the snow starts."

"So the ruins don't actually have any magic mumbo jumbo?" I asked. "Are you sure?"

Rachel shook her head. "Not in the way that you mean. The only magic they have is whatever is in the soil and rocks that helps the flowers grow and bloom year-round, even during the harshest winter. That magic makes the ruins beautiful, but not dangerous."

I stared at the wildflowers. I didn't know about that. Yeah, they were just flowers, but I could almost feel a force emanating from them, some sort of raw, wild energy. As I looked at the photo, the petals and leaves started moving, as though the wind was whistling over them. Slowly, all of the flowers turned in my direction, the streaks, stripes, and stars on their bright petals scrunching up into faces that were staring at me. Suddenly, a scent filled my nose—a light, floral scent that was somehow sweet, sharp, and crisp all at the same time . . .

I shook my head, and the sights, sounds, and scents vanished. My psychometry was acting up again. It was only a photo. But what would I feel when I saw the ruins and flowers in person? I didn't know, but I was going to find out.

Covington hit another button, and the photo disappeared. Ajax leaned over and hit the lights on the wall.

"We will leave at noon tomorrow," Covington said.

"That should give us ample time to get up the mountain, make camp, and find the ambrosia flowers. Don't you agree, Rachel?"

She nodded.

"I'm going too," Rory cut in.

Covington hesitated. "I'm not sure that's such a good idea. From what Ajax has told me, time is of the essence. The more people who go, the slower the group will be. Besides, why would you want to go anyway?"

She looked at the librarian like the answer should have been obvious. "Because there are going to be Reapers there—Reapers that I can kill."

Eyes wide, Covington glanced at Rachel, who sighed.

"Rory, you don't know that Reapers are going to be there," Rachel said.

"Of course they'll be there," I said. "We all know this is some sort of Reaper trap. That's why they used the poison in the first place—so we'd have to come here to get the ambrosia flowers to make the antidote. It wouldn't surprise me at all if Vivian and Agrona were already at the ruins, waiting for us to show up so they can try to kill us."

The three adults exchanged glances, but they didn't contradict me. We all knew they couldn't. The Reapers had lured us here. Now, all we could do was see what sort of trap they had set—and hope we could somehow survive it.

Chapter 20

The others started talking about the things we needed to do, what we should pack, and the route we would take up the mountain to get to the ruins. Rachel and Rory did most of the talking, with Ajax and Covington chiming in. Alexei also offered some opinions. Apparently, he'd done a lot of hiking growing up in Russia. Daphne and Carson put their heads together and started whispering, while Oliver once again pulled out his phone and started texting on it.

Restless, I got to my feet and started pacing around the conference room. Eventually, I found myself peering up at the large gryphon carving on the wall. I didn't get the same familiar, comforting vibe from it as I did the ones outside the Library of Antiquities back home, but gryphons were protectors. For some reason, staring at the carving made me feel a little better about our chances of finding the ambrosia flowers.

After a few minutes, Covington drifted over to me. "You seem very interested in that carving."

"I guess you could say that. What's with all the gryphons?"

He frowned. "What do you mean?"

I gestured at the carving and all the others in the room. "I mean, it seems like there are statues and carvings of gryphons everywhere on campus. On the walls in here, beside the library steps, on top of the rock waterfall in the middle of the dining hall, on either side of the main gate. We don't have nearly this many images of them back home."

"Oh," he said. "That's because there are actually nests of gryphons here in the mountains. Legend has it that when this academy was being constructed, the builders were quite inspired by the creatures. Even to this day, you can see them flying over the academy, although no one knows exactly where they make their homes. Maybe higher up on this mountain or on some of the neighboring peaks."

"Do you have any contact with them?"

He shook his head. "No. For the most part, they avoid us, and we do the same, although every once in a while, a student or professor out hiking will be attacked by one. Rachel should have mentioned them when she was talking about things to look out for on the mountain. Gryphons are wild animals, dangerous, vicious, and completely unpredictable."

I thought of Nyx. I wondered if Covington would think the same of her—that she was a wild, dangerous, vicious creature. Maybe she was, but she was my friend too, my family, and I loved her just as much as I did Grandma Frost and the rest of my friends. I felt the same way about Nyx's mom, Nott, even though she was dead, murdered by Vivian, just like my mom had been.

"Of course, the Reapers don't care how dangerous

the gryphons are," Covington added. "Rumor has it, Reapers come to the area several times a year to trap wild gryphons to add to the ones already in their service, although I don't see how the Reapers manage to control them."

I knew how. Nike had told me the Reapers fed creatures like gryphons, Fenrir wolves, and Nemean prowlers a special poison to keep them under control. Without the daily dose of the poison, the creatures would die, horribly and painfully, so they were forced to serve the Reapers, even if they might not want to. I wondered if the Reapers used some version of Serket sap for that too.

"But Reapers or not, everyone knows that gryphons would just as soon bite your head off as look at you," Covington finished.

He made it sound like the gryphons were the monsters, instead of the Reapers. I didn't think that was true, but I didn't say anything else. It wasn't like I'd had a lot of experience with gryphons. Maybe they were as dangerous as Covington had said. Or maybe they were simply misunderstood, like so many other mythological creatures. Either way, I doubted that I'd run into any gryphons at the ruins. If they were as smart as I thought they were, they'd take one look at us and the Reapers who were probably going to ambush us and fly the other way as fast as they could.

"All right," Ajax said, waving his hand to get everyone's attention. "I think we've got all the details sorted out. Let's go. We've still got a lot to do."

We grabbed our things and left the conference room. Still, just before I stepped through the door, I glanced over my shoulder a final time at the gryphon carving. For a moment, the gryphon's head seemed to slowly swivel through the stone, until the creature was staring straight at me. Its eyes narrowed, and its claws seemed to grow longer and sharper the more I looked at it, as if it wanted nothing more than to break free from the wall, launch itself across the conference table, and tear into me—

"Come on, Gwen!" Daphne called out.

I blinked, and the carving was just stone once more. I shivered and hurried out of the room, not daring to look at it again.

We spent the rest of the day getting ready for our trip. Rachel went back to the dining hall, and she made Rory promise to actually go to her afternoon classes. Covington took the rest of us shopping over in Snowline Ridge, and we geared up with snowsuits, hiking boots, toboggans, gloves, scarfs, backpacks, sleeping bags, climbing rope, and more. We all had our own weapons, but everyone except me bought an extra sword or a few daggers. Everyone wanted to be as ready as we could for whatever might wait for us up on the mountain.

By the time we finished shopping, it was time for dinner, and we trooped back over to the dining hall. Ajax went with us, so we didn't have any problems with the other kids. In fact, everyone seemed to go out of their way to give us as wide a berth as possible. Nobody wanted to mess with an adult who was as strong and as skilled a fighter as the Spartan coach.

After that, we grabbed our luggage from the library and headed down the hill to the dorms. I'd thought that the Powers That Were would have arranged for us to stay in some empty rooms, but Ajax kept right on walking past the buildings and veered onto a path that wound over to the far side of campus. The buildings grew fewer and farther between, although the rows of pines became thicker. Eventually, we reached a small stone cottage nestled in the middle of the trees. It was fronted by a white, wooden wraparound porch. The shutters and gingerbread trim were painted a pale green, although the roof was made out of black slate. Gray smoke puffed up out of the chimney and drifted into the winter sky, mixing with the dark clouds already gathered there.

We stepped onto the porch. The cottage door opened, and Rachel came outside, along with Rory.

I looked at Ajax. "What's going on?"

"Rachel has an extra room, and she offered to put you and Daphne up for the night." Ajax pointed to a similar structure sitting in another stand of trees farther up the hill. "That cottage is empty. The boys and I will stay there. Besides, I thought it would give you a chance to . . . talk with Rachel and Rory. About your father."

Oh. So he knew the whole sad story then. I wondered which one of my friends had spilled the beans to him. I'd told Daphne, who'd no doubt filled in Carson and the others.

"Is that okay?" Ajax asked. "Or would you rather stay with the rest of us?"

I looked at Rachel and Rory. I could feel the curiosity and tension radiating off both of them—and the longing too. "No," I said. "I'd like to stay with them, if it's okay with Daphne."

"Are you kidding?" she said. "*Of course* I want to stay with them. Um, hello, nice warm cottage, beds, sheets, hot water, and, best of all, no guys around to snore in my ear all night long."

I wanted to point out that Daphne snored louder than a race car revved up in high gear, but I didn't say anything.

We said our good-byes to the guys and watched as they trudged up the hill and disappeared into the other cottage. Then, we shouldered our stuff and moved toward Rachel and Rory's place.

Rachel gave us a bright smile and led us inside. "I'm glad you girls are staying with us. Rory and I don't have much company these days."

"Yeah," Rory sniped. "Funny how your parents turning out to be Reapers totally kills your social life."

Rachel grimaced, but she didn't contradict her niece.

The cottage was as warm and inviting on the inside as it was cute and charming on the outside. Pale green throw rugs covered the hardwood floor, and a fire crackled merrily in the fireplace in the main room. Glass knickknacks gleamed on the tops of the antique tables, while a variety of flowers, vines, and trees had been carved into the heavy wooden furniture.

Photos were also arranged on top of the tables, and I drifted over to get a better look at them. One showed Rory sitting between Rachel and another woman who looked just like them, their arms linked together. That must be her mom. Another photo showed Rory with the same woman and a man I assumed was her dad, since he had the same sandy hair and blue eyes as my dad. Rory was grinning in the pictures, but her parents' smiles seemed sad, just like my dad's had always looked to me.

Rory noticed me staring at the photos. She scowled at me, and I moved away from them.

Rachel showed us where the bathroom was, along with the spare bedroom where Daphne and I would be sleeping.

"Have you guys lived here long?" I asked, putting Vic and my messenger bag down on the bed. "Because it's a really cool place."

Rachel smiled at me. "I had just moved in and started my job as one of the junior chefs when . . ." Her smile slipped, then vanished altogether.

"When my parents went all Reaper in the library," Rory added.

Rachel tried to smile again, but after a moment, she gave up. "Covington was kind enough to convince the Protectorate to let me keep my job so Rory and I could stay on here."

"Yeah," Rory sniped again. "He's a real stand-up guy. He just did that so he could keep an eye on us in case we're Reapers too. Him and the rest of the stupid Protectorate."

Rachel sighed. "Rory, you know that Covington has been nothing but nice to us since . . . everything happened."

Her niece snorted. "Whatever. It doesn't change the fact that he killed them. I don't care how nice he's been— or the fact that you have a massive crush on him."

Rachel's cheeks started to burn. Rory kept glaring at her aunt. After a moment, the Spartan girl shook her head.

"And you can't even deny it. Whatever. I'm going to my room."

She stomped away. A few seconds later, a door slammed deeper in the cottage. Rachel winced, then once again tried to smile—and once again failed.

"Anyway," she chirped in a brittle, too-bright voice. "If there's anything you need tonight, just let me or Rory know. We're right down the hall."

"Sure," I said. "We'll let you know."

She nodded, then hurried out of the room.

For a moment, Daphne and I were silent. Then, the Valkyrie shook her head.

"Wow," Daphne said. "And I thought you were moody. I'd say Cousin Rory has one-upped you in that department, Gypsy. Hello, family drama."

I rolled my eyes, grabbed a pillow off the bed, and threw it at her.

Daphne and I spent the next hour getting ready for bed—showering, brushing our teeth, combing our hair, laying out our clothes, and packing our gear for tomorrow. Once that was done, Daphne said she was exhausted and crawled into bed. Within minutes, she was snoring. So was Vic, whom I'd propped up against the nightstand on my side of the bed. His snores rumbled in time with Daphne's, as though they were competing to see who could be the loudest and keep me awake the longest. So far, it was neck and neck.

Since I wasn't going to fall asleep anytime soon, I slid out of bed, grabbed my cell phone, opened the door, and stepped out into the hallway. I called Grandma Frost. She answered on the first ring.

"How are you, pumpkin?"

"I'm fine," I said in a low voice so I wouldn't wake Daphne. "Just a little tired. But I guess that's to be expected. It's been an interesting day."

I told my grandma everything that had happened, everything that everyone had said and done—and all the things I'd learned about my dad.

"Is it true?" I asked, my stomach churning. "Was my dad really a Reaper?"

Grandma didn't answer me for a moment. "Yes and no," she finally said.

"What does that mean?"

She drew in a breath. "It means that your father grew up in a family of Reapers. His father, his mother, his brother. They were all Reapers, and they all embraced the evil that comes along with following Loki. The Forseti family was rather famous for being Reapers—and vicious ones at that."

My hand tightened around the phone. "And my dad?"

Grandma drew in another breath. "Tyr did too—for a while. Then, he met your mother. The Reapers actually sent him to kill her."

"What happened?" I whispered.

"They fell in love," Grandma replied. "Your dad had already started to grow tired of being a Reaper, of the endless battles, the constant fighting, always hurting the people around him. And your mother felt the same way, especially after being Nike's Champion for so many years. So the two of them decided they'd create a new life for themselves—one completely separated from the mythological world. For a while, it worked."

"What happened?" I asked. "And don't tell me my dad died of cancer. I don't believe that. I haven't for a while now."

"I know, pumpkin," she replied. "And I know I promised not to keep any more secrets from you either. But your mom and I didn't want to hurt you."

"Reapers killed my dad too, didn't they?"

Silence.

Then, a sigh. Finally, she answered me. "Yes. A group of Reapers managed to track down Tyr and Grace after you were born. They attacked, and your father sacrificed himself so you and your mother could live."

So many thoughts crowded into my mind—about my dad, about the Reapers, about how he and my mom hadn't been able to escape them or the mythological world no matter how much they'd wanted to, no matter how hard they'd tried. I wondered if I was doomed to the same sort of life, if Logan and I were destined to repeat my parents' fate—or if we already had.

I couldn't stand still, so I tiptoed to the end of the hallway and peered out into the main room. Rory must have gotten over her snit because she and Rachel were sitting in front of the fireplace, playing some sort of board game.

"And what about Rory's parents?" I asked.

Grandma sighed. "I don't know much about them, only that they followed a different path from your dad. They were Reapers, and they always stayed Reapers."

"But why didn't they tell Rory anything about being Reapers? Why didn't they make her one of them? Why didn't they raise her to be a Reaper too?"

"I don't know," she said. "Maybe they wanted her to

decide to become a Reaper of her own free will. Maybe they were secretly hoping that if she didn't know about them, she might choose a different path in life. I can't answer that for you—or her."

I stared at Rory. Rachel said something, and a smile spread across Rory's face, softening the scowl she always seemed to wear. For a moment, she almost looked relaxed . . . and happy. I wondered if it was because none of the other kids were around to sneer at her—or judge her for the horrible things her parents had done.

"Thank you for telling me this."

"You're welcome," Grandma said. "Although I should have told you a long time ago, pumpkin. But with your mom being murdered and you going to Mythos and everything that's happened these last few months . . . it never seemed like there was a good time to bring it up. You'd gone through so much already. I didn't want to cause you any more pain."

"I know you were trying to protect me," I said. "But we both know you can't do that anymore. At least now I know the truth about my dad, even if I don't like it."

"That you do."

We were silent for a few moments before she finally spoke again.

"Be careful tomorrow," Grandma Frost said. "I know your friends are going to be with you, but I don't like the thought of you going up to those ruins. Especially since the Reapers know you're coming."

"I'll be careful. Ajax is taking a lot of precautions. We'll be ready for whatever the Reapers have in mind."

"I know, but that won't keep me from worrying."

"How's Nickamedes?" I asked, realizing she hadn't said anything about him while we'd been talking.

She hesitated. "He's getting worse. He has a fever. Not too high right now, but Metis says it's just a matter of time before his temperature shoots up and the poison starts overpowering her healing magic. He also . . . he can't feel his legs sometimes. The numbness comes and goes. It's another sign of the poison spreading. Metis thinks . . . the paralysis could be permanent, even if the ambrosia flowers flush the poison out of his body."

I rubbed a hand across my head, which was suddenly aching. Here I was, worried about my family drama, as Daphne had said, when Nickamedes was suffering—because of me. But I pushed my worry for him aside and embraced the other emotion blazing through me—determination to find the flowers and get them back to the academy in time.

"I love you, pumpkin," Grandma Frost said. "Be good, and be careful."

"I will. I love you too, Grandma."

We hung up. I went back into the bedroom, shut the door behind me, walked over, put my phone on the nightstand, and crawled into bed next to Daphne. I knew that I should rest, that tomorrow would be even longer and tougher than today, but it was still a long, long time before I was able to tune out the snores and fall asleep.

Chapter 21

For once, I didn't dream of Logan stabbing me. Instead, there was just a deep, quiet blackness that I let myself drift along in until it was time to get up. Maybe my subconscious realized that I'd be in enough danger tomorrow without dreaming about more of it tonight.

We gathered in the dining hall for a late breakfast before shouldering our gear and heading out. Covington was waiting for us at the main entrance. Once again, I stared up at the gryphons perched on either side of the gate. The creatures stared at me like always, but today, their gazes seemed dark and hooded, as if they had some inkling of the Reapers' plans and how dangerous it was going to be for us on the mountain. I sighed and looked away from them. Yeah, I had a feeling it was going to be a *Gwen-fighting-for-her-life* kind of trip.

A large black van was waiting outside the gate, and we climbed inside. Covington steered the van through Snowline Ridge, passing by all of the shops before the road narrowed and started curving upward. Eventually, he pulled the van off the road into a paved lot that fronted a park. A sign by the entrance read SNOWLINE

Ridge Recreation Area. It featured a carving of green pine trees and the rocky gray mountain looming above them. Covington stopped the van. Ajax turned around so he could look into the back where the rest of us were sitting.

"We all know what we're up against," Ajax rumbled. "And we all know what's at stake. Nickamedes is hanging on—for now. But the sooner we get the antidote to him, the better."

I'd called Grandma Frost this morning. She'd tried to pretend that everything was okay, but I'd heard the strain in her voice, and she'd finally told me that Nickamedes had gotten much worse overnight. Metis was now using all of her energy to heal him, but the poison had already started to overtake her magic. Grandma had reluctantly told me that we only had about three more days, maybe less, before Metis's magic failed completely, and the poison raged unchecked through Nickamedes's body.

"But if any of you don't want to do this, I'll understand," Ajax continued. "At the very least, it's going to be dangerous. At the very worst, well, I don't think I have to tell you how bad that could be."

"Worse than the Reapers murdering my mom and killing Nott? Worse than them using my blood to free Loki? Worse than them trying to put Loki's soul into Logan's body?" I asked, staring back at Ajax. "We've been through plenty of bad stuff already. This will just be another twisted version of it. Right, guys?"

I looked at my friends. They all nodded their heads in agreement.

Daphne cracked her knuckles, causing pink sparks of

magic to hiss in the air around her. "Gwen's right. The Reapers will bring it—and so will we."

Ajax stared at us all in turn. Whatever he saw in our eyes seemed to satisfy him because he finally nodded. "All right," he said. "Let's do this."

We got out of the van. It seemed even colder now than it had yesterday, or maybe that was because I knew there wouldn't be a hot shower and a warm bed waiting for me at the end of this day. Instead, we'd find someplace to camp in the ruins, which meant a fire, some tents, and a sleeping bag spread over the snowy, rocky ground—and that was if the Reapers didn't attack us first.

Rachel led us through the parking lot and over to a trailhead, which was marked with a small sign. The wind had worn most of the paint off the wood, but I could still make out the figure of the goddess Eir on the marker, her finger pointing up, as though she was personally directing us to the ruins. I shivered, shouldered my backpack, and fell in step with the others.

Rachel took the lead, followed by Rory, then Covington. Daphne and Carson followed the librarian, with Oliver and Alexei behind them. I was in the back with Ajax trailing along behind me. We walked in silence.

I wasn't really an outdoors sort of girl, preferring to curl up in my room and read comic books and graphic novels, but even I had to admit this was a pretty place to hike. There was more snow on the mountain than down at the academy, several inches in some of the higher drifts. Snow-crusted pine trees lined either side of the trail, while needles that were longer than my fingers and pinecones bigger than my fist stuck up out of the white powder here and there. The sharp tang of the trees' sap permeated the air, mixing with the crisp scent of the snow. A few birds fluttered back and forth in the branches, softly chirping to each other.

Every once in a while, a dark shadow would zoom over the trail and across the forest, causing the other birds to scream and take flight from their warm roosts. The third time it happened, I looked up, trying to figure out what was causing the birds to freak out.

Ajax touched my shoulder. "Gryphons," he explained. "Don't worry. They rarely attack humans, especially a group as large as ours."

Well, that didn't exactly make me feel better, but I nodded and walked on. There was nothing else I could do.

But the farther up the mountain we trudged, the more I became convinced that someone was following us.

I don't know exactly when I noticed it, but I sensed a shadow on my left, moving parallel to me through the forest. This vague shape I could almost see out of the corner of my eye. If I sped up, the shadow sped up. If I slowed down, it did too. Several times I looked straight ahead before snapping my head to the left, trying to get a better look at whatever it was. But I only saw trees and more trees. If Ajax thought my behavior was strange, he didn't comment on it. Then again, it wasn't the weirdest thing I'd ever done.

Finally, I got fed up with trying to spot the mysterious shadow and concentrated on putting one foot in front of the other. If there was a Reaper or someone or something else out there, it seemed content to follow alongside us and not attack. I guessed I'd have to be happy with that—for now.

We'd been hiking for about an hour when Rachel called a halt near a stream. The water running between the two banks was sluggish, since a thin layer of ice covered most of it. But it was a nice spot, and we sat down on the flat rocks along the bank and dug some snacks out of our backpacks.

"Everybody take a breather for a few minutes," Rachel said. "We still have at least another hour to go before we make it to the ruins at the top."

We'd grabbed some trail mix from the dining hall this morning, and I tore into my packet. Dried mango and apricots mixed with tart cherries, big chunks of dark chocolate, slivered almonds, and honey-toasted oats. The flavors exploded on my tongue, a perfect mix of sweet and salty, with a great crunch and a hint of sour from the cherries. Yum. So good.

After we finished our snack and chugged down some water, Daphne, Rory, and I headed into the woods to answer the call of nature, so to speak. All the while, though, I kept scanning the trees for that mysterious shadow I'd spotted earlier. But I didn't see or hear anything, and I didn't get the sense that I was still being watched. Maybe it had just been some animal following us. That's what I told myself anyway, even if I didn't really believe it.

The three of us started to head back to the others when a soft whine sounded.

I froze, wondering if I was only imagining things, but the whine came again. That sounded like . . . Nyx.

I frowned. But there was no way the wolf pup could

be here. She was back at the academy, safe and sound with Grandma Frost. But the small, plaintive wail came again, indicating that some sort of critter was in trouble. So instead of following the others back toward the trail, I veered off into the trees.

"Gwen?" Daphne asked, finally noticing I wasn't following along behind her and Rory. "Where are you going?"

"Don't you hear that? It's coming from this direction."

She sighed and put her hands on her hips. "And of course you're going to go see what it is, despite the fact that the woods are probably crawling with Reapers. Sometimes, Gwen, I think you're going to be the death of me."

I paused long enough to stick my tongue out at her, then headed deeper into the woods. After a moment, Daphne and Rory followed me. I stopped every few feet, looking and listening. I also drew Vic out of the scabbard belted to my waist.

The sword yawned and slowly opened his eye. "What's going on? Are we at the ruins already? Are there Reapers for me to kill?"

"I'm not sure," I whispered. "Stand by."

I kept going into the woods, with Daphne and Rory behind me. The Valkyrie had nocked an arrow in her bow, but the Spartan girl wasn't carrying any weapons. Then again, she didn't need them. Rory could pick up a twig and stab someone to death with it or slice open a Reaper's throat with the edge of a frozen leaf.

"You know there are bears out here, right?" Rory said. "Great big grizzlies. Believe me when I tell you that you do not want to come face-to-face with one of them."

"They can't be any worse than Reapers, can they?" I quipped.

Rory muttered something under her breath about me being flat-out crazy. I grinned and walked on.

The cries grew louder and more plaintive the farther we went, almost as if whatever was out there could hear us approaching and knew that it couldn't escape before we found it. Finally, we crouched down behind a tree several feet away from whatever was making the noise. Even though it sounded like a wounded animal, I wasn't going to rush toward it. Daphne was right when she said the forest was probably full of Reapers, and this could easily be one of their traps.

"What do you want to do now?" Daphne asked. "Because whatever that is, it doesn't sound happy."

"I'll go see what it is," I whispered. "If it is a Reaper trap, maybe we can at least take some of them out before we get to the ruins. Cover me."

She nodded, and so did Rory.

I got to my feet, tightened my grip on Vic, and rounded the tree. I tensed, expecting an arrow to come zooming out of the woods. But when nothing happened, I slowly started moving forward. I'd only gone about ten feet when I stepped into a small clearing and finally spotted the source of the cries—a baby gryphon.

At least, I thought it was a baby. It was still about three feet long from its beak to the fuzzy tuft on the end of its lion's tail. The gryphon's fur and wings were a beautiful bronze that glimmered in what little sunlight slid through the trees to the forest floor. Its eyes were the same mesmerizing shade, although its beak and claws were as black and shiny as ebony.

The gryphon caught sight of me and stopped its struggles, although it narrowed its eyes and sank down onto its haunches, like it was getting ready to leap on me and tear me to pieces.

At first, I wondered what was wrong with the creature, but then I realized why it was crying—its back right foot was caught in a metal trap. Actually, *trap* wasn't the right word. This thing had so many rows of teeth that it looked more like a torture device. The gryphon must have stepped on the trigger, causing the trap to snap shut, and the rows of sharp metal teeth had dug into the poor thing's leg. A thick metal chain secured the trap to a tree, keeping the gryphon from flying away. The creature must have been there a while because the blood in its fur had already matted.

"It's okay," I called out to my friends. "It's not a Reaper."

Leaves crunched, and Daphne and Rory moved to stand beside me.

"That's a snap-snare," Rory said, disgust evident in her voice. "It's like a bear trap, but with more teeth. Reapers leave them in the forest in hopes of capturing gryphons. Fenrir wolves too. The more you struggle, the deeper the teeth tear into your body."

The baby gryphon's tail started lashing from side to side at the sound of Rory's voice, and it studied each one of us in turn. Its bronze eyes narrowed that much more, and it grew very still, except for its tail, which kept whipping from side to side. Suddenly, the creature leaped through the air, its claws aiming for my throat—

But the chain attached to the trap jerked it back, and the gryphon thumped to the ground about five feet in front of me. The creature screeched with surprise and pain, but I could also hear the faintest whimper in its high cries. Despite its tough façade, the gryphon was scared, tired, and hurting. I knew the feelings. Reapers and their cruel schemes had a way of doing that to you.

"Easy, boy," I said, taking off my gloves, holding out my right hand, and creeping toward the creature. "We're not here to hurt you. We're going to get that nasty thing off your leg."

"What are you doing?" Rory hissed. "That gryphon will bite your hand off if you get too close to it. In case you didn't notice, it would have torn your throat out if that chain hadn't stopped it. Are you out of your mind?"

"Have you met Gwen?" Daphne sniped. "Because crazy is kind of her thing. Believe me, this is mild compared to some of the stunts she's pulled."

I shot her a dirty look, then turned back to the gryphon. "It's just scared and confused," I said. "That's why it tried to attack me. I'm not going to leave it here for the Reapers to find. You know what they did to Nott. You know what they'll do to this little guy too."

"Fine, fine. Be all brave and heroic," Daphne muttered. "But don't blame me if it backfires."

I handed Vic to the Valkyrie. Then, I dropped down on my hands and knees, putting myself on the gryphon's level, and slowly crawled toward it. The creature sat on its back haunches and watched me approach, even more wary than before. Its claws started digging into the snow-covered ground as if it was thinking about springing at me again. I could see the suspicion in the gryphon's eyes, but I wasn't leaving it there—even if it did lash out at me again.

Closer and closer, I crept. By this point, the gryphon could have surged forward and swiped at me with its claws—quite easily. But instead, the creature watched me. Maybe it sensed I wasn't an enemy. Maybe it realized I wanted to help. Or maybe it just wanted me to get as close as possible so it could do the most amount of damage to me. I was about to find out. I was three feet away from it, two, one . . .

I drew in a breath, surged forward, and put my hand on the gryphon's front paw.

Chapter 22

The first thing that filled my mind was the baby gryphon's pain.

Every slight movement, every small shift, every shallow breath it took seemed to twist the trap's teeth a little deeper into the creature's back leg, like rows of needles slowly digging into its skin. I grimaced and pushed the feeling aside, sinking deeper into the gryphon's mind, trying to figure out some way to get the creature to trust me long enough for me, Daphne, and Rory to pry the trap off its—his—leg.

The gryphon tried to pull away from me, but I held on, being as gentle as I could with him. I was dimly aware of his face next to mine, his beak snapping close to my nose in a warning to *let go or else*, but still, I held on. If I took my hand from the gryphon's paw, I doubted he would let me touch him again, and then, we'd never be able to help him.

So I tightened my grip and reached for my psychometry again. Image after image flooded my mind, like I was watching a high-speed movie of the gryphon's life. Most of the memories involved the gryphon soaring through the clear blue sky, and a sense of wonder and wildness surged through me—along with one of peace. There was nothing he liked better than spreading his wings wide and drifting up and down on the currents that whipped around the mountaintops. But there were other sights and sounds, as well, mostly of adult gryphons doing the same thing, as if they were flying together in some sort of fancy formation. And finally, there was another gryphon, one who looked larger, stronger, and fiercer than all the others. The leader of the group—and the father of the baby before me. More than anything else, the baby gryphon wanted to grow up to be as big, strong, and tough as his dad. The thoughts, the feelings, the images, made me smile.

Slowly, very slowly, I pushed my thoughts at the gryphon, trying to let him know that I was a friend and not a Reaper who wanted to trap him and take him away from his family forever. I showed the creature images of me fighting Reapers in the Library of Antiquities, the Crius Coliseum, and all the other places I'd battled them. But the images seemed to confuse the gryphon, so instead, I concentrated on my memories of Nott and showed those to him.

But that didn't work either. The gryphon started screeching in my ear and batting his wings against my body, trying to drive me away, as if he thought the Fenrir wolf was going to jump out of my mind and somehow attack him. So I tried showing him images of me playing with Nyx instead, but nothing eased the gryphon's suspicions, and I could tell he was thinking about trying to claw me again.

Finally, in desperation, I called up all the memories I

had of the gryphons on the steps outside the Library of Antiquities back home. The baby gryphon immediately stilled, and I let him feel how beautiful I thought the statues were, how noble, how regal, how brave and strong and fierce. Most of all, I tried to show him how I'd come to view the gryphons as my silent friends and that I wanted to be the same sort of friend to him.

It was so freaking *hard*, especially since the gryphon kept beating his wings against my body and trying to worm himself away from me. Sweat slid down my face, and my hand ached from gripping his paw, but I held my position and poured all of my energy, all of my concentration, all of my magic, into trying to reach the gryphon and put his mind at ease. Finally, I felt the creature settle down and sensed his realization that I wasn't going to hurt him, that I wanted to get the trap off his leg. That would have to be enough for now. I didn't have the strength for anything else.

I opened my eyes, let go of the gryphon's paw, and wiped the cold sweat off my forehead. Then, I looked over my shoulder at Daphne. "Okay. You can pull the trap off his leg now. He's not going to bite us."

Rory looked at me, then at the gryphon, her green eyes wide with surprise. "How did you do that? One second, I thought he was going to tear your nose off or try to beat you to death with his wings. But now, he looks like a puppy you could pet."

It was true. The gryphon had flopped down on his side, exposing his pudgy baby tummy to me. I reached out and carefully ran my fingers over his silky bronze fur, before reaching up and scratching his head. Nyx always seemed to like that, and the gryphon did too, judging from the happy little squeaks he let out.

"What can I say?" I grinned. "I have a magic touch when it comes to animals."

Daphne snorted. "You're touched in the head is more like it."

Still, she handed Vic back to me and dropped down to her knees beside me. With her Valkyrie strength, it was easy for her to reach down and carefully pry open the trap clamped around the gryphon's back leg. Rory lifted the creature's leg free from the metal. Daphne eased the trap shut, then kicked it away.

"Horrible thing," she muttered.

I stayed on the ground next to the gryphon, still petting him. "It's okay, buddy. Everything's going to be just fine now."

I didn't know if the gryphon understood my words or not, but he surged to his feet—and promptly fell back down again. He let out a pitiful screech that told me how much pain he was in.

I turned to Daphne. "Do you think you could work your healing magic on him? He's really hurting, and I don't think he'll let us carry him back to the stream where the others are."

She looked at the gryphon. Doubt filled her black eyes. "I guess I could try. I'm still learning about my magic. But I know what you mean. We can't just leave the little guy out here like that. It's worth a shot."

Daphne put her bow on the ground and slowly crawled toward the gryphon. The creature eyed her with the same suspicion it had me, so once again, I put my hand on his paw and showed him my memories of Daphne and how she was my friend.

"She's going to make your leg all better," I told the gryphon. "It'll be okay. You'll see."

Daphne reached for her magic, and the pink sparks streaking out of her fingertips combined to form a beautiful, rosy golden glow. She leaned forward and gently pressed her hand to the gryphon's side, just above where the trap's teeth had dug into the creature's flesh. The rosy golden glow slowly spread down the creature's body and pooled in the ugly, jagged gashes that ringed his leg. As I watched, the edges of the wounds slowly pulled together and then seamlessly healed. All the while, I felt the soothing power of Daphne's magic, wave after wave of it pulsing off her and sinking into the gryphon. Just being near her when she was using her power made me feel a little stronger and my heart a little lighter, and I knew that if I put my hand on top of hers, I would see the bright princess-pink spark that burned at the very center of her being.

"There," Daphne said a few minutes later. "It's done."

She dropped her hand from the gryphon, leaned back, and let out a long, tired breath. When I looked at the gryphon, the creature's leg was completely healed. Except for the blood still matted in his fur, you would have never known that the gryphon was injured to start with.

The baby gryphon seemed to sense the change too. The creature scrambled to his feet and shuffled back and forth, as if he was testing out his once-injured leg to see how good a job Daphne had done of healing him.

"Hey," I said, stretching my hand out to him once more. "You might want to take it easy—"

But it was too late.

With a loud screech, the gryphon flapped his wings and darted up into the air. Daphne and I scrambled to our feet. The creature hovered in midair for a moment before letting out another screech, zooming up, bursting through the tops of the pine trees, and disappearing into the cloudy gray sky far, far above.

All I could do was crane my neck up and look at where the gryphon had been. I'd wanted to spend more time with the creature, but he was a wild thing, just as Covington had said. I should be grateful the gryphon had let me, Daphne, and Rory help him. At least now he was free of the trap and his leg was healed. I would have to be satisfied with that. Plus, it had been rather amazing to watch him blast up into the sky like a rocket.

"Well, that was weird," Rory said. "Do you guys do stuff like that all the time?"

Daphne and I looked at each other, then at her.

"More often than you might think," Daphne said.

Rory wandered over, squatted down, and looked at the snare-snap I'd kicked to the side. Daphne and I stared at the device too. As Rory had said, it looked like a bear trap—but with more teeth. The gryphon's blood glistened on some of the sharp, pointed edges, making me sick to my stomach.

Daphne nudged me with her shoulder. "You going to do your thing on that? It might give us a clue about the Reapers."

I didn't want to use my psychometry on the trap, but

she was right. So I crouched down, reached out, and touched part of the metal that was free of blood. Images of the gryphon struggling to get free of the trap flickered through my mind, but I pushed them aside, trying to see who had planted the trap in the first place. For several moments, the only memories I saw were of the trap lying on the forest floor, hidden under a pile of leaves and then the snow that had fallen on top of them. I concentrated, going even further back.

A pair of hands popped into my head. I focused in on the memory, trying to pull it into even sharper detail, but all I saw was someone placing the trap in the woods, then piling the leaves on top of it. Frustration surged through me because I didn't even see the person—only their hands. Even worse, they were wearing black gloves, so I couldn't get any sort of sense about whom the hands belonged to, whether it was a man, a woman, a kid my own age.

I opened my eyes, let go of the trap, and got to my feet.

"Anything?" Daphne asked.

I shook my head and put my gloves back on. "Nothing. Just some Reaper putting the trap here."

Rory stared at the trap, then kicked it and sent it flying into a nearby tree. She glared at the metal like she wished she could somehow kill it. Daphne and I glanced at each other, but we kept quiet. We knew all about being angry at the Reapers and not being able to do anything about it.

Daphne reached down and grabbed her bow. "Well, if we're all done playing veterinarian, we should leave. We need to get back to the others."

Chapter 23

Rory, Daphne, and I walked back to the stream. Apparently, everyone had been busy doing their own thing, and no one seemed to notice how long we'd been gone. Oliver didn't even look up from his phone when we walked past him. He was texting *again*. I was surprised that he'd found a signal this high up on the mountain, but, hey, good for him.

Five minutes later, everyone was ready to go, and we started back up the steep, winding trail. I looked left and right and even peered up into the clouds above, but I didn't see the baby gryphon anywhere. I also didn't spot the mysterious shadow that had been in the forest earlier, following alongside us. Maybe it had just been a curious animal after all, wondering what the humans were doing hiking through its turf.

Except for a few brief snatches of conversation, everyone was quiet. My friends kept scanning the forest on either side of the trail, and Ajax kept sneaking glances over his shoulder, as though he expected someone or something to come up on us from behind. We all had our weapons close at hand too—in case the Reapers decided to attack before we reached the ruins.

But the minutes slipped by and turned into an hour, with no sign of the Reapers. I was about to whine and ask how much farther it was when we crested a high ridge. The others slowed and then stopped, and we spread out in a straight line across the trail so we could all see the sight before us.

A swinging rope bridge stretched, swayed, and slightly sagged between either side of a deep, wide chasm. In the distance, the crumbling remains of what looked like a grand stone mansion covered the landscape.

"We're here," Rachel said. "Welcome to the Eir Ruins."

Covington's pictures hadn't done the place justice. Beautiful, blackish stone stretched out as far as the eye could see, the boulders piled in precise heaps, as though the building walls had been dominoes that had fallen on top of each other in a particular pattern. Thick, green ivy vines snaked over, around, and sometimes even through the rocks and the snow that covered them. Farther out in the ruins, I could see small, bright splashes of color, probably the wildflowers and other plants that bloomed in the main courtyard, despite the harsh winter weather.

"Well," Alexei said. "I suppose we should get going."

"Yeah," Carson said in a faint voice, peering over the edge of the trail and staring down into the chasm. "Let's, um, do that."

Rachel gestured at the ropes. "The bridge is fairly sturdy, but I'm not sure it's strong enough for all of us to cross at once. So, just to be on the safe side, we'll go over in groups of two. Rory and I will go first, since we're most familiar with the area. Wait until we're on the other side before sending the next group over."

Ajax and Covington nodded.

Rachel went over to the bridge, grabbed the ropes on either side, and stepped onto the weathered wooden planks. The bridge was free of snow, given all the wind that constantly swirled around it. Rory followed her, and the two of them quickly crossed over to the other side with no hesitation and no problems. Carson's face had a decidedly greenish tint to it, and I could hear his stomach gurgling, but the band geek hurried forward, and he and Daphne crossed second. They were followed by Oliver and Covington.

Then, it was my turn. Alexei stepped up beside me and flashed me a confident smile. He went first. I waited until he'd gone a few steps before walking out onto the bridge behind him.

Just like Rachel had said, the swinging bridge seemed sturdy enough. The wooden boards might have been bleached a pale gray by the sun and wind, but they didn't have any cracks or chips in them, and the ropes were thick and heavy. So I put one foot in front of the other, slid my gloved hands along the rope, and tried not to look down.

I'd made it to the middle of the bridge when a gust of wind whipped up from the chasm below. The sudden rush of air made the bridge sway from side to side. My stomach lurched up into my throat, and my hands tightened around the ropes. All I could do was stand there and hold on.

Alexei glanced over his shoulder at me. "Come on, Gwen," he said. "It's just a little wind. This is nothing compared to the winters in Russia."

"Yeah," I repeated in a faint voice. "Nothing."

Another gust of wind screeched up from the canyon. The high, piercing sound made me think of the baby gryphon, and I remembered that this was exactly how he had felt while he was soaring up and down on the wind currents—and how much he loved the sensation. Sure, he had wings, and I didn't, but thinking about the creature gave me the courage to keep walking forward, one step at a time, until I was on the other side. I hurried forward away from the end of the bridge. Thinking about the gryphon might have made crossing the bridge a little easier, but it wasn't anything I wanted to do again anytime soon.

"Please tell me there's another way down the mountain," I said to Rachel as we watched Ajax navigate the bridge by himself.

She smiled. "Not a fan of the swinging bridge?"

I shrugged.

"There is a trail on the far side of the ruins," she said. "I haven't been down it in years, though. It's much steeper, and it would take twice as long for us to get down the mountain that way. And that's only if there haven't been any rock slides on that part of the mountain to block the path."

In other words, I was going to have to go back over

the bridge when we left whether I wanted to or not. Yippee-skippee.

Once Ajax had crossed, we left the bridge behind and entered the ruins. I'd been right when I'd thought the stone was beautiful. Up close, I could see the flowers and vines that had been chiseled into the smooth surface of the fallen boulders. Even in places where the walls had crumbled and the rocks had scattered over the snowy ground, everything still seemed neat, precise, and clean, as though someone had meant for the ruins to look exactly the way they did. I wondered if it was the goddess Eir or some other magic at work.

And once again, I was surprised by the number of gryphons.

They were everywhere, just like they'd been at the academy. Carved into splintered pieces of rock, painted on parts of walls, looming up out of piles of rubble in statue form. I even saw something that looked like a giant stone column with a gryphon perched on the top of it, as though it was keeping watch over the ruins. The gryphon's eyes met mine and then seemed to follow me. Creepy, as always.

Rachel led us through the ruins, pointing out interesting things, like songbirds that had been chiseled into one of the boulders or the bears that lumbered across another. She even showed us some patches of dill, sage, and other herbs that she picked and took back to the academy to use in the kitchen.

Finally, though, we reached the courtyard in the very heart of the ruins. Once again, Covington's photos didn't do the area justice. The toppled walls and crumbled bits of stone formed a sort of rocky garden at the edges of the courtyard. Then, the flowers took over. Hundreds of thousands of flowers, vines, and small trees crowded into the enormous space. After the endless rows of green pines along the trail, it was like a rainbow of color had exploded at my feet. Pinks and blues and purples and reds stretched out for a hundred yards. The only things that broke up the relentless riot of color were the stream that wound through the courtyard and the stone fountain in the middle. But even they seemed to somehow reflect back the cheery brightness of the blossoms around them. Perhaps the most amazing thing was the scent—a sweet, sharp, crisp aroma that made me think of flowers and water and snow and wind all at the same time.

"If there are any Chloris ambrosia flowers, they should be here," Rachel said. "This is where the goddess Eir had her garden, and as you can see, all sorts of flowers still flourish here today. They're the real magic of the ruins."

I snorted. Well, that was an understatement. A sea of blooms filled the courtyard. I'd never seen so many different types of flowers in so many different colors, shapes, and sizes before. It was a breathtaking sight, but it made my heart sink all the same. Because how were we supposed to find one flower in a field of thousands? I doubted even Hercules could have completed such an impossible task.

The others must have had the same depressing thought because everyone was silent as we stared out at the blossoms. For a moment, the only sound was the sharp whistle of the wind as it gusted through the courtyard, causing the flowers to flutter and a few petals to swirl up into the air like colorful snowflakes before slowly spiraling back down again.

"Come on," Ajax rumbled. "Let's get started. We need to find the ambrosia flowers before nightfall."

Alexei and Oliver helped Rachel set up our tents in a clear patch of ground on one side of the courtyard, then the three of them went in search of some firewood. Ajax and Covington stood guard at the edge of the courtyard, while Daphne, Carson, Rory, and I started looking for the ambrosia flowers.

I moved from one vine and one patch of flowers to another, comparing the plants in front of me to the image on my cell phone. Chloris ambrosia looked sort of like honeysuckle, as Carson had said. A pretty, curling, green vine topped by a white, trumpet-shaped flower. The only difference was the streaks of lavender purple and light gray on the inside of the white petals. So it wasn't enough to pick out the patches of white flowers in the courtyard, wade over, and look at them. You actually had to take the time to lift up the flower, peer inside, and see if it had the streaks of color. And of course every time I went over to a flower and picked it up, it was just white inside and not purple and gray.

Farther into the garden, Carson let out a series of violent sneezes that told everyone how much his allergies were acting up. Rory gave him a slightly pitying look, but they both went back to the search.

"I've never seen so many flowers before in my life," Daphne muttered, picking her way through some vines a few feet away from me. "We're never going to find the ambrosia. All I see are white flowers. Not to mention all the ones that are cream, ivory, eggshell, and every other white and off-white color."

"We have to keep looking—for Nickamedes."

Daphne's eyes darkened. "I know. I'm just worried we won't be able to find it."

"We'll find it," I said, trying to make my voice more confident than I really felt. "We have to."

We kept looking. Alexei, Oliver, and Rachel reappeared, all of them carrying an armload of firewood. A few minutes later, Rachel started a fire in a stone pit close to the tents. I took a break from the search to go warm up. I turned this way and that, letting the heat from the crackling flames soak into the front and back of my body, before diving into the flowers once more.

Another hour passed. By this point, camp had been made, and we were all searching for the ambrosia flowers. But no one was having any luck.

"Anything?" Ajax called out, his voice tight with frustration.

We all shook our heads. He sighed and crouched back down, peering over the flowers in front of him and comparing them to the image on his phone, like the rest of us were doing.

I finished sweeping a section and stood up to stretch out my back. I was close to the right edge of the courtyard, and my heart sank once again as I looked out at all of the plants and vines. We hadn't even covered half of the courtyard yet. We could search for a week and still not come across a single ambrosia flower—and Nickamedes didn't have that kind of time left.

I sighed and leaned against a half-crumbled wall. At least, I tried to. I winced as something sharp dug into my back, poking me even through my purple snowsuit and all the layers I had on underneath. I turned around and realized it wasn't a wall I'd been leaning against—it was a statue of the goddess Eir.

I straightened up and stepped back. "Whoops. Sorry about that. I didn't mean to block your view or anything. I can imagine how much you like to look out over your flowers."

Of course, the statue didn't respond. Instead, it seemed to stare at me.

Somehow, the goddess's head had turned in my direction until her empty stone eyes were firmly fixed on me. I sighed. Every statue stared at me. That was just a part of my life at Mythos. I'd thought that I'd quit being creeped out by it, but apparently not. Or maybe my unease was because a goddess was looking at me—a goddess whose ruins I was standing in right now. It wouldn't surprise me if her eyes suddenly popped open, and a series of poisoned darts shot out and slammed into my chest. That was what always happened in the movies.

I held my breath for a moment, but Eir kept staring at me. Apparently, I wasn't going to get pumped full of poison darts after all. Good. That was good.

The goddess looked at me a moment longer—and then her head began to move.

Seriously, the stone—it just—the statue just *turned*. One second, Eir was peering straight at me. The next, a series of small *scrape-scrape-scrapes* sounded. By the time I blinked again, the goddess was looking in the opposite direction. Not only that, but I swore that I saw her raise her hand, her finger pointing toward the back corner of the garden—almost like she wanted me to go see what was over there.

I eased away from the statue. The goddess kept pointing toward that one spot, although her head swiveled back around in my direction. After a moment, her eyes narrowed, as if she was upset that I hadn't already followed her instructions. Once again thinking of poisoned darts and other nasty traps, I decided to do what she wanted. Probably not a good idea to anger a goddess when you were in her house. Or at least standing in what was left of it.

"Okay, okay, I'm going, I'm going," I said. "Give me a second."

I maneuvered around to the other side of the statue. Then, I leaned down so I could get a better look at the spot where she was pointing. Once I had a bead on it, I headed in that direction.

Everyone else was still busy searching for the flowers, so no one noticed me walking along the crumbled right wall of the courtyard. Every so often, I glanced behind me, but the statue of Eir kept pointing in the same direction. Finally, I reached what seemed to be the right spot. I crouched down, my eyes sweeping over the patch of flowers in front of me. Thick stands of vivid purple lilac mixed with some sort of curling vines that were topped by large, grayish morning glorys. No white flowers and nothing that looked like it could remotely be Chloris ambrosia. Frustration filled me, and I looked over my shoulder at Eir.

"Don't tell me you sent me over here on a wild goose chase," I muttered.

The statue's eyes seemed to narrow a little more, as if

she was displeased with me and my snarky tone. Well, she wouldn't be the first person—or the last.

"Okay, okay," I muttered again. "Who am I to question a goddess?"

So once again I looked at the statue, trying to see exactly what she was pointing at, and I realized her finger wasn't aimed down at the ground but rather at the rock wall in front of me.

I turned my head, raised my gaze—and almost shrieked when I realized I was face-to-face with another gryphon carving.

Seriously, I looked up—and it was *this freaking close* to my nose. I rocked back on my heels and almost toppled over before I managed to find my balance. I drew in a couple of breaths to calm my racing heart. *Get a grip, Gwen.* It was only a carving, one of dozens I'd seen so far in the courtyard. It wasn't like it was a *real* gryphon.

But the more I looked at it, the more I realized it wasn't just a carving of a gryphon—it was one of Eir too. The gryphon stood in front of the goddess with its head bowed. A few small, fragile-looking flowers had actually grown out of the part of the rock that formed the gryphon's beak, making it look like the creature was presenting Eir with the flowers. Okay, that was a little strange, but my unease didn't keep me from peering even closer at the blossoms.

I used my phone to pull up the photo of the ambrosia flowers. Green vine, white flowers. So far, so good. Now came the real test. I held my hand up and gently turned one of the flowers so that I could see inside it.

Purple and gray streaks ringed the petals.

My heart started to pound with excitement, but I made myself study the flowers that much closer. They were tiny, each one barely bigger than my thumbnail, and I compared them once again to the photo on my phone. Green vine, white flowers, purple and gray streaks.

This time, I knew I hadn't made a mistake—and that we had a chance to save Nickamedes after all.

"Hey!" I called out, a grin spreading across my face. "I found them! I found the ambrosia flowers!"

The others hurried over, and we all peered at the blossoms growing out of the rock wall.

"That's them, isn't it?" I asked.

Ajax held his own phone up against the flowers. "It looks like them to me. Rachel?"

She nodded her head in agreement.

"How did you ever think to look in this remote spot?" Covington asked, staring at me instead of the flowers. "We all assumed the Chloris ambrosia would be in the courtyard itself, not out here on the edge."

I shrugged. "I'm just lucky, I guess."

The librarian looked at me suspiciously, but he didn't say anything else. The others started slapping me on the back and congratulating me, but I could still feel Covington's gaze on me. I wondered what Ajax had told him about me—and what he knew from the gossip he'd heard. But there was nothing I could do about Covington and what he thought about me, so I looked at Ajax once more.

"Now what?" I asked.

"Now we wait until midnight," Ajax rumbled.

Chapter 24

Now that we'd found the ambrosia flowers, there wasn't anything left for us to do but wait, like Coach Ajax had said. I pulled out my cell phone and tried to call Grandma Frost, but I didn't have any reception this high up on the mountain. So I hunkered down with the others.

We heated up our dinner—a thick, hearty roasted potato soup that Rachel had made this morning, along with grilled chicken sandwiches topped with fresh vegetables and a spicy, horseradish mayonnaise on herbed focaccia bread. We washed the meal down with some warm apple cider and hot chocolate. Then, I grabbed marshmallows, graham crackers, and thick bars of dark chocolate out of my backpack, and we had s'mores for dessert.

"Only you would think to pack a bag full of sugar on a trip like this." Daphne snorted, but it didn't keep her from fixing herself three s'mores.

I grinned. "What can I say? I brought the important stuff."

After dinner, Carson, Oliver, and Covington left to go

find enough firewood to last us through the night, while Ajax, Rory, Daphne, and Alexei started talking about weapons and fighting techniques. Ajax started demonstrating some moves, and soon, they were all grappling and tossing each other around. That left me sitting by the fire with Rachel. She stared at me for a long time.

"Is there something you want to say to me?" I finally asked.

She shrugged. "You don't look much like a Forseti. Tyson, Rory's dad, had light, sandy hair and blue eyes. So did your dad."

I reached up and tried to smooth down my brown hair, but it only frizzed back out again. "Everyone says I look like my mom. *Violet eyes are smiling eyes.* She used to say that a lot."

Rachel smiled a little. "She sounds like a nice woman."

"She was. She was the best."

"What happened to her?"

"She was murdered by Reapers."

Rachel winced. "Oh. I'm so sorry."

I nodded, accepting her sympathy. "What was . . . what was my dad like? Did you know him?"

Rachel shifted on the rock she was sitting on. "No, I didn't know Tyr all that well. Not as well as I knew Tyson. Then again, I never dreamed that he was a Reaper or that my sister, Rebecca, had followed him down that path. So maybe I didn't know him at all—or her."

She laughed, but it was far from a happy sound. She fell silent for a moment, then looked at me again. "From what I remember, Tyr seemed like a nice guy. He was always making a joke, always trying to get everyone to laugh, even Tyson, who wasn't much for smiling or any sort of humor."

"What happened?" I asked. "My Grandma Frost told me that my dad had a falling-out with Tyson. Do you know anything about that?"

Rachel shook her head. "No, I'm sorry, but I don't. One day, Tyr left, and he never came back. That was when I started to notice how angry Tyson was all the time—and how angry Rebecca seemed to be, as well. But then Rebecca found out that she was pregnant with Rory, and things were better for a long time after that. Rebecca and Tyson . . . they really did love Rory, despite what they did."

She choked on the last few words. Memories darkened her eyes, and I knew she was thinking about her sister, the fact that she'd become a Reaper, and all the people she'd hurt and killed.

"Just because you love someone doesn't mean they'll never hurt or betray you," I said. "Trust me. I know that better than anyone."

Once more, I thought of Logan and that horrible, awful moment when he'd turned around at the Aoide Auditorium and I realized that his eyes were Reaper red. That Vivian and Agrona had done something terrible to him. That I might be too late to save him. It had been one of the worst moments of my life. And now, Logan was gone, and that hurt too. Because this time, he'd left of his own free will, and not because of some Reaper magic mumbo jumbo. He'd gone because he'd wanted to, leaving me with nothing but nightmares.

Rachel gave me a wan smile. "Sad, isn't it? How true that is. That love can hurt so much sometimes."

I didn't say anything else. There was nothing else *to* say. We'd all been wounded by the Reapers, some of us more than others, and we all had to deal with it in our own way. Still, I scooted a little closer to Rachel, and I stayed by her side until the others finished their sparring and joined us.

It grew darker and colder as the sun set and the hours slowly passed. Everyone else snuggled down in their sleeping bags, but unlike the others, I was too on edge to sleep. So I sat by the fire, hunched over as close to the flickering flames as I could get. I'd offered to keep a lookout while the others got some shut-eye. We hadn't seen any sign of the Reapers, but that didn't mean they weren't there somewhere, waiting for the right time to strike. I also kept an eye out for the baby gryphon and the mysterious shadow. But if they were around, they were as invisible as the Reapers were.

Finally, my phone beeped at eleven forty-five, telling me it was time to wake the others. Everyone moaned and groaned a little, but they all got up. We fished some flashlights out of our bags, clicked them on, and headed to the back corner of the courtyard.

The ambrosia looked the same as before—a tiny patch of white flowers somehow blossoming in the middle of the rock wall.

"Are you sure that we have to pick it at midnight?" I asked. "Because it looks the same to me as it did this afternoon. Small and kind of puny."

"That's what Metis said," Ajax replied. "That it has to be picked at midnight, preferably in the middle of a hard frost."

"Well, at least we have the frost," I muttered.

The temperature had been steadily dropping all night long. The lower it went, the more the frost gathered on the rocks and crumbled walls. Now, the entire courtyard looked like a sheet of silver ice—cold and beautiful—although the flowers remained strangely untouched by the gathering frost, as though this were a summer night instead of the dead of winter.

We waited as the minutes slowly ticked by, our breath steaming in the air and then falling away to the ground in clouds of ice crystals. For the longest time, the ambrosia flowers didn't do anything but shiver in the cold like the rest of us.

"One minute until midnight," Oliver announced, peering at his phone, the white glow lighting up his face like a ghost's.

We all stared at the flowers, watching for any change, for any sign that they would do whatever they were supposed to, what Nickamedes needed them to do.

And slowly—very, very slowly—the flowers began to grow.

At first, I thought it was just my imagination. But I blinked and then blinked again, and I realized that they were actually . . . *moving*.

Three small, individual flowers seemed to stretch toward each other, as though the petals were somehow being pulled together by the silvery glow of the full moon so very high above.

"Is everyone else seeing this?" I asked.

"Sshh," Oliver said. "You're spoiling the moment."

I elbowed him in the side, and he grinned. Then, we both fixed our gazes on the flowers once more.

As soon as the petals of the three flowers touched each other, they all seemed to wilt, as though they couldn't stand to be that close together. I sucked in a breath, wondering if something was wrong, if they weren't going to bloom because we were here and we needed them so badly. But as soon as the flowers wilted, a silver light began to burn in the center of each one of them, and the purple and gray streaks on the petals burst into cold flames. For a moment, the colors swirled together, a starry mix of silver, purple, and gray that grew brighter and brighter until I had to close my eyes and look away from the intense light. Then, as quickly as it had begun, the colors and lights abruptly faded away.

I opened my eyes—and was amazed at what I saw.

Somehow, the three small flowers had fused together into one large, beautiful blossom. The petals were now a shimmering silver and had a vaguely metallic look to them, almost as if they would ring like a bell if you tapped on them with your fingernail. White, purple, and gray streaked down the petals, as well, the colors clustered together like they were one stripe. It was one of the most beautiful things I'd ever seen.

Nobody spoke for several moments.

"It's incredible," Daphne finally whispered.

"That it is," Covington said, a strange, almost envious note in his voice. "That it is."

We all fell silent again.

"Well," I said, stepping forward and carefully tugging the flower—vine and all—free of the rock wall and the gryphon's beak. "I don't care how beautiful it is. All that matters is that it did what it was supposed to. Now we can use it to help Nickamedes."

"Of course," Covington said. "Of course."

I carefully slid the ambrosia flower into a long, slender, plastic tube that Ajax had bought when we'd gone shopping for supplies yesterday. Hopefully, the tube would protect the flower so we could get it back to the academy in one piece.

"Now what?" Rory asked.

"We get some sleep," Ajax rumbled. "It's been a long day, and we still have to hike back down the mountain in the morning."

We all headed back over to our camp. Ajax added enough wood to the fire so that it would burn through the rest of the night, while everyone else slipped into their tents and sleeping bags.

Half an hour later, I was in a tent with Daphne. Rachel and Rory would also sleep in here with us later, after they took their turns standing watch. I scooted closer to Daphne for warmth, despite the fact that she was already snoring. Every once in a while, a pink spark of magic would escape from her sleeping bag and flicker up into the air like a firefly before winking out.

I zipped up my sleeping bag, making sure I had one hand on Vic and the other on the tube with the ambrosia flower. The sword's eye opened, and he regarded me with a serious expression. Vic had been quiet today, and we hadn't talked much, but I knew he'd been resting up for the battle that was sure to come. The sword realized the most dangerous part of the journey was still ahead—getting down the mountain and surviving whatever trap the Reapers were planning.

"Don't worry, Gwen," Vic said. "You go to sleep. I'll keep an eye out. No Reapers will creep up on you tonight. I promise."

"Okay, Vic," I mumbled. "I'll leave it to you."

I closed my eyes and let the blackness of sleep take me away.

Chapter 25

The cold woke me.

Sometime during the night, I'd wormed my way up out of my sleeping bag, and the chill in the air had crept down the back of my neck like a ticklish finger. I shivered and snuggled back down into my sleeping bag, until the warmth of my body, combined with the silky material, drove away the worst of the cold. It was early, and Daphne, Rory, and Rachel were all still asleep in the tent with me, but I could tell it was getting lighter outside. It must be close to dawn. With any luck, we'd be back at the academy by noon, then back in North Carolina sometime late this evening.

I lay in my sleeping bag, but it wasn't too long before the others started stirring. Thirty minutes later, we were all gathered around the fire, which had dwindled down to embers overnight. We were all still half-asleep, so nobody felt much like talking. Instead, everyone cracked open some bottled water and dug through their backpacks to find some breakfast. Once again, I tore into a packet of granola. The dried fruit, dark chocolate, oats, and nuts weren't quite as flavorful as they had been yesterday, but they kept my stomach from grumbling too much.

Once we were all more or less awake and fed, we made sure that the fire was completely cold, took down the tents, and packed up our things. Rachel adjusted her pack on her back, then stared up at the sky. The early morning sun had already disappeared, replaced by a heavy veil of dark gray clouds.

"That storm's finally blowing in," she said. "We need to be off the mountain before the worst of the snow starts."

We nodded. None of us had any desire to be trapped up here. It was already cold and blustery enough. I couldn't even imagine how much worse a foot or two of snow would make things. Despite the cold, I didn't put my gloves on. I wanted to be able to pull Vic out of his scabbard without any problems in case of a Reaper attack.

As we shouldered our packs and got ready to head out, I couldn't help the feeling of unease that swept over me. It all seemed too ... *easy*. Except for the attack on the train, the Reapers hadn't made a move against us while we'd been at the ruins. I wondered why—and what they were really up to.

We were about to leave the courtyard when I saw that mysterious shadow out of the corner of my eye.

One second, I was thinking about how long it would take us to hike down the mountain and when and where the Reapers might attack. The next, I realized there was a figure hovering on the edge of my vision—one that seemed to be staring straight at me.

I snapped my head to the left—but no one was there. All I saw were crumbled walls and overturned rocks, with the flowers spread out like a colorful blanket in the middle of the courtyard.

"What's the matter, Princess?" Rory asked, noticing me looking around.

I shook my head. I wasn't sure what to tell her. *Sorry, I seem to be seeing things that aren't really there* didn't exactly seem like the right thing to say—

Caw-caw-caw.

I froze, really, really hoping I was just imagining those sounds.

Caw-caw-caw.

But the high, eerie shrieks came again, echoing from one side of the courtyard to the other and back again, and I knew that I wasn't hallucinating—and that we were in serious trouble.

A second later, a shadow fell over me, blotting out what little sun there was, and a bird swooped down out of the sky. It was an enormous creature, easily twice as big as I was tall, with glossy black feathers shot through with streaks of red; long, curved black talons; and black eyes that contained a hot, burning spark of Reaper red.

A Black roc—and it wasn't alone.

A girl was strapped in a leather harness that was attached to the creature's broad back. A black robe fluttered around her body over her matching black snowsuit. Frizzy auburn hair, bright golden eyes, sneering smile. She looked exactly the same as she did in my nightmares. And just like the roc, her gaze shimmered with that spark of Reaper red. The girl looked at me and grinned.

"Hello, Gwen," Vivian Holler said. "I thought I might find you here."

*   *   *

I immediately threw my backpack down and drew Vic out of the scabbard on my waist. I started to charge forward, but Alexei held his hand out, stopping me. He shook his head in warning, then drew his twin swords out of the scabbard on his back and stepped in front of me. The others dropped their bags and pulled out their weapons, as well, ready to fight the Reaper girl.

When she realized that we weren't going to immediately swarm all over her, Vivian pouted, as though she was disappointed by our restraint. That told me that she'd wanted us to charge her. I wondered why, since it seemed that she was alone. My gaze scanned over the ruins, but I didn't see any other Reapers lurking behind the piles of rubble. They were here somewhere, though. They had to be. Vivian would never try to fight us all by herself. She wasn't that stupid—or brave.

Vivian stared at Alexei, her eyes lingering on the twin swords in his hands. "A bodyguard, Gypsy? Really? Even I don't have one of those. Kind of sad that you feel the need for one, though." She clucked her tongue in mock sympathy. "Then again, I can take care of myself, and we just can't say the same for you, now can we?"

"Oh, I don't know," I drawled. "I think I'm doing okay. After all, you haven't managed to murder me yet. Kind of a big epic failure on your part, isn't it? Especially since I'm so weak and pitiful and helpless? What's wrong with you that you can't kill one geeky girl, Viv? Aren't you supposed to be this great warrior with such powerful magic? Bet Loki's not too happy about all that—that his Champion hasn't been able to carry out this one simple order. Who knows? If you keep sucking like you do, he might decide to name a new Champion. Maybe even take away your telepathy magic. And wouldn't that just be *so* humiliating for you."

Her golden eyes glimmered, and that eerie Reaper red spark burned a little brighter and hotter in her gaze. Her hands tightened around the roc's reins, like she was thinking about urging the creature forward and making it plow into me. After a moment, Vivian relaxed her grip, but I knew I'd pissed her off. Good. I was planning to do a lot more of that—before I killed her.

Still, I couldn't help feeling that Vivian had already sprung her trap—and all that was left was for the teeth of it to sink into our throats, like the snap-snare had done to the baby gryphon's leg. Once again, my eyes scanned the ruins, but I didn't see anyone, and the only sound was the whistle of the winter wind whipping around the crumbled stones.

Vivian unbuckled herself from her harness and slid to the ground, grabbing a sword out of the scabbard that was tied to the roc's harness. She stepped in front of the bird and held up the sword by the blade, so that the hilt was showing. After a moment, I stepped up next to Alexei and did the same thing with Vic.

"Lucretia," Vic hissed.

A Reaper red eye snapped open on the hilt of Vivian's sword and glared right back at him. "Vic," she purred in a low, feminine voice. "So nice to see you again, especially looking so dull and tarnished. But you are getting up there in years, aren't you?"

"Dull? Dull *and* tarnished? Why—why you—" Vic was so incensed that all he could do was sputter.

Lucretia laughed at his anger, her dark chuckles mirroring the ones coming out of Vivian's mouth.

Finally, when they'd both quit laughing, I looked at Vivian again. "What do you want? What is this all about?"

Vivian pouted once more. "Getting down to business already, Gwen? If you want to die sooner rather than later, well, that's fine with me."

She grabbed the sword's hilt, then lifted Lucretia high overhead. I tensed, wondering what she was doing, but I got my answer a second later when another Black roc dropped down from the sky.

It plummeted into the ruins, landing beside Vivian's. Another familiar figure was riding the enormous bird—Agrona Quinn.

She too looked the same as in my nightmares—silky blond hair, tan skin, intense green eyes. She wore a long black robe that fluttered in the wind, showing off her silver snowsuit and boots underneath. Despite the cold, she wasn't wearing gloves, and a ring flashed on her left hand, just as it had in my dreams. She must be wearing more of the Apate jewels she'd stolen from the Library of Antiquities. The ones she'd used to control Logan and turn him against me.

But the thing that caught my eye was her right hand. It almost looked like one of the roc's curved claws. Agrona's fingers were purple, swollen, and twisted together at an awkward angle. She noticed me staring at her hand, and she scowled and dropped it down out of sight, not wanting me to see her weakness.

I frowned, wondering what was wrong with her hand, and then I remembered—I'd done that to her.

During the fight at the Aoide Auditorium, I'd used Vic to smash Agrona's hand to try to destroy the heart-shaped Apate ruby she'd been wearing as a ring. It looked like her hand hadn't fully healed from the injury. It must have been because I'd used Vic to break her fingers. The damage was incurable since he was a powerful artifact in his own right. Maybe it was wrong, but a wave of dark satisfaction filled me that I'd been able to hurt Agrona like that. She deserved it for what she'd done to Logan and his dad. She deserved that—and worse.

"Agrona," Ajax growled. "I should have known you'd be behind this."

She smiled, but the expression was anything but pleasant. "So nice to see you again too, Ajax. Tell me, how is my dear stepson doing? I'm disappointed not to see Logan here among your little band of warriors."

"He's fine," I cut in before anyone could say anything. "Despite what you did to him."

Agrona laughed. "Of course he is. He's so fine that he's not by your side like you want him to be. Right, Gypsy?"

I didn't say anything, but once more, my stomach tightened with worry that the Reapers had somehow captured Logan, like Vivian had claimed. I held my breath, waiting for Agrona to crow about how Logan was being tortured to death right now.

Agrona must have seen the hurt, anger, and fear in my face because she laughed again and waved her good hand in the air. "No matter. Logan isn't important anyway. Not anymore. But some of you are—or rather the things you brought with you." Her green eyes focused on Vic, and a spark of jealousy flickered in her gaze.

Maybe it was Agrona's covetous look or maybe it was the way the weak winter sun glinted off Vic's blade, but I flashed back to two days ago when I'd been staring up at the flat ceiling inside the Library of Antiquities. Instead of the fresco of my friends and me fighting the Reapers, I'd only been able to see the weapons we carried—not who was actually wielding them.

My eyes went from one of my friends to the next. Daphne holding Sigyn's bow, ready to let loose the arrow nocked on the golden strings. Alexei slowly twirling the Swords of Ruslan around and around in his hands. Carson with the Horn of Roland hanging off the side of his bag. Me with Vic in my hand and Ran's net stuffed into my backpack.

"Artifacts," I whispered. "That's what this is all about."

Agrona raised an eyebrow, apparently surprised that I'd figured it out. She glanced at Vivian, who shrugged.

"I didn't say anything," Vivian said. "I was waiting for your grand entrance."

Agrona shot her a pointed glare, but Vivian gave her an angelic smile in return. After a moment, Agrona turned back to me.

"Well, I hate to ruin the surprise, but, yes, Gypsy, this is all about artifacts," she said. "According to my spies, you've been searching for artifacts lately—artifacts that I am very, very interested in. And surprise, surprise, you've actually managed to get your hands on at least one of them that I know of—Ran's net. What made you decide to start looking for artifacts?"

I kept my face blank. I wasn't going to tell her about the mission Nike had given me to find artifacts and keep them out of the Reapers' hands.

Agrona shrugged when she realized I wasn't going to respond. "Your answer doesn't really matter. All that does is that you walked right into my trap, just like I thought you would." Her eyes met mine. "At first, I was disappointed you didn't drink the poison I'd so thoughtfully sent your way, but this will work out even better. Now, we won't have to figure out some way to steal your sword from the academy. We'll just take it from your cold, dead body."

"That's why you poisoned Nickamedes?" Carson asked, pushing his glasses up his nose. "To get us here? In hopes that we'd bring our weapons along with us?"

"Not your weapons," Agrona sneered. "Your *artifacts*. Sigyn's bow. The Horn of Roland. The Swords of Ruslan. And, of course, Vic."

"Well, naturally," the sword crowed, his voice swelling with pride. "I do put the *art* in *artifact*."

I looked down at him. "Really?" I whispered. "You're really going to talk about how awesome you are at a time like this?"

"Certainly," Vic said. "Why wouldn't I?"

I rolled my eyes.

"We knew that if we poisoned Nike's Champion you would all be just *frantic* to find an antidote," Agrona said. "So frantic that you would forget about everything else, like the fact that it was so obviously a trap. It was simply a matter of picking the right poison and making sure you went exactly where we wanted you to. Fools. Don't you realize we've been watching you ever since you left North Carolina?"

"We realized," Ajax said. "But we had to come anyway. You made sure of that."

"Yeah," Daphne chimed in. "We take care of our friends no matter what. Something the two of you wouldn't know anything about."

Vivian clutched a hand to her heart. "Oh Valkyrie. I'm so very hurt by your words."

Daphne looked down her arrow at the other girl. "You'll be hurt when I put an arrow through your black heart."

Vivian raised Lucretia. "Bring it."

Agrona shot Vivian another warning glare. After a moment, the Reaper girl lowered her sword, although she kept glaring at Daphne.

"And of course you all obliged me by bringing along your artifacts, then traipsing up here to the ruins. Not only that, but you actually found the ambrosia flower, which will be a nice bonus," Agrona said. "So sad that you only want to use it on Nickamedes. It's quite powerful, you know. It has all sorts of uses. Why, legend says it can even heal the gods themselves."

Her words made me think back to the night Vivian had used my blood to free Loki at the Garm gate. The evil god had been powerful, but I'd also sensed weakness in him—that all the long centuries of being trapped in Helheim had taken their toll on him. Loki's weakness was the reason the Reapers had tried to put his soul into Logan—so the evil god would have a young, healthy body.

A numb feeling spread through me. "You're going to use the ambrosia flower to make Loki stronger."

"Well, well, Gwen. Look at you, being all smart again. But you're exactly right," Agrona purred. "We are going to give the ambrosia to our lord. It won't return him to his full strength, but it will take care of some of his . . . difficulties being in the mortal realm once again."

I didn't need to glance at the others to realize they were as horrified as I was. We'd thought the Reaper trap was only about killing us, but they had a plan within a plan within a plan just like they always did. Whatever happened, whether we lived or died, we couldn't let the Reapers take our artifacts—and we most especially couldn't let them have the ambrosia flower.

"Well, too bad none of that is going to happen," I said, trying to make my voice sound stronger and more confident than I felt. "You're not getting anything. Not one thing. Not our artifacts, not the ambrosia flower, not our lives."

Agrona laughed again. "Oh Gypsy. You always play the part of the fool so well, don't you?"

My fingers tightened around Vic's hilt. "Maybe. But I'd like to see you try and take my sword away."

Agrona smiled. "Gladly."

She jerked her head at Vivian. I tensed, expecting the Reaper girl to raise her sword and finally rush forward and start the fight. But instead, all Vivian did was put her fingers to her lips and let out a loud, earsplitting whistle.

Oliver gave her a mocking look. "What good do you think that's going to do you—"

Caw-caw-caw.

Caw-caw-caw.

Caw-caw-caw.

A series of harsh cries rang out, drowning his voice. One moment, the only things in the sky were the snow-laden clouds. The next, Black rocs filled the space above the ruins. One by one, they dropped to the ground beside Vivian and Agrona, forming a solid line in front of us. There must have been more than a dozen rocs, all with a Reaper or two riding them. The Reapers' long, black robes fluttered in the wind, while the rubber masks covering their faces seemed especially hideous, mirror images of Loki glaring at us.

"Get ready," Ajax murmured, cracking his knuckles. "On my mark, raise your weapons and retreat back into the courtyard. Make the Reapers come to us. Engage them at will, but stay in groups and stay away from the rocs. Otherwise, the birds will tear us to pieces with their beaks and talons. Daphne, you stay behind all of us and pick off as many of the rocs as you can with your bow."

She nodded and started easing backward. The others tightened their grips on their weapons and raised them into attack position.

One by one, the Reapers unbuckled themselves from the rocs, slid to the ground, and started creeping forward. I drew in a breath and brought up Vic, ready to fight once more—

A hand snaked around my waist from behind. Before I could react, before I could move or try to fight back, cold, sharp metal pressed against my throat—a dagger.

But even more surprising was the person holding it.

"Don't make a move," Covington hissed at my friends. "Or Nike's Champion dies."

Chapter 26

Everyone froze.

I hadn't seen or heard Covington move, but he had to be a Roman to have gotten behind me that fast. My friends looked back and forth between the dagger at my throat and the Reapers still creeping toward us. My psychometry kicked in, showing me flickers and flashes of all the people Covington had killed with the dagger—and how he planned to do the same thing to me.

"Covington?" Ajax asked, the shock apparent in his voice. "What are you doing?"

"What I've been doing for years," the librarian said in a sly, satisfied tone. "Ensuring the downfall of the pathetic Pantheon one death and one artifact at a time."

"What do you mean?" I asked.

He laughed in my ear, the sound even more chilling than the air around us. "Who do you think has been helping the Reapers find so many artifacts lately? I've been using the resources in the Library of Antiquities to track down the objects that we need—that Loki needs—to finally defeat the Pantheon and win the second Chaos

War. But time and time again, you and your little friends have been there first. You've already gotten Sigyn's bow, the Swords of Ruslan, and the Horn of Roland, and you almost stopped Agrona from getting the Apate jewels. How are you doing it? How do you know so much about artifacts?"

I didn't answer him, but my eyes met Oliver's, and I could tell he was thinking about the same thing I was—the drawing he'd done for me of all the artifacts, people, and creatures that Nike had shown me. The one I had stuffed in my backpack right now. Another thing I couldn't let the Reapers get their hands on.

"Tell me!" Covington screamed and pressed the dagger into my throat.

I winced as the blade sliced into my skin, but I didn't answer him. I wasn't telling him about the drawing or the fact that I knew there were other artifacts out there—ones that might make the difference between who won and who lost the looming Chaos War. I wasn't telling him anything—not one damn *thing*.

I didn't get a chance to respond before Rachel stepped forward, a horrified look on her face.

"Rebecca . . . Tyson . . . You said they attacked *you*. That they were trying to steal artifacts from the library. You said they murdered those students, and that you had no choice but to defend yourself against them—against the *poor, misguided Reapers*. That's what you called them."

"They were fools," Covington sneered. "They agreed to break in to the Library of Antiquities and steal artifacts to make it look like a robbery and a Reaper attack gone wrong so suspicion wouldn't fall on me. But at the last moment, they changed their minds and tried to stop me."

Rory moved to stand beside Rachel. Anger made her cheeks burn and her eyes flash, and her hands were clenched into tight fists. "Why? Why did they try to stop you?"

"They were unhappy," he sneered again. "They didn't want you to grow up to be like them. Boo-hoo. They were even talking about leaving the Reapers completely. But they should have known better. No one leaves us—*ever*."

"So you framed them," Rory said, her voice raspy with rage. "You framed them for what you did."

"Oh, grow up, you stupid girl," Covington snapped. "Your precious parents were hardly innocent. They were Reapers for years—*years*. You have no idea the things they did, all in service to Loki."

Tears streaked down Rory's face, but she didn't bother to brush them away. Rachel was crying too, but she had the same hurt, determined expression on her face as Rory.

Covington laughed at their tears and anger. "And do you know what the best part is? That you two were dumb enough to come up here with the rest of these fools. Why do you think I asked you to be our guide?"

Confusion filled Rachel's face, but I had a sinking feeling I knew exactly what he was getting at.

"Because I'm the only one from our group who will go back to the academy alive," Covington answered. "There will be a Protectorate investigation, of course, but in the end, it'll look like I finally took care of the rest of the Forseti family of Reapers."

So not only was he going to help Vivian and Agrona

kill us, but the librarian was also planning to frame Rachel and Rory for our murders. And of course everyone would believe him, given the fact that Rory's parents had been Reapers. Cruel—very, very cruel.

"You're not going to get away with it," Rory vowed. "I won't let you."

More tears slid down her face, but she slowly started advancing on the librarian. So did Rachel. Meanwhile, the Reapers crept up on my friends, who were standing their ground. My friends hesitated, wanting to attack the Reapers, but they couldn't—not as long as Covington had his dagger against my throat—which meant that I had to find some way to free myself or we were all dead.

I quickly considered my options. Sure, I had Vic clenched in my right hand, but I couldn't raise the sword and attack the librarian with it. Not with Covington right behind me. So I concentrated on exactly how and where he was standing. He had his left hand around my waist, and his right one at my throat, still holding the dagger. Warm blood trickled down my neck from where he'd cut me already.

No, I couldn't use Vic, not without getting my throat sliced open, but the sword wasn't my only weapon—I had my touch magic too.

That's what I'd used on Preston Ashton when he'd stabbed me with the Helheim Dagger. I'd pulled the Reaper boy's life force into my own body and healed myself with it—and Preston had died as a result. Killing him had been horrible enough, but Vic had wanted me to do the same thing to Logan, to keep him from murdering me when he'd been under the influence of the

Apate jewels. But I'd refused. I hadn't wanted to hurt Logan. I hadn't wanted to use my Gypsy gift that way. Not again—*never* again.

But Covington was a Reaper, he was my enemy, and he'd happily led me and my friends into Agrona and Vivian's trap. Not only that, but he'd framed Rory's parents for something they hadn't even done.

Killing Preston with my touch magic had sickened me, and the thought of using it on Covington was making me ill right now, but I didn't see any other way out of this. My friends couldn't defend themselves until I was free, and this was the only way I could slither out of the librarian's grasp.

So I focused on Covington's hand wrapped around my waist. I was holding Vic in my right hand, but my left hand was hanging down by my side. Slowly, very, very slowly, I started moving my free hand up toward the librarian's.

"Stand still or I'll cut your throat!" he snarled.

I froze, my hand no higher than my hip. I couldn't move it the rest of the way or he'd make good on his threat. Frustration filled me because I needed my skin to touch his. That was how my magic worked. But I realized there was another way I could use my Gypsy gift on the librarian—by getting him to touch me instead.

Covington's fingers brushed up against the collar of my snowsuit as he held the dagger against my neck. I shifted on my feet, trying to get his fingers to slip up over the edge of the cloth and press against my skin, but the angle was wrong, and I couldn't get it to work. More frustration surged through me, and my gaze went to my friends. They'd moved together, forming a tight ring in the middle of the courtyard, even as the Reapers kept advancing on them, slashing their curved swords through the air in anticipation of cutting into my friends. And I realized I was almost out of time—and there was only one option left.

If I couldn't get Covington to touch me, then I'd have to touch him instead. All I had to do was turn my neck into the blade at my throat. It was a risky plan, and I didn't know how much damage the dagger might do to me, but it was the only way I could save myself and my friends.

Out of the corner of my eye, I noticed that Vivian was watching me, a frown on her face, and I felt a sharp, sudden pain in my head, as though a pair of fingers were digging into my brain. Vivian was using her telepathy magic to peer into my mind. After a moment, her eyes widened. Too late, she realized what I was planning.

"Covington! Don't let her move! Don't let her touch you—"

I gritted my teeth and turned my neck, trying not to scream as the dagger sliced into my skin. Covington jerked back in surprise, but I kept turning, turning, turning my neck, even as the blade cut deeper and deeper into my throat.

Finally, just when I thought I couldn't stand the pain a second longer, I felt the librarian's cold fingers scrape against my bare, bloody skin—and then I *yanked*.

Covington's thoughts and feelings flooded my mind the second his skin touched mine.

The dark jealousy that seeped through every part of his being almost took my breath away. One after another, I saw images of him over the years. Working in the library, looking down on all the students and professors, meeting with Agrona and other Reapers, gleefully doing whatever foul thing Agrona asked of him. Metis, Nickamedes, and Ajax were even in a few of his memories, when Covington had visited the North Carolina academy. I felt his deep, burning hatred of them, particularly of Nickamedes and the fact that he was in charge of our Library of Antiquities, a job Covington had always secretly coveted.

I blinked, and another memory roared to the surface of my mind—Covington arguing with two people dressed in black Reaper cloaks. They weren't wearing masks, so I could see their faces—the same faces, the same people, I'd seen in that photo with Rory. I knew I was watching her parents—Rebecca and Tyson.

"You'll have to find another way . . . we're not going to do it . . ." Rebecca's voice sounded in my mind. "We're tired of this . . . of the Reapers. All we want to do is live a nice, quiet, peaceful life with our daughter . . ."

Tyson nodded, agreeing with her.

The two of them walked away, and Covington picked up the sword he'd hidden underneath the library's checkout counter. Quiet as a whisper, he advanced on them and raised the weapon high, even though their backs were turned—

The rest of the memory rushed by before I could latch on to it, but I knew how it ended—with Covington murdering Rory's parents.

But a new image took its place—one of Covington alone in the library, poring over book after book, looking at pages covered with plants, herbs, and flowers. Searching for a poison—the poison the Reapers had meant for me . . .

I drew in a breath and pushed the images away. Instead, I let myself sink even deeper into the librarian until I saw the black spark flickering at the very center of his being—the ugly thing that made Covington who and what he was. I imagined closing my hand around that spark, and then I *yanked* again—even harder than before.

Covington screamed as I pulled his magic, his power, his life into my own body. The wounds on my neck healed, and I could feel myself growing stronger and stronger even as the spark inside his body started to dim. At that moment, I wanted nothing more than to snuff that spark out completely—and kill the librarian where he stood.

"Let go of her!" I heard Vivian scream. "You're dead if she keeps touching you!"

Covington let out one more agonized scream. Then, he dropped the dagger from my neck and shoved me away. I stumbled forward and fell to my knees in the rocky rubble.

"You!" Covington snarled. "You think you can use your pitiful psychometry to kill me? I'll show you how wrong you are, Gypsy!"

He raised his dagger high. I brought up Vic, although I knew I wouldn't be quick enough to block his attack—

A figure darted between us. It took me a second to realize it was Rory—and the Spartan girl had her hand locked around the librarian's wrist. Rory's free fist snapped up, and she punched Covington in the face. He cursed and staggered back, and Rory smoothly plucked his dagger from his hand.

She twirled the weapon around a few times, getting a feel for it, her green eyes glinting with that Spartan combination of anger and anticipation of the fight to come. "I've got this, Gwen," she said in a cold voice. "You help the others. Covington is *mine*."

"Alive!" I heard Ajax yell. "We need him alive, Rory!"

Covington tried to back up, even going so far as to duck behind a pile of rocks, but Rory followed him, stalking him as coolly as a Fenrir wolf would its prey. A second later, the librarian screamed. Rory must have sliced him open with his own dagger. I just hoped she'd let him live, like Ajax had said. No doubt the coach wanted answers about the Reapers—answers Covington might be able to give us.

Those were the thoughts that raced through my mind as I scrambled to my feet. I raised Vic, ready to fight whoever came my way—and immediately had to duck down as a Reaper's sword whistled by my head.

Clash-clash-clang!

The Reaper and I fought, exchanging blow after blow after blow, before I was finally able to cut through his defense and bury Vic's point in the man's chest.

"That's my girl!" Vic crowed. "On to the next one!"

I pulled the sword free, stepped over the dead Reaper, and started forward. Then, I stopped, unsure where to go.

Because the ruins were in complete chaos.

The Reapers had launched themselves at my friends, their black robes whipping around them like a wave of death spilling forward into the flower-filled courtyard.

Ajax, Alexei, and Rachel were at the front of the fight, holding the first surge of Reapers at bay. Ajax and Rachel were using their swords to battle the evil warriors, along with their daggers, while Alexei swung his twin swords every which way, cutting into all the Reapers he could reach.

Behind the Reapers, the Black rocs screamed out their fierce battle cries. Some of the Reapers slapped the creatures on their sides, urging them to zoom through the air, join in the attack, and dive-bomb my friends from above.

But every time one of the Black rocs took flight, Daphne raised her bow and loosed a golden arrow. She was one of the best archers at Mythos, and her aim was true. Roc after roc plunged to the ground, already dead before their bodies hit the rocks. Carson and Oliver flanked Daphne on either side, protecting her from the Reapers who managed to slip past Ajax, Alexei, and Rachel.

"Gwen!" Alexei shouted.

He used his twin swords to cut down first one Reaper, then another. But before he'd taken more than a half dozen steps in my direction, two more Reapers had moved to block him.

I waved him off. "I'll be okay! Help the others protect Daphne! She's the only way we can keep the rocs from joining in the attack!"

Alexei didn't like it, but he nodded and started working his way back to the others.

"Oh good," a voice purred behind me. "She's sent away her bodyguard."

I turned to find Vivian and Agrona standing behind

me, along with their two rocs. Both of the Reapers were holding swords. They slowly advanced on me, and I raised Vic once more. Vivian was still holding Lucretia, and the red glow of the female sword's eye was even brighter than before.

"Look," Lucretia purred. "Dull little Vic might finally get some use in the fight after all. If my first blow doesn't just snap his puny blade in two."

"Lucretia!" Vic shouted. "Come over here and say that!"

"With pleasure!" the other sword crowed back.

And those were all the insults they were able to exchange before Vivian and I charged at each other.

Clash-clash-clang!
Clash-clash-clang!
Clash-clash-clang!

We battled through the ruins. Over rocks, around rocks, ducking and darting, moving back and forth and up and down, trying to get every little advantage we could to hurt the other girl as much as possible. We trampled the flowers underfoot, our boots smashing the beautiful blossoms into runny smears of color. Petals whipped through the air at our frantic movements, and the crisp scent of the flowers took on a thick, coppery stench as blood spattered onto the blossoms from the nicks and cuts Vivian and I were able to inflict on each other.

Finally, I managed to drive her back against a large boulder and slashed out with my sword. Vivian ducked to one side just in time to keep me from taking off her head, but I still managed to open up a deep gash on her right cheek.

Vivian gasped in pain and surprise and brought her fingers up to her face. She pulled them down, staring in disbelief at the blood on her hand.

"You cut me," she said. "You cut my *face*."

I twirled Vic in my hand. "I'll do more than that, before this fight is through."

"Not so fast, Gypsy," Agrona said.

Up until now, she had just watched the two of us fight. At first, I'd wondered why Agrona hadn't joined forces with Vivian, but then I'd realized she was holding her sword at an awkward angle, as though she wasn't used to wielding it with her left hand. Her right hand—her sword hand—must have been too badly damaged by Vic to be of any use. All she could do was watch—until now.

Agrona snapped her fingers, and her Black roc charged forward.

I threw myself to one side, barely managing to avoid the vicious swipe of the roc's talons. If I'd held my ground, I would have been dead, my chest ripped wide open by the creature's claws. But the roc was faster than I was. I'd barely gotten back onto my feet when the roc whipped around and slammed one of its wings into my left shoulder. I grunted, and the force of the impact threw me five feet to the left. My legs went out from under me, and I stumbled to the ground, landing on my hands and knees. The roc launched itself into the air, hovering over me like an evil black helicopter. It pumped its wings once, then surged forward, its claws extended toward my throat—

A figure darted between me and the roc. At first, I thought it was Rory again, and it took me a moment to realize it was a guy my own age. He charged the roc, spun to one side, and managed to grab hold of the creature's harness. The guy yanked on the long leather reins as hard as he could, causing the creature to stop two feet short of me. But he wasn't finished. He moved forward again, tossing the leather straps over the roc in such a way that they bound the creature's wings to its sides. The roc hit the ground with an audible *thud*, even as it *caw-caw-cawed* and frantically tried to tear off the leather straps with its beak.

Then, the guy turned to me, and my breath caught in my throat.

Ink-black hair, intense ice-blue eyes, and a crooked smile that made a warm, fizzy feeling explode in my heart.

"Logan?" I whispered.

His smile widened. "Hey there, Gypsy girl."

Chapter 27

My gaze locked with Logan's. No matter how happy I was to see him, I couldn't help thinking of my nightmares and how he had hurt me in them over and over again.

But instead of that awful Reaper red, his eyes were sharp and clear and as blue as they could be—the most beautiful blue I'd ever seen.

"Gypsy girl?" he asked. "Are you okay?"

"But how—when—why—" I sputtered like Vic had a few minutes ago.

Logan flashed me another smile and helped me to my feet. "Talk later. Fight now. Okay?"

I was so stunned that all I could do was just stand there. The roc got free and threw itself at Logan. Out of the corner of my eye, I saw Vivian sneaking up on Logan's blind side, and I put myself between her and the Spartan.

"Protecting your boyfriend's back? Aw, how sweet," Vivian muttered. "Not that it's going to do either one of you any good."

She raised her sword and charged me. I tightened my

grip on Vic and stepped up to meet her. Vivian attacked me over and over again, trying to use her Valkyrie strength to cut through my defenses. Red and purple sparks crackled in the air every time our blades met. Off to my left, Logan kept battling the roc, darting back and forth to keep out of range of the creature's sharp, snapping beak.

Finally, the roc zigged instead of zagged, taking Logan by surprise. His feet went out from under him, and the roc launched itself into the air once more.

"Logan!" I screamed, knowing he wouldn't be able to get out of the way before the creature dive-bombed and tore him open with its claws—

A golden arrow zipped through the air and buried itself in the roc's side. The creature collapsed, its body barely missing crashing into Logan's. He rolled to the side, trying to shake off his daze from hitting the ground.

"You're welcome!" Daphne shouted across the courtyard.

I waved at her and turned my attention back to Vivian. This time, I threw myself at the other girl.

I attacked Vivian with all the strength, skill, and fury I could muster. The intensity of my attacks seemed to surprise her, as though she was the only one of us who could be so fierce and vicious. I'd told Daphne before that the Reapers hadn't seen my crazy yet—but I showed it to Vivian.

I attacked her with everything I had.

All the moves Logan had shown me. All the sneak attacks Oliver and Kenzie had taught me. All the positions Ajax had drilled me on in gym class. All the passion and intense ferocity Daphne gave to everything in her life. All the fluid grace of Alexei's movements. All the quiet devotion Carson showed to his friends. All the pain, anger, and frustration Rory and Rachel had felt these last few months. All the love Grandma Frost, Nyx, and Professor Metis had always given me. All the cranky concern Nickamedes and Vic had for me.

I hacked and slashed at Vivian with all of that and more. And for the first time, it actually seemed like *enough*. I couldn't hurt her—not seriously—but she couldn't break through my defenses either.

The longer we fought, the more frustrated she grew, until her eyes were glowing like two pools of molten lava in her face.

"Why won't you just die?!" she hissed.

"You're going to fail again, Viv," I mocked. "Because you're not killing me today. Not by a long shot. Not with those weak-ass moves. And look. The rest of your friends are losing too."

Vivian's gaze darted around the ruins. By this point, Daphne had killed all of the rocs, except for Vivian's, and the Valkyrie was now picking off the Reapers one by one with her bow. Ajax and Alexei were battling three Reapers, while Carson and Oliver had cornered two more. Rachel was off to the side, fighting the last one, and I could still hear Covington screaming, which meant that Rory had him under control. One by one, the Reapers were falling. It was only a matter of time before my friends finished off the rest of them and came to help me against Vivian.

The Reaper girl knew it too. She cursed and lashed out at me with her sword, causing me to leap back.

Then, she turned and raced toward her roc. Agrona had realized the tide had turned against the Reapers, and she was already trying to climb up onto the bird's back, although her damaged hand slowed her down. Vivian used her Valkyrie strength to shove the other woman up and onto the roc, then climbed in front of her.

"Go, Gwen!" Vic shouted, his voice slightly muffled by my sweaty palm over his mouth. "Go! Don't let them get away again!"

I started toward them, but Logan was quicker. The Spartan got to his feet and hurried toward the roc, quickly outpacing me. By this point, Vivian was on top of the creature and had the reins in her hands. All she had to do was slap them down, and the bird would take flight. But instead, she looked at me, a cruel smile curving her face.

"No! Logan!" I screamed. "Stop!"

But he didn't listen to me. Instead, he kept running as fast as he could because he had his own score to settle—with his former stepmom.

"Agrona!" Logan shouted. "Face me!"

Agrona leaned forward and whispered something in Vivian's ear, and the Reaper girl's smile widened. I raced along behind Logan, but I knew I was going to be too late—*again*.

Logan was ten feet away from the roc and closing fast. Seven feet . . . five . . . three . . . Just as he started to launch himself through the air and onto the roc, Vivian let out another high, earsplitting whistle. The roc darted forward—and jabbed its beak into Logan's side.

All of his forward momentum abruptly stopped, and he tumbled backward to the ground.

"Logan!" I screamed again.

He groaned and didn't answer me, although his legs kicked out, sending up sprays of petals.

"Finish him!" Agrona hissed. "Now!"

Vivian let out another whistle, and the roc darted forward once more—but this time, I was there.

I put myself between Logan and the bird and swung my sword in a vicious arc. The roc jumped back to avoid me.

"Forget them!" Agrona screamed. "Get us out of here!"

But Vivian wasn't about to give up this chance to finally murder me. Again and again, she urged her roc forward. Again and again, I lashed out with my sword, keeping the creature from killing me and Logan. It was bizarre, fighting something more than twice my size, but maybe all those mornings of weapons training had finally started to sink in because I actually held my own against the creature. Then again, it was also burdened by the two riders on its back, whereas all I had to do was avoid its raking claws and sharp, stabbing beak.

"Gwen!" Daphne screamed behind me. "Duck!"

I immediately dropped down on my knees. A second later, a golden arrow zipped over my head. But Vivian had heard Daphne's shout too, and she managed to maneuver her roc out of the way of the arrow, which sailed over the creature's head.

"Stay down!" Daphne shouted and loosed another arrow.

Vivian and her roc managed to avoid the second arrow, as well.

"Get us out of here!" Agrona screamed again. "Now!"

This time, Vivian listened to her. She slapped the leather reins down against the roc's back. The creature let out another loud, screaming cry before it flapped its wings, zoomed up into the sky, and disappeared.

I waited a few moments to make sure that Vivian and Agrona weren't going to come back for another strike, then turned to Logan. He'd gotten back up onto his feet, although he was holding his hand to his side.

I hurried over to him. "Are you okay?"

He smiled, although I could see the pain in his eyes. "I'll live, Gypsy girl. Just a little scratch."

"Are you sure? Let me take a look at it—"

"No!" he said, violently twisting away before I could touch him. "Don't touch me! Just . . . don't."

I stood there, my hand stretched out toward him. Logan must have seen the hurt in my face because he blew out a breath.

"I'm sorry," he said. "I just . . . I'm sorry. I'll be okay. Really, I will be. Nothing to worry about."

I dropped my hand and stared at him, not sure what to do, not sure what to say. This was the moment I'd longed for ever since he'd left. To see Logan again. But now that he was here, now that we were face-to-face, I realized things still weren't right between us—and I didn't know how to make them that way again.

"Gwen! Gwen!" My friends' voices echoed through the ruins.

A second later, they were all crowding around me and

Logan. Daphne, Carson, Oliver, Alexei, Ajax, Rachel, even Rory, who shoved a bloody, bruised, and disheveled Covington along in front of her.

My eyes scanned each one of them. Except for Daphne, everybody had some lumps, bumps, and bruises. Carson was limping and using his staff to stand upright, as though he'd twisted his ankle, while Ajax's right arm appeared to be broken from the awkward way the coach was holding it against his side and grimacing. Rachel and Oliver both had bloody faces and scraped knuckles, and blood dripped from a series of deep cuts on Alexei's left arm. But no one seemed to be seriously injured. At least, nothing Daphne couldn't take care of with her healing magic until we could get back to the academy. I let out a quiet sigh of relief that no one had been hurt worse.

"Are you okay?" Daphne asked.

"I'm fine. Just a little beat up, bloody, and bruised. Nothing to worry about," I said, echoing Logan's words.

Once they realized I was okay, they all looked at Logan, who shifted under the weight of their curious gazes. Everyone seemed surprised to see him—except Oliver.

Oliver saw me watching him and winced. I thought of all the times he'd been texting on his phone the past few days. I'd thought he'd been talking to Kenzie back at the academy, but now, I knew better.

I narrowed my eyes. "You were texting with Logan this whole time. That's why you were so certain he hadn't been captured by Reapers. You knew he was here."

A guilty flush crept up Oliver's neck, but he didn't say anything.

"Um, hello. Totally lost right now. Who is this guy?" Rory asked, jerking her thumb at Logan. "And why are you all looking at him like you've just seen a ghost?"

Logan winced, but he stared at her. "I'm Logan Quinn."

Rory's brow furrowed in confusion, but after a moment, her face brightened. "Oh. You're the guy who went all Reaper on Gwen and tried to kill her. Right?"

"Yeah," Logan muttered. "That's me."

Rory opened her mouth, but Daphne elbowed the other girl in the side and shot her a warning look. Rory glared at her and took a step forward, like she was going to shove Daphne, but Rachel stepped between them.

"That's enough," she said, her eyes darting around the ruins as if she expected more Reapers to appear at any second. "We need to get out of here—right now."

Oliver gestured at the Reapers' bodies. "But what about them? Don't you want us to check them? They might be able to give us a clue as to where Vivian and Agrona went."

Ajax shook his head. "There's no time. Vivian and Agrona could come back with reinforcements, not to mention the snow that's going to start coming down soon. We need to get off the mountain and back to the academy as quickly as possible. So let's move."

We all hurried to grab our backpacks and other gear from where they had fallen. Five minutes later, we walked out of the ruins, leaving nothing behind but dead Reapers, dead rocs, and a courtyard full of crushed, broken, blood-covered flowers.

Chapter 28

We headed toward the rope bridge at the edge of the ruins, weapons drawn, still keeping an eye out in case the Reapers had planned a second ambush. Despite the danger, I fell in step beside Logan at the back of the group.

He was carrying a curved, bloody sword that he'd gotten from one of the dead Reapers. Seeing him with the weapon made me think about how he'd stabbed me with a similar blade at the Aoide Auditorium, but I shoved the memory away. Logan was here now, and I had so many things I wanted to ask him—and so many things I wanted to tell him too.

"I think we can walk and talk at the same time," I said. "Don't you?"

For a moment, I thought he might rush on past me, but he finally sighed and nodded. The two of us walked a few feet behind the others.

"So," I said. "You're here."

"Yep. I'm here."

"You want to tell me about it?"

Logan sighed again. "Metis called my dad the night

that Nickamedes was poisoned and let us know what was going on. I couldn't sit around and do nothing, especially when Oliver told me you were coming out here to look for a cure—and that it was most likely a Reaper trap. So I got on one of the Protectorate's private planes and flew out here. I arrived a couple of hours before you guys did."

"And what did your dad think of that?"

Logan shrugged. "He didn't like it, but he let me come. Mainly because I told him that if he didn't, I'd go to the nearest airport and buy a ticket to fly out here on my own."

"So what? You've been following us this whole time?"

He nodded. "I was already at the train station when you guys showed up. I even had a seat in your car, but I got up and moved to another one before you could spot me. My dad arranged for me to room in one of the guest dorms at the academy and then for a car to take me up to the park entrance. There's another trail that runs parallel to the ones you guys used, so it was easy for me to follow you. I camped on the other side of the bridge last night, in case the Reapers decided to attack from that direction. I was packing up my gear to leave when I heard the rocs. So I raced across the bridge to come help you guys."

I thought of all the times over the past few days when it seemed like someone was watching me. "So you were at the train station, and it was you I saw in the stacks in the library. And you were watching me through the trees as we hiked up here yesterday."

"Guilty as charged."

I reached over and punched him in the shoulder. "Well, you scared the crap out of me. I thought you were some Reaper spy. Why would you do that? Why not let everyone know that you were here? And that you wanted to help? Why not let *me* know?"

Logan stared at me, a troubled, haunted look in his eyes. "Because I still don't trust myself. Especially not when it comes to you, Gypsy girl."

Guilt filled his face, and he dropped his gaze from mine. I'd been so focused on my own nightmares, on my own anger, on my own pain, that I hadn't stopped to think that Logan might have had the same kinds of feelings. That he might have spent the last few weeks reliving how Loki had infected his mind and forced him to attack me, just as I'd seen it dozens of times in my dreams.

"Didn't you get my letter?" I asked in a soft voice. "None of it was your fault. It was all Vivian and Agrona. There was nothing you could have done against them. And I flashed on the letter you sent me. I saw how hard you fought against Loki himself—how hard you fought to keep from hurting me."

Logan let out a bitter laugh. "But I *did* hurt you. Sure, I fought—I fought Loki with all my might, but in the end, it wasn't enough to keep me from stabbing you. I almost killed you. And who's to say I won't do that again? Maybe next time, you won't be able to use your touch magic to get through to me. Maybe next time, Daphne and Metis won't be there to heal you. Maybe next time, you'll just be *dead*."

His voice cracked on the last word. More than anything else, I wanted to hug him and tell him it was okay, that everything was going to be okay, but he'd just side-step me again before I could get too close to him. Even now, when we were walking, Logan made sure he was out of arm's—and sword's reach—of me.

"You won't attack me again," I protested. "You're free of Loki now. I saw that too. And I see it in your eyes now."

He gave me a grim smile. "Only because you used your psychometry on me. But you're not always going to be around. What if he comes back? What if I go all Reaper again? What if I hurt someone else? I can't take that chance—especially not with you."

His words broke my heart all over again, especially since I could see how much he was hurting. He could barely look at me, and even when he did, guilt twisted his features.

"So what happens now?" I asked, forcing out the words through the hard knot of emotion in my throat. "After we get down the mountain? Will you come back to Mythos with us?"

Logan shook his head. "I'll return to the academy to make sure Nickamedes is okay—but I'm not staying. After that, I'll go back to be with my dad."

"For how long?" I whispered.

He shrugged again. "I don't know. I just don't know. I'm sorry, Gwen. Really, I am."

Logan gave me a sad smile, then quickened his pace, leaving me alone at the back of the group. But I didn't mind too much. At least this way, no one saw my face pinch tight with pain or heard the sob that escaped my throat. Logan might be here, but he was still as far away and lost to me as ever, and I didn't know how to fix it— I didn't know how to fix *us*.

Now, I wondered if it was even possible—or if Logan and I were as crumbled and broken as the ruins around us.

We reached the rope bridge a few minutes later. My heart was still aching, but I kept my emotions in check. As Ajax had said, we were still in danger, and turning into a weeping, wailing mess wouldn't help.

Ajax held up his hand, and we stopped. The coach looked this way and that, just like the rest of us did, but there was no sign of Vivian, Agrona, or any other Reapers. Ajax took a few steps out onto the bridge, testing it, but it seemed as sturdy as when we'd first come up here. It looked like the Reapers had expected to kill us in the courtyard and hadn't bothered to sabotage the bridge.

"All right," Ajax said. "Let's get this over with. And keep your eyes open. There could still be more Reapers waiting on the other side to ambush us."

Ajax and Oliver crossed the bridge first. I held my breath, but they made it over to the other side safely, and no Reapers came rushing out of the forest to attack them.

Rory went next, prodding a dagger into Covington's back to get him to shuffle along in front of her. She'd used some of the climbing rope we'd brought along to tie his hands together. The evil librarian hadn't said a word as we'd been walking, although he kept giving us all murderous glares.

Rachel hurried after her niece, and Daphne and Carson followed them. Alexei hesitated, but I waved him on ahead.

"Logan and I will cross last," I said.

Alexei looked at me, then Logan. After a moment, he nodded and set off across the bridge. He made it to the other side without any problems.

"You first, Gypsy girl," Logan said.

I started to step onto the bridge—

Caw-caw-caw.

I froze.

Caw-caw-caw.

The roc's shrieks sounded once again, although for some reason, it seemed as if the cries were coming from the ground beneath my feet, rather than the clouds above. I moved away from the bridge, raised Vic, and turned this way and that, searching for the roc—and the Reapers that would be riding the creature.

A second later, instead of dropping down from the sky, a Black roc soared up out of the chasm below. The creature smashed right through the middle of the bridge, snapping the boards and ropes in two like they were made of nothing more substantial than brittle matchsticks and thin thread. The splintered debris seemed to hover in midair for a moment before it silently floated down into the canyon far, far below.

The Black roc swooped back down, with Vivian and Agrona on its back. I tightened my grip on Vic, expecting the creature to dive-bomb forward and attack me and Logan, but instead, the roc only hovered above the chasm.

"Good luck getting off the mountain now, Gwen!" Vivian yelled.

She slapped the reins against the creature's back, and

they zoomed off into the sky. A golden arrow followed them, shot by Daphne, but the wind sent it skittering sideways, and it sailed off into the ruins.

Stunned, all I could do was stare up into the clouds and then back down into the yawning chasm in front of me. Slowly, the reality of the situation broke through my surprise.

Now, only empty air lay between me, Logan, and the others—and the Spartan and I were trapped on the wrong side of the bridge.

Chapter 29

I stared in disbelief at the canyon. We'd gotten the ambrosia flower, learned that Covington was a traitor, and had survived being attacked by Vivian, Agrona, the other Reapers, and their rocs. I'd thought we were finally free and clear.

I really should have known better by now.

"Gwen!" Rachel shouted, the wind whipping her words over to me. "You'll have to take the other trail on the far side of the courtyard! It's the only way you can get off the mountain now!"

I remembered her talking about the trail before—the steep, winding trail that she hadn't gone down in years and that had probably been made impassable by falling rocks. Terrific. But Rachel was right—it was the only option we had.

"Where is it?" I shouted at her.

"Look at the map in your backpack! Go to the south side of the courtyard!" she yelled back. "It starts there! You can't miss it!"

"Get as far down the trail as you can!" Ajax yelled,

his voice booming across the open space. "We'll come up and get you as soon as we can!"

He didn't say it would take hours—if not longer. My friends would be lucky if they made it back to the academy by lunch. By the time they geared up for a rescue mission, dark would be approaching, and it would be too late to come searching for us without putting everyone in danger—which meant that Logan and I were most likely spending the night on the mountain.

Panic rose up in me, as cold and biting as the winter wind tearing through my hair, but I pushed it down. I couldn't afford to panic. Not now. Instead, I plastered a smile on my face and waved at my friends.

"See you at the bottom!" I yelled.

They all stared at me, their faces pinched with worry. But there was nothing they could do—there was nothing any of us could do. So I forced myself to turn away from them.

Instead, I looked at Logan. Fear and unease flickered in his blue eyes, and his face was twisted into a painful grimace. He held his hand against his side where the roc had injured him, as though the wound was bothering him more and more, although I couldn't see how bad it really was, given the heavy black snowsuit he wore.

"Please tell me you brought your supplies over to this side of the bridge."

He winced. "Sorry. I left all my gear behind when I came over to help you guys fight the Reapers."

That meant we only had what little food and water I had left in my backpack, along with my sleeping bag. But I didn't know how warm it would keep us tonight with no tent to help keep out the cold.

As if being separated from my friends and low on supplies wasn't bad enough, a few fat, fluffy flakes of snow started to drift down from the sky. The storm was here—and Logan and I were going to be stuck in the middle of it.

"We need to get moving," I said.

"I know." He hesitated, then handed me the sword he'd grabbed from one of the dead Reapers. "I want you to take this—and use it on me, if you have to."

I reached out and took the sword. I hefted it in my hand a moment, then turned and threw it into the chasm. Logan sucked in a surprised breath, but he didn't say anything. I faced him once more and slid Vic back into the scabbard on my waist.

"I trust you, Spartan. You're not going to hurt me. Not again."

No matter how many horrid nightmares I'd had. They weren't real. Logan was—*this* Logan. He was real, and he was what mattered.

"But what if I—"

I held up my hand, cutting him off. "I don't want to hear another word about it—not one more *word*. In case you haven't noticed, it's snowing. That means that big monster storm is almost here. We at least need to get down a little lower on the mountain and find some fire-wood and a place to camp for the night. Otherwise, we'll freeze to death. I'm more worried about that than I am about Loki suddenly popping into your head and you going all Reaper on me again. We can . . . talk about things later. After we're somewhere safe for the night. Okay?"

Logan stared at me, but, in the end, neither of us had a choice, and we both knew it.

Finally, he nodded, his face still grim. "Okay. Let's move."

I found the trail easily enough on the south side of the courtyard, right where Rachel had said it would be. Before we'd left the park, Rachel had given each of us a map of the mountain, the ruins, and the various trails, so I dug that out of my backpack and tried to make sense of all the squiggles, lines, and symbols.

"It looks like the trail down this side of the mountain is twice as long as the one coming up, just like Rachel said," I muttered. "Wonderful."

Logan didn't say anything. He was still being careful to stay at least five feet away from me at all times. I put the map back into my pack, grabbed my gloves out of it, and zipped it up. Then, I pulled my gloves on and started down the trail. After a moment, Logan fell into step behind me.

It was slow going, just like Rachel had said it would be. The trail was so steep and narrow that we had to be careful with every step we took or risk our feet going out from under us and starting a slide that would be hard to stop—if not impossible. It would be all too easy to slip right off the edge of the trail—and fall hundreds of feet to the rocks below.

For some reason, the wind was more intense on this side of the mountain, until it almost seemed like fingers constantly clawing at my jacket, scarf, toboggan, and gloves. I bundled up as best as I could, but nothing seemed to keep out the cold that crept into every corner of my clothes, boots, and even down into my socks.

And then there was the snow.

It picked up speed and intensity with every passing minute. We hadn't even been walking an hour, and there were already several inches on the ground. The only reason I could still see the trail was because it was the only part of the mountain that wasn't covered with trees.

Logan didn't talk, and neither did I. We didn't want to waste our breath or energy. Even as we picked our way down the steep slope, I scanned either side of the trail, trying to find someplace where we might find shelter from the snow for the night. Five feet to my left, the land dropped away in a sheer vertical drop, so no help there. Five feet to my right, a solid row of pine trees ran alongside the path, and I had no way of knowing how far we might have to go into the forest before we found a cave—or if we'd even find one. All I could see was snow, rocks, and trees. So we walked on.

We'd gone maybe two miles down the mountain when I realized Logan wasn't keeping up with me anymore. He had maintained his distance, but I couldn't even hear him shuffling along in the snow behind me. I turned around and realized he was about fifty feet behind me, staggering around like he was drunk. For the first time, I noticed his black snowsuit had a wet, almost shiny spot on it—right where the roc had stabbed him with its beak. A sick, sinking feeling filled my stomach as I worried he was hurt worse than he'd let on—a suspicion that was confirmed a moment later when I saw the blood dripping off the ends of his fingers and spattering onto the ground.

"Logan?"

"Sorry," he said, lumbering toward me, his face white with pain. "I don't think ... I can ... go ... any farther ..."

He crumpled to the snowy forest floor.

Chapter 30

"Logan!"

I raced over to the Spartan and dropped down on my knees beside him. He smiled up at me, but I only had eyes for his wound. I carefully lifted his hand and pushed aside the tattered edges of his snowsuit and his clothes underneath so I could get a look at his injury. The roc had left a deep, ugly gash in his left side—one that kept oozing blood.

"Why didn't you say anything?" I asked.

"I didn't want you to worry," he rasped. "I was going to get Daphne to heal it after we left the ruins."

Daphne wasn't here—but I was. I might not have her healing magic, but I'd picked up some first-aid skills at Mythos. That was another thing Coach Ajax drilled us on in gym class, along with weapons training. I slung my backpack off my shoulders, unzipped it, and rummaged through the items inside until I found two extra gray turtlenecks I'd brought along. I used Vic to slice up the turtlenecks and placed a couple of squares of fabric over the wound. Then, I wrapped the rest of the cloth all the way around Logan's waist and tied the whole thing together as tightly as I could. I tried not to notice how quickly the blood seeped through the fabric, even as I helped Logan put his clothes and snowsuit back in place.

"You need to leave me behind," he said in a soft voice.

I shook my head. "Don't even think about that. We stick together, remember? That's the best chance we have to get off this rock. That's our *only* chance. It always has been, and it always will be."

Logan gave me a crooked smile, the one that always turned my heart into a pile of mush. "I've missed this about you."

"What?"

"Your determination," he said. "I seem to have lost mine the second Agrona snapped that damn Apate collar around my neck."

He rubbed his throat, as though the gold band with its glittering jewels was still cinched tight there. Pain and memories darkened his eyes.

"Well, I've got enough determination for both of us," I said. "And I'm determined that we're both getting off this mountain—alive. You wouldn't want to make me a liar now, would you?"

Logan looked at me. After a moment, his face softened into a smile once more. "No, I wouldn't want to do that."

"All right then. Let's get you up. We still have a long way to go."

I managed to get him back up on his feet, although he was staggering even worse than before. But there was nothing I could do about that—there was nothing I could do about any of this but keep going forward.

So I put my arm under Logan's shoulder, helping him as much as I could, and together, we stumbled forward into the storm.

I managed to half-drag, half-carry Logan another mile down the trail before he passed out. One moment, he was hobbling along as best he could. The next, he was facedown in the snow.

"Logan? Logan!"

I turned him over and shook his shoulder, but he didn't respond. I bent down and put my ear over his mouth. His warm breath rasped against my skin, and his chest rose and fell with a steady rhythm.

I let out a quiet breath. He was still breathing, still alive.

But for how long? It was even colder now than it had been before, and the wind was howling like a pack of Fenrir wolves. Plus, I still hadn't seen anyplace where we could take shelter from the storm. I wanted to scream and cry and beat my fists against all the stupid rocks and trees around us. I would have, if I thought that my knuckles wouldn't crack and bleed and that the tears wouldn't have frozen on my face and added to my misery.

"Now what are you going to do?" a voice interrupted my thoughts. "Because the Spartan is pretty much done for."

I looked down at Vic, who was still snug in his scabbard around my waist. I'd been so focused on getting down the mountain that I'd pretty much forgotten about the sword, but he was peering at Logan, his purple eye bright against the white wash of snow.

I knew what Logan would say if he were still awake—that I should leave him behind. That there was no way he could get off the mountain now, and that I should save myself. But no matter what Logan said, I wasn't leaving him out here in the cold. He'd freeze to death—or bleed out from the roc wound. No, I needed to keep moving, and I needed to figure out some way to take him with me.

"Gwen?" Vic asked again. "You need to make a decision—fast."

"I'm going to save him—and us too."

I opened my backpack, digging through all of the items inside, hoping one of them would give me some sort of spark of an idea about how I could get us down the mountain.

Matches, extra clothes, a couple of comic books, my cell phone, a flashlight, a pack of granola, a bottle of water. Important items, but nothing that would help me right now. I was just about to zip the bag back up when I noticed something thin and fragile at the very bottom of it—Ran's net.

Desperate, I pulled out the net and held it up. Thin strands of gray seaweed woven together and tied off with a series of tiny, brittle knots. It looked even smaller and more pitiful than I remembered. I started to wad it up and shove it back into my bag when I thought about what the ID card in my bag said about the net—and what it claimed the artifact could do.

This net is thought to have belonged to Ran, the Norse goddess of storms, and was rumored to be among her favorite fishing gear. Despite its fragile appearance, the net is quite strong and can hold much more than it should be able to, given its relatively small size. The braided seaweed itself is thought to have the unusual property of making whatever is inside it seem much lighter than its actual weight...

I looked at the net, then at Logan—and I finally got the idea I needed so badly.

I closed my backpack and put it on my shoulders again. Then, I wrapped the net around Logan. At first, I didn't think there was going to be enough seaweed to cover him, but every time I reached down, there was more and more of the net to use. Finally, I looped the last bit of it around his shoulders. I propped him up into a sitting position, wrapped one arm around his waist, and put my shoulder under his. Then, I drew in a breath and lifted him. To my surprise, I was able to pick him up as if he weighed no more than a couple of dumbbells.

"Come on, Spartan," I said. "Back on your feet."

"Okay..." Logan mumbled, his eyes fluttering open before sliding shut again. "Okay, I'm up..."

Slowly, I started down the trail once more. Oh, it was still awkward, with Logan half-clinging, half-hanging off me and me trying to keep the net from slipping off his body, but he was much, much lighter than before. I could at least hobble down the mountain, even though I was moving much, much slower than before. Still, every step I took was one that got us closer to the bottom.

"Thank you, Ran," I murmured, although I doubted the goddess was even listening to or interested in my troubles.

I don't know how long I guided Logan down the trail. It might have been five minutes, it might have been an hour. Time ceased to have any meaning. There was just cold and snow and wind and trees. More than once, my boots slipped in the snow, and I almost sent both of us sliding down the trail, but I managed to stop myself before my feet went out from under me.

I'd just kept myself from dumping us in the snow for the fifth time when I realized there was something on the trail ahead of me.

I froze, Logan hanging off my side like some sort of weird, extra limb, and squinted through the flakes. What was that shape up ahead? For a moment, I thought it might be a Reaper, someone who'd been stationed on the back side of the mountain to finish us off if we made it this far down the trail, but the shape didn't seem dark and slender enough for that. It looked . . . big. That was all I could really tell about it. Maybe a boulder had fallen across the path, like Rachel had said. Well, wouldn't that just be terrific.

I sighed, tightened my grip on Logan and the net, and surged forward once more. Maybe it would just be a tree or rock that I could find some way to get over or around.

I'd almost reached the shape—whatever it was—when a sharp, fierce screech cut through the swirl of snow.

I froze again. I'd lowered my head against the cold,

looking down at the trail, so I had a perfect view of the lion's paw right in front of me. It was easily larger than my hand and featured long, sharp, curved claws that glittered like ebony against the white snow.

I swallowed and slowly raised my head.

A gryphon stood in the middle of the trail, looming over me and Logan.

Chapter 31

I stared up at the huge creature.

Lion's body, eagle head, bronze fur, wings, and eyes. The creature looked even larger than the Black roc that Vivian and Agrona had flown away on, probably a male, from the size of him. I stared down at his claws again, before my gaze drifted up to his curved beak. It too glinted like ebony, despite the snow.

Finally, I raised my gaze to the creature's eyes. They glowed like bright, warm, bronze lanterns in the midst of the swirling snow. I stared into the orbs, but I didn't see any trace of Reaper red in the creature's eyes. So this was a wild gryphon then, and not one the Reapers had caught and forced to serve them. I didn't know if that made things better or worse. Because a wild gryphon could kill me and Logan as easily as a Reaper-controlled one could. Claws were still claws, after all.

"Crikey," Vic said from his scabbard. "He's a big fellow, isn't he?"

"Sshh," I said, talking out of the side of my mouth. "Don't make him angry."

The gryphon stood in the middle of the trail, staring

at me. Just . . . staring at me, as though I were some sort of bug he was examining. After a few more seconds of scrutiny, the gryphon's gaze flicked to Logan. The creature studied the Spartan with the same intensity before his eyes dropped down to Logan's side. He could probably smell the blood that was no doubt still seeping through the bandages I'd wrapped around the Spartan.

I tensed, then turned my body so that I was standing between the gryphon and Logan. I thought about pulling Vic out of his scabbard, but I'd have to let go of Logan to do that, and I didn't want to drop him in the snow, not when he was so badly injured already. But I'd go for the sword if I had to. Because whatever happened, the gryphon was not going to hurt Logan.

At least, not until he had eaten me first.

Seconds ticked by and turned into minutes. The silence stretched on and on, and, still, the gryphon didn't move. Finally, I drew in a breath. Because I still had Logan to think about, and we were both growing weaker and colder with every passing second.

I drew another breath and took a step to my right.

The gryphon didn't move. The creature could have been one of the statues outside the Library of Antiquities for all the emotion he showed. So I took another step to my right. Then another, then another, until I was no longer directly in front of the gryphon.

And then, I started to walk forward.

The trail wasn't all that wide, and the creature's wings brushed against my snowsuit as I stepped past it. The gryphon turned his head, watching me, but I kept walking. I'd never wanted to just run, run, run as badly as I did in that moment, but I forced myself to keep my panic down and put one foot in front of the other. Slowly, carefully, cautiously, and mindful of the mythological creature at my back the whole time.

"What are you doing?" Vic said.

"What I have to," I said. "Now shut up. Maybe he likes to eat things that make unnecessary noise."

"Unnecessary noise? Unnecessary noise? Hmph!" Vic sniffed.

But thankfully, the sword didn't say anything else.

I kept walking, my shoulders tense. At any second, I expected to feel the gryphon's claws sinking into my back or his beak tearing into my neck. But nothing happened. Maybe the creature had lost interest in us. I hoped so. I'd gone about fifty feet down the trail when I felt safe enough to look behind me.

Once again, I found myself staring into the gryphon's eyes.

The creature was about five feet behind me, his head stuck out and down as he peered at me. Despite his size, I hadn't heard the gryphon move through the snow. Once again, curiosity glimmered in his gaze, and I realized I wasn't a bug he was staring at—I was a mouse.

A tiny, tiny, little mouse—one that could be eaten at any second.

I swallowed down a hard knot of fear, along with a scream that was stuck in my throat, turned my head, and started forward once more. Every fifty feet or so, I stopped to look back, but the gryphon was always right there—following me.

Seriously, the creature was trotting along the trail behind me like Nyx running after me across the quad.

Okay, that was creepy. But since the gryphon wasn't attacking us, I slogged on.

Logan drifted in and out of consciousness as I hauled him down the mountain. Occasionally, he would mumble a few words, but I was so focused on following the trail that I didn't pay any attention to what he was saying, although every once in a while, he called out my name.

"Gypsy girl..." he mumbled. "Can't fight it...can't fight him...run, Gwen...run!"

Logan thrashed against me, lost in his memories of our fight and the moment when he'd stabbed me. I wasn't the only one with some serious nightmares. But there was nothing I could do for him, so I gritted my teeth, pretended I couldn't hear his anguished cries, and trudged on.

I don't know how much farther I'd gone before I noticed the baby gryphon.

For the longest time, the trail ahead was a mix of snow and wind. Then, I glanced up, and the baby gryphon was there, like he'd just popped out of the trees. I slowed, then stopped, wondering if this was what the adult gryphon had been waiting for. If the creature had been following me and Logan this whole time because he knew that his baby was waiting and this would make it easier for both of the creatures to tear into us at once. I was so cold and exhausted that it took me a moment to realize why that would be a Bad, Bad Thing. Getting eaten by gryphons? So not cool.

Once more, I stopped and waited to see what the creatures would do.

The little gryphon crept closer to me. The baby eyed

me the same way the adult had. Finally, after what seemed like forever, the baby let out a sharp, squeaky cry.

The adult gryphon screeched back some sort of response. Before I even realized what had happened, the adult gryphon had lunged forward, hooked his beak through Ran's net, and pulled Logan away from me. One moment, I had my arm around the Spartan's waist. The next, the entire net was dangling from the gryphon's beak, with Logan swinging back and forth like he was relaxing in a summer hammock.

The gryphon gave me a long, almost pointed look, then darted off the trail and into the trees.

I was so stunned that I stood there for a moment. Then, the reality of the situation hit me.

"Hey!" I shouted. "Come back here with him!"

But the gryphon ignored me and moved deeper into the forest, taking Logan with him. I drew Vic out of my scabbard and plunged into the trees after them.

I'd thought the gryphon might spread his wings wide and soar up into the sky, but instead, the creature loped through the forest at a slow, steady pace, like a lion running through the plains of Africa, despite the fallen trees, rocks, and other obstacles that littered the forest floor. I followed as fast as I could, not caring that my boots slipped in the snow with every step and that I was in danger of falling and breaking a leg. All I could think about was Logan and how I couldn't let him get eaten by the gryphons.

Apparently, the baby gryphon thought this was some sort of game because the creature hopped through the snow right beside me, occasionally letting out little screeches of excitement. Well, I was glad someone was having a good time because I certainly wasn't.

I don't know how far back into the trees we'd gone when the adult gryphon finally stopped. The creature stared at me another second before plunging into a dark opening that led into some sort of cave. The baby gryphon let out another happy screech and followed the older creature into the darkness.

I sucked down a breath and raced after them. Yeah, maybe running blindly into a cave wasn't the smartest thing to do, but I couldn't leave Logan to the gryphons' mercy—or lack thereof.

So I ran forward and found myself in an enormous cavern. The walls were made out of some shiny, reflective, phosphorescent rock that gave the interior a soft, golden glow, almost as if there were lanterns flickering in the stone. The ceiling rose a hundred feet above my head, while piles of pine needles and dried summer grasses lined the floor inside, stretching from one side to the other like the flowers in the courtyard ruins. It was also surprisingly warm in the cavern—much warmer than it should have been—and I sighed in relief as the higher temperature chased away the chill that had sunk into my bones.

Too bad the gryphons were waiting for me.

There must have been a dozen of the creatures in the cavern, and before I realized what they were doing, they all crowded around me, forming an unbreakable ring and cutting me off from the exit. My steps slowed, then stopped, and I looked from one creature to the next, expecting them to leap forward and tear into me, the crazy

Gypsy girl who'd been stupid enough to run right into the middle of their nest.

"Um, Gwen?" Vic asked. "You know how not good this is, right?"

"You just better hope they don't like to eat shiny things too," I muttered.

But instead of chomping down on me, the baby gryphon skipped over and put his head against the back of my leg, nudging me forward. I swallowed again, but all I could do was go where he wanted me to.

The baby kept pushing at me until I was near the back of the cavern. The adult gryphon who had grabbed Logan was there, standing next to a series of shallow pools. The surface of the water gleamed like a coin under the golden glow from the rocks, adding to the airy, enchanted feel of the cavern.

The gryphon had laid Logan down next to one of the pools of water. A bit of steam rose from the surface, and I cautiously stepped forward, pulled off my glove, leaned down, and dipped my hand into it. To my surprise, the water was warm, and I realized that the cavern must house some sort of natural hot springs—and that maybe the gryphons didn't plan on eating us after all.

"You didn't bring us here to hurt us, did you?" I asked the adult gryphon as I straightened back up. "You brought us here to keep us warm ... to save us from freezing to death in the storm."

The gryphon nodded, agreeing with my words. I hesitated, then slid Vic back into his scabbard, pulled off my other glove, and slid them both into a pocket on my snowsuit. Slowly, I walked toward the gryphon and stretched out my bare hand. The creature watched me approach with solemn eyes, as if he knew exactly what I was going to do. I drew in a breath, reached out, and gingerly touched his wing.

Images and feelings flooded my mind. I felt the gryphon's strength, his pride, his love of sailing through the clouds. The gryphon had been flying high when he had heard his baby wail. The creature had swooped down into the trees to see me and my friends helping. A wave of intense gratitude washed over me, that I'd helped save his baby from being turned into a Reaper slave.

There were other images too, of the gryphons hiding in the ruins, watching my friends and me fight against the Reapers. So it was they I'd sensed peering at me. I felt the creature's burning hatred of the Reapers and his sadness at how the Reapers forced the Black rocs to do their bidding. And finally, I saw the gryphon watching me help Logan through the forest and his admiration for how I kept going, even though he knew we wouldn't make it through the night without finding some sort of shelter.

I opened my eyes, dropped my hand, and looked at him. "Thank you," I whispered. "For bringing us here. For saving us. You didn't have to do that."

The gryphon stared at me, and I felt a wave of pride wash off him—that yes, he did have to bring us here. That he'd felt honor-bound to help us just as we'd helped his baby.

I carefully ran my fingers across the gryphon's wings. The creature let out a little snort, but I could tell he liked it. The baby nudged his head against my legs again, and I dropped down to my knees and petted him too. Then I turned my attention to Logan, who hadn't stirred the whole time we'd been in the cavern.

The gryphons gathered around and watched while I unwrapped Ran's net from Logan and carefully placed it to the side. He didn't come to, not even when I unzipped his snowsuit and pulled his clothes up so that I could check his wound. Blood had seeped through the crude bandage I'd wrapped around it, and I slowly untied the cloth and peeled it away. Thankfully, the wound had finally clotted, and Logan wasn't bleeding anymore. I didn't know how much more blood he could afford to lose.

I used Vic to slice up the last of my extra clothes, then went over and dipped the cloth into the hot springs. I'd expected the water to have a sour, sulfur stench, but instead it smelled light and floral, with a fresh, clean, almost vanilla scent. I used the cloth to wipe the dried blood off Logan's wound. The roc had left a nasty gash in his side, and he probably needed stitches, but that wasn't something I could do. It didn't look like the wound was infected, though. Maybe Logan would be a little stronger in the morning—or at least well enough to walk the rest of the way down the mountain.

I used the last of my cut-up clothes to bandage his wound again, then covered him back up with his other clothes and made sure he was comfortable on the bed of needles and grasses. I also pulled my sleeping bag out of my backpack and covered him with it. Logan slept through the whole thing. I stroked his black hair back from his forehead, then leaned down and kissed him on the cheek. Logan sighed, but he didn't wake up.

I unbuckled the scabbard from my waist and propped

Vic against one of the rock walls so he could see out into the cavern and keep watch. Just because I was surrounded by gryphons didn't mean Vivian and Agrona couldn't show up with more Reapers and rocs.

"Get some sleep, Gwen," Vic said, realizing how exhausted I was. "I'll stand guard tonight, just in case one of these oversized fuzzballs decides to make a move."

The gryphon leader snorted at that, but one by one, the creatures all settled down around me, the combined warmth of their bodies adding to the steam rising up from the hot springs.

There was nothing else to do but wait for the storm to pass and morning to come. So I lay down and drifted off to sleep, with the gryphons cocooning me.

Chapter 32

I fell into a dark, dreamless sleep and woke up some-time later.

At least, I thought I was awake—until I realized I was standing in the middle of the cavern staring down at my sleeping body lying next to Logan's. I blinked and blinked, but the image remained the same. I turned around and around, but all of the gryphons were sleep-ing, as well, and I was the only one who seemed to be awake—or whatever this was. It didn't feel like another nightmare, though. It felt . . . *real.*

"Crikey," I muttered, echoing Vic's earlier sentiment.

I glanced around the cavern, but everything was the same as before. Gryphons arranged in a circle around me, the pools of water giving off heat, the walls glowing with those strange golden rocks. Finally, I looked to-ward the mouth of the cavern. For a moment, all I saw was a solid sheet of white as the snow continued to pour down outside. But then the flakes parted, as though the wind were whipping them back like curtains, and a fig-ure appeared outside the cavern.

Her long, white dress was the same shade as the snow swirling around her, although the curled ringlets of her hair glimmered with a polished, bronze sheen. Wings arched up over her back. They too were the same white as the snow, but the soft feathers didn't ruffle, despite the fierce wind. She stood there, her hands clasped together, like she was patiently waiting for me to notice her. Her eyes met mine, and, once again, I was struck by what an unusual, vivid color they were—all the different hues of purple and gray mixed together to create one vibrant, twilight shade.

Nike, the Greek goddess of victory, stared at me for a second longer, then turned and walked out of sight of the entrance. Well, if the goddess wasn't going to come in here, I supposed that I would have to go out there to her.

I tiptoed through the sleeping gryphons, even though I probably didn't have to. Since, you know, I was in this weird sort of a world, and they weren't. At least, I didn't think they were, since I was awake and they weren't. Or I was dreaming, and they weren't. Or whatever exactly it was that I was doing that they weren't. I shook my head and pushed the thoughts away. Thinking about how real or not this dreamlike world was always gave me a headache.

I reached the entrance. To my surprise, the snow had stopped falling, although more than a foot of the white powder covered the ground like fluffy frosting on a cake. I stepped outside and realized I didn't feel cold, despite the fact that I'd left the warmth of the cavern and the gryphons' bodies behind.

I noticed a movement out of the corner of my eye and

turned in that direction. The goddess was perched on a wide, flat rock several feet away. Her face creased into a smile.

"Hello, Gwendolyn," Nike said.

I looked around at the snow, the rocks, and the pines that towered above us. Everything looked exactly the same as I remembered from when I'd first gone into the cavern. I don't know how much time had passed, but it must have been close to dawn, because the streaks of silver and lavender in the sky were slowly giving way to a pale orange sunrise.

"Hi," I finally replied to Nike. "So we're doing that weird dream thing again, huh?"

The goddess kept smiling at me. "If that's how you wish to think of it."

"If I try to think of it any other way, I'm pretty sure my head will explode."

She laughed, the sound washing over me like the high, lilting melody of wind chimes tinkling in the breeze. She patted the rock, and I walked over and plopped down next to her. We sat there in silence for several moments.

"So," I asked. "Does this mean that Logan and I are going to get off the mountain alive?"

"Why would you think otherwise?"

I shrugged. "Well, it was a little touch and go there for a while. What with all the snow, Logan being injured, me trying to get us both down the mountain. It hasn't exactly been a fun trip."

"No, I suppose it hasn't," Nike murmured. "But you did what you needed to do."

"What do you mean by that?"

But the goddess didn't answer me. Instead, she got to her feet. "Come," she said. "Let us walk."

Mystified, I got to my feet and followed her deeper into the forest. Nike seemed to glide over the snow, as if she were a cloud drifting along, and I noticed she didn't leave any footprints behind in the dense powder. I turned around and realized I wasn't leaving any indentations in the snow either. In fact, I couldn't even feel the wet weight of it pressing against my legs. Creepy. I shivered and hurried to catch up with her.

Nike stopped at the edge of a large clearing, and I crept up beside her. Snow was piled all around us, the drifts two and even three feet deep in places, but inside the clearing, wildflowers had somehow bloomed, their green stems sticking up through the powder, and their blue, pink, purple, red, and silver petals glistening like jewels that had been spilled across a white marble floor.

A woman stood in the middle of the clearing. Her long, velvet gown was the same rich green as the pines, although the edges of the fabric seemed to shimmer with all sorts of opalescent colors—pinks, blues, purples, reds, silvers, golds. She wasn't beautiful, not like I considered Nike to be, but her face was kind and gentle, although her lips were turned down with a hint of sadness. Her black hair was short, with ends that curled under. Her skin was as pale as snow, which made her eyes seem that much greener. Something about her features seemed familiar, as though I'd seen her before, although I couldn't quite place when or where.

As I watched, the woman moved through the clearing. She didn't have on any shoes, but the snow didn't appear to bother her, and she didn't leave any footprints in her wake. Her head was bent, and she was speaking softly, as if she was talking to the carpet of wildflowers that surrounded her. I couldn't make out her words, but the flowers seemed to respond to her voice, their stems turning and their bright petals arching toward her, as if they were trying to show off their best sides just to please her.

"Who's that?" I whispered.

"That," Nike replied, "is Eir."

So that was why her face looked so familiar. I'd seen it in the carvings and statues at the ruins.

"That's the Norse goddess of healing?"

Nike nodded. "Eir is one of my oldest, dearest friends—and strongest allies."

We watched Eir move among the wildflowers. Suddenly, a shadow darted across the snow, and a gryphon dropped down from the sky—the same gryphon who had saved me and Logan from the snowstorm. I wasn't quite sure how I knew that, but I did.

The gryphon bowed low to Eir, then gently tugged some wildflowers free from the snow and presented them to her, just like in the carving I'd seen at the ruins—the one where the ambrosia flowers had been. Eir smiled and returned the creature's bow before carefully taking the flowers from his beak. She brought them up to her face and inhaled deeply. Perhaps it was my imagination, but I almost thought I could smell the same thing she did—the sweet scents of the flowers mixing with the cold crispness of the snow.

Eir whispered something to the gryphon, and he soared back up into the air, darted toward a nearby tree, and grabbed something out of the top of it. He landed in the clearing again a moment later. Eir bent down and plucked a green plant from his beak—something that looked like a clump of mistletoe. After a moment, she turned. Her green eyes met mine, and I was again struck by the kindness in her face. She radiated the emotion the same way Nike exuded victorious power. Eir started walking toward us, while the gryphon padded along at her side.

"There are few things Eir loves more than her wild-flowers," Nike said. "But her gryphons are one of them."

"So they're Eir gryphons then?" I asked. "Like Fenrir wolves and Nemean prowlers and Maat asps?"

Nike nodded. "Exactly like that, although few mortals remember the gryphons' proper name anymore, just like they've forgotten Eir is the goddess of mercy, as well as healing. But Eir has always had a fond place in her heart for the creatures. That's one of the reasons she built her home here on the mountaintop—so they could make their nests nearby and she could watch over them."

"Why are you telling me all of this?"

Nike smiled. "You'll see."

Eir and the gryphon stopped in front of us. The goddess tilted her head to the side, her green eyes boring into my violet ones as if she could see all the secrets of my soul just by looking at me. Maybe she could. I straightened up to keep from shivering under her intense scrutiny.

"I see it now," she said, her voice as soft as a breeze rustling through the wildflowers. "Why you have such faith in her. She is strong-willed. Young, but very strong."

Nike's smile widened, and, for a moment, I felt like a puppy the two of them were oohing and aahing over in some pet store window. Like I'd just done some sort of trick to win their approval, although I had no idea what it might be.

Eir kept staring at me, as if she expected me to say something.

"Um . . . thanks," I said. "Thank you, goddess. That's a very nice compliment."

"It was not a compliment, merely a statement of fact." She once again tilted her head to the side. "Sometimes, I think I will never truly understand mortals. They are so strange in their sentiments."

The gryphon screeched his agreement, and I wondered what I'd said that was so wrong. But the goddess seemed thoughtful instead of upset, so I supposed I hadn't put my foot into my mouth too badly.

"You were merciful to one of my gryphons," Eir said. "One of the few mortals who has been so in a very, very long time. For that, I have a gift for you."

She took the wildflowers and the clump of mistletoe she was still holding and began to twist them, as if she was going to make a daisy chain with the green stems and colorful petals. A bright silver light flared, leaking out from between her fingers, almost as if the flowers were some sort of metal the goddess was working with. The light was so intense that it hurt my eyes, but I didn't dare look away.

"There," Eir said, a few moments later. "It is done."

Something *clinked*, and I felt a small weight on my arm. I looked down and realized a thin silver bracelet had appeared on my right wrist. The chain itself was made out of strands of mistletoe, with several small petals dangling off it. All put together, it reminded me of a charm bracelet that Carson had given Daphne awhile back.

The bracelet was touching my bare skin, and I waited for my psychometry to kick in—but it didn't. In fact, I didn't get any big flashes off the bracelet—just the same sort of calm, kind vibe that I got from Eir herself.

Curious, I held up one of the petals. It was small, silver, and more like a leaf than a true flower, but I recognized the shape of it. My eyes flicked up. The heart-shaped leaves exactly matched the ones in the wreath on top of Nike's head. Laurels—the symbol for victory.

"The laurel is a curious plant," Eir said. "And silver laurels are exceedingly rare. I'm the only one who grows them anymore, but even that has been all but forgotten—along with their properties. Mistletoe is also quite powerful, although all that mortals seem to use it for these days is kissing."

She made a face, as though she didn't like the idea, then paused.

"And . . . what are their properties?" I asked, since it seemed as if she wanted me to say something.

"Silver laurels can be used to heal even the most grievous wounds," Eir said. "Or they can be used to kill the mightiest foe. In some cases, silver laurels can even destroy the gods themselves."

My breath caught in my throat, and my fingers curled

so tightly around the leaf that the metal edges pricked my skin. Was she saying—did she mean—could I possibly *kill* Loki with the laurels?

When Nike had shown me the artifacts in the fresco on the ceiling of the Library of Antiquities, I'd thought that I'd been holding a silver arrow or spear, some weapon that would help me defeat the evil god. But what if what I'd seen was the bracelet? What if it was at least part of the answer? I glanced at Nike, and the goddess nodded, as if she knew what I was thinking. She probably did. She always seemed to.

"The other interesting thing about silver laurels is that whether they heal or destroy depends entirely upon the will and intent of the user," Eir said. "So wield them with care, Gwendolyn Cassandra Frost. Because your choices will affect us all."

Her green eyes bored into mine, and she held out her hand to me, as if she wanted to say good-bye. I hesitated, then brushed my fingers against hers. For a moment, her power washed over me, and I felt her wonderful kindness toward all creatures great and small, her love for her gryphons, her delight when mortals used her wildflowers to heal the sick and injured.

And I also felt her utter ruthlessness.

Like victory, mercy could be a great and terrible thing. Giving mercy, accepting it, rejecting it, withholding it—all of those things had a price someone had to pay. And I realized that in her own way, Eir was just as cold, terrible, beautiful, and powerful as Nike was—as all of the gods and goddesses were, including Loki.

Then, Eir's fingers slipped away from mine, and the

feelings vanished, although I still got that same calm, kind vibe from the bracelet around my wrist. I stared at the metal leaves and vine-like chain. I wondered if Eir had given Nike the crown of laurels that the goddess of victory wore—and I wondered what I was supposed to do with the ones I now had. How could such simple-looking leaves heal anyone? Or possibly kill a god? How was I supposed to use them? Were they the key to destroying Loki and ending the Chaos War? Or did they have some other purpose? And what was the mistletoe for, if anything?

Those questions and a dozen more burned on the tip of my tongue, but Eir had already returned to the center of the clearing, with the gryphon walking by her side. The goddess bent her head again, and the wildflowers strained toward her once more. A smile curved Eir's face as she started murmuring to them and the gryphon.

"Come," Nike said. "She has given you the only gift she can. Let us leave Eir in peace, as she has asked of me."

We walked back through the woods until we reached the cavern. Instead of going back inside, I stared at the bracelet, then at Nike.

"You're always playing some sort of game, aren't you?" I couldn't hide the bitterness in my voice.

"What do you mean?"

I threw my hands wide. "I mean—this. All of this. Me. My friends. Coming here. The Reapers poisoning Nickamedes. You planned it all, didn't you? So I would come here, and Eir would give me the laurels and mistletoe."

She shook her head. "I did not plan anything, Gwendolyn. The Spartan librarian being poisoned was what was always going to happen. You and your friends made your own choices, and you used your own free will, just the way you always do."

I didn't understand how some things could seemingly be predetermined, while my friends and I still had free will about others. Trying to puzzle it out made my head hurt, like always. Still, I kept staring at the goddess. There was more to all of this than she was telling me, and I let her see the questions and suspicions in my eyes.

After a moment, she nodded her head.

"I admit that I had . . . hopes you would prove yourself to Eir, that you would show her the goodness in your heart," Nike said. "She had been . . . undecided about getting involved in the Pantheon's fight against Loki. But you convinced her to give us a weapon that we needed, that *you* needed."

I stared down at the silver laurels once more. "A weapon? So is this how I'm supposed to kill Loki then? With these? I thought I had to find a spear or something—that mysterious shadowy thing that's on the fresco on the ceiling of the Library of Antiquities that you showed me."

Nike shook her head. "You know I cannot tell you that, Gwendolyn. I can only give you the tools you need to fight Loki and his Reapers. How you use them is up to you."

"Of course you can't," I sniped. "Because that would just be too freaking easy. Because that would just make too much *sense*."

She kept staring at me.

"Call it whatever you want," I finally muttered. "It just sounds like gods and their games to me."

"War is nothing *but* a game, Gwendolyn," she replied. "One with a winner—and a loser."

I didn't tell her I was tired of being part of her games—and most especially the Reapers' tricks. If Nike didn't know that by now, well, she wasn't as smart as she seemed to be—or as powerful. But there was nothing I could do but tuck the bracelet under the sleeve of my snowsuit. I would have to add it to my list of things to research. Sometimes I thought I spent more time in the library looking through books these days than Nickamedes did. My heart twinged at the thought of him. I wondered how he was doing—and whether he was even still alive.

"I know you are upset with me, Gwendolyn," Nike said. "But it is not easy, trying to win a war, especially against an enemy as foul as Loki."

I sighed. "I know. I just hate that I'm caught in the middle of it all. I never wanted this, you know?"

"I know," she replied. "I never wanted it for you either. But it is what must be done."

I frowned, wondering what she meant, but the goddess leaned forward and kissed me on the cheek, the way she always did whenever our time together was coming to an end. It was a brief touch, just a whisper of her lips against my skin, but once again, the cold, fierce waves of her power washed over me, giving me the strength I needed to continue. And this time, the cold didn't seem to vanish—instead, I felt it seep into the silver laurel bracelet, until it felt as if a string of snowflakes was encircling my wrist. But the sensation wasn't unpleasant. If anything, it was a reminder of the goddess—and her faith in me.

Nike straightened up and stepped back, and the snow began to swirl around her once more. "Be well, Gwendolyn."

She bowed her head and clasped her hands together once more. She stood in front of me for a moment longer. Then, she was gone, swallowed up by the snow, as if she'd never even been there to start with.

Chapter 33

I woke with a start.

One second, I was outside by myself in the snow. The next, I was in the middle of the gryphons' cavern. I sat up, yawned, and rubbed the crusty sleep out of the corners of my eyes. I glanced to my left to see that Logan was sitting up and staring at me.

"You're awake," I said in a soft voice so I wouldn't disturb the still-sleeping gryphons.

He gave me a wan smile. "You didn't think I'd miss the rest of our trip, did you, Gypsy girl?"

I snorted. "Oh no. Why should I get to have all the fun?"

He laughed, then gestured at the creatures that were sprawled around us. "You, um, want to tell me how we wound up here? And why we're both not a pile of bones yet?"

I told him how Daphne, Rory, and I had helped the baby gryphon on our way up the mountain and how the creatures had returned the favor by saving us from the storm.

When I finished, Logan nodded, but then his face turned serious. "Well, gryphons or not, I want to thank you—for taking care of me. I know it would have been easier if you'd left me behind on the trail."

"I couldn't leave you behind. I would never do that."

His mouth flattened out. "Maybe you should have."

I stared at him. Ink-black hair, ice-blue eyes, muscled body. On the outside, Logan looked the same as always, but I could see the difference in him—in the droop of his shoulders, in the shadows that haunted his eyes, and most especially in his smile. It wasn't the fun, confident, teasing grin I remembered. No, now his smile just seemed . . . sad. The same sort of sad smile that Rory's parents had had in their photos—and my dad in his. I was so *sick* of seeing those sad, defeated smiles.

I knew Logan was hurting, but I was too. Maybe it was my frustrating conversation with Nike, maybe it was all the nightmares, or maybe it was simply everything that had happened over the past few weeks, but once again, that mix of hurt and anger bubbled up inside me—and this time the anger won.

"Oh, quit feeling sorry for yourself."

Logan blinked. "Excuse me?"

"You heard me," I said, my voice growing harsh. "Quit feeling sorry for yourself. Yeah, something horrible happened to you, and the Reapers tried to turn you into Loki's little soul puppet. But you know what, Spartan? Horrible things have happened to all of us now—and more terrible things are in store. So suck it up and get back in the fight."

"I don't understand," Logan said, his eyebrows

drawing together in confusion. "I thought you weren't mad at me."

I let out a breath. "I'm not mad at you because you attacked me. I'm mad at you because you're giving up—because you're *quitting*. I thought Spartans never quit."

Logan sighed. "But you don't understand. I could be a danger to you and the others. Loki ... I could still be connected to him. I don't want to risk hurting you again."

I couldn't stop the tears from filling my eyes or the words from tumbling off my lips. "You've already hurt me. You broke my heart by leaving, by going back on your promise to me. You said you'd always be there for me, fighting right by my side against the Reapers, and you left—you just *left*. Without even giving me a chance to say good-bye, or to tell you that I understood."

"I was afraid you'd try to convince me to stay," he whispered. "And that I'd let you."

"I know," I whispered back. "I know that you just wanted to get away after what Agrona and the Reapers did to you, but it hurt all the same. It still hurts, knowing that you'll be leaving again the second we get back to the academy and Nickamedes is okay."

Logan didn't say anything. I got to my feet and turned away so he wouldn't see me brushing the tears from my eyes. I'd just finished wiping the last of them away when I realized I could see daylight through the cavern entrance—real daylight and not the twilight world I'd been in with Nike and Eir.

I drew in a breath, lifted my chin, and faced Logan once more. Because no matter how much I would have liked to find someplace to curl up into a ball and cry, we still had to hike the rest of the way down the mountain so we could get the ambrosia flower to Nickamedes in time.

"It's light outside," I said in a dull tone. "We should get moving. Ajax and the others will probably come searching for us soon."

Logan nodded. We didn't look at each other as we got ready to leave.

I packed up my sleeping bag, grabbed my backpack from the bed of needles and grasses, and hoisted it onto my shoulders. I also walked over to the wall where I'd propped up Vic last night. The sword let out a wide, jaw-cracking yawn, then regarded me with a sleepy purple eye.

"Good," he said. "You're up. That means I can finally get some sleep. Don't wake me unless there is something to kill."

Before I could even say anything, he'd snapped his eye shut. Less than a minute later, he started snoring and talking in his sleep.

"Bloody Reapers..." he mumbled. "Going to kill them all..."

Vic didn't stir as I picked him up and belted the scabbard around my waist.

With that task complete, there was nothing left to do but to finally turn and face Logan again. He had gotten to his feet, although he was a bit wobbly. He clutched at his side, but he seemed to be a little stronger than the day before. I took a sip of water from the bottle I'd been carrying in my backpack, then gave him the rest. He downed it in one gulp. I also offered him the last packet of granola that I had, but he shook his head, telling me he didn't want it. Neither did I, so I stuffed it into one of my pockets.

"Can you walk?" I asked. "Do you want me to check your wound again?"

He shook his head. "I can make it, with your help. I think we should leave the bandage alone. Otherwise, the wound might start bleeding again."

I nodded, stepped forward, and slid my arm under his shoulder. We fell silent, although he leaned on me as we slowly headed outside.

When Logan and I stepped out of the cavern, the cold was like a slap in the face, and the bitter chill instantly seeped through all my layers of clothes.

But the worst part was the snow.

More than a foot of the white stuff had fallen overnight—a thick, heavy, wet snow that would be difficult to walk through even if Logan wasn't injured. Not to mention the fact that we were deep in the forest, and I didn't have a clue as to where the trail was—or how to find it.

"Where's the trail from here?" Logan asked, voicing my thoughts.

"I have no idea. Maybe the gryphons can take us back to it."

Our movements in the cavern had woken the gryphons, and they'd followed us outside, screeching, yawning, and stretching, shaking off the last of their sleep as Logan and I had. I helped Logan lean against the side of the cavern while I went in search of the leader. He was standing outside with the others, with the baby snuggled by his side.

I looked at the adult gryphon, wondering if he'd really been with Eir in the clearing earlier, but I had no way of knowing.

I cleared my throat. "Um, so I was wondering how my friend and I can get back to the trail? You know, so we can walk the rest of the way down the mountain?"

The gryphon cocked his head to the side, as if he didn't understand what I was asking. I pumped my arms up and down by my sides and marched in place, trying to show him what I wanted. The gryphon stared at me a moment longer, then dropped down onto his belly in the snow. He screeched, spread his wings wide, and then waggled them at me before making a little hopping motion, like he was about to take off into the air. He did that over and over, but I didn't understand him any more than he did me. I looked at Logan, but he shrugged.

"Don't look at me," he said. "I don't speak gryphon."

"Oh, it's so bloody *obvious*," Vic grumbled. "He wants you to ride him."

I looked down at the sword. "I thought you were going to sleep."

"Hard to sleep with all this bloody screeching going on," he muttered. "Apparently, I have to translate as well as stand guard. My work is *never* done."

I ignored the sword's snit and faced the gryphon again. "Do you really want us . . . to ride you?"

He nodded.

I shook my head. "I don't think that's a good idea."

The gryphon narrowed his bronze eyes and screeched again. He wasn't going to take no for an answer. And really, we didn't have another choice anyway. Not if we wanted to get off the mountain in time to get the ambrosia flower back to Nickamedes.

"Come on, Gypsy girl," Logan said, grinning. "It'll be fun."

I sighed, thinking that his idea of fun was far, far different from mine.

I helped Logan climb up onto the gryphon's broad back; then I got up in front of him. I also grabbed Ran's net out of my backpack and used it to tie Logan, Vic, and myself to the creature—because I really, *really* did not want to fall off. I also hoped the net would make the three of us that much lighter. I'd seen Black rocs carry more than one rider, and the gryphon probably had the same sort of strength, but I figured it wouldn't hurt.

The gryphon seemed amused by my wrapping the net around and around all of our bodies, and he gave a little huff, as if he was laughing at me.

"What?" I muttered. "In case you haven't noticed, you're the only one with wings here. Logan and I can't fly like you can. If we fall off, well, we won't even have time to scream on the way down."

The gryphon let out another huffing laugh.

Finally, when I was as ready as I could be, I gently put my hand down on the gryphon's head and smoothed out his bronze fur.

"Please take us back," I said.

The gryphon let out a loud, fierce, wild cry and launched himself into the air. In the space of a few heartbeats, we'd shot up hundreds of feet into the sky. My hands tightened around Ran's net, and I felt Logan's arm slide firmly around my waist.

"Easy," he murmured in my ear. "If Vivian and Agrona can do it, so can we. The gryphon isn't going to let us fall. So just relax and enjoy the ride."

It took me a few minutes to unclench my fingers and jaw enough to do that. The gryphon flew at an easy pace, his wings spread wide, sailing up and down on the air currents. Slowly, I began to enjoy the high, airy, weightless sensation. It was almost like we were a feather floating this way and that on the breeze. Eventually, I was able to look over the side of the gryphon's body. For a moment, I wished I hadn't, as the forest, trees, and rocks zipped by us below, becoming a white, green, and gray blur. But I slowly got used to the sensation, and I realized just how wonderful it was—like being completely, utterly free.

I wondered if this was how Vivian felt whenever she rode her Black roc. I wondered if she got any happiness out of soaring through the sky on the creature—or if she ever enjoyed anything besides hurting other people. But I pushed thoughts of the Reaper girl out of my mind, determined to enjoy this moment for as long as I could.

The other gryphons joined us in the air, even the baby, and they formed a sort of honor guard around us. I found myself laughing and waving at the creatures, even as the wind tore away my happy chuckles and sent them sailing down to the ground so very far below. Behind me, I could hear Logan laughing and cheering, as well. He was enjoying the ride just as much as I was. Even Vic chimed in on occasion with a *Jolly good show. Jolly good show, old boys.*

We flew down the mountain, and I got glimpses of the winding trail that we'd first come up. Once he sensed us relaxing, the gryphon picked up the pace, pumping his wings back and forth, and flying faster and faster. Soon, we left the mountaintop completely behind and were zooming over Snowline Ridge. Below, the people and cars on the streets looked like tiny toys half-buried in the snow. I leaned over the gryphon's side and waved, although I doubted anyone could see me. A few people looked up as the gryphons' shadows slid over their heads, but they quickly ducked back into whatever shop they'd come out of. I kept laughing.

Finally, though, the academy came into sight. Like everything else, snow covered the grounds, but I still spotted the wall that ringed the campus, as well as the buildings on the main quad.

I leaned forward. "Set us down there," I told the gryphon. "Right in the middle of everything."

The creature nodded, let out another screech, and started circling down toward the ground.

One kid looked up and caught sight of the gryphons. He started yelling at his classmates, and, soon, everyone's heads were turned up in our direction. All I could hear was the wind roaring in my ears, but I could imagine the chatter of conversation on the ground.

People came rushing out of all the buildings, mouths

open, eyes wide with shock. It took me a few minutes, but I finally spotted my friends among the mix. All I had to do was look for a splash of head-to-toe pink, and I saw Daphne, with the others standing beside her. I waved, even though I wasn't sure they could see me.

Finally, the gryphons glided to the ground right in the center of the main quad. Whispers swirled all around me, but I ignored them as I untied Logan, Vic, and myself from Ran's net and the gryphon's back and slid to the ground.

I pulled off my glove and put my bare hand against the gryphon's side. "Thank you," I whispered. "For everything."

And then I closed my eyes and concentrated, trying to show the gryphon how much I appreciated his helping me and Logan—and saving our lives.

The gryphon bowed his head, then nudged me with it. I knew what he wanted, and I laughed and scratched the top of his head. Once more, I felt the creature's warm feelings of friendship and gratitude wash over me.

"You know," I murmured, "if you're ever out in my mountains, I'd love to take another ride sometime."

The gryphon dipped his head, and I knew it was a date.

Logan touched my shoulder, then jerked his head, and I realized we'd attracted quite a crowd. Students were holding up their phones and snapping photos, but no one dared approach the gryphons—no one but my friends.

Daphne. Carson. Oliver. Alexei. Ajax. Rory. Rachel. My friends, old and new, stood in a row before me, their eyes moving back and forth between me, Logan, and the gryphons.

"Hey, guys," I said.

No one spoke for a moment.

Finally, Rory shook her head. "I'll give you this, Princess. You sure do know how to make an entrance."

I just grinned.

Chapter 34

I said good-bye to the gryphons a final time. Then, as one unit, the creatures spread their wings and soared up into the sky, spiraling higher and higher. A sense of awe rippled off everyone on the quad as they watched the creatures—and disappointment, too, that the creatures weren't going to hang around longer. I had a feeling the gryphons would be back, though—sooner than anyone thought.

Once the gryphons were gone, all eyes turned to me and my friends as we left the quad behind. Well, I was trying to leave. Everyone else was still walking slowly and staring up at the sky, hoping to catch one more glimpse of the creatures.

Daphne finally lowered her gaze and shook her head. "Only you would make friends with a gryphon and have it pay off later."

I thought of the silver laurel bracelet Eir had given me. "I don't know about that."

"What was it like?" Rory asked in an eager voice. "Actually getting to ride on one?"

I sighed. "It was *amazing*."

I told them all about my trek down the mountain with Logan and how the gryphons had saved us from the storm. I didn't say anything about my visit with Nike and Eir or my argument with the Spartan. But my friends could tell something was going on between me and Logan. More than once, Daphne raised her eyebrows at me, then at him. I shook my head, telling her we'd talk about it later.

As soon as I finished my story, Ajax pulled out his cell phone and started making arrangements for us to take a plane back to North Carolina as soon as possible. I handed the coach the container with the ambrosia flower, and Ajax tucked it inside his jacket. I didn't tell him about the bracelet, though. It was still hidden under my snowsuit and layers of clothes. I didn't know what I was going to do with the bracelet—or when I would do it.

Daphne used her magic to heal the roc wound in Logan's side, and she took care of all of my bumps and bruises, as well. Once that was done, we went back to Rachel's house, while the guys headed up the hill to the empty cottage where they'd been staying. Apparently, my friends had been packing up their gear and getting ready to hike back up the mountain to find me and Logan when the two of us had landed on the quad with the gryphons.

Daphne and I grabbed our things and went out into the front room. Rachel and Rory were looking at the photos on one of the tables—the photos of Rory's parents I'd noticed before. From Rachel and Rory's red eyes and flushed cheeks, it was obvious they'd both been crying.

Daphne looked back and forth between me, Rory, and Rachel. "I'll go on up to the other cottage and help the guys," she said. "It always takes Carson *forever* to get ready."

I wanted to point out that it took her just as long, but she was giving us some time to say good-bye, so I nodded. Daphne stepped outside and shut the door behind her.

Rory, Rachel, and I were silent for a moment. Finally, I cleared my throat.

"So I guess this is good-bye," I said. "Thanks for all your help. My friends and I wouldn't have made it off the mountain without the two of you."

Rory and Rachel both nodded.

I looked at the older woman. "What will happen now? To Covington?"

She sighed. "Right now, he's in a cell in the academy prison. Ajax alerted the Protectorate that Covington was a Reaper and that he killed all of those people in the library. The Protectorate is sending some folks to question Covington to see what he knows about the Reapers' plans. Hopefully, now that we know what really happened, Rory and I can try to clear Rebecca and Tyson's names—at least about what happened in the library. And ours too."

She smiled at Rory, who returned the expression. The phone rang. Rachel gave me a quick hug good-bye, then excused herself to go answer it.

Rory looked at me and shook her head. "You know, I heard all those stories about you, and I never believed they were true. But you sure do impress, Princess."

"So do you, Spartan," I replied. "You kicked some serious Reaper ass up there in the ruins."

She smiled, but her eyes were still dark and sad. "Some, but not enough. Not nearly enough. Not for what Covington did to my parents and how he planned to frame me and Rachel."

"I know. I'm sorry about that."

She brightened. "But at least now you know that you're not really related to a family of Reapers. Or at least that not all of us are Reapers. I just wish . . . I just wish my parents had told me what they were and that they wanted to change."

"Oh, I think family secrets are a way of life for us Forseti girls," I said, trying to make my tone light. "But you know they loved you. That will help. Maybe not today or tomorrow. But someday, it will help."

She nodded and stared at the photo of herself with her parents. "I know."

"Whatever happens, don't let what they were affect who you are—or who you want to be."

She snorted. "As if. Rachel says that I never listen, anyway. Apparently, being stubborn is another Forseti trait."

"Well, I think it's a good one," I replied. "If you're ever in North Carolina, come say hi. Because we've got plenty of Reapers to fight out there."

Rory grinned at me. "I may just take you up on that, Princess."

I returned her grin. "I hope you do. I really hope you do."

Rachel finished her phone call, and the three of us stepped outside. My friends were waiting on the porch, and Rory and Rachel walked with us down to the main gate, through Snowline Ridge, and all the way over to the train station.

Twenty minutes later, my friends and I had our faces pressed against the windows, waving good-bye to Rory and Rachel. All too soon, though, the train started down the mountain, and they disappeared from sight. Yeah, there might be Reapers everywhere, but I had made some new allies, some new friends, these past few days. That made me feel better about things. Maybe I could actually pull off all of the missions Nike had given me. Finding artifacts. Killing Loki. Saving the world.

We made it down the mountain without incident, and an hour after that, we were at the airport in Denver, getting ready to board the plane home to North Carolina. While the others carried their luggage on board, Logan gestured at me. I stepped over to one side of the tarmac with him.

He hesitated. "I'd like to fly back to the academy, if that's okay with you. I want to make sure that Nickamedes is okay."

"Of course," I said. "He's your uncle. I always thought you would fly back with us."

"It's just . . . after what you said to me in the gryphons' cavern, I didn't know if you'd want me to come along or not."

We'd been so busy getting back to the academy, packing up, and then getting to the airport that Logan and I hadn't really talked since our argument. He may have been traveling with us again, but he'd kept his distance from me on the train, sitting with Oliver, Alexei, and Carson. He still didn't trust himself around me, and I didn't know what I could do or say to change his mind.

Everyone had told me that Logan needed some time. I knew that—really, I did—but that still didn't make it hurt any less.

"Gypsy girl?" he asked, breaking into my thoughts.

"Of course I want you to come along," I said, finally answering his question. "I never said I didn't."

I just don't want you to leave and break my heart all over again.

That's what I really wanted to tell him, but I kept my mouth shut. I might be hurt and angry, but I didn't want to add to Logan's guilt. He had enough of that already.

He opened his mouth, but Ajax stuck his head out of the plane's door.

"Come on, you two," the coach said. "We need to get in the air as soon as possible."

Logan hesitated again, then held out his hand. "After you."

I climbed up the steps to the plane with him behind me. I sat down next to Daphne, while Logan moved past me and took a seat next to Oliver, keeping his distance from me yet again.

I could feel Logan's eyes on me, but I put my head down and pretended to look for something in my messenger bag so he wouldn't see me blink back the tears scalding my eyes.

I hadn't asked Logan what he would do after we got back to the academy and gave the ambrosia flower to Nickamedes. I didn't have to because I already knew the answer.

Logan was planning on leaving the academy, on leaving me—again.

Chapter 35

It was late that afternoon when we finally got back to North Carolina. The others had managed to sleep on the plane, but I couldn't. Oh, I wasn't worried about having any more nightmares. Not now, when I knew Logan was safe from the Reapers. But too much had happened the past few days—and too much was still on my mind.

We all kept an eye out for Reapers, but, for once, we managed to make it to our destination without getting attacked.

Metis and Grandma Frost were pacing back and forth in the waiting room of the infirmary. Grandma looked tired, the wrinkles on her face deeper and more pronounced than usual, the colorful scarves drooping off her body. Metis also seemed exhausted, and much thinner than I remembered, but her face brightened when Ajax handed her the tube containing the ambrosia flower. Metis and Ajax disappeared into the back of the infirmary without another word, leaving the rest of us to sit and wait—just wait.

I hugged Grandma and pulled her away from the others. "How is Nickamedes?"

She smiled, but it was a tight, weary expression. "The poison progressed faster than Metis thought it would and faster than her healing magic could handle. She's been using her magic on Nickamedes pretty much nonstop for the last six hours now, and all she's been able to do is keep him alive. It's a good thing you got back when you did, pumpkin. Now, we'll just have to wait and see."

I let out a breath. We sat down at the far end of the infirmary, away from the others, and I told Grandma Frost everything that had happened—including what I'd found out about my dad and Rory's parents.

"Why didn't you tell me anything about my dad? And Rory and her family?"

Grandma shifted in her chair, and her violet eyes took on a distant look, almost as if she was peering back into the past. "After your father was killed by Reapers, Tyson finally managed to track down me, you, and your mom. Tyson told Grace he was sorry for what had happened, and he also told her to keep you as far away from him and the mythological world as possible. He said that he had a daughter too, and that he was trying to figure out some way to keep her safe from the Reapers. I guess he never did."

We fell silent for several minutes.

Finally, I looked at her again. "So is this it? Or are there any more deep, dark, horrible skeletons in our family closet that I need to know about?"

Grandma shook her head. "As far as I know, this is it, pumpkin. No more secrets."

I grimaced. "Well, I wouldn't say that. Because I have one to share with you."

I turned to the side so my friends wouldn't see what I was doing and showed her the silver laurel and mistletoe bracelet that Eir had given me. I also told Grandma what the goddess had said about how the laurels could be used to heal—or destroy.

"What do you think I'm supposed to do with them?" I asked. "Do you think—do you really think that I can kill Loki with the laurels?"

Grandma reached out and ran her finger across one of the silver leaves. "I don't know, pumpkin. But Eir and Nike wanted you to have them for a reason. You'll figure out what it is when it's time. I know you will. You always do."

I wanted to tell her that I was sick of mysteries and riddles and having the fate of the world resting on my shoulders, but I kept my mouth shut. It wouldn't help. This was my life, for better or worse, good or bad, and all I could do was make the best of it—and try to do the right thing in the end.

Even if I was starting to think I didn't have a clue as to what that right thing might be.

The hours slipped by. We all stayed in the waiting room, although one by one, we drifted off to sleep. Daphne. Carson. Oliver. Alexei. Logan. Vic. Grandma Frost. Even I went to sleep eventually, despite the fact that I couldn't quite get comfortable in my chair. One second, I was shifting in my seat for the hundredth time.

The next, I felt someone gently shaking me awake. I opened my eyes.

Metis was standing over me, her hand on my shoulder. "Nickamedes is awake," she said in a soft voice. "He's asking for you."

I blinked away the last of my sleep, sat up, and got to my feet. I tiptoed past the others, being careful not to wake them, and followed Metis into the back of the infirmary. Nickamedes was in a room by himself. The librarian looked thin and pale, and his blue eyes were duller than I remembered, but his face was soft and relaxed as he turned his head in my direction.

Metis went over and pulled his blanket up. "Are you comfortable? Do you have everything you need?"

"Of course," he said, reaching out and grabbing her hand. "You've taken excellent care of me, Aurora. Just as you always do."

She smiled, but her expression was a little sad, and she quickly pulled her hand away from his. "Yes. Just like always."

Nickamedes frowned at her. Apparently, he had no idea how she felt about him. Maybe I'd have to do something about that, when he was well.

Metis touched my shoulder again. "I'll give you two a minute," she said, pulling the door shut behind her.

I went over to his bed and stood there, not quite looking at the librarian. What did you say to the person who'd been poisoned because of you? Who'd suffered so much pain? Who'd almost died because of you? *I'm so sorry* just didn't seem like enough.

"Thank you," Nickamedes finally said. "Metis told

me what you did for me. How you went to the Eir Ruins and all the dangers you faced along the way."

I shrugged and picked at one of the silver laurels on my bracelet just to have something to do. "It wasn't just me. We all went—together. Daphne. Carson. Oliver. Alexei. Ajax. And Logan was there too."

He nodded. "I know, but if you hadn't figured out what the poison was, I wouldn't be here right now. So thank you for that, Gwendolyn."

I shifted on my feet, uncomfortable with his gratitude.

"I'm sorry," I said, finally raising my eyes to his. "I'm so, so sorry that I wasn't able to stop you from drinking the poison. That you got sick instead of me. If I could go back and change things, I would. I'm so sorry the Reapers hurt you."

I swallowed, trying to dislodge the hard lump in my throat. Because now came the hard part—telling him something that had been on my mind ever since that horrible night in the library when he'd first collapsed.

"Maybe—maybe I shouldn't work at the library anymore," I said in a low voice. "The Reapers could always try it again, you know. They probably *will* try it again, and I don't want you or anyone else getting hurt because you're in between them and me."

Nickamedes stared at me in disbelief. Then, his blue eyes blazed, and his features fixed into that firm glare I knew so well.

"Absolutely *not*," he snapped. "I will not hear of any such *thing*."

I blinked. I'd expected him to accept my resignation

with no questions asked. In fact, I thought he'd be rather glad to get rid of me. "But—"

"But nothing," Nickamedes interrupted, his voice as fierce as I'd ever heard it. "I won't hear of you quitting your duties simply because of one measly Reaper attack. You're my best worker."

I blinked again. "I am?"

"Yes." He paused. "Despite your perpetual tardiness."

I rolled my eyes, but I couldn't help smiling. His snippy words and the huffy tone to his voice told me Nickamedes was going to be okay. I started to excuse myself to let him get some rest when he frowned and nodded at my hands.

"What's that you're fiddling with?" he asked.

I looked down and realized I was toying with one of the laurel leaves. I started to pull my hoodie sleeve down and tell him it was nothing when another idea occurred to me.

"Actually, I, um, found something else besides the ambrosia flower while we were out in Colorado," I said. "Some sort of . . . artifact, I guess you would say. Do you feel like taking a look at it?"

Nickamedes straightened his shoulders. "Of course. I may still be a little under the weather, but I'm not dead yet, Gwendolyn. You should know by now that I'm always interested in artifacts."

So I pushed my sleeve up and held the bracelet out where he could see it. He leaned forward and ran his fingers over the leaves just as Grandma Frost had earlier. Nickamedes turned one of the laurel leaves this way and that, studying it with his usual intensity.

After a moment, his eyes brightened with wonder. "The mistletoe chain is quite beautiful, but this looks like a silver laurel leaf. They all do. Where did you get so many of them? Silver laurel is even rarer than ambrosia flowers. I've never actually seen them myself, not in person, just pictured in books in the library."

"Oh, it was just something I...picked up in the ruins," I said, not quite ready to tell him the whole story yet. "I need to know how to use the leaves and what they can do. Do you think...you can help me with that? Please?"

Back at the ruins, Covington had bragged about how he'd been researching artifacts for the Reapers. I figured it couldn't hurt to have Nickamedes do the same for the Pantheon—and for me too.

He smiled again, looking more and more like his old self. "Of course. I wonder if I could convince Ajax to bring me some books from the library. Well, actually, you can go get them. You'll be able to find them quicker than he would anyway. I know just the place to start researching this. Hand me that piece of paper and pen, will you? Quickly now, please. I want to make some notes before I forget them..."

I handed the librarian the items he asked for, and he started muttering to himself and scribbling down all the books he wanted to use to start researching the silver laurel. Instead of leaving, I sat down in a chair in the corner and listened to him talk, happy that he was going to be okay and that everything had worked out, despite the Reapers' plans.

For now at least.

Chapter 36

Things slowly got back to normal over the next few days.

Once Nickamedes was out of danger, my friends and I went back to our regular schedule of classes, homework, and weapons training and tried to catch up on all of the assignments we'd missed while we'd been away. Rumors swirled around campus about what had happened in the Library of Antiquities the night Nickamedes had been poisoned and about where my friends and I had gone, but I ignored the stares and whispers. All that mattered was that he was getting better. Besides, I doubted the other kids would believe everything that had happened anyway. I could hardly believe it, and I'd been there.

A few nights later, I was back in the library, sitting behind the checkout counter, working my usual shift. Alexei was standing against the glass wall behind me, while Aiko, the Protectorate guard, was at one of the study tables, reading a book. After the attack, the Powers That Were at Mythos had decided to assign Aiko to watch over me, as well. It wouldn't do much good, though. If the Reapers wanted to get to me, they would get to me. All I could do was just keep trying to become a better warrior so that when I faced Vivian again, it would be for the last time. So that I would finally manage to defeat her.

It was a slow night in the library, and most of the kids had already left to go back to their dorms for the night. I'd grabbed several books out of the stacks and was poring over them, comparing the pictures on the pages to the artifacts on the map Oliver had drawn for me. Since the attack at the Eir Ruins, I was more determined than ever to find the artifacts before Vivian, Agrona, and the rest of the Reapers did—

Tap-tap-tap. Tap-tap-tap.

I glanced behind me. Nickamedes slowly shuffled out of the glass office complex. With his left hand, he cradled some books to his chest. With his right hand, he leaned on the cane that he was using to help him walk. The librarian was still feeling the aftereffects of the poison that had damaged his legs, and his steps were slow and a bit unsteady.

Tap-tap-tap. Tap-tap-tap.

Nickamedes was getting around well enough, and Metis had said he would probably make a full recovery, but the faint, hollow sound of his cane hitting the floor caused a fresh wave of guilt to surge through me—because it should have been me hobbling around instead of him. As soon as we figured out exactly what the silver laurel did, I was going to use one of the leaves on him to make him as strong and healthy as he'd been before.

Still, despite my guilt, I made myself smile as Nickamedes walked over to me and carefully slid the books in his arm down onto the counter.

"Anything?" I asked.

I wasn't the only one doing research. As soon as he'd been released from the infirmary, Nickamedes had started stockpiling books to go through in hopes that they might contain some information about the silver laurel leaves.

He shook his head. "Not in these books. But don't worry, Gwendolyn, we'll find out more about the laurels. It'll just take some time."

I looked at his too-thin face, the tired slump in his shoulders, and the way he had to lean on the cane just to stay upright. More guilt surged through me, along with anger. Not for the first time, I made myself and Nickamedes a silent promise—that the Reapers were going to pay for what they'd done to him.

"Gwendolyn?"

"Yeah," I said, pushing my dark thoughts away and forcing myself to smile a little bigger and brighter. "I know you'll find out something about the leaves. It'll just take some time, like you said."

"Anyway," he replied. "You can shelve those. I've got some more books to go through in my office. I want to start researching the mistletoe too, in case it has any special properties."

I nodded. Nickamedes gave me a tired smile before he slowly turned and headed back through the glass door. I watched him out of the corner of my eye, making sure he made it back to his office and was seated at his desk again.

I had reached for the books so I could go shelve them when footsteps sounded. I looked up to see Logan walking toward me.

My heart lifted at the sight of him. I hadn't seen much of Logan these last few days, since he'd been spending a lot of time with Nickamedes, making sure the librarian was resting and taking it easy like Metis had ordered him to. I also hadn't had any more nightmares about Logan stabbing me. Our time together on the mountain had at least put those fears to rest.

My eyes traced over Logan's face. His chiseled features looked as handsome as ever, but something seemed . . . different about him. Maybe it was the square set of his shoulders or the way his gaze fixed firmly on my face instead of skittering away as it had so often on the mountain. He just seemed . . . better.

Logan stopped in front of the counter and tucked his hands into the pockets of his dark jeans.

"Hi," he said in a soft voice.

"Hi."

He stared at me, and I looked right back at him, wondering if this was the last time I'd ever see him. But after a few seconds, I couldn't stand the silence anymore—or the way my heart clenched with dread at the thought of him leaving again.

"Come to say good-bye?" I asked, wanting him to just say the word and go. At least that way, I could hurry off into the stacks where no one but Alexei and Aiko would see me cry.

Logan shook his head. "No, not to say good-bye—to apologize."

I frowned. "Apologize for what?"

He looked at me, his blue eyes serious. "For running away, just like you said."

This time, I shook my head. "I didn't mean that. Not really. I know you needed some time to think about things. I'm the one who should be apologizing. You were the one the Reapers hurt—not me. I was just being a selfish, whiny bitch, back in the cavern. You're the strongest, bravest person I know, Logan. What the Reapers did to you was horrible, but you survived it. That's the only thing that matters. I'm sorry for all of the mean, hurtful things I said to you—sorrier than you will ever know."

Over the past few days, I'd had a lot of time to think about me, Logan, and what the Reapers had done to him. Yeah, I was still hurt and angry, but I'd also realized that part of me was jealous of Logan—and the fact that he could walk away from the Reapers and everything else when I couldn't. But being in danger, being a target, being hurt over and over again, was part of being a Champion—part of being Nike's Champion. And it was something I was just going to have to deal with until the second Chaos War was decided—one way or the other. But in the meantime, I wasn't going to take my emotions out on Logan, not when he'd suffered just as much as I had—maybe even more.

I drew in another breath. "So anyway, I'm just—I'm just *sorry*. For everything. I hope you can forgive me."

"There's nothing to forgive," Logan said. "Because you're right. I did run away. It was easier to leave, rather than staying here and facing you."

"You didn't want to see me and be constantly reminded of how you'd hurt me. I get it—really, I do. I probably would have done the same thing, if our positions had been reversed."

He shook his head again. "No, you wouldn't have. You would have stayed here. You would have sucked it up and done what you had to do in order to defeat the

Reapers and keep everyone safe. Because that's the kind of person you are, Gypsy girl. And it's the kind of person I want to be too."

"What are you saying?" I whispered.

"I'm saying that I'm back," he said. "I'm back at the academy, and I'm back in the fight, right here by your side, Gypsy girl. I love you, and I don't ever plan on leaving again."

So many emotions surged through me at his words—hope, relief, happiness, and just a touch of fear. That it wouldn't last. That something else would happen. That he would leave again. But I made myself stare into his eyes, and I let him see how important this was to me.

"Promise?" I whispered again. "Promise that you'll stay no matter what happens? Because I don't know—I don't know what I'll do if you leave like that again."

"I promise."

He drew an X over his heart—the same sort of off-center X that the scars on my own chest and hand made. Then, he grinned, and it was *his* grin again—Logan's crazy, crooked, sexy, teasing grin that I loved so much. There was no guilt in his blue eyes. No hurt. No fear. Just his determination—and his love for me.

And just like that, all the anger, hurt, and guilt I'd been carrying around ever since Logan had stabbed me and left the academy vanished. Maybe it was crazy, but all the pain was just ... gone, and all I felt in its place was a dizzying rush of love and concern for him, the emotion so intense that my body trembled with it. Logan had told me once that we'd already spent enough time being apart, and he was right.

I closed my eyes and drew in a breath. Then, I shuddered it out, hopped off my stool, ran around the check-out counter, and threw myself into his arms. Logan stepped forward to meet me, burying his face in my neck. The heat of his body melted into my own, driving away the chill I'd felt in my heart ever since he'd gone away.

I pulled back, stood on my tiptoes, and pressed my lips to Logan's in a hot, fierce kiss, not caring who saw me or what they thought about it.

His lips met mine, and everything else just fell away. All I was aware of was the press of his lips on mine, our breath mingling together, our arms holding each other that much tighter, and all the warm, soft, fizzy, dizzying rush of love flowing from him to me and back again.

Finally, the kiss ended, and I stared up into his face.

"I love you," I whispered.

He gave me another crooked grin. "You know, I think that's the first time you've ever said that to me. In person, anyway. I thought girls were supposed to say *I love you* first, along with all that other mushy stuff."

I rolled my eyes, stepped back, and lightly punched him on the shoulder. "There you go again, Spartan. Ruining the moment."

His grin widened.

I stood up on my tiptoes and pressed another kiss to his lips. Then, I jerked my head at the checkout counter.

"What is it?" Logan asked. "What's wrong?"

"Nothing," I said. "But now that you're back, we have work to do. Feel like helping me with something?"

He grinned again. "Always, Gypsy girl. Always."

I threaded my fingers through his, then led him around the checkout counter to show him the map of artifacts that we were going to go after—together.

BEYOND
THE
STORY

Wondering how Gwen retrieved Ran's net before the start of *Midnight Frost*? Read on for a blow-by-blow account.

GWEN'S DIARY

Today, Daphne, Alexei, and I went to the Crius Coliseum to look for a possible artifact, but things didn't turn out quite like I expected . . .

"Do you really think the artifact is here?"

I shrugged. "I don't know."

Daphne Cruz, my best friend, stopped in the middle of the room, put her hands on her hips, and glared at me. Princess pink sparks of magic streamed out of the Valkyrie's fingertips, telling me she wasn't exactly happy with me right now.

"Well, if you don't know, then what are *we* doing here?" she asked. "And by *we*, I really mean *me*."

Here was the Crius Coliseum, a museum on the outskirts of Asheville, North Carolina, devoted to all things mythological. Most folks who visited the coliseum thought it was an interesting look back at ancient times, with its rooms highlighting Greek, Norse, Russian,

Roman, Japanese, Chinese, and all the other peoples, cultures, and gods of the world.

What they didn't realize was that it was all *real*.

That those in the mythological world were locked in a struggle that had carried over into modern times—and that it was up to warrior whiz kids like me and Daphne to make sure the good guys of the Pantheon won.

That's right. Me, Gwen Frost, the Gypsy girl who touched stuff and saw things, was officially responsible for saving the world. Something I wasn't doing so well at so far, since I'd gotten my ass kicked more times than I cared to remember by some seriously bad guys. But no matter how terrible things got, I kept on fighting. It was the only thing I could do.

I'd come to the coliseum in search of a net that had supposedly belonged to Ran, the Norse goddess of storms. Nike, the Greek goddess of victory, had tasked me, her Champion, with finding such mythological artifacts and protecting them from the Reapers of Chaos. Something else I wasn't doing so well at.

"Well?" Daphne asked. "What do you have to say for yourself, Gwen?"

I looked at the brochure I'd grabbed from a metal rack by the front door. "That the net is in one of the rooms in the back. So come on."

The Valkyrie kept glaring at me, but I was used to her temper. Daphne's bark was always worse than her bite—unless you were a Reaper.

I batted my eyelashes at her. "Pretty please?"

"Of course it's in the back," Daphne muttered, but she fell in step beside me.

It was a cold afternoon in late January, just before

closing time. Given the bitter winter chill and snow showers outside, we were the only ones in the coliseum, besides a few staff members wearing long white togas who were taking inventory in the gift shop.

None of the staff gave us a second glance, despite the sparks of magic Daphne was still giving off. Mythos Academy students like us came into the coliseum all the time to look at the exhibits and gather information for reports, essays, and other homework assignments. Most of the staff members were former Mythos students themselves, so they knew all about the mythological world and the Valkyries, Spartans, Amazons, and other warriors who inhabited it.

We walked through the main room of the coliseum, which was filled with glass artifact cases. The silver and bronze swords and spears all glinted with a dull, bloody light, while the jewels in the rings and necklaces winked like evil eyes opening and closing, following my every move. The gauzy silks hovered in midair, as if they were ghosts about to break free of the wires holding them up, burst through the glass, and attack.

I shivered and quickened my steps. Bloody weapons. Winking eyes. Ghostly garments. My Gypsy gift was acting up again.

"Geez, Gwen," Daphne muttered again. "Slow down. It's not a race."

I bit my lip to keep from telling her that it *was* a race—us against the Reapers—and forced myself to walk at a more normal pace. We left the main room behind and stepped into a long hallway.

"It's all the way in the back," I said, pointing up ahead. "In a room next to the library."

Daphne sighed, and another shower of pink sparks streaked out of her fingertips.

"Look," I said. "I know you're getting tired of chasing after artifacts, but the net I saw on the coliseum's Web site looked like the one we're searching for. So I figured we might as well come and check it out. Besides, it's not like we were doing anything else important."

"Oh no," she sniped. "It's not like I wanted to spend the afternoon with my boyfriend or anything."

"I asked Carson to come too," I said, referring to her boyfriend, Carson Callahan, "but he had that band meeting about rescheduling the winter concert that the Reapers ruined."

Daphne snorted. "Ruined is a bit of an understatement, don't you think?"

I grimaced. She was right. *Ruined* didn't even come close to describing the horror show the concert had turned into when Reapers had crashed the event, killed members of the ruling Protectorate, and taken others hostage, along with Mythos students. The Reapers had intended to murder everyone at the Aoide Auditorium as a blood sacrifice to the evil Norse god Loki. I'd stopped their plan, but it had cost me—more than I cared to remember.

"Well, at least Gwen decided to look for this artifact during the day," a voice with a cool Russian accent chimed in. "Instead of dragging me over to the Library of Antiquities in the middle of the night like she did last week."

I looked over to my left at Alexei Sokolov. With his dark brown hair, tan skin, and rugged features, Alexei was as handsome as any movie star, but he was also the Bogatyr warrior who served as my bodyguard.

"You're just grumpy Oliver couldn't come with us today," I said.

Alexei smiled, and his hazel eyes softened at the thought of Oliver Hector, the Spartan he was involved with. "Maybe."

"And you're just grumpy Logan's not here," Daphne sniped again.

Her words surprised me, and I stumbled over my own feet, even as my heart twisted in my chest.

Daphne caught my arm and pulled me upright with her great Valkyrie strength. She winced at the miserable expression on my face.

"I'm sorry, Gwen. I didn't mean that—"

I held up my hand, cutting her off. "No, it's fine. We all know it's true. I am grumpy about Logan."

Another understatement. Spartan Logan Quinn was the best fighter at Mythos Academy. Over the last few months, he'd taught me everything I knew about weapons and how to use them.

He was also the guy I loved—and the one who'd attacked me and then left the academy.

"Gwen?" Alexei asked.

I snapped out of my dark thoughts. "I'm fine. Let's see if the net is here."

We hurried to the end of the hallway and the last exhibit room in this part of the coliseum. According to a sign on the wall, this area was devoted to gods and goddesses of the sea, the sky, and all the storms that raged between them. I put my messenger bag down in the corner, then went from one case to the next, staring at all of the artifacts. They included everything from splintered planks of the doomed boat that the Greek warrior Odysseus had tried to sail home in to a couple of gold tridents that had supposedly belonged to Poseidon, the Greek god of the sea. Finally, I spotted a bronze plaque that read *Ran's fishing net*, and I stepped over to that case.

A net made out of something that looked like light gray seaweed lay beneath the glass, along with a small white ID card. I'd have to remember to take that with me too. Hopefully, it would tell me what was so important about the net. I leaned even closer to the glass, studying the artifact.

Thanks to my psychometry, I never forgot anything I saw, so I was able to pull up my memories of the drawing that featured the artifacts I was supposed to find for Nike. I compared the net before me to the one in the drawing. It was a perfect match.

"Here it is!" I called out.

Daphne and Alexei moved over to stand beside me. They both looked down at the net.

"What do you think it does?" Daphne asked, her black eyes narrowed in thought.

I shrugged. "I have no idea. But Nike showed it to me, so it must be important."

"Now what?" Alexei asked.

I shrugged again. "The usual. I'll call Metis, and she and Nickamedes can come and get the net—"

I saw a flash of silver out of the corner of my eye, and I instinctively jumped back.

The Reaper's sword missed my head by an inch.

One second, Alexei, Daphne, and I were alone in the exhibit room. The next, six Reapers had appeared, all wearing black robes and twisted rubber Loki masks and all carrying curved swords.

"Reapers!" I screamed, even though my friends had already spotted them.

The Reaper next to me raised his sword again, and I pivoted and lashed out with my foot, kicking him in the stomach. The Reaper stumbled back, giving me the chance to grab my own weapon—the sword in the black leather scabbard that was belted around my waist.

I raised the blade up into an attack position, and a purplish eye on the hilt snapped open. Instead of being plain, half a man's face was inlaid into the hilt of my sword, complete with a nose, an ear, and a mouth that I could feel curving into a satisfied smile under my palm at the thought of the battle to come.

"Reapers!" Vic, the sword, said with dark relish. "Let's kill them all!"

Beside me, Daphne slung an onyx bow off her shoulder and nocked an arrow on the thin golden strings, while Alexei pulled two matching swords out of the gray leather scabbard strapped to his back.

I tightened my grip on Vic and charged into battle.

Clash-clash-clang!

I swung my sword at the Reaper over and over again, mercilessly hacking and slashing my way through his defenses until I was able to bury my weapon in his chest.

"Way to go, Gwen!" Vic crowed as I pulled him free of the Reaper's body. "On to the next one!"

I turned to face the next Reaper coming at me—

Thwack!

A golden arrow zoomed past me and buried itself in the Reaper's chest, and he too fell to the floor. My head snapped around.

"You're welcome!" Daphne shouted.

I raised Vic and saluted her with the sword. She grinned before bringing up her bow and using it as a sort of shield to fend off another Reaper. Daphne stepped forward and punched the Reaper in the face, her Valkyrie strength throwing him back against the wall. I knew she'd be okay so I charged over to where Alexei was fighting two Reapers. The Bogatyr's swords flashed through the air like streaks of silver fire as he moved back and forth, attacking first one Reaper, then the other.

"Get the net!" one of the Reapers screamed at the sixth and final man.

The last Reaper smashed his sword into the case, reached through the broken glass, and grabbed the gray net. He threw the seaweed over his shoulder and raced toward the open doorway.

"Go!" Alexei said, slicing his sword across first one Reaper's chest, then the other's, making them both scream with pain. "I can handle these two!"

I hurried after the last Reaper. He turned to see how close I was and slammed into another artifact case, knocking it over. The Reaper tripped and hit the floor hard, sliding to a stop just inside the doorway.

"Get him, Gwen!" Vic shouted.

I leaped over the smashed case and brought the sword up, ready to bring it down on the Reaper.

And that's when he threw the net at me.

I ducked to one side, but the net still clipped me. It was heavier than it looked, and I felt like someone had slammed a couple of lead weights into my shoulder. I grunted, spun around, and managed to fling the net off me, although the left side of my body ached from the strangely hard impact.

But that gave the Reaper enough time to scramble to his feet and lurch out of the exhibit room and into the hallway. I picked up my pace, running after him. He wasn't going to get away. Not if I could help it—

The Reaper stopped in the hallway, turned, and tossed something that looked like a black rubber ball in my direction. I stopped short just as a flash of fire exploded in front of the doorway, separating me from the Reaper. Through the flames, I watched as the evil warrior ran down the hallway and out of sight. I looked around, but of course there wasn't another exit from this room, which meant I couldn't chase after him.

I cursed, ripped off my gray hoodie, and used it to beat down the flames. Whatever the Reaper had thrown at me wasn't all that powerful, because I was quickly able to smother the fire. I coughed, waved the wisps of smoke away from my face, and stepped out of the room.

Empty—the hallway was empty, the Reaper long gone.

I cursed again, but there was nothing I could do to catch him, so I went back into the exhibit area to check on my friends. Daphne and Alexei were already moving from one body to the next, tearing off the rubber Loki masks to reveal the Reapers' real faces underneath. I went over to Daphne and touched her shoulder.

"You okay?" I asked.

She nodded.

"Alexei?"

"I'm fine," he called out.

I let out a quiet sigh of relief. Alexei might technically be my guard, but he was a friend too, and I was glad that he and Daphne were all right.

Daphne noticed the worry on my face, and she slung her arm around my shoulder. "Relax, Gwen. We made it through the fight, and they didn't. Why, my hair didn't even get messed up."

She used her free hand to smooth back the golden locks in her long ponytail. Daphne grinned, and I found myself smiling a little.

"Well, as long as your hair's okay, I guess we're good."

She nodded. "Don't you know it."

Across the room, Alexei crouched over one of the Reapers' bodies and used his cell phone to take a photo of the dead man's face. He did the same with all the Reapers, then put the phone to his ear. He was probably calling Professor Metis and the rest of the academy's security council to let them know about the attack. This wasn't the first time something like this had happened in the last few weeks, and it certainly wouldn't be the last, as long as I kept searching for artifacts.

"You did well, Gwen," Vic said. "I'm proud of you."

I raised the sword up so I could look him in his one eye. "Thanks, Vic."

He stared back at me. "Although you really should have killed more Reapers. And you especially shouldn't have let that last one get away ..."

And he was off on one of his rants, talking about exactly what we should do to track down the Reaper and how much Vic was looking forward to cutting him to ribbons. The sword was totally bloodthirsty that way. I rolled my eyes at his violent chatter, but I let the sword talk. It was just easier.

While Vic muttered to himself about all the Reapers he wanted to kill, I looked out over the exhibit room. Blood and bodies covered the floor like dolls that a child had thrown down in a tantrum. Several of the artifact cases had been destroyed, and bits of glass glittered like diamond shards among the Reapers' black robes. Déjà vu. This was the third time now that I'd seen such a scene at the coliseum. At least the Reapers were the only ones who were dead this time, and not kids from my school like before.

Screams echoed in my head, and all the shadows in the room took on a bright, glossy sheen, like they were puddles of blood tainting everything with their horrid, coppery stench—

I shook my head, banishing the thoughts back to the bottom of my brain.

"What's wrong?" Daphne asked, noticing my weary expression.

I shook my head again. "I was just thinking that I'm really starting to hate this place."

Mythos Academy Warriors
and Their Magic

The students at Mythos Academy are the descendants of ancient warriors, and they are at the academy to learn how to fight and use weapons, along with whatever magic or other skills that they might have. Here's a little more about the warrior whiz kids, as Gwen calls them:

Amazons and Valkyries: Most of the girls at Mythos are either Amazons or Valkyries. Amazons are gifted with supernatural quickness. In gym class during mock fights, they look like blurs more than anything else. Valkyries are incredibly strong. Also, bright, colorful sparks of magic can often be seen shooting out of Valkyries' fingertips.

Romans and Vikings: Most of the guys at Mythos Academy are either Romans or Vikings. Romans are super-quick, just like Amazons, while Vikings are superstrong, just like Valkyries.

Siblings: Brothers and sisters born to the same parents will have similar abilities and magic, but they're sometimes classified as different types of warriors. For example, if the girls in a family are Amazons, then the boys will be Romans. If the girls in a family are Valkyries, then the boys will be Vikings.

However, in other families, brothers and sisters are

considered to be the same kind of warriors, like those born to Spartan, Samurai, or Ninja parents. The boys and girls are both called Spartans, Samurais, or Ninjas.

More Magic: As if being superstrong or superquick wasn't good enough, the students at Mythos Academy also have other types of magic. They can do everything from heal injuries to control the weather to form fireballs with their bare hands. Many of the students have enhanced senses as well. The powers vary from student to student, but as a general rule, everyone is dangerous and deadly in their own special way.

Spartans: Spartans are among the rarest of the warrior whiz kids, and there are only a few at Mythos Academy. But Spartans are the most dangerous and deadliest of all the warriors because they have the ability to pick up any weapon—or any *thing*—and automatically know how to use and even kill someone with it. Even Reapers of Chaos are afraid to battle Spartans in a fair fight. But then again, Reapers rarely fight fair. . . .

Gypsies: Gypsies are just as rare as Spartans. Gypsies are those who have been gifted with magic by the gods. But not all Gypsies are good. Some are just as evil as the gods they serve. Gwen is a Gypsy who is gifted with psychometry magic, or the ability to know, see, and feel an object's history just by touching it. Gwen's magic comes from Nike, the Greek goddess of victory.

Bogatyrs: Bogatyrs are Russian warriors. They are exceptionally fast, and most of them use two weapons at once, one in either hand. Bogatyrs train themselves to always keep moving, to always keep fighting, which gives them great endurance. The longer a fight goes, the more likely they are to win, because they will still be going strong as their enemies slowly weaken.

Want to know more about Mythos Academy?
Read on and take a tour of the campus.

The heart of Mythos Academy is made up of five buildings that are clustered together like the loose points of a star on the upper quad. They are the Library of Antiquities, the gym, the dining hall, the English-history building, and the math-science building.

The Library of Antiquities: The library is the largest building on campus. In addition to books, the library also houses artifacts—weapons, jewelry, clothes, armor, and more—that were once used by ancient warriors, gods, goddesses, and mythological creatures. Some of the artifacts have a lot of power, and the Reapers of Chaos would love to get their hands on this stuff to use it for Bad, Bad Things.

The Gym: The gym is the second largest building at Mythos. In addition to a pool, basketball court, and training areas, the gym also features racks of weapons, including swords, staffs, and more, that the students use during mock fights. At Mythos, gym class is really weapons training, and students are graded on how well they can fight—something that Gwen thinks she's not very good at.

The Dining Hall: The dining hall is the third largest building at Mythos. With its white linens, fancy china, and open-air indoor garden, the dining hall looks more like a five-star restaurant than a student cafeteria. The dining hall is famous for all the fancy, froufrou foods that it serves on a daily basis, like liver, veal, and escargot. Yucko, as Gwen would say.

The English-History Building: Students attend English, myth-history, geography, art, and other classes in this building. Professor Metis's office is also in this building.

The Math-Science Building: Students attend math, science, and other classes in this building. But there are more than just classrooms here. This building also features a morgue and a prison deep underground. Creepy, huh?

The Student Dorms: The student dorms are located down the hill from the upper quad, along with several other smaller outbuildings. Guys and girls live in separate dorms, although that doesn't keep them from hooking up on a regular basis.

The Statues: Statues of mythological creatures—like gryphons and gargoyles—can be found on all the academy buildings, although the library has the most statues. Gwen thinks that the statues are all super creepy, especially since they always seem to be watching her. . . .

Who's Who at Mythos Academy—
The Students

Gwen (Gwendolyn) Frost: Gwen is a Gypsy girl with the gift of psychometry magic, or the ability to know an object's history just by touching it. Gwen's a little dark and twisted in that she likes her magic and the fact that it lets her know other people's secrets—no matter how hard they try to hide them. She also has a major sweet tooth, loves to read comic books, and wears jeans, T-shirts, hoodies, and sneakers almost everywhere she goes.

Daphne Cruz: Daphne is a Valkyrie and a renowned archer. She also has some wicked computer skills and loves designer clothes and expensive purses. Daphne is rather obsessed with the color pink. She wears it more often than not, and her entire dorm room is done in various shades of pink.

Logan Quinn: This seriously cute and seriously deadly Spartan is the best fighter at Mythos Academy—and someone who Gwen just can't stop thinking about. But Logan has a secret that he doesn't want anyone to know—especially not Gwen.

Carson Callahan: Carson is the head of the Mythos Academy Marching Band. He's a Celt and rumored to have come from a long line of warrior bards. He's quiet, shy, and one of the nicest guys you'll ever meet, but Carson can be as tough as nails when he needs to be.

Oliver Hector: Oliver is a Spartan who is friends with Logan and Kenzie and helps with Gwen's weapons training. He's also one of Gwen's friends now too, because of what happened during the Winter Carnival.

Kenzie Tanaka: Kenzie is a Spartan who is friends with Logan and Oliver. He also helps with Gwen's weapons training and is currently dating Talia.

Savannah Warren: Savannah is an Amazon who was dating Logan—at least before the Winter Carnival. Now, the two of them have broken up, something Savannah isn't very happy about—and something that she blames Gwen for.

Talia Pizarro: Talia is an Amazon and one of Savannah's best friends. Talia has gym class with Gwen, and the two of them often spar during the mock fights. She is currently dating Kenzie.

Helena Paxton: Helena is an Amazon who seems to be positioning herself as the new mean girl queen of the academy, or at least of Gwen's second-year class.

Morgan McDougall: Morgan is a Valkyrie. She used to be one of the most popular girls at the academy—before her best friend, Jasmine Ashton, tried to sacrifice her to Loki one night in the Library of Antiquities. These days, though, Morgan tends to keep to herself, although it seems she's becoming friends with Savannah and Talia.

Jasmine Ashton: Jasmine was a Valkyrie and the most popular girl in the second-year class at Mythos Academy—until she tried to sacrifice Morgan to Loki. Gwen battled Jasmine in the Library of Antiquities and managed to keep her from sacrificing Morgan, although Logan was the one who actually killed Jasmine. But before she died, Jasmine told Gwen that her whole family are Reapers—and that there are many Reapers at Mythos Academy....

Preston Ashton: Preston is Jasmine's older brother, who blamed Gwen for his sister's death. Preston tried to kill Gwen during the Winter Carnival weekend at the Powder ski resort, although Gwen, Logan, and Vic eventually got the best of the Reaper. After that, Preston was locked up in the academy's prison.

Alexei Sokolov: Alexei is a third-year Russian student who most recently attended the London branch of Mythos Academy. He's a Bogatyr warrior who is training to become a member of the Protectorate. Alexei has met some of Gwen's friends before, including Daphne, Logan, and Oliver.

Rory Forseti: Rory is a first-year student at the Colorado branch of Mythos Academy. She's a Spartan and Gwen's cousin, since her dad and Gwen's dad were brothers. Rory's parents were Reapers, although they never told her about that. However, everyone at the academy now knows about her parents, and Rory has a lot of pain and guilt about all of the terrible things that her parents did as Reapers.

Who's Who at Mythos Academy and Beyond—
The Adults

Coach Ajax: Ajax is the head of the athletic department at the academy and is responsible for training all the kids at Mythos and turning them into fighters. Logan Quinn and his Spartan friends are among Ajax's prize students.

Geraldine (Grandma) Frost: Geraldine is Gwen's grandma and a Gypsy with the power to see the future. Grandma Frost makes her living as a fortune-teller in a town not too far away from Cypress Mountain. A couple of times a week, Gwen sneaks off the Mythos Academy campus to see her grandma and enjoy the sweet treats that Grandma Frost is always baking.

Grace Frost: Grace was Gwen's mom and a Gypsy who had the power to know if people were telling the truth or not just by listening to their words. At first, Gwen thought her mom had been killed in a car accident by a drunk driver. But thanks to Preston Ashton, Gwen knows that Grace was actually murdered by the Reaper girl who is Loki's Champion. Gwen's determined to find the Reaper girl and get her revenge—no matter what.

Nickamedes: Nickamedes is the head librarian at the Library of Antiquities. Nickamedes loves the books and the artifacts in the library more than anything else, and he doesn't seem to like Gwen at all. In fact, he often goes out of his way to make more work for her whenever Gwen is working after school in the library. Nickamedes is also Logan's uncle, although the uptight librarian is nothing like his easygoing nephew. At least, Gwen doesn't think so.

Professor Aurora Metis: Metis is a myth-history professor who teaches students all about the Reapers of Chaos, Loki, and the ancient Chaos War. She was also best friends with Gwen's mom, Grace, back when the two of them went to Mythos. Metis is the Champion of Athena, the Greek goddess of wisdom, and she's become Gwen's mentor at the academy.

Raven: Raven is the old woman who mans the coffee cart in the Library of Antiquities. Gwen has also seen her in the academy prison, which seems to be another one of Raven's odd jobs around campus. There's definitely more to Raven than meets the eye....

The Powers That Were: A board made up of various members of the Pantheon who oversee all aspects of Mythos Academy, from approving the dining hall menus to disciplining students. Gwen's never met any of the board members that she's aware of, and she doesn't know exactly who they are, but that could change— sooner than she thinks.

Vic: Vic is the talking sword that Nike gave to Gwen to use as her personal weapon. Instead of a regular hilt, a man's face is inlaid into Vic's hilt. Gwen doesn't know too much about Vic, except that he's really, really bloodthirsty and wants to kill Reapers more than anything else.

Linus Quinn: Linus is Logan's dad and the head of the Protectorate. He is also a Spartan and has always pushed Logan to be the best warrior he can be. However, Linus and Logan's relationship is often strained, due in part to the murder of Logan's mom and sister. Linus feels that Logan should have done more to protect his mom and sister that terrible day, which adds to Logan's guilt that he survived the Reapers' attack.

Agrona Quinn: Agrona is Logan's stepmom and a member of the Protectorate. She is also an Amazon.

Sergei Sokolov: Sergei is Alexei's dad and a member of the Protectorate. He is also a Bogatyr.

Inari Sato: Inari is member of the Protectorate. He is also a Ninja.

Rachel Maddox: Rachel is a chef who works in the dining hall at the Colorado branch of Mythos Academy. She's a Spartan and Rory's aunt, since she and Rory's mom were sisters. Like Rory, Rachel has a lot of conflicting feelings about the fact that her sister was a Reaper.

Covington: Covington is the head librarian at the Library of Antiquities at the Colorado branch of Mythos Academy. He is friends with Coach Ajax.

Who's Who at Mythos Academy—
The Gods, Monsters, and More

Artifacts: Artifacts are weapons, jewelry, clothing, and armor that were worn or used by various warriors, gods, goddesses, and mythological creatures over the years. There are Thirteen Artifacts that are rumored to be the most powerful, although people disagree about which artifacts they are and how they were used during the Chaos War. The members of the Pantheon protect the various artifacts from the Reapers, who want to use the artifacts and their power to free Loki from his prison. Many of the artifacts are housed in the Library of Antiquities.

Black rocs: These creatures look like ravens—only much, much bigger. They have shiny black feathers shot through with glossy streaks of red, long, sharp, curved talons, and black eyes with a red spark burning deep down inside them. Rocs are capable of picking up people and carrying them off—before they rip them to shreds.

Champions: Every god and goddess has a Champion, someone that they choose to work on their behalf in the mortal realm. Champions have various powers and weapons and can be good or bad, depending on the god they serve. Gwen is Nike's Champion, just like her mom and grandma were before her.

The Chaos War: Long ago, Loki and his followers tried to enslave everyone and everything, and the whole world was plunged into the Chaos War. It was a dark, bloody time that almost resulted in the end of the world. The Reapers want to free Loki, so the god can lead them in another Chaos War. You can see why that would be a Bad, Bad Thing.

Fenrir wolves: These creatures look like wolves—only much, much bigger. They have ash gray fur, razor-sharp talons, and burning red eyes. Reapers use them to watch, hunt, and kill members of the Pantheon. Think of Fenrir wolves as puppy-dog assassins.

Loki: Loki is the Norse god of chaos. Once upon a time, Loki caused the death of another god and was imprisoned for it. But Loki eventually escaped from his prison and started recruiting other gods, goddesses, humans, and creatures to join forces with him. He called his followers the Reapers of Chaos, and they tried to take over the world. However, Loki and his followers were eventually defeated, and Loki was imprisoned for a second time. To this day, Loki seeks to escape from his prison and plunge the world into a second Chaos War. He's the ultimate bad guy.

Mythos Academy: The academy is located in Cypress Mountain, North Carolina, which is a ritzy suburb high in the mountains above the city of Asheville. The academy is a boarding school/college for warrior whiz kids—the descendants of ancient warriors, like Spartans, Valkyries, Amazons, and more. The kids at Mythos range in age from first-year students (age sixteen) to sixth-year students (age twenty-one). The kids go to Mythos to learn how to use whatever magic and skills they possess to fight against Loki and his Reapers. There are other branches of the academy located throughout the world.

Nemean prowlers: These creatures look like panthers— only much, much bigger. They have black fur tinged with red, razor-sharp claws, and burning red eyes. Reapers use them to watch, hunt, and kill members of the Pantheon. Think of Nemean prowlers as kitty-cat assassins.

Nike: Nike is the Greek goddess of victory. The goddess was the one who defeated Loki in one-on-one combat during the final battle of the Chaos War. Ever since then, Nike and her Champions have fought the Reapers of Chaos, trying to keep them from freeing Loki from his prison. She's the ultimate good guy.

The Pantheon: The Pantheon is made up of gods, goddesses, humans, and creatures who have banded together to fight Loki and his Reapers of Chaos. The members of the Pantheon are the good guys.

Reapers of Chaos: A Reaper is any god, goddess, human, or creature who serves Loki and wants to free the evil god from his prison. Reapers are known to sacrifice people to Loki in hopes of weakening his prison, so he can one day break free and return to the mortal realm. The scary thing is that Reapers can be anyone at Mythos Academy and beyond—parents, teachers, even fellow students. Reapers are the bad guys.

Sigyn: Sigyn is the Norse goddess of devotion. She is also Loki's wife. The first time Loki was imprisoned, he was chained up underneath a giant snake that dripped venom onto his once-handsome face. Sigyn spent many years holding an artifact called the Bowl of Tears up over Loki's head to catch as much of the venom as possible. But when the bowl was full, Sigyn would have to empty it, which let venom drop freely onto Loki's face, causing him great pain. Eventually, Loki tricked Sigyn into releasing him, and before long, the evil god plunged the world into the long, bloody Chaos War. No one knows what happened to Sigyn after that....

Maat asp: A Maat asp is a small snake with shimmering blue and black scales. It is named after Maat, the Egyptian goddess of truth. The Protectorate uses the asp to question Reapers, since the snake can tell whether or not people are telling the truth. The asp's venom can be poisonous—even deadly—to those who lie.

The Protectorate: The Protectorate is basically the police force of the mythological world. Among other duties, members of the Protectorate track down Reapers, put them on trial for their crimes, and make sure that the Reapers end up in prison where they belong.

Don't miss Gwen's ultimate showdown with Loki,
coming next March!

KILLER FROST

Myths, Magic, Mayhem . . .

I've battled the Reapersof Chaos before—and survived.
But this time I have a Bad, Bad Feeling
it's going to be a fight to the death . . .
most likely mine.

Yeah, I've got my psychometry magic, my talking
sword, Vic—and even the most dangerous Spartan
on campus at my side, in Logan freaking Quinn, but
I'm no match for Loki, the evil Norse god of chaos. I
may be Nike's Champion, but at heart, I'm still just
Gwen Frost, that weird Gypsy girl everyone at school
loves to gossip about.

Then someone I love is put in more danger than ever
before, and something inside me snaps. This time, Loki
and his Reapers are going down for good . . . or I am.